A Darkness so SWEET

II

ALSO BY EMMA HAMM

Deep Waters
Whispers of the Deep
Song of the Abyss
Echoes of the Tide
Call of the Fathoms

Seven Deadly Demons
The Demon Court
The Demon Crown
The Demon Prince
The Demon Mark

Dragon of Umbra
Fire Heart
Bright Heart
Brave Heart
Torn Heart
Taloned Heart

and many more...

Emma Hamm

Copyright © Emma Hamm 2025

Visit author online at www.emmahamm.com

Cover Design by Feyspeaker
Underside Dustjacket by Andrea Corsini
Hardcover Design by BookishAveril
Interior Artwork by JaneDark7

For every girl who was told she was too loud, too much, too everything...

I hope you find someone who makes you comfortable enough to be all of those things and more.

You deserve it.

Chapter 1

Maia stood outside the door that would change her life forever. She could hear her heart thudding in her chest, and the sound of her own ragged breathing. In through her nose and out through her mouth. It felt like she was going to die, right here, right now.

This was all she'd ever dreamt of. Every opportunity that had ever been given to her, all rolled up into one moment that meant so much and she could not mess it up. If she did, then her entire career might as well be over.

Perhaps it was a little dramatic, but having the chance to create floral arrangements for the royal wedding itself? She'd never see this happen again in her lifetime. The king had only one child—his daughter. Her wedding would be the grandest display this kingdom had ever seen and, if she played her cards right, everyone would know who Maia Fremont was afterward.

Taking another steadying breath, she lifted her shaking hand and knocked on the door. The sound was too loud, even to her ears. But she was standing in a cavernous hallway. The cathedral ceilings over her head ended in arched peaks, so tall she swore she could see clouds building in them. The gray stone was familiar, though. How many peasants like herself had stared at the pristine marble castle and wished they might see the interior at least one time in their life?

Sixteen guards stood on either side of her. Each of them wore gleaming silver chest plates that reflected her red features and the crazed curls that billowed around her head. When she'd first gotten here, she had sworn those curls were tamed. That had very much changed by the time she'd made it up the massive stairwell to the castle.

She smoothed her hands over the red locks, trying not to make it obvious that she was staring at her own reflection on the chest of the nearest guard. He shifted, almost as though he had turned toward her and made her reflection a little easier to see.

"Thank you—" she started to say, only to be interrupted by the door opening.

A stately woman stood on the other side. Her expression was severe, her dark hair pulled back so tightly that it made her features seem pinched. A beak for a nose must have been put there to stare down at other people, like an arrow pointing toward something the woman didn't like.

"You're late," the woman hissed. The words struck through the air like the crack of a whip.

"I'm sorry," Maia replied. "I was told noon."

"It is nearly half past noon."

It wasn't, though. She'd been punctual, and had arrived nearly an hour early. Maia had made certain that nothing, not even an unexpected circumstance, could ruin this opportunity.

But she couldn't just say that the woman was lying. Clearly this woman worked with the princess, and to argue with someone who had that much power was folly.

Anger made her cheeks burn even more. A part of her wanted to argue, but Maia had learned a long time ago to stay quiet, even if she was angry. If they wanted flowers for the wedding, she was contracted to do so. They couldn't find someone else this late. Maia opened her mouth to apologize for her supposed tardiness, only to snap it shut again as the woman stood aside and gestured with her hand.

"Come on then," the words were angry and clipped. "Get inside."

She did what she was told.

Maia still had the question of why she was even meeting with the princess. As far as she had guessed, she would meet with the head of staff or whoever oversaw the wedding. There was no reason for her to meet with the princess herself, or any of the royal family.

Yet, when she'd gotten to the castle, the first thing they'd done was send her right up the stairs to this room. She wasn't one to question why she was getting those orders, if only so she could see more of the castle itself.

But still, it was odd to walk into a building so full of opulence. Her flowers had been taken the moment she'd stepped foot onto the castle grounds, and she'd never felt like her arms were so empty.

All the oddities were worth it to see this particular room, though. Where the rest of the castle was gray, this haven for the princess was glistening white marble. The ceilings were painted blue with clouds dancing across them that looked so real Maia wondered if she could touch one. The bed in the far corner looked plush and comfortable, with its sky blue blankets and gauzy white fabric hanging from the posts.

This room was larger than her entire cottage was big. There was a dresser taller than Maia, a seating area with six different chairs, and a podium that was placed right in front of a mirror that must have taken years to perfect with its massive silver frame. Then there was the balcony. Four doors opened up to the entirety of the kingdom, laid out like a child's play set before her eyes. It was hard not to stare at the town. All the little, quaint homes painted different colors with wisps of chimney smoke above them.

But then her gaze turned to the right, and she was frozen yet again. The most beautiful woman in the entire kingdom stood just beside that podium. Golden hair coiled in waves down her shoulders, and spilled nearly to the small of her back. Not a single, glistening strand was out of place. Tiny, pointed ears were just barely visible where they poked through the gilded strands. The princess wore a white dress that tucked in at her ridiculously tiny waist. Even Maia thought if she wrapped her hands around the woman's torso, her fingers might meet.

Not that she would. There was bound to still be dirt underneath her nails.

Sky-blue eyes matching the ceiling and the world beyond the balcony turned to look at her. The princess was lovely in body as well as face, it seemed. Tiny bow lips, perfectly plush, were contained within a face that was porcelain smooth and certainly never reddened like Maia could feel her own doing.

"You're beautiful," Maia stuttered, before grabbing fistfuls of her brown dress and dropping into a curtsey.

Princess Liliana laughed, and the sound was like the tinkling of bells. "My goodness, aren't you charming?"

No one had ever called her that before. People forgot that Maia even existed. She wasn't charming, she was odd and slightly cloying to be around. Or at least, that was what her father used to say when he'd been alive. He'd always suggested she stay on a separate side of the house before anyone had come over.

But correcting a princess seemed inappropriate. And besides, when the princess said it, it made Maia feel like she was, perhaps, slightly charming.

She stayed in the curtsey for too long before straightening. "It's an honor to create the florals for your wedding, your highness."

"Ah, yes, that's what you're doing here. I thought perhaps you were another maid."

The princess smoothed her hands down the intricately beaded bodice. Maia took a step closer, and realized the tiny pearlescent beads were actually woven in a pattern. They were roses. Shimmering roses that spilled down her chest into a smooth satin skirt that swayed with her movement. She was exquisite. The true depiction of all the elven blood the royal family shared. Nearly half blooded, if the rumors were true.

Maia needed to remember where she was. She certainly needed to not gape at the princess like she was a complete dolt.

But it was hard being in the presence of a half-elven woman when she herself only had the merest drop of elvish blood. It was like standing in front of the sun.

"I hope the flowers are to your liking. It's an honor to be part of the first royal wedding in many years." She cleared her throat, trying hard not to stare at the pillowy cushions of the princess's breasts, which really were impressively high. How did she get them to stand up like that without it hurting?

The princess wandered over to the podium, stood on it, and

admired her reflection. "A royal wedding that will chain me to a beast. What a wonderful thing it will be."

She could hear the bitterness in the words, and pity flooded through her chest. "You are not... I'm sorry. Did you say a beast?"

"You haven't heard? My father is marrying me off to the trolls. It's a bid for peace, although I highly doubt such creatures are capable of controlling their baser instincts."

Maia felt all the blood drain out of her face. She grabbed for the nearest object, a chair at the vanity, as she listed to the side. "Trolls?"

She'd never seen one herself, of course. They were rarely seen in these parts, but she'd heard they were getting closer. Attacks on the outskirts of the kingdom were becoming more regular. Rumors abound that trolls were tunneling through the ground and coming into homes from the basements. Everyone knew to fear the beastly creatures.

They hardly even fought with weapons. They liked to use their massive fists, pounding a man's skull until it popped into nothing more than gore and brains.

"Your father wouldn't marry you off to one of them... would he?" she asked, her voice quiet as maids suddenly poured into the room.

Six maids, each of them in the same black and white outfit. Their skirts kissed the floor, their hair pulled back just as tightly as the beak-nosed woman who still stood at the door. They all lined up against the wall, waiting for Princess Liliana's command.

"I'm a princess. I don't get to choose who I marry." Then she looked over her shoulder at Maia, and she swore there was a calculating look on the princess's face. "Do you get to pick who you marry... I'm sorry, what was your name again?"

"Maia, your highness." It was so strange that a princess wanted to know her name that she almost forgot the original question. Clearing her throat, she shifted from foot to foot as she tried to find the right words. "I cannot marry."

"You cannot? What an odd choice of words."

"My father..." She shouldn't even be talking about this, but the words still poured out of her. "When my father died, I was his sole heir. If I want to keep the business in my name, and I very much do, then I cannot marry. Whatever I inherited from my father would transfer over to my husband, and there are very few suitors out there who wouldn't sell the whole thing."

Her father's business had hardly been his in the end. Maia grew the flowers into the perfect blossoms. She cut them at the right time, making sure all the arrangements were perfect. And yes, it was hard. Few people had a reason to spend money on flowers when there were more important things. But plenty of nobility used to sponsor her father simply so that their homes looked more impressive when people came to visit.

Then he'd died. Fewer nobles wanted to give a woman money when she was running the business, even though the product hadn't changed.

The princess turned, looking perfect even though more maids had rushed to attach more fabric onto her back, weaving through the strands of her hair beneath a veil. They draped jewels over her throat and rings on her hands. But the princess's eyes were on Maia.

"Come here," the princess said, her voice low and melodic.

An icy cold wind coiled around her. It seemed to take root in her chest, twisting painfully the longer she stood still. She had to move, even though she didn't want to. Maia drifted forward as though in a dream, taking one of those bejeweled hands when one was offered to her.

She stared in shock as the princess turned her hand over, looking at the callouses on her palm and the dirt underneath her nails before gently kissing her fingertips. "You and I are the same. Stuck in a life we didn't choose. Unknowing who our husband will be, or if we even want to marry. I feel such kinship with you."

"Kinship, your highness?"

"You are alone, are you not?"

That stabbed her right in the heart. Because yes, she was. Her mother had died when she'd been very young, and her father had passed last year. It had been hard ever since. Maia had worked her entire life for her father until she'd been little more than skin and bones some years. Even during a good year, she hadn't time to find friends or even suitors.

But it was hard to believe a princess was ever really alone.

It was almost as though she said the words out loud. The princess smiled, but it didn't quite reach her eyes. "You can be surrounded by people and never feel like a single one truly knows you."

Again, that icy cold sensation stabbed at her. What was it? Magic? It felt like some kind of power coiling throughout her entire body.

Maia supposed that made sense. Swallowing hard, she tried to tug her hand out of the princess's grip, only to find that the other woman was gripping onto her a little too tightly.

"Your highness?" she asked, trying not to look too afraid in front of the other women in the room. "Are you well?"

"I'm fine," the princess said, but she didn't appear to be well. "It's rare to find someone who is so alike me. I'd like you to be in my wedding party, Maia."

She... what?

"Excuse me?" Maia asked, certain she hadn't heard the princess correctly.

"I think you would look lovely standing up there next to me. I need someone who won't look afraid as the trolls come in. You seem like you have a spine of steel and clearly have your wits about you, as a business woman."

But why would a princess want her? They'd never met before today, and even if they had known each other for years, it simply wasn't done. She wasn't even remotely nobility. Not in the slightest.

"I don't think—"

The princess snapped her fingers and all the maids moved away from her as one. It was strange to watch them. Every step was synchronized, as though they had planned every moment of this.

"I would like Miss Maia to wear a gown of the finest quality. She will stand beside me as the brutes enter our castle grounds, and she will be the first they see. No one will question if she's afraid, or if I am afraid." That smile appeared on her face again, so perfect made her appear to be made of stone. "She will be the only one to accompany me to the altar."

"I don't really want to—"

"I won't take no for an answer," the princess interrupted her. Her bright blue eyes turned steely, as though she was unused to anyone even beginning to say the word no to her. "Or would you like me to ask my father to ensure you are there?"

No, she didn't want to catch the attention of the king. He was known throughout their lands for his iron fist and his speed to kill. She'd heard many artisans who came to the castle never returned to their home because their product didn't provide him with what he needed.

"No need," she whispered. "I'd be honored to be there with you on your wedding day."

Some of the tension leaked out of the princess. She held out both of her hands, waiting for maids to appear underneath and help turn her back toward the mirror. "Good. I simply don't believe I could do it without you."

What strange words they were, as two more maids gestured for Maia to follow them and drew her toward a dressing room.

It was an odd day already, and apparently it was only going to get more strange by the hour.

A Darkness So Sweet

Chapter 2

Splashing water over his face, Ragnar tried to still his thoughts. They'd been rushing for the better part of two months now. A hundred thoughts, a thousand of them, voices screaming in his mind over and over again.

What he had agreed to do was wrong.

No, it was more than wrong. It was repulsive. Helping his people in any way that he could—that was the honorable thing he had chosen to do. But marrying a human?

He wasn't sure he'd be able to stomach it. He'd walk down that stupid aisle and he'd throw up right at her feet. Not in fear, but in knowing that he was going to marry one of her kind. Humans were creatures he had never found attractive, and yet now he would be bound to one. Not just in life and in marriage, but offspring were expected as well, which would require...

Gagging again, he shook his head and braced himself on the edge of the leather basin. He could do this. He had been bid by his king to make this connection, even if it was a lie.

The human king James had asked for peace. The troll king Egil had laughed and said the only peace would come from elven blood. And that was when the treaty had been signed. It was King James who had offered up his own daughter. A woman who was half elven. Her blood was pure, far more pure than Ragnar's own, that was certain.

His people needed those bloodlines. They were tired of the baser instincts that came with being made of mud and fur. It had taken centuries for them to build up as much elven blood as they already had. The magic that ran in their veins was stronger than most humans would ever see, but it still wasn't enough.

The troll king had no interest in using his own offspring for this treaty, however. No. He would not give a prince to a mortal woman.

That was where Ragnar came in.

The flap to his tent opened, the supple leather barely making a sound as another massive troll walked through the opening. His brother, Gunnar, was the spitting image of their father. Broad shoulders, darker green skin, and tusks that were so large they nearly curved up to his cheekbones. His flat features were what made him so handsome to the troll women, but it was the faded stripes on his skin that set him even more apart.

They had the same set, he and his brother. Markings that made them blend into the foliage when they moved through the birch groves that dotted their mountain home. But Ragnar had not been blessed with the same deep green skin. He took after their mother, with plum and mulberry streaked beneath the tattoos across his arm and chest.

"You look like we're sending you to the gallows, rather than a wedding," his brother said with a laugh. He leaned forward and smacked Ragnar's shoulder hard enough that he knocked into the basin and nearly sent it to the floor. "Careful. Your troll wife will wish to know her husband is strong."

He could still taste the bile on his tongue at the thought of her. He groaned, "You know I have no interest in humans."

"Yes, you've always found them so disgusting. Why was that again?"

"Because they are weak. Their skin is far too pale. They have no talons, no claws, nothing even remotely pretty about them. Instead they are just—"

Gunnar interrupted him because he'd heard this rant far too many times. "Fleshy bags of weakness that should be hunted into the next realm?"

"Yes!" He burst out. "That's exactly what they are, and I have no patience for it. I understand the king having no wish to marry his son to one of them, believe me. But why is he sending me, of all people?"

"Because you are the best of us."

The best of them.

He'd heard it countless times. And he knew that there was some sense to the claim. He was larger than most trolls. Both he and his brother were massive beasts, even among their kind. His chest was broad, his waist trim, his tusks were sizeable but not overwhelmingly large. Their mother had been nearly a quarter elf, which gave both him and Gunnar impressive magical abilities. Any woman would be glad to have him.

Ragnar reached for a few of the piercings in his ear, tugging at the ones that he'd gotten for his wife. Each of them had meaning, but the rings at the very tips of his pointed ears showed her that he had plenty of elven blood to gift their children. There were more piercings as well. Countless of them.

Ones he had gotten for her. The famed mate he had dreamt of his entire life, who would now prove to be a nightmare.

Sighing, he shook his head. "I am not the best of us. If they were looking for that troll, then they should have chosen you."

Gunnar grinned, his tusks only marginally getting in the way of the expression. "Ah, yes. But I am not meant to have a troll wife yet."

It was always the same excuse. The same reasoning. Those who were meant to have troll wives were found in the smoke and mirages of those who could see the future. Just like he was now supposed to go see their Bone Reader. The seer who would tell him that he was, indeed, about to meet his mate for life. Confirming what he already knew, because the king's Smoke Breather had already deemed it so.

Sighing, he ran his hand over his head, scratching at the newly shaved sides that were already growing sharp stubble. "I shaved my head for her. For this woman who I know I will not wish to have as a troll wife."

"And yet, you look like a mate." Gunnar opened the flap of his tent and a spear of light filled the room. "Come, brother. Morning is upon us and the Bone Reader grows antsy to get home."

"At least she can go home alone," he muttered, and followed his brother out into the sunlight.

He lifted a hand to cover his eyes, the burning light of the sun a blinding white that took long moments for him to get used to. Trolls were not creatures who regularly found themselves in sunlight. Many of them still had the slitted gaze of a cat, or the rounded wide-eyed vision of owls. Twilight was the time when trolls saw best. Not at high noon like this.

Grumbling under his breath, he weaved through a crowd of his brethren. Women and men, trolls of immense power, created a wall between him and his fate. He pushed through muscular bodies, all while listening to the sound of clinking piercings and gnashing teeth. The flashing of fangs and tusks and claws filled his vision until he pushed through the many-colored bodies to the center of their tented circle. And there she sat.

The Bone Reader.

She swayed on the ground, her legs crossed beneath her. Her dark hair was dreaded and piled atop her head in intricate designs. There were bones woven throughout those strands. The remains of creatures she called upon when she wished to see the future. Her eyes were milky white, and her skin a pale lavender that was so thoroughly tattooed it was almost impossible to see what her skin color really was.

She sat cross-legged on a rug someone had laid out for her, a low hum building underneath her breath as she swayed. The other trolls fell silent as Gunnar shoved him into the middle. They all watched, waiting for the moment when they would witness the confirmation of a mated pair.

His stomach rolled again. He did not want this to be his moment. Ragnar had always prayed that he would find a troll wife with certain traits he'd find beautiful. Rounded muscles in her arms. Tusks that were perhaps smaller than his own, but ones that would scrape against his as he kissed her. Light blue skin, the color of the sky just before the clouds came in. And pitch black hair, like coals in a fireplace.

Now, he would find none of those things in the partner he had been thrust upon.

The Bone Reader reached out her hand, her palm full of tiny animal bones. Some of them were rabbit, he knew that from memory. Others, he thought, might've been the individual ribs of a snake. They all rattled in her hand as she shook them.

"Ragnar, Seed of Frode, Son of Ingvild. You stand before me in search of a troll wife."

No.

No, he didn't.

He didn't want a troll wife, not like this. He wanted a woman who desired him. Who could see the beauty in the world they shared together. He wanted a wife who didn't hate his people, like a human certainly would.

But the bones never lied. They rattled in her hands on their own now, magic coursing through them as the icy tendrils of their power coiled around his body. He was forced to take another step closer, bit by bit, until he was right in front of her.

He stared into those milky eyes, feeling the icy shards of her power crawling through him, and he envisioned the troll wife he wanted. He thought of her bravery, in the face of all odds. He thought of the kindness in her heart, and how she looked at all trolls with love and not judgment. But above all else, he thought of a bride who loved him dearly and with every ounce of her being.

The icy power radiated through his body until he was on his knees before the Bone Reader. Her eyes were level with his, and he could see the power in her gaze. It sparkled through her body, making her veins glow with a strange darkness that he could see like a web through her skin. She was powerful. He wondered how they'd gotten such a powerful seer to risk her life and come this close to a human settlement.

The Bone Reader trailed her fingers along his ears. They weren't as long as hers, but his points were prominent.

"A good bloodline," she said quietly. "You got these from your mother."

"My father had less elven blood than she did."

"And so you will follow in your father's footsteps. A man who sees true goodness in his children, regardless of what they look like. You have a good heart, Ragnar, but I fear you are short sighted."

He wasn't following the last bit. Or the first, really. The princess was supposed to be well over half elven and that should mean his children would be even more than that. "Has the king lied to us?" he asked without thinking.

But she did not answer his question, because that was not the reason she was here. The bones in her hands rattled free. They clacked against each other, skittering across the ground into a pattern that meant nothing to his eyes, but everything to the Bone Reader.

She poured over them, her back arching as she hunched over the skeletal remains. She murmured under her breath, nudging a bone here and there as though it displeased her. But then she leaned back on her haunches.

He could see the disappointment in her gaze. The answer was not the one he wanted either, and he felt the need to reassure her that he already knew the damage was done. He would suffer with a bride he did not want. Their lives would be miserable and he would give up the future he had once dreamt for himself, all because the king thought he was the right troll for this job.

Instead, she gestured for a man at her side to come forward with a bowl of white paint. "A troll wife is a responsibility. She weaves herself around your soul like the roots of a tree."

The Bone Reader pressed her palm to the bowl of paint and then over his thundering heart. It was all he could hear. The pounding in his chest nearly drowned out the sound of her words as she continued to speak.

"I open your heart to the woman who walks into your life. It is your responsibility to take care of your troll wife. You will keep her safe, keep her happy, and you will put her needs above all others. Even your own."

He could hear the crowd murmuring in agreement. To them, the creation of a mated pair was nothing short of holy. They were bound, body, mind, and soul. There was no getting out of a mated pair without death. Not even if he begged the gods themselves to free him from the torment.

The Bone Reader dipped both of her hands into the paint this time, a grim expression on her face as she met his gaze. "You have been blinded by too many years of fighting and hatred, Ragnar. Your troll wife waits for you beyond the walls of that city. You will stride into the wedding with your heart locked away because what you see is far beyond what your heart can stand to reason with. But the gods have spoken. The gods have sent her to you. I will do my best to open your gaze."

She reached forward and pressed the palms of her hands into the hollows of his eyes. Her fingers reached beyond his temples, into the short strands of hair he'd shaved just yesterday. Leaving the handprints behind, she met his gaze once more with a sad expression.

As the trolls behind him went wild, their chants echoed through the clearing. "Troll wife! Troll wife!"

"The hunt is on," the Bone Reader said. "The gods have chosen wisely for you. Even if you do not believe it to be so."

"I know you are lying," he quietly replied, standing and towering above her. "It will be a hard path for both of us to walk."

"I suspect you will make it harder for her to walk than it has to be. I know my words will change little to nothing in your eyes, but Ragnar, hear me. It is not the end of the world to be mated to a human."

"I don't see you mated to one."

He turned toward the crowd of trolls behind him and lifted his fist into the air. They all cried out, stomping their feet on the ground and repeating the chant of *troll wife*. They would hunt tonight. They would go out into the human realm and bring back his mate.

They didn't care that he didn't want one. Nor did they care he didn't want her.

This was his path to walk. No matter the consequences of what waited for him at the end.

Chapter 3

This is... white."

"No, no, dear. It's cream. This is the one that the princess chose."

And she was getting a very bad feeling about all of this.

Maia knew for certain that the dress they had shoved her into wasn't cream. She was staring at it in the mirror. Anyone with eyes could see that this was, in fact, a white dress. It was simple, but beautiful. A square neckline wasn't too risque and the satin bodice tucked in around her ribs and then poured from her hips in a delicate waterfall of clinging fabric that left very little to the imagination.

On someone who was born noble, it likely would have been even more elegant. Maia's arms were left exposed and the muscles there were far too prominent for any noble woman to have. But the dress was pretty.

They'd brought her into a back room that was just as nice as the princess's. The bed in the corner was clearly unused, and while the view wasn't quite as nice, it was still larger than her entire cottage and filled with fine velvet. And the smell of it. The room smelled like fresh strawberries, and she really had no idea how they were doing that.

The maid next to her tsked. "It needs more lace."

"I don't understand why I need more lace at all. I'm going to be standing up there next to the princess. Shouldn't I look... plain?" Maia snapped her mouth shut as the maid started snickering.

Apparently, no one was concerned that Maia would outshine the princess. Honestly, she wasn't all that concerned with it, either. But it was awfully strange to be wearing a white gown next to the woman of the hour.

She should say something. She knew she should. A part of her screamed to just open her mouth and say she wasn't going to do this.

Maia could figure things out if the royal family pulled out of the flower contract. But they wouldn't. Anyone with their head on straight would know it was far too close to the wedding—less than an hour away—for any contract to be dissolved.

Unless they didn't want flowers. But that would be the scandal of the next ten years if they didn't have flowers at the princess's wedding.

Maia talked herself out of arguing. Saying anything would just make her look even more foolish, and she didn't want to look foolish in front of these people. So she wouldn't. She would keep her mouth shut. Even if it made her very uncomfortable. Even if alarm bells were screaming in her head that this wasn't right and she should be looking at the finer details.

Like that veil they were carrying to her.

"Oh, no." She put her hands up and backed away from the mirror. "No, I don't need that. That's..."

"What the princess asked. When the trolls enter the room, she has decided she would like your face to be covered. It only makes sense that they should see her features and not yours."

But that wasn't a face covering. It was a veil. Like the kind a bride would wear.

She was in white. There was a veil. Something was definitely wrong with this situation and she didn't like where it was heading. She just needed a few seconds to get her head on straight and then she could confront everyone in this room.

All it would take was for her to say that something felt wrong. The maids here weren't paid well enough to lie for anyone, after all. They were cut from the same cloth she was. Maia wasn't born into this life of riches and wonderful things. She was like them.

But then the maid shook her head and sighed. "What do you think is happening here, flower girl? You're just lucky the princess even looked at you. Who wouldn't want this opportunity?"

"I suppose," Maia murmured, but she still didn't let them walk toward her with that veil. "I don't expect anything to be happening. It's just all rather odd. Don't you think?"

"Rude," the maid said. "You're ridiculously rude. This is the opportunity of a lifetime. You want a contract with the castle that never ends? You put on the veil."

It would be life changing if the castle signed a contract with her that declared her the official florist for every function that they had. The castle had more money than they knew what to do with. If the princess liked her, then they might do just that.

Still, this was all too odd. The warning bells going off in her mind wouldn't let her agree to all this without pushing back some. "I just don't think—"

Her stomach interrupted her complaints. The angry growl filled the room with an embarrassingly loud noise.

Yet again, the maid looked at her with pity. "We'll get you some food once the ceremony is over, too. We'll do something about that hair of yours, and then you can head out to be with the princess again. Yes?"

She tried. She really did. The words were right at the tip of her tongue, and a part of her screamed to stand up for herself. All it would take was a single word. But they were all staring at her. They all had expectations, and they were, unfortunately, in a position of power. These maids knew the royal family better than anyone else. They were the ones getting her dressed, and she had to listen to them.

Even if it felt wrong.

So she nodded and let them work on her hair. They curled it, coiled it, made it look entirely unlike her. All her curls were smoothed out and piled atop her head. They were so pretty and she wasn't... that. Winged eyeliner made her eyes seem bigger. Bright red rouge burned when they put it on her lips, making them so red it was almost comical to look at. When they were done, they had created a different person.

She bit her lip, horrified at what she saw. This wasn't her. It wasn't even remotely her.

"Stop doing that," one of the maids said before smacking her shoulder. "Now we'll have to fix your teeth."

Baring said teeth, Maia realized she had gotten some of that rouge on them. The bright red streak seemed like an omen for what was about to happen, and she had no way of stopping it.

They scrubbed the three teeth affected by her mistake and then covered her hair and face with the veil. Why now? She had no idea. All she knew was that they were then tugging her out of the room and down the halls again.

All she could hear were the repeated clacks of their heels on the stone floor. She could barely see at all through the veil, just shadowy figures behind the white that all moved past her. Even then, it was distracting to feel her own hot breath pressing back against her face. Her breath puffed the veil out and still, she couldn't see anything until the maids suddenly let go of her hands and then she was... alone?

Why were they leaving her alone? Why were they doing any of this?

She reached for the veil to remove it from her face.

"I wouldn't do that if I were you," a deep voice said. "You'll ruin all the hard work of the women who prepared you."

Not alone, then. A cold sweat broke out over her entire body and she froze. She wasn't proud of it. Maia had always been that person, though. A piece of her knew she was in danger and instead of fighting or running or even just being scared, she was the first person to appease whatever caused her danger. Her father had likened her to a fawn, once. A creature who made others want to help her, even if they had originally hunted her.

A long exhale puffed the veil out just enough to reveal scuffed wooden floors before it dropped back into place. She returned her hands to her side and replied, "They did work awfully hard."

"I should thank you. My daughter was very pleased you showed up when you did."

His... daughter?

Maia's knees went weak. She stopped being able to breathe, although that might've been the tightness of the dress. Certainly, it wasn't the king himself in this room with her. The king, who everyone in this kingdom knew to fear.

Rumors about him fluttered through her head like a flock of birds had suddenly taken flight. He'd loved to behead trolls in the war when he had been a young man. Humans didn't satisfy him any longer, and the women who were brought to his bedchamber never left. He used to be known for wearing a necklace of troll ears around his neck, their multi-colored skin and pointed tips obvious to all who saw him.

And then there were the darker rumors. The ones that said he bled young women dry and had his daughter drink the life force to keep her young. Someone had once said he hunted down strong young men in the hedge maze at the center of his castle because he grew tired of hunting animals.

That man was now standing behind her. She could feel his breath toying with the faint hairs at the nape of her neck. Then his fingers as he trailed his hand along the back of her neck to her shoulder.

This was bad. This was very bad.

Was he going to sacrifice her at the start of his daughter's wedding? Why was he even here? He was the king. Surely there was something very important for him to do. Like be in the wedding.

She had to say something. Had to figure out what he wanted.

But what came out of her mouth was, "I just arranged the flowers, your highness."

He chuckled, but the sound had no happiness in it. "Of course you did. I thought I heard wind that you arrived with a cart full of flowers that you had harnessed to your shoulders like you were a work horse."

She didn't have the money for a horse or a donkey. So she had to do it herself. That was something this man would never understand.

He continued speaking, "No, that is not why I'm thanking you. My daughter is a particular young woman. You could say she doesn't make friends easily, nor is she all that interested in doing so. When she came to my rooms claiming that you were going to be standing up there with her, I was rather surprised."

"Truth be told, so am I."

"I'm sure you are." He walked around in front of her, his shadow blocking out the light in the room, and then slowly, he lifted her veil.

She'd heard he was handsome, and he was. Though his hair had turned silver, there was still strength in his square jaw. The once broken ridge of his nose might have been ugly on anyone else, but on him, it was austere. Shrewd brown eyes stared into her very soul, making it hard to look at anything but them.

Still, she looked. She looked at the golden crown on his head and the gold tunic he wore. But mostly, she looked at the malice in his eyes.

This was a man unused to being kind. Maia had been around people like him her entire life. She'd come to learn how to read them, and in this moment, she knew he wanted to hurt her.

The king's hands came down on her shoulders, squeezing just a little too hard. "Are you loyal to your kingdom?"

The change in subject was so unusual, she wasn't exactly sure how to respond. "I am."

"Are you certain?"

"I love this kingdom with all my heart. It's my home, and I'm proud of it." Was that what he wanted? She could continue if he needed to hear her say other parts that she loved.

He sighed, those hands squeezing harder until she thought her bones might break. But then he released her, and Maia had to lock her knees so she didn't fall onto the floor.

"You're shaking like a leaf," he grumbled. "My daughter claimed you were far braver than that."

How would the princess know? She had seen Maia for only a few moments before she'd made some insane decision.

Breathing hard, Maia licked her lips and tried to sound like the brave person they wanted her to be. "I can be, your highness. Although, I will admit, your daughter does not know me."

"She sees into souls," he replied. He glared at her as though her performance had been lacking. "She sees deep into the hearts and minds of those who stand before her. If she says you are brave, then you are."

Was that what the ice cold sensation had been? Maia had thought the woman was controlling her like a puppet master, reaching into her mind and forcing her actions. Perhaps the princess was skilled at both talents. Neither of which would be surprising, considering the amount of elven blood that ran through her veins.

"I..." What did he want to hear? What could she say that would convince him to leave her alone? "I suppose I have not had many opportunities to be brave."

Of course she had. She had spent her entire life keeping her mouth shut when men like this one threatened her. She had stood by her father when he'd gotten sick, learned every part of their business, broke her back day in and day out in the gardens and then prettied herself up for the customers in the afternoon. Maia had been brave every single moment of her life, but this man made her feel as though none of it had been all that impressive.

The anger in his gaze softened. "My dear, sweet girl. You are going to be braver today than you have ever been. You will be there when the trolls arrive. You will greet them. You will be the person they see before all others. In that moment, you will have to be brave."

"What do you mean I will greet them?"

But then he flipped the veil back down, placed his hand on her back, and shoved her forward. Suddenly thrown out into the light, she could do nothing other than walk where he drew her.

There were more shadows. All of them moving and bobbing in front of her. Almost as though there was a crowd surrounding the two of them. Then sound hit her. The murmurs of people, hundreds of them, all standing in this room.

Were they already at the wedding? Maia tried to straighten her spine a little more, making sure she wasn't slumped over beside the glowing beacon of the princess.

The king's booming voice silenced them all. "My people! It is a great honor to have you all here. I beg you all to steal your hearts and your minds, for it is now that the trolls will enter."

She tried not to tremble, but it was hard not to in the sudden silence that filled the room. And she couldn't see anything at all. Not a single thing through the damn veil, but they had said she would be the person to greet the trolls, which made little sense.

That twisted feeling in her gut grew worse. She thought she might vomit. Something was terribly wrong.

Maia turned to leave, only to find that heavy hand at her back again. Not just a hand. Something sharp pressed against her spine, right between her ribs, with its tip against her hammering heart.

"Do not move a muscle," the king growled into her ear. The threat made her freeze even more, like ice had filled her veins.

That was when she heard them. The whooping cries, the animalistic snarls, nightmarish noises filled the room with their haunting song.

The trolls had arrived.

Chapter 4

Trolls scattered around him. They all lunged in different directions, their chests bare and their tusks on full display. Ragnar and his brother strode through them, hearing the calls of "Troll wife" in their language.

The humans called it the black tongue. They were so afraid of what the trolls were saying in their deep voices and their chanting calls, they assumed it was dark magic that would threaten their lives. Or perhaps steal their souls right out of their bodies. The humans feared everything the trolls did, though. They feared his people for just existing.

The air in the castle was thick with smoke. It coiled out of sconces on the walls and made it hard to breathe. Black smudges darkened the walls. Not to mention the ever present scent of body odor that clung to these people. They tried to hide it with perfumes and bundles of herbs they wore around their necks, but he could smell it.

He bared his teeth, flashing tusks at women who fainted at the sight of him. One of them, who wore a bright yellow dress that puffed up around her body like some kind of crazed flower, toppled right into the man behind her. He caught her for a moment, only to freeze when Ragnar caught his gaze. The man released his hold on the woman and allowed her to fall onto the floor with a hard thud.

It was hard to hear over the chanting calls of his people, but he did. Humans weren't even capable of protecting their own kind. How was he to endure one as a wife?

Gunnar grinned as they made their way up to the podium where King James stood. Ragnar had never met the human king, but he knew what the man looked like. Silver hair. Angry eyes. A crown on top of his head that had been poured out of gold stolen from his own people. Not to mention the gemstones on it that had been set by troll hands.

Beside him stood a smaller figure. She wore the customary white that he had been warned she'd be in, but her face was covered by a veil.

It was strange. He'd figured his bride would be tall and willowy, and had expected the lithe body of a nearly half elven woman. Instead, the woman he saw was rather broad shouldered. She had strong arms revealed by the dress she wore. Her biceps were remarkably defined for a woman of her lineage, and he had to wonder what had given a princess arms like that. Although, he supposed, he knew very little about her people.

The veil rustled with her breath. In and out, a little too fast. There was the fear he had expected. The terror that he was going to eat her alive.

Some part of him found a thrill in that. She should fear him. He was massive in comparison to her, strong arms or not. The king barely came up to his shoulders, and this woman only came up to his chest. She should tremble knowing that it would take so very little for him to snap her neck or rip her head clean off her shoulders if he wished.

He did not, though. Because his own king would be livid if he killed the princess that was supposed to end all this fighting. At least for now. Perhaps someday King Egil would give him leave to rid himself of her shackles.

The human king had his arm behind his daughter with a smile on his face that didn't reach his eyes. "It is an honor to meet the troll worthy of my daughter."

Ragnar tilted his head to the side, knowing the sconces on the walls would gild his sharpened tusks. "Is it?"

Again that veil annoyingly shuddered. Had he said something wrong? Somehow, he felt like he was making all of this worse. But that wasn't entirely his fault. The two of them had to marry each other, and she was a human woman who knew nothing about his people. Of course she would think him blunt and callous.

Gunnar nudged him from behind. And that was another sign that he was being too gruff. So he ground his teeth together and bit out, "Princess Liliana, it is a rare treat for one such as me to be before one such as you."

The veil stilled. There was no sound at all now. Not even the sound of her panting.

The calls for his troll wife died down, and there was sudden silence. Just him, staring down at this woman in white with her face hidden from him. What did she look like beneath? He hadn't been at the meeting between kings, nor had anyone even offered to tell him about her appearance.

He hoped her hair was at least dark. If she had black or perhaps even deep brown hair, he could suffer through this. At least then, if he turned her around, he could pretend she was a troll.

The king lifted one of his hands and raised his voice. "The trolls have arrived! From this day forward, with a marriage to my daughter, our kingdoms will be united. No more fighting. No more war. Together, we will walk into a new era."

A pretty speech, but not one that Ragnar readily believed. None of the trolls did. This was a bid to perhaps see if the humans could keep their word. Did the trolls believe it was the end of fighting with them? Certainly not.

The king moved behind his daughter and another man stepped up. This one wore a long black robe with a stiff white collar around his neck. The man looked at Ragnar's bare chest and gulped.

"We are gathered here today to witness a ceremony of binding. Together, these two individuals will walk into the future, hand in hand, soul with soul." On and on he droned more useless words about giving and taking in life. Yet, he was right. A relationship was a give and take, but in his case... well, it would mostly be take.

He turned toward the woman beside him instead of the priest. She kept her gaze firmly on the floor, which he found to be rather odd. There was much to look at beyond the pattern on the floor.

Ragnar was a troll standing beside her, and she wasn't even curious about him. He'd at least expected her gaze on his claws that flexed at his sides repeatedly with stress. He wanted this all to be over with, and he'd never been particularly good at hiding how he felt. But no, she didn't look at his claws or his bared skin, or even the tattoos visible on his massive thighs.

She was covered far more than he was, and he found himself ready to see what she looked like.

Gunnar leaned over beside him, lips nearly touching his ear. "Do you think she's hideous?"

"What?" he hissed.

"Is that why they covered her face?"

By all the gods, he hoped not. "She's half elf."

Elves were beautiful creatures. They were lithe and cunning, but they were mostly known for their stunning beauty that nearly blinded anyone who looked at them. A princess with such high elven blood content would be just as beautiful as a natural born elf.

Right?

But then he found himself staring at the veil and trying to see beneath it. Was that a pretty, sharp nose? Or was it the blunted end of a snout?

The priest continued on until suddenly everyone was staring at him. Silence rang through the room yet again, and he realized he hadn't been listening to a word the man had said. He looked over at his brother, who was trying hard not to laugh.

"The priest asked you to kiss your troll wife," he said in the black tongue.

Kiss her?

He felt all the color drain from his cheeks. That was the very last thing he wanted to do. He didn't want to kiss the creature before him, no matter what she looked like. Besides, he was quite certain she was repulsive, and that was why the king was so ready to give her away.

Even the king seemed to hesitate. "I don't think that's necessary."

"Your highness, it is tradition," the priest blustered.

But it was the little princess in front of him who answered for all of them. He was surprised to hear her voice at all. The raspy tones didn't fit the elven bloodline, which should have made her voice sound like the tinkling of bells.

"It's fine," she breathed. "I'll do it."

As if it was something she had to endure. At least they both shared the same mindset.

He reached forward and lifted the veil from her face, slowly revealing a long neck that was both graceful and beautiful. For a moment, he was reassured that he would be getting a bride with high elven blood. At least then he knew what to expect, even if he didn't find their kind physically attractive.

But then he revealed... spots. Dark little flecks that spread across her jaw and even dusted over her far too red lips. Her nose was a little crooked, something he'd only seen in his own kind after they'd been in a fight. Dark eyes, faintly green and faintly brown, looked up at him. They were a little too wide set on her face. And red hair. Bright, flame colored hair that framed her face. They'd clearly tried to tame her curls, but already a soft halo of baby hairs had escaped.

She was... fine, he supposed. As far as humans went, she could have been a lot worse. But she wasn't what he had expected, either.

She looked up at him, her chest rising and falling more quickly the longer he stared at her. Perhaps he was making her uncomfortable. It was just that he wanted to know every inch of his troll wife's face before he bound himself to her.

Those ruby red lips parted, and she whispered, "Did you not want to?"

"He does," Gunnar snarled, before giving him a hard shove between the shoulder blades.

But he didn't. And she didn't want to either, he could tell. Kissing her in front of all these people felt wrong. That was a private act. Even worse, if she was against it.

Her eyes widened a bit, and he wondered how much of his thoughts had been plastered across his face for her to see. She swallowed hard, and then a tiny hand landed on his chest.

"It's all right," she said quietly. "It's all mostly for show, anyway."

He'd make the decision for them then. He slotted his massive hand at her waist, hearing her sharp intake of breath, before dragging her against his chest. The harsh slap of both of her palms against his skin echoed in the church, but he used his free hand to hide her face from the crowd. He cupped her jaw, his fingers spanning most of her head.

Leaning down until their lips nearly touched, he realized these were the first words he was going to say directly to her. No one would hear what he said. No one would know what was shared between breaths.

"I am not your husband," he murmured. "And I never will be."

There it was again. That little gasp that made every part of his body crawl with revulsion. But then he leaned back and turned her toward the crowd, as though they had kissed after all.

Cheers from his people turned thunderous. They shouted their pleasure and pride that he had taken a troll wife. Ragnar wasn't looking at his own people, though. He was looking at hers.

At the confusion on their faces. How some of their expressions were odd before being wiped clean, like they didn't want any of his people to notice. When he looked down at the princess, however, she appeared dazed. Confused as well. Perhaps it was merely that he did not know how to read humans that well.

Gunnar leaned forward again, already walking back down the aisle. "Let's not give them a chance to change their minds, brother. Take your troll wife and let's go."

He didn't need to be told twice. Ragnar bent at the waist, jammed his shoulder into her hips, and lifted her. There was the faintest squeak from the princess as he tossed her over her shoulder, but even that sound was drowned out by the calls of his people.

King James did not argue. He merely stood there with his stolen crown on his head and watched as his daughter left.

A pit boiled in Ragnar's stomach at that. What father didn't say goodbye after losing his child? What father didn't insist upon just a few more moments with the little girl he'd raised?

He would not pity this woman. He could not, and should not, entertain the thoughts in his mind that she might have had a hard life.

No, he had to focus on all the things he did not like. He was not here for a pet or for mercy. He was here because his king had bid him to do so, and now he had done what his king had asked.

Ragnar strode out of the castle with her on his shoulder. Not a single troll said anything until they had passed the castle walls and moved out into the open air and fields where his people were much more comfortable. Soon enough, they would disappear into the forest and be almost impossible to find.

With the woman still on his shoulder, and cleaner air in his lungs, he felt better. But still, he could smell her now. The musk of her body, the stink of her sweat, and the scent of fear that clung to her skin. Her people didn't bathe often, from what he'd heard, they only bathed once every other week. And even when they did, they cleaned themselves with nothing more than a quick rinse of water only. A bath was in order. And quickly.

"That was too easy," Gunnar said in the black tongue, appearing beside him with a frown on his face.

"I agree."

"She's the princess. They should have fought to keep her."

Such was the reason King Egil hadn't offered his own child. A son of a renowned general, yes. But his own son? Never.

Ragnar turned his gaze to the forest. "Perhaps we should run, then."

"Prepare your woman, brother. I have a feeling she won't like running in her current state."

Right. She would be jostled on his shoulder, and the bone of it would jam into her shoulder and make her ill. He should tell her to prepare herself, because the journey would be long and grueling. What he said was, "Do not throw up on me."

The princess planted her hands on his back and shoved herself upright. "Why would I throw up?"

She'd figure it out on her own. He was certain of that.

As he picked up his pace, feeling her jolting on his shoulder, he could admit he admired her spunk. Every jolt of his body rammed his shoulder into her stomach and likely stole the air from her lungs. She didn't complain, she just wheezed and tightened her stomach muscles. Those strong arms helped prop her up a bit until he really started running.

"But wait—"

She almost slid off his shoulder twice before he planted his hand on her bottom. He could hold her in place like this, but he was surprised to find how plush her ass was. Soft enough to be tempting, and he'd never thought that about a human woman.

He was losing his mind already. He wasn't tempted by a human. He pitied her. Because the moment he looked at her face again, all he would see was a disgusting creature that, somehow, he would have to fuck.

Chapter 5

What the actual fuck was happening to her?

Maia had always had a problem saying no. It was why she'd gotten herself into the whole situation with her father in the first place. He'd been an ailing man, begging her not to let his life's work die, and frankly, she enjoyed gardening. But did she really need to take it all on? Of course not. She could have married. She could have gone on a great adventure without the ties of an ailing father, who had taken up so much of her time.

Instead, she'd stayed. She'd continued his work even after his death. Which had led her to this moment, slung over the muscular shoulder of a troll who was significantly farther from the ground than she'd ever been before.

And what did he tell her? Not to puke on him.

Her mind whirled at the reasoning for that until all of a sudden, he started to run. Not just trot, not even a slight jog with the rest of them. No, the trolls turned as one and they bolted toward the forest with an unnatural speed.

She went from just being uncomfortably slung over his shoulder to having her stomach slammed down on his muscles, again and again. The repetitive strikes sent her meager breakfast up into her throat and it took every part of her to focus on not vomiting.

Which was probably a good thing. At least she was focused on not embarrassing herself rather than the way the world changed in front of her eyes. EverythingE familiar disappeared all at once. She barely managed to lift her head and stare at her entire world disappearing.

The castle faded into the distance. The rolling hills that had always framed her home like emerald swaths of fabric disappeared. They ran through waist high fields of wheat, likely shoulder height for her. Sunlight burned against her back until the world sank into darkness.

The stark difference of being in the forest was hard to ignore. The air was colder. Icy shadows lingered on her spine and danced down her legs until it was difficult to remember what warmth felt like. The sun disappeared, left only to be seen in the dappled marks on the ground through the leaves that soaked up all the heat from their rays. As she lifted her head again, pressing her hands against the small of the troll's back so she could see what they passed by, all she could see were trees.

Maia had spent her entire life living in fields of golden wheat and verdant grass. She had never left the safety of the castle's shadow, nor had she ever traveled. She'd seen the forest, of course. It surrounded large portions of her home, but it was always far away.

When she was young, other children used to talk about these woods. They whispered how dangerous they were, and how people died when they went into it. Monsters roamed among the trees. Not just trolls, but beings that were far older than that.

Slumped over this troll's shoulder, she could see why children would believe those stories. So many of these trees were ancient. She couldn't have fit her arms around them if she stretched herself. The bark was textured, some trees pale silver and others almost white. But the more she stared at them, the more it felt like something was looking back.

Her mind played tricks on her. She swore she could see movement in between the trunks, in the darkness that lingered between the silhouettes of straight lines. It was impossible. There was no one standing there, watching as a woman was taken from her home in the worst case of a miscommunication anyone had ever heard of. But she could still feel their eyes on her.

Swallowing hard, she flopped down when her arms gave out. Her biceps trembled and her stomach ached. Worse than all of it, she feared what the trolls would think once she told them the truth.

She wasn't the princess. Obviously, they had made some kind of deal with the king, but what was she supposed to do about the deception? With a knife at her back and the king himself threatening her, there hadn't been a choice. She'd had to do what the king had told her to do, or be stabbed in front of hundreds.

King James hadn't wanted to give up his daughter, that much was certain. She could appreciate that. No one wanted to be married to a troll, and certainly not the most beautiful woman in the kingdom.

What would the trolls do to her when she told them the truth? They clearly thought she was the princess, and they had made a deal with her people. She hadn't been thinking about any of this when the king had thrust her forward. All she'd thought at the time was that she wanted to stay alive. And if she was going to do that, then she had to do whatever that priest had said. Parrot the words back. Kiss the man in front of her. Marry, when she had promised herself she wouldn't do that and risk everything she'd worked for.

Now, she regretted doing what she was told.

Bracing herself again once her arms had rested, she peered over the shoulder that still dug into her belly and looked at the creature who now believed he washer husband. A troll. He really was a troll.

She'd thought she was hallucinating when he'd pulled back the veil. How strange it was indeed to realize, without question, that the monster she'd seen was real. The dappled sunlight played across his pale lavender features, blending into the tattoos that marred his face. The white paint that had been spread across his eyes and torso had been smudged by his hands when he'd wiped his eyes.

He had tusks. Sharp teeth that curved up from his bottom lip and glinted in the meager sunlight. They were the first thing she'd noticed about the strange creature who had agreed to marry a human. His mouth was broader than her kind, his jaw wider to make room for such impressive teeth. His nose was broad as well, flatter than a human's and more cat-like. But his eyes. Those eyes were as human as her own.

Maia's first impression had been maybe he would be kind. He had the eyes of a kind man, and she'd easily read the thoughts that were filtering through them. It had almost appeared that he hadn't wanted to be there either. The thought of marrying her had turned his stomach, and in that, they shared the same opinion.

But then he'd leaned forward and whispered that he would never be her husband, and Maia felt again the charge of terror that came from those words.

Or maybe that was just vomit pressing against the back of her throat.

"Stop," she hissed out, trying hard to not spew it all down his back.

"No," the monster growled.

"Stop, or I'm going to vomit all down your back."

"I told you not to do that, woman."

She slapped her hand hard against his spine, not caring if he beat her for the action. If he didn't stop, she was going to embarrass herself even further. She wanted to tell him that not vomiting wasn't an active choice, but all that came out was a horrible retching sound.

He stopped immediately and tossed her from his back.

Maia landed in a heap on the ground. Some of it was soft moss, so at least her knees didn't hurt when she landed, but her right wrist cracked against a fallen log. The blinding pain was a distraction only for a moment before everything heaved out of her body in one impressive projectile mess.

Her captor made a low hissing noise, one that she was certain was meant to be an expression of disgust. She was disgusted with herself, too.

But maybe, if she could pull herself together, she could get home. All she had to do was explain to him that she was in the wrong place, at the wrong time. He'd wanted a princess for a wife! She certainly wasn't that.

Just look at her. There was mud on her wedding gown. It splattered over her knees and left dark wet patches all down her chest. She'd managed not to get vomit on the dress, but the puddle of it in the moss was humiliating enough.

She stared down at the fabric and could only feel angry at what the king and princess had done to her. "Cream," she muttered. They'd truly expected her to believe that, and she had.

What a mess she was. None of this would have happened if she had just said something. Her entire life was filled with moments like this because she was too scared or too passive to speak up. All of this was her fault and somehow, that made it even worse.

"What did you say?" the troll asked, his deep voice different from anything she'd ever heard before.

The accent there was similar to how the other troll had spoken. She'd never forget the way that green creature had sounded. Everyone always talked about the black tongue and how just hearing it could curse a person.

But it had sounded so lyrical. Like a song or a hymn the other troll had hummed through words, and that made her feel like an absolute idiot even thinking so pleasantly of him. Because so far, all she had seen from these people was callous treatment and vomit.

She ran her hand under her weeping nose. "I said nothing."

"I have better hearing than humans." He crouched down in front of her, sinking onto his haunches and not even caring that his pants were loosely tied onto the sides of his legs, and his movements revealed more skin than it should have.

She averted her gaze, just in case it was rude for her to stare. "I know you can hear better, and see better. There are many stories humans tell of your kind."

"What do you know of trolls? You won't even look at me."

Why did he want her to? He didn't want to be around her, and he certainly didn't want her as a bride.

So she stared at everything but him. The forest was just as unforgiving, though. She'd always thought there was a romantic quality to the hidden trees and space between the glens. But now, all she saw were the sharp edges of the twigs and the ominous silence that surrounded them.

"I used to dream about walking through this wood," she whispered. "It was always forbidden for any of us to come in here. But I always wondered what magic was hidden within the trees."

"There is no magic hidden here."

"No." Her voice cracked around the word, and she tried hard to rein those feelings in. "I fear there is very little here for anyone but trolls."

Even the rocks that poked through the moss were hard, sharp. Her wrist ached where she'd struck it against the log, and her stomach felt bruised. She feared he'd injured her just by carrying her. Her mind whirled, the truth pressing against her tongue even as hopelessness set in.

She should tell him now. This was all just a horrible mistake. If she didn't tell him the truth soon, he would think she was part of the plan. Would he kill her? Would he do what others had said the trolls did? Skin her alive and then hang her body from the trees?

Finally looking over at the monster that crouched in front of her, she stared at all the pieces of him that could so easily harm her.

His claw tipped hand rested on his knees. The black claws were curved like a falcon's and left little dimples in his skin, as though even he could not escape their sharpness. They could tear out her throat, even if the massive size of his hands didn't give away that he could kill her without a moment's thought. All he would have to do was grab onto her head and twist. The power in the size of his shoulders, in the towering height of him, all of that proved he was a walking weapon.

This troll was a monstrous being, one who had fought her kind for centuries and who would continue to fight them, no matter how much she wished it wasn't true. And now she was married to one. Bound to him before the gods, and there was nothing she could do to change that now.

Exhaling, she wiped her nose one more time and curled her

fingers in her lap. He gave her a look of disgust, but then when wasn't he looking at her like that?

"I think there's been some grave misunderstanding," she said, her voice hoarse from vomiting.

"Indeed."

Had he figured it out without her having to tell him? Perhaps it had become clear to him that Maia was obviously not the princess. She swallowed hard, "Then perhaps you would bring me back to—"

"I was promised a princess who was lithe in figure and light in form. One whose bloodline ran deep with elven magic, and who would gift our sons with true power. You are not what I was promised, princess. And in that, I have no trust that your king knows how to tell the truth at all."

No, no. He had it all wrong. He still thought she was royal, and she wasn't at all. The words stuck in her throat, too jumbled with all her arguments, that they kept coming out wrong. "Well, that's because—"

He stood and all her words dissolved. This troll really was massive. Seated as she was on the ground, staring up at his body, she was forced to face the reality that they were even more different from what she'd thought. Her eyes danced over the swirling tattoos that meandered down his thighs, his bulging calves, all the way down to his bare feet.

She hadn't noticed he wasn't wearing shoes. But the tips of those toes were still marred with claws. Black tipped and terrifying, his feet flexed in the soft moss before he made a noise like a growl.

Maia blinked up at him, ripping her gaze from the sight of those strange feet.

"I have no faith in humans. Nor do I have any respect for your kind. I should have known, elven blood or not, that you would be little more than a dirty creature who only knows how to wallow in the muck. Now, get up."

Tears stung Maia's eyes. She was more than that. She was a talented woman who knew how to make plants grow and how to give people happiness at the sight of bright flowers. But in this moment, clothed in only a ruined wedding dress and the tattered remnants of her pride, she stood.

He watched her with a cruel gaze before clasping his clawed hand around the back of her neck. That massive, warm palm felt like a shackle that closed around her neck.

"You have wasted my time," he snarled. "Now we must make camp here for the night. It is not a good place for us to sleep, but your foolishness has cost us too much time."

He was the one who had thrown her over his shoulder. He was the one who had pushed her to the end of reason.

But she remained silent and seething as he marched her through the woods like a misbehaving child. Figures appeared in the shadows, moving out from behind trees where the trolls had been listening. They stood there watching her. Their gazes burned as he moved her through the crowd until they came upon a little stream.

Was he going to drown her? She wouldn't put it past the monster who gripped the back of her neck.

He gave her one hard shake that made her teeth rattle. "Do humans not bathe?"

"We do," she ground out through gritted teeth.

"When was the last time you bathed?"

"Last week."

Filtered laughter rose from the trolls who had followed them. Her gaze slanted to the side, seeing the wall of multi-colored flesh and muscles. No one here would give her even an ounce of pity. No one would step in on her behalf.

The troll who had his hand around her neck released her as though she had said she was ill with the plague. "Trolls bathe daily. Sometimes more if the work is hard."

"That's how you get sick." The words slipped out, a little too bitter and biting to be safe. She knew better than to talk like that. Maia knew what happened when she talked back to men. Curving in on herself, she waited for the slap or the shove that would send her onto her knees.

Instead, there was a long pause, and then deep guttural laughter.

They were all laughing at her. Every single one of them.

She curved her body tighter, rounding her shoulders and trying to make herself smaller. Then came the hand that she knew would hurt. He planted his palm between her shoulder blades and shoved her into the stream.

Her feet slipped on the algae-covered rocks and she fell onto her hands and knees again. Not quite as painful as the last time, but still making her wrist scream in pain.

But she ground her teeth and didn't let them know it hurt. She'd never let anyone know it hurt.

Her husband's laughter died to a snarl. "Clean yourself, troll wife. And take off those rags. I'll return with clothing more suited for you."

He turned to leave, weaving through the trees with the other trolls. They almost made no sound as they moved, leaving her alone with her desolate thoughts.

53

Chapter 6

He didn't like being cruel, but she would have to be tougher to be a troll wife. This creature had barely lasted a few hours on his shoulder before vomiting.

Humans were delicate. He would need to ensure she ate and drank enough water during their travels to keep her alive, but he did not know how much of either she needed. Clearly, she would have different needs than his own kind. Her people were more delicate, softer than the trolls. He wasn't sure if she could go a full day without food, let alone a week like his own people could.

Regardless, she would need to be capable of significantly more than what he'd seen thus far.

He was... worried. And that feeling didn't settle well with him. He didn't want a wife he had to worry about. He'd wanted a sturdy woman who knew how to hunt and fish and all the things she would need to do while he was out in the war bands as their healer. She would need to be able to take care of herself while he was gone. And this little creature?

He doubted she could even bathe herself regularly. She thought it made her sick.

Striding through the trees and toward a clearing nearby, he was pleased to see the rest of the trolls had already started making camp. The black dyed hides were hand stitched with gold threads in runes for protection, good rest, and warnings in case anyone snuck up on them while they were asleep. Among those rune borders were markers for each family. He and Gunnar had the same stitchings on theirs. Twin bears, both of them fighting each other in a great battle until the end of time.

Their father would have been proud to see his family story still on the war tents. After all, it was their great-great grandfather who had found the two bears all those years ago. Their lineage was that of the bear tamer, the troll who had found the bears and brought them home with him.

Gunnar waited for him at their tents, seated outside of one with a fire already started. "You left her in the stream?"

"You saw?"

His brother grinned and shook his head. "The entire campsite is talking about the troll who shoved his wife into the water. We're taking bets on what she takes in retribution. Your cock or your ears. I bet on the cock."

If only. Trolls valued a woman who knew how to fight, and troll wives were known to be the fiercest among them.

"My troll wife is meek," he muttered before ducking into the tent his brother had set up for him.

"What?" His brother's squawk echoed before Gunnar thundered into the tent after him. "What do you mean, she's meek?"

"I mean, she's little more than a ground mouse hidden in a hole.

I scolded her, ordered her around, shoved her into a stream, and not a single word. She's delicate, fragile, everything she should not be." And that terror was already consuming him.

His brother had done little to set up the tent's interior. Normally he would have layered plush rugs inside this late in the evening. They would keep her feet warm in the icy wind that always crept through the forest this time of year. He'd have to get those out of the crates, along with the clothing he wanted to bring her.

But none of the bridal clothing he'd made for her would fit. He had spent his entire life learning how to stitch and sew and design clothing that would befit a troll wife, but all of it had been made for a much larger bride. A creature who would have, without a doubt, been his match in every way.

Two crates in the corner held all of his travel gear, and he marched over to them and opened up the one on the right. There were furs there for the bed he would eventually make, and the bridal clothing that he'd brought with him.

Bright baby blue leathers would have made any troll wife hiss a happy sound. He'd taken time to learn how to string pure silver into a thread he stitched into them. The dress was designed to hang off the shoulders of his wife, showing the graceful lines of her neck, which were his favorite part about women. The strong lines of her shoulders would be bare for him to linger on and kiss, to drag his tusks along the muscles there. But the dress was far too large, and the pattern wouldn't fit her.

His troll wife wouldn't want to wear anything that told the history of the trolls. She wouldn't care about the time it had taken him to carefully stitch, line by line, how his people had been born from mud, fur, and scales. How the elves had created them, and how the trolls had freed themselves.

Besides, allowing her to wear such a garment felt like a denial of the bride who should have been. Sighing, he reached beyond the beautiful blue fabric to grab one of his own shirts. It was plain cotton, but it would have to do for now.

Standing, he turned to face his brother's frown.

"What now?" Ragnar snarled.

"You would give her that to wear?"

"What else should I give her? I didn't have enough time to stitch her anything else. The bridal wear was made for a troll, brother. She's hardly the size of our children, let alone a full grown troll wife."

There it was again. More anxiety. More nerves churning in his belly because she was so much smaller than he'd expected. Would she even be able to keep up with them? Would he be forced to carry her for the rest of their days? What would he do when he was older and incapable of carrying her such a great distance?

Gunnar clapped his hand on his shoulder, giving Ragnar a little shake. "She deserves the honor of any troll wife. I know you're struggling with this, brother. But it will look bad in the eyes of our people."

For her to be covered in little more than cotton? Of course it would. The entire camp would think he was ashamed of her, but what else could he do?

"I have nothing else to give her," Ragnar grunted.

Gunnar searched his gaze for a few moments before nodding. "Of course you don't. I don't know why I assumed there would be more. Allow me to set up your tent while you go and gather her. Make sure she's dry."

Helplessly, he stood there, facing his brother's disappointment. All he could think to say was, "She thinks bathing will make her sick."

His brother blinked in surprise. "She does?"

With slow steps, Ragnar backed to the trunks and sat down hard on top of one. He crushed the shirt in his hands, wringing it like there would be some answers in the fabric. "What do I do with a creature who believes the mere act of cleanliness will harm her? I knew the humans were backward and knew far less than our kind, but I didn't realize I would be bringing an animal into my home. What disease does she already carry? What little else will she know?"

"I didn't realize the humans were so..."

They stared at each other, at a loss for words. There was no chance for Ragnar to feel better. This troll wife of his was more than disappointing. She was a waste of time.

Gunnar sighed and ran a hand over his head. "Well, I don't know what to tell you. She's your wife now."

"Not yet. There is still another step."

"She will be," Gunnar insisted. "The Bone Reader saw it, as did the king's seer. You will be her husband and she will be yours to take. You can fight it all you want, or you can accept it and learn how to..."

"Don't say it."

"I wasn't going to say love her, brother. I was just going to say learn her." Gunnar circled his hands in the air. "Her. Learn. All of it. There are differences here perhaps you do not understand, but it's a choice. This is the first time any troll has mated with a human, but it's for the betterment of all our people. You will bring about a new age of elven blood."

Would he? Ragnar reached for the tips of his ears, slowly dragging his fingers along the piercings there. "She doesn't have pointed ears, Gunnar."

"Maybe humans don't."

"Even with elven blood?"

Something was wrong here. He could feel it. He might not have been the warrior that his brother was, or the tactician their father had been, but Ragnar had always trusted his gut. And right now, his gut was saying something was terribly wrong.

Perhaps Gunnar felt the same way. His brother's gaze narrowed before he said, "There is no way to know unless you ask her. Go get your troll wife, Ragnar. There are many reasons for you to speak."

He supposed there was. But he was enjoying his time away from her. In the tent alone, he didn't fear what she would say next, or what she wouldn't say. There was something off about how she took whatever he yelled at her. She didn't seem to care when he was rude or downright mean. She just curled into herself, even when the others laughed at her fears about the water.

A troll wife should argue. She should fight. She should shout at all the others to not laugh at her because she didn't know these things. Then she should demand someone teach her.

Perhaps he would have to do it for her. The mere thought made his heart skip a beat in his chest. If he fought all her battles for her, then when he was gone, she would have no one to fight on her side. She would be picked on by all the other trolls. She would be the weakest among them.

Heading out from his tent, Ragnar stomped through the woods and told himself that his fears were unwarranted. She could take care of herself. He would return to the stream and see she'd already made her escape attempt. He'd track her through the woods easily, because there was no human who could hide from a troll in their own home, but it would reassure him that she at least had some sense. A hunt like that would do them both good.

He would be able to hunt her down and ease some of the anger in his chest. She would be able to get some of her own anger out in attempting to trick him through all of her tracking knowledge. And once he finally found her, perhaps much of their fears would lessen about the other.

When he arrived at the stream, already prepared for the hunt, he did not find a trail of scent growing cold and footsteps hidden in leaves. Instead, his dirty little creature was seated on the edge of the stream in the muck. She was plucking handfuls of sand out of the water and scrubbing her skin nearly raw. In some way, he understood why she was bathing like that, but now there was sand all through her clothing.

Clothing she still had on.

Why would she bathe with her clothes still on? The wedding dress had been ruined when she'd fallen from his shoulders, smeared with mud and specks of vomit. The fabric wasn't meant to get wet. Already he could see some of it disintegrating and floating away in the shallow current.

He crouched, watching as she lifted her arms to her hair and... Was she rubbing sand into her hair as well? That was going to take forever to get out.

She'd bring sand into his bed tonight. The absolute horror.

Not to mention she still hadn't realized he was right behind her. Where was this creature's sense of self preservation? At the very least, she should have felt his eyes on her. The hairs on her arms should have stood up in fear, but no. She was just grunting and grumbling under her breath as she washed herself. Not a single realization that there was a hunter watching her every move.

Ragnar only had so much patience. He lifted a stone beside him and tossed it into the stream. The heavy plunk caught her attention before she looked over her shoulder and realized he was crouched there.

A myriad of things then happened in rapid succession. She let out an ear-piercing shriek, tried to stand, slipped on the rocks, and then fell backward into the stream. A wave of impressive volume splashed around her, nearly reaching his toes, before surging back into her face as she tried to sit up. It pushed her back underwater, and for a few moments, all he could see were her flailing limbs.

Was she going to drown in knee-high water?

He wasn't all that certain what to do, considering he was the catalyst for all of this, so he remained where he was. Watching until her head finally crested the water, free of sand now that she'd been flailing about so badly. Spluttering, she shoved all that red hair away from her face and stared at him. Wide eyed. Far too concerned for his liking. Black streaks dripped down her cheeks, likely from the makeup they'd painted all over her. A smear of red streaked from her lips across her cheek as well.

"What are you doing?" she wheezed, her breath sounding a little ragged in her lungs. Likely from inhaling too much water.

"I brought you clothing," he said, lifting the shirt in his hand. "Don't you need to remove your dress to bathe?"

"No."

"How do you get everything underneath clean?"

She stared at him a little longer before rasping, "You just reach up under there and clean it."

Perhaps she believed that was sound logic, but he didn't think so. The corset alone covered too much of her ribcage for her to appropriately clean her torso. Not to mention the heavy skirts would make it hard for her to see if there was anything left that she had missed while wiping at all the other bits. Their kinds weren't so different that he couldn't imagine everywhere she needed to take care of.

That dress would be the death of her, not the stream. She was so convinced it was cleanliness that would be her downfall, but that just wasn't true. Keeping wet clothing on her body for long periods of time could actually make a person sick. She would need to dry off. And, like an idiot, he hadn't brought her a blanket with which to do so.

His shirt would have to do. It was thick enough to soak up much of the water, and he likely had another one lingering somewhere. He wasn't one to wear a lot of shirts, though.

His stomach churned and his chest grew tight with that anxiety again. He didn't want to be known as the man who lost his wife to something as stupid as the cold.

"We're not taking the dress back with us," he declared.

"Excuse me?"

"Take it off. We're not returning to camp with that."

Her mouth parted, those berry red lips dropping open. "The dress stays on."

"It comes off."

"I don't want to wear the shirt you have in your hands. It's not a dress and hardly enough fabric to cover me." She crossed her arms over her chest, as if those meager biceps were enough to shield herself from his sight. "It's simply not done to walk around men I do not know with my legs showing."

"You're no longer with the humans." He stood, letting her gaze trail over his much larger form. She needed to understand that when he told her to do something, it wasn't because it was a choice. He wanted to keep her safe. "Take the dress off, or I will take it off for you."

Her features paled at his order. But she nodded, even if the muscles in her jaw jumped a bit as she did so. "Fine. If that's how it is."

Ragnar held the shirt out for her. "Good. I'm glad you've finally seen reason."

But she still stared at him, seated in the water, while her lips started to turn purple. "Are you going to turn around?"

"Why would I do that?"

"A gentleman would."

Ragnar tried very hard not to let any emotion show on his face. "What makes you think I'm a gentleman?"

Gentlemen were the nobles who hunted trolls down in the middle of the night. Gentlemen were the humans who went out of their way to leave his people dying painful deaths and then hang pointed ears around their necks. He did not want to be like any of those people.

Still, considering how pale she was, he supposed he could relent. Shaking the shirt in his hand, he slowly turned and then held it out behind him. "Quickly, fire hair. My patience grows thin."

They had very little time. The forest was dangerous at night, and there were many creatures who hunted in the silver light of the moon. He needed to get her back to the tent site, back where there were fires to keep away the creatures who would attack even a troll.

He listened to the sounds of rustling fabric and her soft breaths before he felt the slightest tap on his forearm. Glancing down at her, he ground his teeth at the delicate sight. All that red hair had turned dark as blood, plastered back from her face and revealing those strangely rounded ears. But even more than that, she just looked... small. Fairly swimming in the shirt he had given her. The hem reached her knees, and the arms pooled around her fingertips.

"Ready?" he asked, his voice perhaps a little softer.

At her nod, he grabbed the back of her neck and guided her through the woods to his tent.

Chapter 7

She'd never felt so exposed in her life. The shirt he'd given her revealed far more of her body than she'd ever shown to anyone. Not even her father had seen her bare legs since she'd been a child. And this beast had put her in a shirt that was hanging off her shoulders and then paraded her through an entire camp of terrifying trolls.

Maia supposed she should have known they wouldn't reach the troll kingdom in a single day. But, she didn't actually know where the trolls lived. No one did. Humans assumed that the trolls had homes. The rumors were that they dug underneath the ground to live, which was entirely possible. It made sense that they wouldn't be living so close to the human homes.

Still, it hadn't been her greatest worry with all the other things happening. With a throbbing wrist and an aching stomach, there were so many other things for her to think about. Walking into the campsite full of trolls, she was starkly reminded of that.

The trolls looked different in the dim light. Most of them were seated in front of their black tents, their long legs crossed as they rested on animal skins. She wasn't sure what kind of animal had such glistening white fur, or how they kept each of the rugs so clean. It was as impressive as it was intimidating. Fires were built before each tent, all of them surrounded by what looked like crystals. The fire glinted in each of the pillars, reflecting light in prisms all around the ground.

The tents glistened in the dying light as well. She could just barely make out the golden stitches before her new husband thrust her in front of a pair of tents that were rather close together.

"This one is ours," he grunted, shaking out his hand as though touching her had made him dirty. "Go inside."

She hated how he ordered her around. Maia was her own person; she could make her own choices. What if she wanted to stay outside by the fire he was surely going to build? What if she wanted to look at the other trolls, ask questions, and try to get her bearings? They were married now, after all. If he didn't kill her, then she would have to make this her home as well. He wasn't even giving her a chance to do that.

Another troll came out of the other tent. Though it was hard for her to see him very clearly, she thought he was the one who had stood beside her husband at the wedding. Maia hadn't been able to get a good look at him. All she knew was that his skin was a deep green.

He nodded at her, then gestured toward her husband. "You found her, I see."

"Didn't even attempt to run."

Why did that sound like a derogatory statement? Her husband said it as though he was disappointed she hadn't run, when she had been told to stay in the stream and wash!

Rubbing her hand up and down her arm, she decided to introduce herself before ducking into the tent. "My friend's call me Maia."

The green troll looked her up and down before his gaze flicked to her husband behind her.

This was her moment. All she had to say was, but actually, I'm not the princess. You have the wrong person.

But then her gaze caught on the weapons resting by the fire. The sharp edge of the axe leaning just beside the trolls glinted in the firelight. She looked farther, seeing the rest of the trolls all staring at them. Some of them were stroking the knives at their waists, some of them were even sharpening swords.

Not here, she told herself. Once she was alone with the man she'd somehow married, then she would tell them. So instead, she said nothing.

This troll's tusks were larger than her husband's by far. Even those seemed like weapons as her heart raced.

"Gunnar," the green troll said. "You can call me Gunnar."

"It's nice to meet you, Gunnar."

"Lovely wedding you had."

"Thank you," she whispered, trying so hard to be polite while also feeling as though she might topple over at any moment. "I didn't have anything to do with it."

But that wasn't true, now was it? She'd been the one to bring the flowers. All the flowers that had hung over their heads, draped along the columns and bannisters that the trolls had walked by. She was the only one who had turned that entire room into a wonderland of brightly colored wisteria and hydrangeas dripping from every inch of cold gray stone.

Her husband snorted behind her. "Lovely? The only thing lovely about that room were the plants. And you can't convince me any of the royals had a single thing to do with that."

He'd like her flowers?

Cheeks burning, she rushed into the tent. It was dark inside, so all she could see was the shadowy outline of the interior. Strangely spacious for a tent, she could easily stand and walk fifteen paces from one end to the other. Her feet were immediately cushioned by plush rugs, as well. Maia curled her toes in them before groping for what looked like a few trunks. She could sit there and wait for him.

Primly, she sat her bottom down and held her aching wrist. A heartbeat now resided underneath the skin, likely prevented by the icy cold stream. Maia was only distracted from the pain for a few moments by the sheer size of the trunks, which left her feet dangling above the ground when she sat down. She would tell him everything, and she would make him listen.

Too much time had already passed. The moment they had exited the castle, she should have been begging him to let her go. All of this was a mistake. She was a foolish girl who was in the wrong place at the wrong time. All he had to do was look at her to believe her. She didn't have a high blood content of elven magic. The last person in her family who had even a drop of elven blood had been centuries ago. It was why her only talent was with plants.

She'd just come right out with it. She'd tell him everything that she'd seen in the castle, and all the details he might need, then she'd beg to go home. Yes, she wasn't entirely able to do that, considering they were married in the eyes of her kingdom. But maybe this would be a good thing.

She planned out her argument while she waited for the troll to enter the tent. If they remained married, then she could just ask him to sign over everything to her. Her father's business would remain safe.

Why would a troll have any reason to take that from her? And even if he wanted her to pay him a small sum every year, she could do that. After all, everyone would know that she was the one who worked on the royal wedding.

Clearly, they had intended the princess to marry this troll. She'd been in a wedding dress, after all. Or had all of that been a ruse? Perhaps they were intelligent enough to seek out one of the few people in the kingdom with no family, no friends, and who wouldn't be missed. Then they'd lured her to the castle, popped her in a wedding dress, threatened to kill her, and voila. The princess was free.

Her plan wouldn't work if the entire kingdom knew what happened. If this was the plan the whole time, then she was certain the king would insist that everyone knew.

People would know she was married to a troll, and they wouldn't want to work with her. So she'd have to fake his death. Or perhaps try to swing it that they'd gotten a divorce. Which also wouldn't work, because if they had gotten a divorce, then he would have the rights to her business. Not her.

Damn it. Was there no way out of this?

The flap covering the tent's opening swung open, revealing a small glimpse of the outside world. As she'd suspected, a fire now burned in front of the entrance. The golden light burnished the muscles of his thighs, outlining his massive form as he bent low to enter. He was a god straight out of a fairytale. A massive warlord come to claim his prize.

Gulping, Maia shrank a bit on her perch. She'd never felt smaller than she did in this instance. His shirt was too big. The trunk made her feel like a child sitting here with her feet swinging, and now he was staring at her with those strange eyes. He looked back at the entrance for one moment, and she swore she saw his eyes glow like a cat's did in the dark.

But then the flap swung closed, and she was stuck in this tiny tent with him.

"Troll wife," he said, his voice a command that could not be denied. "Why are you sitting in the dark?"

"There are no candles," she replied. Even if there were candles, she had no flint or match to light them.

He reached above her head toward a metal contraption hanging from the ceiling. With a slight twist of his fingers, fire bloomed within it.

Her jaw dropped open as she stared at the small metal cage now illuminating the space. There was a heavier metal bottom, filled with some kind of fuel she could only imagine, and now a tiny flame merrily dancing and filling the room with golden light.

"I've never..." She cleared her throat. "I've never seen such a thing."

He grunted before walking to the back of the tent. "I'm not surprised."

Maia narrowed her eyes at the man who was now her husband, watching as he slapped at the furs in the back. She thought she could hear him grumbling about how Gunnar never set the bed up correctly, but surely that wasn't the bed he expected her to sleep in?

"You don't think very highly of my kind, do you?" she mused, not realizing the words were out until they hung before the two of them.

"It's hard to think well of a species who are so beneath me," he replied, before gesturing toward the bed. "You can go to sleep now."

"I'd like to talk, if that's a possibility."

"It is not." He crossed his arms over that massive chest and glared down his nose at her. He really was an imposing figure, but he hadn't hurt her yet.

So Maia took a deep breath. "I think there's been some misunderstanding between the two of us. And I would like to rectify that before we go any farther."

He just watched her beneath those hooded lids in a way that made her feel so small and so insignificant. But he wasn't arguing with her, so there was that much, at least.

"It's just..." How was she going to say this without him killing her? "I think it's a situation of wrong place, wrong time. I'm not supposed to be here."

That apathetic expression disappeared from his features. Instead, she could easily read something akin to hatred on his face now. "I know very well what your kind is like. I know the lies to expect from you, and the way you will try to twist the truth. I have seen what your people are capable of, fire hair."

"That's not what I'm saying—"

Suddenly, he was right in front of her. Looming in the dark and so big, her tongue tied in her mouth. It was hard to think when there was a massive creature bent down and bracing his arms on either side of her. "Silence, troll wife."

But she couldn't stop her tongue now that it had started. "Why do you call me that?"

"It's what you are."

"It feels like you're trying to erase who I am. You haven't even asked for my name."

He seemed to freeze. Those dark eyes reflected a strange glow as the light from the metal contraption reflected in his gaze. "You already told Gunnar your name."

"But you have never asked me for it."

He blinked. "I do not need to. I know your name is Maia."

Right, of course he did. But that didn't mean... She took a deep breath and told herself to be brave. "Then may I ask what your name is?"

The troll sucked in a deep breath, and she thought for a moment that she'd asked something wrong. Perhaps she wasn't ever supposed to ask for her husband's name. Maybe that was against their traditions. "You know my name. It was told to you by my king and all others when your father and him made this deal."

But she hadn't been there. "That's what I've been trying to tell you—"

"It's Ragnar," he snarled. And there was anger in those words. "You forget the name of your mate and yet insist I remain a gentleman? You have followed none of the rules that were set out for you. You are a weak mate, a delicate creature who will be broken in these woods long before you learn to walk in them."

Suddenly those big hands were around her waist, lifting her from the trunk and carrying her toward the bed. Her legs dangled in the air, and though she grabbed at his wrists for stability, she was once again too small. Too weak. Everything that he said she was.

Ragnar placed her down on the furs, surprisingly gentle for the rage that seemed to blister through him. Maia lost her breath as he planted his knee between her legs, pinning her in place by the shirt he'd given her.

And now she was surrounded by him, his scent, his clothing. The furs smelled of him. A strangely citrus scent that was both clean and surprisingly... nice. She hadn't thought a troll would smell nice, and yet, here it was. Here he was.

Crouched above her, one thick thigh parting hers and anger on his features. But he was still gentle as he reached for her hair. He caught a curl between his fingers, then wrapped it around his massive pointer finger.

"I prayed for a troll wife," he murmured, his voice deep and low. "A beautiful woman with lavender or pale blue skin. A wife who would let me tattoo my clan markings onto her skin, and who would wear my piercings with pride. But your pale skin would crack and bleed."

That blunt finger trailed along her bottom lip, and she drew in a deep breath at the sudden sizzle of awareness that flooded through her body. At his touch, all she could think was that he felt... heavy. A weight she welcomed because it calmed and stilled her anxious mind. He prodded her lips, willing her to open them so that he could trail the pad of his finger along her teeth.

"No tusks," he said. "Not even fangs. You cannot understand the qualities I am missing from the wife I was promised."

Pity made her heart ache. She knew she wasn't what he'd expected, but from the sounds of it, neither was the princess. "I thought you wanted someone with elven blood?"

His gaze hardened. "What use have I for a bride with porcelain skin and fragile glass appendages? I wanted a sturdy wife, a hard wife, one who would survive the harsh winters and the beckoning skies. What shall I do with an elven bride?"

But then his eyes flicked to her ears again, and something deeply troubled crossed his expression. Because he had to know now, in some way, that she wasn't who he'd been promised.

She opened her mouth to tell him just that, only to freeze as his knee came up and pressed against her core. They both froze at his movement, staring at each other as heat flooded through her body. She didn't know why she was reacting like this, only that she was surrounded by him. His scent. His need. It all swelled around her and she was overwhelmed by it.

Ragnar leaned closer, his lips nearly pressed against hers. She could feel the heat of him spreading through her entire body. Her own breath came in tiny pants, puffing against the stone wall of his body.

"We wouldn't even fit," he murmured, before he was gone. Cold air rushed in where he had been and she took in a deep, shuddering breath. The light went out, and the tent flap swung as he left.

Chapter 8

There was the slightest hint of a fight in her, Ragnar realized that night. She'd been trying to tell him something and even though he had interrupted and pushed, she'd still tried to speak. Even then, though, she had only the most meager arguments.

Fear dogged his steps all night. He tried to consider all the things that could possibly go wrong. His little wife needed food more than anything else. Of course, he would have to carry more water for her as well when they were running. He'd caught her sipping from the stream while she bathed, so she must have been thirsty.

Clothing would be the most necessary, though. She wasn't warm enough with fall edging away from summer and toward winter. Not with the shirt that he had brought her, and certainly not with that wedding dress.

So he'd spent his evening bartering. There were things he could do that others couldn't. His healing touch was renowned among the trolls, and if he offered those services, then he was usually able to

get something in return. Shoes that would fit her feet a little better, although they had been created on this journey. A dress that might fit her form, although it had been made for a much younger troll. A cloak that wasn't yet finished, so it was considered far too short for the owner just yet. Pieces and parts of what he should have already had for her, and yet, he hadn't the time to prepare for a human.

It took him the better part of the night. And when he'd returned, she'd been tucked underneath his furs so deeply that he'd thought he had lost her for a few moments. Then he'd seen the small lump beneath the blankets rising and falling with her deep, even breaths.

It was enough. At least she hadn't died in her sleep. Perhaps there was hope for her yet.

Glowering at her for the rest of the night, he stared as she slept through even the loudest ruckus. His people rarely slept as much as humans, and if they did sleep, it was only for brief spurts. Apparently, that was not the same for humans.

She slept through the revelry of his people and he missed it all because... well, he was just looking at her. Only the peak of her forehead and the tip of her nose showing through his furs, and still, he was fascinated by the sight of it.

So many differences. So much he did not know about this woman.

He wanted to ask her more questions than he knew how to verbalize. What was it like growing up with her people? Did she know how to hunt, to fish, to live as she was meant to live? Probably not. She didn't hear the earth singing the way the trolls did, nor would her people be able to find the deep mines where the crystals and gems had been birthed.

She was weak, with tender limbs that he would have to be careful were not overused.

Ragnar planned all evening and into the early hours until she stirred. Then she blinked those eyes open, forest-hued and flecked with gold, and he didn't know what to say. She'd caught him staring at her, appearing like he cared about her well-being. Somehow, that made him feel like he was something wrong.

So he stood abruptly. "We leave now."

"Now?" she asked, sitting up slowly. Her hair billowed around her head into a wild red tangle. Like flames that had been stoked ever higher by her rest. The shirt he'd given her slid off of one shoulder, revealing those dots along her face also traveled down to her shoulders.

The peaks of her arms were red, he realized. Burned by the sun and travel just from the castle to the forest. She'd been injured already, and he'd had no idea.

Frowning, he pointed to the pile of clothing he had left her. "Those should suffice for our travels. Come, troll wife. Today, you prove to me that I am wrong about humans and that you will not be a burden for the rest of our lives."

He noted the way her jaw tightened and her eyes narrowed. His words had made her angry. Good, they should have. She had a lot to prove. Not just to him, but to his people as well.

Ragnar ducked out of the tent before he did something foolish, like help her. She could figure out how to put clothing on herself. All clothes were the same.

Gunnar waited for him on the other side. His brother had already set up breakfast over a fire, two dozen quail eggs sizzling in a pan while he heated up the dried ham they'd brought with them. Others had legs of deer on spits that they had caught this morning, and a few even had fish from the stream.

"You're surly this morning," his brother said with a short, coughing laugh. "I thought a newly mated man would be a little less... tense."

"Keep your mouth shut this morning."

"It's hard not to tease my brother when he insists that the woman he's mated to is not the woman he wants." Poking at the eggs, Gunnar failed to hide the grin that stretched his mouth. "I take it you did not indulge yourself in... husbandly duties?"

"If you do not stop talking, I'll turn your breakfast onto the ground."

"That would be a waste, considering it's your breakfast, too."

"Then we'll both go hungry for your stupidity," Ragnar snarled. But he did not dump their breakfast into the dirt. Instead, he sank down next to the fire and stared into the flames that merrily danced along the crystals.

What was he to do? They were days away from Trollkin mountain. Days where she would have to prove she could take care of herself. She had to prove that she was worthy of being a troll wife before he would bind their blood and magic.

But even he knew that was a lie. He would take her because that was what the fates said he should do. Unfortunately, he didn't understand their reasoning.

It took a long time for the flap of his tent to pull back and for the human to come outside. This pretty little fire hair who had no idea what she'd done by turning his life upside down. Then...

Gunnar lifted his hand to his mouth, but he wasn't quick enough to hide the snort that came out. His brother's shoulders then shook, and Ragnar tried to convey through a very unimpressed look that no one was supposed to laugh.

The look failed.

Gunnar burst out into bright, vivid laughter as his troll wife walked over to them.

"What?" Maia asked, her face already screwed up with concern. "What is it?"

Besides the fact that her shoes were on the wrong feet, the dress he'd gotten her was also backward and inside out. At least no one would notice the last part. Most of their clothing could be worn however it was picked up, but they certainly would notice that the deep "v" which was supposed to be in the front was in the back for her. Odd creature. At least the cloak in her hands wasn't on. She'd probably put that on her front like a complete fool.

"You're wearing those all wrong," he muttered, lifting his hands. "Come here, I'll set you to right."

"I'm wearing them wrong?" She looked down at herself and lifted her arms as though that would give her a better view. "What do you mean? I thought this made the most sense."

It didn't. He sighed as she strode up to him, and then was struck by how small she was. There were so many moments like this for him, but he hadn't realized that she could stand between his legs and be at eye level. She looked right into his gaze, without having to stoop to see him.

How strange. It made something in his chest flutter in a way that he wasn't sure he liked. Ragnar rubbed at the feeling before grabbing the shoulders of her dress. "Arms up."

"Please don't make me get undressed with everyone looking," she whispered.

It wasn't the first time he'd wondered why she wasn't ordering him around. Especially in this. If she felt so strongly about not getting undressed before the eyes of his people, then shouldn't she be shouting at him? Instead, she pitched her voice low, as though she didn't want anyone else to hear it.

Ragnar was horrified to feel himself soften. Troll wives demanded. They argued. They fought for everything they wanted with tusk and claw. This little one merely asked permission. Her fear would have been endearing if he were a weaker man.

Instead, he just grabbed the shoulders of the dress and lifted it up. "There is room for you to still be dressed, fire hair. Tuck your arms into the dress and I will spin it."

"Oh." Her cheeks turned a lovely shade of bright pink. "I suppose I should have thought of that."

Maia tucked her arms into the dress, clearly crossing them over her chest, and he turned the fabric around. It took very little effort, considering the garment was still far too big for her. One spin and then it was exactly how the dress was meant to be worn. But as he let it settle against her skin, his eyes were drawn down to the deep gap between her breasts.

A troll's shoulders were wider than humans'. Her shoulders and broad chest should have stretched the fabric, so it didn't reveal quite so much skin. But on her, the leathers dipped nearly below her breasts. Instead of just seeing a hint of that flesh, he was treated to an unhindered view of all the freckles that dusted over her collarbone, down between her breasts, and even underneath the faint shadow of the globes that were suddenly far more interesting than they should have been.

She looked like she tasted sweet, as though her skin was dusted with sugar and granules of bee pollen. His mouth shouldn't have watered at the feast laid out before him, but he was suddenly a starving man. He wanted to taste her. He wanted to draw his tongue along the shadows hinted at beneath her breasts and brand her taste to his memory.

As it was, he could not do that. He didn't want to be married to her. He didn't want a human for a troll wife, and he did not want her.

Blowing out a long breath, his gaze flicked up to hers. Her pupils were dilated, turning that bright green into black. Scared? Perhaps. He had been staring for a long time, and even Gunnar was suspiciously quiet.

"I see now why you put it on the way you did," he rasped. "Let's turn it back around."

Because he had the sneaky suspicion that if he caught anyone looking at his wife the way he had just been staring at her, he'd get into a fight. He'd rip their eyes out of their head if they saw what he did, even his own brother. Those were sights for his gaze only.

Ragnar lifted the sleeves of her dress again, this time allowing her to turn while he held the fabric still. She seemed to want to cover herself even faster than he did.

But then she was facing away from him, and the revealing fabric showed him the graceful line of her spine. He'd marveled at the muscles in her arms, but they were nothing compared to her back. Strong muscles flexed with her movements, an impressive show of strength as the wings of her shoulder blades moved. The valleys and hollows there were almost enticing.

Now his mind was back in that tent. When he'd leaned over her, he swore he had smelled honey, spun sugar, pretty things that melted on the tongue without ever having to chew. Unbidden, Ragnar leaned forward until his nose almost touched the valley between her shoulders. And there it was again. That scent that drove him wild and made his mouth water as nothing ever had before.

His mind spun. He clenched his claws into fists, hoping that the pricks of pain would ground him, but all it did was made him want to sink his claws into something else. It was either anger or desire. That was all he could feel in his moment and he hated her for it.

Growling low under his breath, he grabbed onto her waist and turned her again. "You've got your shoes on the wrong feet like a child. You know nothing about my people."

"Considering I've never met one of you before, I don't think that's so surprising."

Ragnar wasn't expecting the fight from her. He wasn't expecting that she would call him out for what was arguably outrageous behavior on his part. He was trying to throw her away. To get her to run from him or at least go back into the tent so that he could breathe a little easier.

Instead, she called him out on what was the stupidest thing he'd said yet, and that made him like her all the more. There was a hint of fire in her after all, and not just on the top of her head.

He was frozen in shock, unsure if he should argue back or if he should just shut up. But then a snort from his brother broke through his awareness and Ragnar leaned to the side to glare at the offending fool.

"What?" Gunnar said, then he shrugged. "She's right, you know. You expect her to know how to put on our clothing, but you've seen what the humans wear."

"Constricting nonsense that makes it hard for them to move," Ragnar snarled.

His troll wife looked between the two of them and then eased around him. She sat on the opposite log, carefully removing her shoes and revealing tiny, delicate feet. He hadn't looked at those much last night. But he was surprised to see that there were small cuts on the bottoms of them.

Angry that he'd missed it, he pointed at those wounds and demanded, "Where did you get those?"

"I slipped in the stream and cut my feet."

"Why did you not tell me?"

Her head lifted. Locks of that bright red hair fell in front of her features, but he could easily see her eyes widen and her mouth drop open. "I didn't think you'd care."

She didn't think he'd...

That was ridiculous. He was her husband. He was supposed to care about everything that came with her well-being and if she wouldn't even tell him when she was bleeding, then what else would she hide? He was a healer! Everyone came to him with their wounds and the knowledge that his own wife wouldn't?

He stood abruptly and started to leave. But then he remembered she was a meek little thing and apparently needed to be ordered around. So he marched right back to the fire and pointed in her face.

"Eat," he snarled. "We have a long day ahead of us. I will not slow down for you again. Do not embarrass me before all the other trolls."

And then he stalked away before he did something else stupid. Like hold those delicate little feet in his hands and heal every single wound. Like throw sand in his brother's face and then lock tusks with him just because Gunnar got to eat breakfast with her and he didn't.

Chapter 9

Maia quickly realized her new husband had not been joking about the travel she would have to endure. Ragnar, she was coming to find, didn't embellish much. When he said it was going to be a hard travel day, he meant exactly that.

At first, he'd tried to throw her over his shoulder just like he had the first time they'd traveled together. Unfortunately, that had worked for only a few minutes before she struggling against him, swearing that she was going to vomit again.

That was a lie. She hadn't felt sick at all, but the bruising on her stomach had hurt significantly worse than she'd thought it would. Not to mention her injured wrist made it impossible to brace herself on his back like she had before. A little lie didn't hurt anyway, and besides, she knew that speed was important to him.

Instead, she'd offered to hold on to his back. If they needed to run at this breakneck speed, she couldn't keep up. But she wasn't weak, and she could cling to him with her arms and legs.

He let her, and that meant they traveled even faster. She'd had to press her face against his neck and pray to all the gods that would listen to her because the speed at which the trolls ran was terrifying. She'd only ridden a horse once in her life, but this was the same sensation. All she could do was trust that he wouldn't run them both into a tree, because she certainly couldn't tell if they were going to or not.

By nightfall that first night, she stumbled into bed and fell asleep so fast she didn't even remove her clothing. It felt like her eyes had only just closed before he was waking her again. They ran. For days on end. And at the end of the second day, he started dunking her in whatever pool of water he could find. Sometimes it was a stream, sometimes it was a vernal pool, but every single day she fell asleep with her head on his shoulder and woke to him tossing her into frigid waters.

He claimed it was her stench. She thought it was more likely that he just enjoyed hearing her squawk of disapproval.

Her patience was wearing so thin. Soon enough, she feared she would explode. She'd start yelling at him, screaming that he wasn't treating her right and that he was a beast of a man who had no idea how to treat a woman.

Except, she knew she wasn't what he had wanted in a partner, either. The other trolls laughed at the way she had to wear their clothing, and they thought it was hilarious that her own mate had to convince her to wash.

Maia was just waiting to get sick. Soon enough, she would feel the dripping of her nose and the sniffles that wouldn't leave. A cough would set into her chest, and she would lose her voice.

He was making her wash every single day, which meant she was at risk of getting sick, but strangely, it hadn't happened yet…

No, she wouldn't admit that he was right. She didn't care that she felt better after she washed. She didn't care that her mind even felt lighter after washing the day's grime off her body. It didn't matter. She would not fall into his trap and believe that her own people were wrong.

A troll didn't know more about her own body than she did.

Sitting up in bed, she stared at the flap of the tent and waited for Ragnar to come through. But the light filtering through it this morning looked a little different. Brighter, somehow. As though he'd let her sleep in.

But that couldn't be possible. He'd woken her as the sun crested the horizon for three days straight now. Maia was just getting used to this grueling torment and was ready to get onto his back and hold on until her arms were quaking and her thighs ached.

She should have told him days ago. But the longer she let it go before telling him that she wasn't even the princess, the more it seemed likely he'd kill her once she did tell him. Why did she let it go this long? It just hadn't felt like the timing was right, or worse, that she had knowingly withheld the information rather than being such a pushover that the words just refused to leave her tongue.

The longer she stared at the glimmering light, the more she was certain it was later in the day. He hadn't come for her.

A small glimmer of hope blossomed in her chest. Maybe, if she was lucky, he'd decided she wasn't worth the trouble and would just leave her in the woods. At this point, she thought that was preferable. She knew nothing about surviving in the forest by herself, but maybe she could figure it out.

Still, she should make sure she was alone. No use getting her hopes up if he was about to stomp in here and yell at her again.

Maia rolled out of bed, sighing as her feet touched the ground and her thighs started to ache again. Just using them flared all that pain bright and hot once more. Limping over in nothing but the shirt he gave her to sleep in, she eased the flap aside and squinted her eyes in the bright sunlight.

There were four trolls around the fire in front of the tent. One she recognized, but she'd recognize him anywhere. She'd been mapping the goose bumps on his back while pressed against him for days now. But the other three she didn't know at all.

Stepping closer, she realized they were women. Female trolls, which she hadn't realized she would see this early in her journey.

They were all thinner than their male counterparts, and smaller. But they still looked strong, with broad shoulders and bulging muscles that set them apart from any human woman she'd met before. It was interesting to see them and how different they were. All the women had tattoos, and some of them had piercings in their ears that jangled when they moved.

They were all speaking in the black tongue. The melodic, rhythmic speech was something that Maia was still getting used to. But it wasn't quite so strange to hear it now, even if she didn't know what they were saying.

Ragnar looked over his shoulder at her and then stood. "Good, you're here. We are soon for Trollkin Mountain. They'll help you prepare."

"P-prepare?" she stuttered. Maia had no idea what was going on.

Was he leaving? He was. He just walked away without another glance. But that left her here by herself, with three women staring at her like she was supposed to know what was happening.

And she was in nothing more than a threadbare shirt.

Tucking a strand of hair behind her ear, she tried to clear her throat, but it came out as more of a garbled, throaty sound. "Hello. I'm sorry he didn't introduce me, but my name is Maia. It's lovely to meet all of you."

The troll women all looked at each other, then back at her. It gave Maia a few moments to drink in their differences. Their clothing was what Maia supposed she was meant to be wearing. Leathers that were dyed a particular color and beaded around the edges. Gemstones and jewelry dripped from their forms. Rings, multiple necklaces, and bracelets that danced up their arms and created a light metallic song as they moved.

One of them was significantly younger, and slate gray. Perhaps part of why Maia could tell her age was that she had fewer tattoos. There were only a few dark marks on her body. The swirls even looked newer than the others'. Less faded. She also only had two piercings on each elongated ear.

The next troll woman was a little older, a darker blue, although still young looking. Her ears were full of piercings, and her entire body appeared to be tattooed from head to toe. Large black patches covered a significant amount of her skin, as though someone had intended to create bars of black rather than intricate designs like Maia had seen so far.

The last woman, however, was elderly and wrinkles bisected her green coloring. Her hair was nearly white as snow and pooled down her shoulders like foam. Her eyes were worn, with wings around the edges that crinkled when she caught Maia's attention. Though she was also heavily tattooed, she had more piercings than either of the two trolls who sat beside her. Her markings were worn, just as her skin was a little faded as well.

"Maia," the old woman said, standing with a hand pressed against her back. "It is good to meet you. We were chosen to guide you into your role as troll wife. Although, from what I've heard, you have very little guidance needed."

Maia frowned. "I need all the help I can get. I don't know what's going on, to be honest."

The three women looked at each other. And that was when she realized she'd said something wrong.

Apparently, the princess was supposed to be studying what it meant to be a troll wife. Perhaps they had sent instructions to the king that the princess should have read. There were preparations that the princess had been meant to do, and here Maia was completely ignorant of those.

Maybe now was when she told them? It seemed as good a point as any. These women weren't as scary as the troll who had just left.

"All of this is a great misunderstanding," she tried again. "You see, I'm not supposed to be here."

The trolls looked at each other, and then a soft smile spread across the old woman's face. "Indeed. But no troll wife feels certain when it is her time. You were promised to Ragnar by the Bone Reader. Therefore, you are right where you're supposed to be, princess."

"But I'm not a princess," she said, desperately trying to find the right words to punch through the wall of her anxiety.

The older woman reached out a hand for her to take and drew her with the other two. "We'll refresh your memory, dear one. You'll learn with us the best we can teach you. For now, let us introduce ourselves. I am Hulda, a troll crone."

A what? Maia opened her mouth to ask more questions, but then the one who appeared around her age spoke. "I am Inkeri, a troll wife. Just like yourself."

The youngest then waved her hand. "I am Rota, a troll maiden. The three of us represent the three stages of a troll's life. We are the maiden, wife, and crone."

She'd heard of something similar, but only whispered in secrets. Witches, her people called them. They twisted the magic of the elves that was in their bloodline and used it for dark magic. At least, that was what the rumors were. She knew plenty of people who were very quick to go to said witches for magic, however.

"It's nice to meet you all," she said again, only to pause as they all stared at her. Clearly, she was meant to say something else. Maia licked her lips and finally said, "I am Maia, a troll wife?"

Hulda clapped her wrinkled hands. "Yes! She learns quickly, this one."

They drew her through the camps then, and the other trolls murmured blessings and hellos as they passed by them. If Hulda didn't know them, then Inkeri or Rota did. It appeared almost all the trolls here knew each other. Which went against everything she'd heard about them. Trolls were solitary until they banded together for war, and that was only because they enjoyed raiding human settlements.

But this seemed as though they all knew each other deeply. And soon enough, she found herself enjoying the jabs they gave each other as they walked by. Inkeri certainly thought she was prettier with those new earrings. Hulda looked remarkably straight backed for such a hunched old lady. Rota still looked so young with those soft cheeks! The teasing endeared them all to her, as though she knew them, too.

The deep sense of community lulled her into a sense of peace until she realized the women had drawn her into the forest with them. Soon enough, they came upon a stream and that was where they stopped her.

Hulda drew her to a large stone and sat her down on it. "I was once a troll wife, and it is my honor to be the one to bring you into the fold. Troll wives stick together. We are a family even more than the husbands are."

"I don't know what any of this means," she replied with a slight laugh. "I'm sorry. I feel like you expect me to know what's happening."

A flash of dark tattoos caught her attention as the youngest sat down beside her. Rota grabbed her hand, and Maia stared down at the massive slate gray hand that held hers. Rota curled those claws around her, holding tightly. "Don't worry. It won't hurt that much."

Maia's skin went cold with a flare of panic. What did she mean it wouldn't hurt?

"Why would anything hurt?" she asked, before her gaze flicked over to Inkeri. She'd drawn out a long needle from her pocket. It was nearly the length of Maia's finger, and thicker than any she'd seen before. The sunlight of the glade caught along the edge and made it seem sharp as a sword the more she stared at it.

"What are you doing with that?" Maia asked, and then she realized she couldn't get away. Rota had placed a hand on her back as well, holding her in place on the rock.

"It is the duty of the troll wives to give you your first," Hulda replied. "I am pleased to see no one has broken skin on you before."

Were they going to shove that into her eyes? What was the point of this? Perhaps now she would find out why the trolls were considered so cruel.

"Please," she whispered, squeezing her eyes shut. "Don't do this."

Her heart fluttered in her chest. She could feel the rhythm of it knocking off what it normally would be, and suddenly, there was no rhythm at all. She was going to die of her heart exploding in her chest long before she felt the pain of whatever they intended to do. They were going to make her suffer, she could feel it. She would never live through this, she wouldn't—

Inkeri grabbed her right ear. "Take a deep breath, fire hair. It's not as bad as you're thinking."

And then the needle slid through the lobe of her ear. She felt the sharp tip first, pressing hard against her skin. Then the pop as it slid through and the heat of a sting that seared through the flesh.

She released a long breath, hissing out the sound as though that might help with the sting. But then she opened her eyes and looked up at Inkeri, who was staring down at her work. "I think that's centered. Don't you?"

Hulda leaned closer to look it over before nodding. "And barely any blood. Good job."

"Now the next," Inkeri said. But she didn't go to the other ear. Instead, she placed the needle against the harder part at the top of Maia's ear.

"Wait," she said, trying to reach for Inkeri's hand, but found herself held in place by Rota. "I don't need one there. My lobe is enough."

"A troll wife always gets her first four piercings after the mating. Stay still."

They made quick work of the other three. Her ears burned afterward, but it wasn't as bad as she'd thought. Maia had never gotten anything pierced in her life. Some women had their ears done, but her father hadn't been able to afford earrings. Why would she have holes in her ears that would just heal over?

Hulda produced pretty gold rings and gently put them into each of the punctures that Inkeri had made. There was a reverence in her touch, one that made Maia sit very still so that she didn't mess this moment up.

"A troll wife's first jewelry is usually provided by her husband," Hulda said. "But yours did not bring the piercings. I believe he thought we would be meeting in our home. But that is all right. I knew to bring some of my own."

"These are yours?" Maia asked, then lifted her hand to touch them.

"They were the rings my husband gave me when we first met. He told me only the prettiest troll in the land would be worthy of them." Hulda looked at each ear before cupping Maia's face. "You may not be a troll, but they still look lovely on you."

For some strange reason, tears pricked Maia's eyes. She didn't want to cry in front of these women, but she couldn't remember the last time someone had told her that she was lovely. Her father hadn't cared to. None of the men who came to the house ever cared about her. They cared about the business and the money they might be able to make. Perhaps her mother had once told her she was pretty, but Maia didn't remember her at all.

"Thank you," she whispered.

"Now, I'm sure you feel silly for being so afraid."

Her cheeks burned just as hot as her ears did. "A bit."

Inkeri chuckled, and Rota let out a bell like giggle that filled the clearing. The youngest of them all said, "Can you imagine how afraid Ragnar was when he got his husband piercings? What you just did is nothing compared to what he endured."

"Husband piercings?" she asked.

The three troll wives went quiet. They all looked at each other, then at her.

Hulda was the first to ask, "Yes? I assume you felt them if you did not see them."

"I haven't..." Maia wasn't sure how to say that she hadn't even seen her husband for a few days other than hanging onto him. "Was it his ears? Those didn't seem worse than this."

A loud snort erupted from Inkeri's mouth. "Fuck, no. That's hilarious. Silly little thing, we meant the ones on his cock."

Again, silence. All Maia could hear were the birds that twittered in the trees around them and the faint hush of the wind moving through the leaves. All three of the troll women looked at her expectantly, as though she were supposed to laugh or reveal that this had all been a giant joke on her end. But she didn't know what they were talking about.

"Did you say piercings on his cock?" she asked, although the last word she could barely get out.

Inkeri's face paled. "Oh, you haven't—"

"Oh dear," Hulda said before pressing her hand to her mouth.

Rota was the only one with the absolutely ridiculous nature to burst out laughing and shout, "She hasn't seen his cock yet!"

The forest burst into movement as the loud noise scattered birds into the trees around them. And all the while, Maia couldn't help but wonder what a pierced cock would even look like.

A small laugh bubbled out of her as well, then a longer one, and soon they were all braced against each other, laughing until tears ran down their cheeks.

"I really am sorry," Inkeri stammered out. "I just assumed after four days of being mated that you would have at least seen the damn thing."

"I haven't!" Maia said with another laugh. "But what kind of piercings does one even put on a cock?"

Hulda gathered them all up, forcing the younger women to stand

and then nudging them all forward. "Back to the camp with the lot of you. We aren't answering that question, fire hair. That's a question for your husband."

And what a shame that was, because Maia was married to a man who had very little use for her at all. Questions? He wouldn't answer a single one of them. And she certainly wouldn't be asking him about his cock.

Chapter 10

Today was the day. The last day where he might be able to wriggle out of this. They traveled closer and closer to the blood witch, the one who would see into their future and deliver them news of their children. She would mingle their magic, and that would bind them until the end of time. All he had to do was make it to this point, and then, maybe, all his questions would be answered.

He'd successfully avoided his human for multiple days now. Nearly a week of travel and he'd slept in Gunnar's tent. The other trolls were starting to wonder why his mate was so unworthy of their healer, but he'd never paid mind to gossip.

The more he could hold himself back from her, the better. Ragnar barely even looked at her when he stopped in front of their tent to pick her up and run. It didn't matter what she looked like. It didn't matter now if she was even clean. All he could think was that if he could just hold off until the blood witch, then everything would be easier.

He didn't want to get to know her. The less he knew her, the easier it would be for him to let her go.

He'd denied her this long. The blood witch would know. She would sense that they were not a good match and that their children would suffer because of it.

Stopping in front of their tent, he took a deep breath and steadied himself. Just one day with her alone. One day where he couldn't distract himself by talking to the other trolls or pretending to be out of breath while he ran. This was easy enough.

But then Maia walked out of the tent as though she knew he was waiting and all the breath in his lungs rushed out.

The piercings in her ears. He had known they'd done it, but he hadn't expected her to be so lovely wearing them. The gold sat on her skin better than anything he would have chosen for a troll wife. They were delicate and thin wired, not so flashy that they were the first thing anyone saw, but still lovely all the same. When she moved, her red hair tangled around them, leaving little sparks of gold in the strands.

He suddenly had a vision of what he would make her. Golden clasps for her hair. He'd braid it into intricate weavings and then seal those braids with golden caps. She was a woman made for gold. Perhaps he would inlay rubies in a necklace as well, because those would look so pretty sitting against that graceful throat, bouncing against her pulse.

And then he scowled at his own thoughts. He would not decorate her with anything at all. She was a human, and he did not want a human for his troll wife. He never had. He would not bend now simply because she hadn't complained at all during this journey.

"Come," he said, holding out his hand for her to take. "We see the blood witch today."

"Who is that?"

He just impatiently thrust his hand toward her, waiting until she would wrap her arms around his neck and they could be off. Usually she was quick to jump when he ordered her, but this time, she did not. Instead, she sidestepped his hand and wrapped her arms around herself.

"I'd prefer to walk if it's not far," she said.

She didn't meet his eyes when she said it, but it was the first time she'd ever asked him for anything. Progress. He wanted her to tell him when she needed something, even if he wasn't going to keep her. He shouldn't.

But he still found himself nodding. "We can walk."

No, he did not want to walk! He didn't want to give her a chance to start talking to him because that was the very last thing he should be doing. She was the enemy. A creature of terrifying abilities to do more damage than he could ever dream up. She and her kind were the monsters in this realm, not his.

Yet he walked with her. He guided her away from the camp until it was just them. There was only the sound of their footsteps in the forest as they meandered away from the others. The companionable silence was well enough for him. It wouldn't convince him to change his mind, but then she started talking and he just... listened.

"The forest always frightened me when I was young. People told stories about all the terrible things that lurked in the dark and all the awful ways we would die if we went beyond the treeline." He watched her press her fingers to the bark of an old tree, using it to help her over a fallen log. "But I don't think the forest is so scary now."

"There are beasts in these woods that are dangerous. Dire wolves, stone bears, even the Weavers, which are similar to large spiders, but they can speak." Ragnar shrugged. "Those stories were likely told to keep you safe."

"I suppose so. But I wanted to thank you for giving me the

opportunity to learn that it isn't all bad. I think my life is better for having known that not everything in these woods is terrifying."

He hated that he liked what she said. Ragnar had been the one to show her there was more to this world than just what she had seen through her human eyes. He was the one who had given her the gift of the forest's beauty.

Damn it, he had other things to do here. Like keep himself held away from her so the blood witch would change her mind.

He told himself to say something, anything, that would make her angry at him. There were words that could fly between them, and keep her at arm's length. That was all it would take. A single sentence that would fill her with rage or fear of him.

"The blood witch can determine if we are not compatible," he said, clearing his throat at the sheer wrongness of saying that. "She is the final test before you become my bonded mate."

Maia staggered. He grabbed her elbow, certain she had tripped. But there didn't appear to be anything that she'd caught her foot on.

Quickly she stammered, "What do you mean, the final test?"

"There are many seers for us to meet with before we can truly become mates."

"But we're married?"

He didn't see how this was any reason for her to look so surprised. "In your human ways, yes. We are."

Her mouth opened, closed, mimicked being a fish for a few moments before she gasped, "But we said vows before a priest. Nothing can change that."

"In the human kingdom we are married. Not yet in mine." He released her and shook off the sensation of her on his hand. No matter how many times he touched her, she lingered on his skin. Everywhere burned whenever he touched her. The heated sensation was distracting.

He continued forward, listening to her follow him after a bit of time. He knew it would take her a while to say anything, so he indulged himself in enjoying a sunny day in the forest. Ragnar focused on the beauty of the leaves, how pretty the song of the birds was, but then it grew too much.

Finally he turned around, crossed his arms over his barreled chest, and asked the question that had been burning in him for ages now. "Why do you not argue with me?"

She froze like he was a hunter who had come across a deer. Her eyes widened, her limbs tensed as though preparing to flee, but she didn't. She stood there and said, "Do you want me to argue with you?"

He blew out a frustrated breath. "I want you to say what you're thinking. I do not enjoy that you play coy and pretend to be some weak little thing. There is fire in you. A fight. It lives in all things just as the dragons of old breathed fire. You hold yourself back, and I do not understand why."

She swallowed hard, her throat bobbing with the emotion. "Most people don't want to fight."

"Troll wives do. You dishonor me by not speaking your mind."

He watched as she blinked and then drew her body in on herself. But she didn't quite curve like normal. Instead, she took a deep breath and looked him in the eye. "When I was growing up, I was told the sound of a woman speaking was grating on the nerves of men. My opinions did not matter. My knowledge about any subject also did not matter. I was to be silent, seen but not heard. That's how I was raised."

It made sense. But what didn't make sense was why she still clung to those flawed teachings. "You are free from such expectations. You are now a troll wife. Act like one."

He turned to go, assuming this conversation was over, but then heard her bitter laugh. He turned again, his brow arched in surprise.

Maia stood there in the glen, her arms raised as if in shock. "You think that's it? You just say I don't have to be like that anymore and an entire lifetime of discipline will disappear?"

"Yes. I gave you permission to let those memories go."

"That's not how it works!" It was the loudest he'd ever heard her.

Maia's eyes widened as she registered her own volume. But this was what he had wanted. This was the person he thought might live inside of her. It was the same woman whose eyes had glittered with rage at their wedding.

He took a step closer to her, everything in him insistent that he push. "It sounds to me as if you are clinging to these old ideals. You are the one who wishes to be silent and meek."

"That is not who I am."

"You could've fooled me. Since the first moment I met you, you have been silent. Quiet. Lingering in the shadows like a mouse, flinching at every loud noise. You are nothing like a troll wife should be."

He could see the red gathering at the base of her neck, slowly moving up her throat as massive emotions filtered through her body. And still, her voice was only mildly loud when she replied, "I do not cling to anything, troll! I've lived my entire life under a certain set of circumstances that kept me safe. I made my own rules, and they got me to where I am now."

"Those rules bind you. You created your own chains and your own prison. This is foolish human nature and why you will never be worthy." He walked ever closer to her, close enough to touch her if he lifted his arm.

She glared up at him. "It's not a prison if it keeps me safe!"

"A prison is four walls from which you do not allow yourself to leave. You stare out at the world beyond, and you wish to live in it. You've told me so. The forest scared you? Everything seems to scare you, fire hair."

"Don't call me that."

He arched a brow, making all of this worse. "I'll call you whatever I want. Human scum. Weak woman. Fire hair, troll wife—I'll call you whatever I want because you don't fight back."

"Enough." That red had reached her face now. Tomato red cheeks matched her hair. If she had been a troll, she would have smacked him already.

"It will never be enough. I will torment you for the rest of your life because you do not have a single bone in your body worthy of me."

And just like that, she exploded.

Both of her hands came down on his chest and shoved with surprising strength. She even pushed him back an entire step with the force of her anger. "Worthy of you? I know nothing of this world you brought me into. I'm not even supposed to be here! You don't listen to me, you don't do anything right according to the other trolls I've spoken with!" she seethed. "You dress me in rags and someone else had to pierce my ears and give me jewelry from her own husband! Nothing about you makes me wish I was worthy of your attention. You've wasted both of our times and I hope to all the gods in the sky and everyone who can hear me that the blood witch finds us incompatible, you absolute beast!"

Ragnar stared at her, watching as her chest rose and fell with the power of rage that coursed through her veins. She glared at him, bright red and angry. Her nostrils flared and her eyes were so green that he swore he could see the forest in them. Her hands curled into fists, perhaps ready to punch him if he pushed back at her in the slightest.

Instead, he raised his hands and nodded. "For a moment, I believed perhaps you had a spine after all. More of that, fire hair, and you'll do just fine."

She somehow turned even more red. "Excuse me?"

"You show your true strength when you're angry. Such is power. When you let that fuel you, you can see more than what you did when you were trying to hide. I didn't realize you were disappointed in my treatment of you."

"How could I not be?" Maia burst out, shouting it into the forest.

And still, he grinned even wider. "I didn't think you cared how I treated you."

"You were the one who said you would never be my husband on our wedding day." She turned her nose up at him and sniffed. "I'm just informing you that you were right."

He wanted to kiss her. He'd wipe that snotty expression off her face and bring her down onto the bed of leaves at her feet. He'd ravage her right here in the forest until she screamed so loud the other trolls would hear her. All just to wipe that smug expression off her face. But she wouldn't welcome that. Not when she was so angry at him.

Instead, he gestured for her to follow him. "The blood witch will determine if you are right."

"I'll make sure she sees reason," Maia snapped before stomping in front of him.

He walked behind her, only giving her directions when she started going the wrong way. And what a view. He'd never noticed how round her hips were beneath that shirt, nor had he noticed how her bottom swayed with every step. It was quite the sight. Almost enough to make him like her.

But then the blood witch's hovel appeared out of the trees. Her kind always lived in earthbound homes. This hut had sunk into the forest floor. It looked like a hill covered in fallen branches, earth, and moss. Hard to notice at all, unless one knew what they were looking for.

"There," he said, pointing at the door that was barely a door. "We're going in there."

The worn wood, half rotten, swung open on its own. The smell of mildew and mushrooms filled the air as smoke poured out of the room beyond.

Maia gulped, her throat working to swallow her fear. But she didn't cower like he'd expected. Instead, she just gave him a determined nod. "Looks inviting."

Ragnar chuckled and followed her into the shadows. He'd known it was a bad idea to be alone with her. But now that he'd discovered her ire, he found he rather liked her.

Chapter 11

Maia was shocked by how good it had felt to just let loose. But the moment the angry words had crossed her lips, she had frozen, waiting for him to shoot back angry barbs. Surely he would make her feel awful about herself. He'd spit words that would remind her how she was beneath him, and everyone else.

But those words hadn't come. Ragnar might've been a terrifying man with far more power than he deserved to have in just his pinky, but he wasn't her father. He wasn't like the man who had beaten her down into a mere smudge on the floor compared to what she wanted to be. Even in death, the man who'd raised her still lived inside her head. He still whispered in her mind that she should know her place, and that had kept her exactly where he had wanted her for years.

It would take more time to feel confident and able to say whatever was on her mind, but... Damn. It had felt good.

It was for that reason that she could look at the hovel rising out of the ground before her and not be afraid. Or perhaps not as afraid as she might have been if she wasn't fueled by her anger. There was still an air of warning about the mist that flowed out from the door that swung open on its own. And from the house itself.

As they walked toward it, she stared up at the greenery that covered the roof. Sprigs of grass poked through the emerald blanket of moss that covered it, though some of it was flopping over the side as though they were lacking in water.

Something twisted inside Maia's chest. Plants had always called out to her when they were in need. She could feel their pain in her chest. As Ragnar walked through the doorway, she reached above her head for a split second and let her fingers brush through the strands. The grass sent a pulse of happiness through her skin and she felt them wake with the slightest amount of magic she poured into them.

It wasn't much. Not even enough to really be called magic. But it was a bit more than what they currently had, and they were grateful for her intervention.

Breathing out the tension that had knotted in her, she walked into the darkness after the troll.

The interior of the home was barely lit. There was a small fire in the far back, but even that wasn't casting light the way it should. She could hear dirt crunching underneath her feet when she walked. There was no floor in this place. Only earth. The air was filled with smoke, but not from the fire. As she breathed in, she recognized the scent of burning pine, sap, and something similar to rosemary, but she wasn't sure why that would be burning.

Turning her gaze toward the massive shadow to her right, she assumed it was Ragnar. He blended into the darkness of this place, but why wouldn't he? The trolls were made for the dark. They all lived underground, just like this woman did.

Blood witch, the words echoed in her mind.

What did that entail? What would a blood witch see that no one else had already?

Nerves spun in her belly, twisting and curving throughout her guts until she wondered if she might throw up. The bravery she had clawed and scraped to get disappeared the moment something else shifted in the darkness.

Her nerves were a warning. Out of the shadows, an ancient troll uncoiled herself. Her back was bent in on herself, but worse were the scars. She was decorated in them. The moment her face turned toward the light, they looked like worms dug underneath her skin. Each scar was so raised, Maia thought perhaps they were the thickness of a fingertip. They cast shadows on the troll's face, more markings and scars that were even more intimidating than before.

Sucking in a deep breath, she found herself frozen as the witch reached for a small glass orb beside her and lifted it to her mouth. Blowing into the glass bubble, she awakened a wisp that apparently was trapped inside. But that white glow illuminating everything made this place seem all the worse.

The blood witch was covered in tattered garments, little more than strips of fabric that were all woven around her form and sticking out in all directions. The dirty brown fabric clung to her rail thin form. All the other trolls Maia had seen were healthy. They were muscular and thick legged, some of them with rounded bellies from the comfortable life they led. This troll was anything but that.

Her bones were painfully visible through the thinness of her pale yellow skin. Sickly. Maia could see her ribs expanding as she breathed in and out. Her collarbones were so prominent that Maia feared only a single touch would shatter them. As the blood witch reached for

Ragnar, she swallowed hard. She could see the two individual bones in the woman's arm. Like there wasn't even muscle there at all, just bones.

Ragnar leaned down to catch Maia's attention. "The blood witch does not speak the common tongue. I will do my best to translate for you."

"Oh," was all she managed before they spoke in the black tongue.

It was hard to focus on anything but the state of the woman before them. Even though Ragnar drew her toward a table in the center of the room, all she could think was that someone needed to help this witch. Clearly, they were mistreating her. Clearly, someone needed to get some food into her, perhaps some water, and a blanket would go a long way as well.

"Maia," Ragnar said, his voice hardened with emotion. "Stop staring at her."

"Is she all right?"

Her gaze flicked to his, and she saw something shift in him. Like he'd thought she was judging this witch for her state, not worrying about her well-being. His expression softened. And there was the slightest feeling in her chest like she'd done something right for once.

"Ah," he said, his voice pitched low. "She's fine. Blood witches create their magic through pain. She has dedicated herself to a life of suffering so that she can see the magic inside people."

"The what?"

He placed his hand on the table and nodded toward the blood witch. "She will look into my magic now. Watch, fire hair, and perhaps you will understand better than my words can explain."

She wasn't all that certain anything would make sense. But she kept her mouth shut and watched as the witch lunged for Ragnar's hand. Her fingers and claws scraped down the thick base of his thumb, and then she traced the wrinkled lines across his palms all the way to his fingers.

Her voice rose and fell like the cresting of a wave. And though Maia didn't understand a word, Ragnar was quick to speak the words for her to understand.

"A strong hand. The hand of a man who has worked all his life and will continue to do so. This is not the soft palm of a troll who has known an easy path. Instead, it is the hand of a man who will walk the hardest path by choice." He winced. "It is the truth, unfortunately."

"The last bit was your own commentary, I assume?" She tried very hard not to smile at him, because she understood this was a very serious matter.

Ragnar's expression turned grave. "Don't try to make me like you, human. It won't work."

And still, she had a feeling he was lying. That new, brave version of her whispered, "Are you sure?"

His lips quirked just the slightest. And then the tail of his brow moved as well. She had to wonder if he was having a hard time keeping his own smile from his face.

But then he hissed out a low breath and Maia's head whipped back to the blood witch, who had scraped her claws down his hand. Beads of red welled from the wounds that were now deep furrows across his palm. As strange as it was, the first thought in her head was that she hadn't known trolls would bleed red.

It was eerily human to see that red blood. To see it welling up in the lines of his hand and then dripping down onto the table. The blood witch leaned forward, smearing her hands in the thick liquid and spreading it across the worn wood. It was grotesque to watch, but she couldn't stop staring, either.

The witch suddenly flattened her hands on the table, sucking in a deep, long breath. Then she looked up at Ragnar and spoke again.

He did not translate this time, but he didn't have to. Small droplets of blood on the table rolled together and then they lifted into the air. She watched, her lips parting in shock as the blood then drew together, hovering in a ball the size of her fist before, all of a sudden, light bloomed inside of it. White light that was so blinding it was difficult to look at.

Then the witch spoke, and Ragnar translated: "He is powerful in healing magic. There is much inside of him that knows the bodies he touches. A broken bone is not too much to heal, nor is the fragmentation of the mind. He could easily become stronger with the connection of a powerful troll wife. If given a strong wife, then his power will magnify tenfold. He would be able to heal an entire battlefield and prevent death itself should he wish."

Suddenly, what was happening all barreled toward her.

They weren't looking into the soul of a person and weighing if she was good enough for him. This troll was revealing how much magic was inside of them. And though her husband had a lot of power, soon enough, he would know she had very little.

She was supposed to be the princess. She was supposed to have more magic than any of the trolls could guess at, because she was supposed to be half elf.

Her time had run out to tell him the truth. If only she had pushed herself harder. If only she'd been brave enough to let it all blurt out of her mouth without wondering if he would kill her for it. If only she wasn't… Maia.

Because now he would know. He would believe her omission of her true identity was a direct attack against his people. Perhaps he would even believe she had been part of all this. He'd accuse her of working with the king, and maybe he'd drag her before his own. She didn't want to see the troll king, nor did she want to know what their people did in retribution for those who lied.

Her breath caught in her throat, but then she heard a sound behind her. Turning to look, she saw a wall of multi-colored flesh standing in the doorway. They hadn't been alone on their walk after all. Nearly all the trolls who were in their war band were waiting on the other side of that door. They were all here to see how much power she had.

She was supposed to bring them safety, she realized. With her tied to Ragnar, somehow, the magic was supposed to give them certainty that they could not lose a battle.

And she'd ruined that.

Maia didn't even have time to get up and run. The blood witch reached for her hand and drew it onto the table. When she tried to pull away, Ragnar placed his hand on her forearm and held her down.

Eyes wide, knowing that her fear must be visible, she begged. "Please, let me go. I don't want to do this."

"It is our way."

"I have to tell you something beforehand, Ragnar. You have to listen to me this time." Her heart threatened to beat out of her chest. She couldn't breathe, but also knew she had no idea how to say the words. "I'm frightened, Ragnar."

He sucked in a deep breath, but his hand didn't move. "Fear is what limits us. You can let it control your life, or you can control it. The choice is up to you."

She hated how poetic he was. A proverb about fear didn't help her right now when all the trolls were going to realize that she wasn't who the king had claimed her to be. She'd tried to tell him, but he hadn't listened. Or perhaps she just hadn't found the right words.

Panic made her breaths saw in and out of her lungs. The blood witch trailed those claws down her hand, following the lines of her palm. And as the other woman spoke, Maia stared up at Ragnar as his brows furrowed in confusion. "These are the hands of a woman who has worked hard, as well. A woman who has suffered much at the hands of those who should have cared for her. The death of her family lingers in these palms, not because she is responsible for their loss, but because their souls linger to taint every step she takes. The path she walks will never be easy until she lets those old ghosts go into the underworld where they belong."

Confusing words for a princess, Maia was certain.

But then sharp spikes of pain stuck through her skin. She let out a little sound of pain as her injured wrist throbbed along with the new aching that joined the bone deep pain that had plagued her since she'd fallen into the stream. Her blood streamed down her wrist onto the table and she saw her entire life flash before her eyes.

The moment the chanting began again, she knew she was done for.

Her blood rose into the air between them, a smaller bead than Ragnar's. And then a light. A glowing green light that was so dim it was almost hard to see. Just the barest of lights, but it was there.

And for a moment, with the smoke swirling around them and that green light sparkling in her eyes, all her fears filtered away. Instead, there was only the sense of awe.

Maia had spent her entire life knowing there was something inside of her that awakened when plants were around her. She loved them. They loved her. It was the only thing that was constant in her upbringing. The support and undying love of green things growing and it had rooted deep inside of her. Now she was looking at that power.

There was so little elven blood in her family that she had thought it was entirely gone. She'd believed she was just making up her power in her head.

But no, it was there. A tiny green light, like the spark of a seed, and that was inside of her. Just waiting to bloom.

The blood witch chanted more, and she seemed to frantically begin moving. There was a sense of urgency as her hands blended the blood together. Moving ever faster, even as Ragnar seemed to freeze beside her.

Until it all came crashing down.

A snarl came first from the doorway. Then another voice muttering, "It cannot be."

Then Ragnar's hand tightened on her forearm. His claws scraped the table rather than her flesh, but the sound ripped her from her sense of peace. The blood witch let the spell drop and there was only silence in the room. The silence before a storm that would soon unleash upon her.

"You have no magic," he spat.

She stared at their blood pooling on the table, mingling into the fair color of ferns. "I do have magic," she whispered. "Just not as much as *her*."

Chapter 12

The rage among the trolls was palpable. Ragnar should never have let them trail along in their path. Being followed by other trolls was always tricky to discover, but he'd chosen to let them in the hopes that it would give others some peace. But he hadn't trusted his gut that something was off about this redheaded beast they'd been given so easily.

The humans never were honest. They wouldn't have handed their princess over so quickly, not to a troll. Not to someone they deemed little more intelligent than an animal. Of course King James had done everything in his power to fake this alliance, although Ragnar couldn't understand why this king didn't realize that he was risking his entire kingdom by tricking them.

Still, Ragnar had fallen for it. They all had. Perhaps it was her pretty hair, or those wide eyes that welled with tears whenever she was being yelled at. He'd wanted to protect her, even though it was against everything his people were.

He had failed them all.

The rage that boiled in his chest became a mist that hid everything in front of him other than her. She had lied to him. She wasn't the princess. There wasn't a chance that she was. The princess was half elven. She had more power in a sneeze than this woman did. And now he was bound to the weakest wife he could have been given, all because the blood witch had frantically finished the ritual.

This woman was a stranger to him. He had no idea who Maia was, if Maia was even her name, and now he knew better than to trust her.

Grabbing her by the back of the neck, he drew her up and thrust her toward the door. The rest of the war band waited for them. Trolls who would tear her limb from limb. This had to be a mistake. The seers had claimed she would be his troll wife, but they had been looking at the princess. Not this woman. Surely they hadn't looked at this fire haired creature and deemed her to be the person for him.

He would throw her to the other trolls, would enjoy watching them torment her. For the lies and for all the things that her king had done to them, they would exact their revenge. It would be easy for him to pull out her hair. Then the others would rip out her nails, both from her fingers and her toes. Only at the end, when she was begging for mercy, would they start to pull off her limbs. One by one. First her arms, then her legs, making her stay alive until the very last moment when she bled out at their feet.

The blood witch's voice raised, and he stopped halfway to the door. The rest of the trolls hovered there, unable to enter without the witch's permission.

"She's still yours, you know," the blood witch said, her old voice shaking with the effort after the magic she had cast. "She's yours, Ragnar, more than I've seen in a hundred years. That woman was made for you and you for her."

It made every inch of his body turn ice cold. It wasn't possible. He was meant to have a powerful bride, to serve his people in a way that only he could do. He was the healer who would deny death itself.

But not with her. Now, he would be forced to walk a different path. Ragnar had known his future since he'd been a boy. Changing that now was terrifying.

He stared down at the shaking creature in his grasp. Maia shuddered with fear as she froze in his grip, her eyes locked on the enraged trolls who waited for her beyond that door. She knew there would be punishment for what she had done. She knew there was nothing she could do to stop that judgment from coming.

And yet...

In the black tongue, he answered the blood witch. "How can it be her? How am I supposed to have a troll wife who would make our children even more weak than I?"

"Your prophecy may speak of your son, not you. She will not make your children weaker, she will keep your bloodline as strong as it is now. But perhaps it is not you who needs to be stronger." The blood witch stood, bracing her hand on their mingled blood. "You will give her strength, Ragnar, just as she will give you a place to rest."

He swallowed hard. The decision he had to make was not an easy one. His people wanted their revenge, and so did he. But he also did not want to deny a troll wife if she was... his.

A choice had to be made. Finally, he released his hold on her neck and instead stooped to grab her waist. As he had before, he slung her over his shoulder and charged out through the door.

He was certain his people were confused by his actions. Likely, they wouldn't understand it for many weeks to come. But he bolted through them, ignoring the claws that raked down her back and grasped for her hair. He felt them tugging at her, heard her screams of pain as they tried to rip her from his arms, but he would not allow that to happen. Not when he was owed answers.

Ragnar darted through all of them and wriggled free from the crowd. And then he was off. Sprinting through the woods as the howls of his people trailed after them. The trolls in this war band were good hunters. They would follow him for a long time yet, but he knew how they hunted.

First, he took her over the stream, making sure his feet were soaking wet so that his scent wouldn't linger in the area. Then he took off up a steep incline, allowing his feet to slip and slide over it before hopping up to the top of the ledge. Crouching low, he took his time slithering through the woods until he circled back on himself.

He stayed still and quiet as a small group of trolls headed up that steep incline, and then he was off again. Throughout it all, Maia was suspiciously quiet. Almost as though she had passed out on his back. She might have, he supposed. It was a terrifying thing to be hunted by trolls.

But finally he didn't hear the others for the better part of the afternoon and he knew he had shaken them. Heaving her off his shoulder, he let her hit the ground harder than he should have. He heard the breath wheeze from her lungs and tried not to see the blood that now stained the shirt he'd given her. There was more of it than he'd expected. His people had cut through the cotton and left harsh streaks of blood in their wake. They'd torn into her flesh while he'd run past with her, and he hadn't even noticed.

Perhaps he'd smelled it, but he had ignored the pain she had been in. The healer in him screamed out for him to heal her. First, though, he needed answers.

She backed away from him, scuttling like a crab as she tried to get away, only to find her back pressed against the side of a mountain. There was nowhere for her to run. Nowhere for her to escape.

"Who are you?" he growled, his voice thunderous.

"I tried to tell you—"

"I don't want to hear any of your excuses. Speak, woman. What treachery were you part of?" He knew it had to be something devious. The human king wouldn't have done this without a plan.

"I don't know."

"No more lies."

"I really don't know a single thing about this. I haven't lied to you about anything."

"More lies!" he roared before dropping onto his hands and knees. He crawled over her, every bit the animal she thought him to be. It was so easy to loom over her, to wrap his clawed hand around her thin little neck and shake her so hard her head hit the stones behind her. "You will tell me everything your king has planned for my people, and why he would insult us so gravely."

Her shaking hand came up to rest on top of his. Little fingers, warm and gentle as she held onto him. "My name is Maia. I'm a florist. I grew up near the castle, and my father provided the flowers to many nobles in the area. When the king asked me to create flower arrangements for the royal wedding, I did what I was asked. When I showed up, there was clearly another plan."

"I don't believe you."

"I don't care if you do," she wheezed. "I've told you from the beginning, I was not meant to be here, and I don't know why I was the one you married. I haven't lied to you. Never."

He hated how he believed her. Truth rang in every single word.

She hadn't known what the plan was. She was a pawn in all of this.

"A florist?" he repeated, his grip easing on her neck. "Is that what the magic helped you with?"

She nodded, although her eyes were still too wide for his comfort. She was terrified and thought he was going to kill her. He was still considering it. His people would expect that he do exactly that.

But the blood witch's words still ran in his head. She was the one who'd been made for him, and he had searched his entire life for that person. Why did it have to be her?

He trailed his claws down her neck, watching the bright red welts that rose in their wake. "I should kill you for what you have done to my people. The trolls do not forgive easily, and you have betrayed us."

"I don't think I deserve that," she said, her voice shaking with nerves, but he was proud to hear her argue with him.

"Why not?"

"I didn't actively take part in this plan. If I had known what the king was going to do..." She trailed off.

"If you had known?"

Her jaw clicked shut, her throat working through the emotion. "I likely would have still gone through with it. The king is not someone to cross. I've seen what he does to those who disagree with him, let alone those who outright deny him. It's said that his previous brides were all skinned alive because they didn't please him. I'm not so brave as to fight a man like that."

"My people have fought with him for decades." Ragnar's hand trailed down to the rip in her dress right over her heart. He could just barely see the swell of her breast, so plush that it distracted him for a few moments. "Trolls are far braver than humans, though."

"You're very much correct. From what I have seen in a very short amount of time, I think there's a lot I could learn from your people." Taking a deep, steadying breath, she forced herself to calm. He could feel her heart slowing beneath his fingers as he pressed them against her skin. "I ask your forgiveness, husband."

Husband.

The word thrummed through him. It rocked throughout his entire being. This was the first time she had called him such, and he hadn't realized what it would feel like.

This delicate, tiny creature looked to him to keep her safe. Big eyes stared up at him, her heart still and slow underneath his fingers as though she trusted him. No matter what decision he made.

"Beg me," he said.

"For what?"

"For your life." And also because he wanted to hear her beg. It made his blood boil and his cock harden. He wanted her to beg for her life in whatever way she saw fit.

He watched her chest rise and fall. Watched her eyes widen for a brief moment before she nodded.

"Please," she whispered. Then her hand moved from his wrist to his chest. It was the first time she'd willingly touched him, not that he'd given her a lot of opportunity to do so. For a woman who had been pressed against his back while they ran, he didn't really know what she felt like. Now, her fingers spread wide across his chest.

Her fingers lingered between his pectoral muscles and then dipping down to his stomach. He felt his muscles clench against her touch, even though he didn't want to react to her.

"Husband of mine, I beg you to spare my life." Her warm touch slid farther down, skating over the edge of his pants that he could already feel tenting just from this simple touch. "I will do anything you desire, anything you wish for. But please, spare my life."

He grabbed her hand just before she tried to slip it underneath the leathers. "Wife," he snarled.

As he said the word, a wave of gooseflesh rose on her skin. He watched it spread from her arms, across the skin of her chest that was just barely revealed, and up her neck. All the hairs on her body rose at that single, deep toned word.

So, she wasn't unaffected by him. Good. Because he felt like he was losing his mind.

"Isn't that what you wanted?" she breathed.

"When I take you for the first time, wife, you'll be dripping for me. Not a single moment sooner." He drew her hand back up his chest. "But your begging will need to be improved. Long before I give you what you want."

They were both breathing hard, staring at each other as they realized just how far gone they were. He had always wanted a troll wife that would be his match in every way. If the seers saw something in her that meant she was the best option for him, then who was he to tell them they were wrong?

He'd keep her alive. For now.

"You live," he said. "For as long as I wish you to live. But I would have you tell me your real name first."

"My name is Maia."

"Not the lie."

She shook her head, her lips so close to his that he could feel her breath fanning across his tusks. "My name is Maia. I did not lie to you. I've never lied to you. Not about my love of flowers, not about who I am, and certainly not about my name."

It was a start. He didn't know why he believed her, but he did.

Maybe it was the words of the witch sinking in. The woman who was meant for him wouldn't lie to him, not about this. But, at his core, he knew it wasn't just that.

This woman hadn't complained once on the journey here. She had proven herself stalwart and enduring, even if she wasn't brave or fierce like his people. And perhaps there was some merit in that.

"Good," he breathed. "We start here today then, wife. No lies between us."

"Are you agreeing to be my husband? Really?"

He sighed. "I rarely go back on my word, but yes. You were born for me, fire hair. And so I will keep you."

Chapter 13

Maia sat in the same place and watched him prepare a makeshift campsite for the night. Ragnar refused to bring her back to the others after their conversation, but she wasn't pushing for him to. She could still feel their claws raking down her spine and how easily her skin had split. The experience had been similar to cutting herself on her father's sharpest knife, and she simply did not wish to endure that again. Let the trolls' anger fade with time. Perhaps they wouldn't be so inclined to kill her in a few days.

Although she understood their anger. She would have been mad too if she had discovered the trolls had tricked her people.

Huddled as she was, she could see everything Ragnar did. He was quick to build a circle of stones, not crystals. He kept his eye on her the entire time. She wasn't sure if he thought she was going to bolt, or if he was just worried about her in general. She wanted to bristle at the thought. Maia had always taken care of herself.

But she was bleeding quite badly. She could feel the shirt sticking to her skin where the blood had soaked through the fabric and her wrist was aching terribly. Her palm hurt where the witch had bled her. Everything in her ached, even the top of her head.

So she stayed right where she was. She didn't offer to help, nor did she care to do so. Ragnar worked hard to get the fire going and then left once more, returning with armfuls of leaves over and over again until he'd created a sizable pile that was clearly meant for sleeping on. It wouldn't be the most comfortable bed she'd ever slept in, but it would do just fine for the night. Hopefully, they were going back and not just... staying here forever.

The thought terrified her. She felt all the blood drain out of her face as he returned with a rabbit and pulled his knife out of his pocket. At least this time he sat down with her, slowly skinning the poor fluffy beast that he'd killed to feed her.

"Are we staying here?" she asked.

"Yes."

"Forever?"

He looked at her with a frown. "No, not forever."

Maia was ashamed to admit that she sagged a bit in relief. "Oh, good."

He paused in skinning the creature, then pointed the bloodied knife at her. "Did you think we weren't going back to the other trolls?"

Well, when he said it like that, it sounded a little silly. Shuffling her feet and sticking her toes into the soft dirt, she shrugged. "Well, I don't know what your plan is. You don't tell me anything. All I know is that they wanted to kill me just a few hours ago. I'm still the wrong human to be here, and that can't be easy for them."

"It isn't," he muttered. That knife made quick work of the rabbit and soon enough, he was threading the meat onto a stick. "You leave that part up to me. They're not a forgiving lot, but they'll accept you if

I ask them to."

"Is that because you're..." She struggled to find the right word. "Noble doesn't sound correct for your people. Or do you have nobility? Well, you must. You have a king, so that means there must be others. A duke is what we would call someone like you, perhaps. Or an earl?"

She was rambling at this point. But trying to make some sense of what had happened to her helped with the panic attack currently coiling around her heart.

All the while, the damned troll sat there looking at her. Slowly, he extended his arm, easing the meat over the open fire. "Trolls don't look at it that way. Nobility, like what you're saying, has to be earned through deeds, not through bloodlines. We don't give our respect to others so easily."

"Oh," she breathed. "I like that."

His mouth twisted into something similar to a smile before he looked back down at the fire. "So on your terms, I would be the son of a 'noble'. My father was a grand general who won many battles for our people. All know of him, and all think of him as a... grandfather to them. He was a good man, with many impressive deeds."

"Ah." Maia nodded as though that made sense. "And you're a healer? At least, that's what the blood witch said."

He nodded again, turning the rabbit over the open flame. "I am."

"How long have you been a healer?"

"My entire life."

Right, because that was his magic. Trolls were far more tied to the magic they were born with. Though, she supposed if she was born with more magic than what she currently had, she would have used it more.

And she was running out of things to say. He didn't have a lot to say, even when she asked very specific questions. Maia was distracted by the pain in her back and the sensation of numbness running from her wrist into her fingers. It was hard to think about superficial things to talk about, especially when the creature in front of her didn't want to talk.

Still. She had to try. He'd all but agreed to be her husband and that was progress. She wasn't in a one sided marriage anymore and she didn't want to be married to someone who hated her.

Clearing her throat, she tucked her aching wrist against her belly and tried again. "What's your favorite food?"

Both his brows shot up. "What?"

"What is your favorite food?" she repeated, a little louder this time.

"I heard you, I just... What kind of question is that?"

"I just want to know you a little better than I do. I don't know what you like to eat, or what you hum when your mind is bored. I don't know what your favorite color is, your favorite flower, or how often you think about your future. I want to get to know you. If we're married, that only seems fair."

There was a long moment of silence. Eventually, she gave up on hoping that he would even respond. Maia listened to the crackling sound of the fire and scooted a little closer to it for the warmth as the sun dipped below the horizon. Crickets started up, their chirps likely the last before winter set in. She'd miss their song, but she also loved the first snow. When the world was blanketed in white, and all was still, she had a wonderful feeling of peace.

Eventually, he shifted, shaking himself off as he stood. The evening chill didn't seem to affect him at all as he walked over to her with that rabbit in his hands.

"Here," he said as he reached her side of the fire. "Eat this."

"Oh," she let out a little startled squeak as he handed the hot, dripping stick to her. "Thank you."

She ripped off a small steaming piece, trying very hard not to get it all over her already ruined shirt, and then handed the stick back to him. But he shoved her hand back into her lap, ignoring the grease that spilled onto the ground and moved behind her.

"What—" Maia cleared her throat. "Aren't you going to eat?"

"It's for you."

"I can't eat a whole rabbit."

"You'll try." He settled onto the ground behind her, and she was terrified to look back. She had no idea what he was doing, and didn't want to look. The firelight set his features into a terrifying grimace.

But then his hands came down on her back, light and soft, as he parted the long gashes in her shirt to look at her wounds. His claws weren't so terrifying as he peered at her wounds. Then, with a low hum, she felt the first wash of his power. Cool and calming, it was a balm to the heated wounds that were burning long before his touch.

Sighing, she tried to lean back into his hands. He nudged her forward again.

"Eat," he said, and she did.

Maia put the strip she'd ripped off in her mouth and let the flavor explode on her tongue. Rabbit really was good. She'd had it a few times, perfectly bathed in wine beforehand and braised to perfection. But this was somehow better. This was wild rabbit that he'd caught with his bare hands, charcoaled over an open flame while crisp clear air surrounded them.

It was better this way. Filled with wild abandon that eased some knot inside of her.

Or maybe that was the healing magic that dripped down her back, like he was painting her. Long slow strokes of magic, even though he wasn't touching her.

Then his deep voice quietly interrupted her thoughts. "There is a certain kind of mushroom in my homeland. The trolls are known for growing it. We can do much with that mushroom, but my favorite is to cook it simply with garlic and butter from our cows. You've never tasted a sweeter mushroom in your life, and it feels indulgent to eat it. Even if it is common to grow in Trollkin."

"Do you know what my people would call it?"

"I believe you call them morels."

She'd seen them before. They were delicious when cooked right, and a little finicky to grow.

Now, she wasn't sure what to say next. Morels were hard to find where she was from. Few people knew how to grow them, and even fewer knew how to find them in the woods. It wasn't like a lot of people were wandering into the forest, anyway.

She couldn't have thought of another thing to say because he started to hum. His voice was already a baritone, but it dropped into a voice so deep it was like the earth itself was singing. Like the depths of a mountain had opened up, and the call was the very roots of trees that had grown for a thousand years. The song was simple, more like a nursery rhyme, but it moved through her bones and vibrated every part of her being. So lovely. So deep that it made her bones rumble.

And when he stopped singing, she wanted to ask him to continue. To keep going, even though it might seem strange that she wanted to listen to him hum. Was it odd to ask?

But then he stood up again, and she didn't say a single word. He'd think her a silly little thing with her head not quite screwed on right. After all, he'd probably just been humming to keep himself concentrated on healing.

Her back no longer ached, like even the bruises were gone from where she'd fallen on rough stones.

"That feels much better," she murmured, rocking her shoulders a bit. "Thank you for that. You didn't have to heal me."

He grunted before shifting her so her side was facing the fire. Then he sat down in front of her and took her hand in his lap. Unfortunately, that meant he also grabbed onto her wrist.

At her little high-pitched noise of discomfort, he froze.

Right, she should just tell him, so he didn't think she was hiding that too. "When I fell in the creak that first day, I think I hurt my wrist. I don't think it's all that serious. I can still rotate it. It just... hurts to do."

His frown deepened, but then he rotated her wrist for her. Up and down, side to side, watching for when she tensed or flinched in pain.

"Green," he muttered.

And she hadn't the faintest idea what he was talking about. "Green?"

He nodded. The cool touch of his power flared again between them, this time in a shackle around her wrist that tightened with a pinch before she felt it start working.

Was he losing his mind? Or did he have some odd way of focusing his magic? She wasn't sure what he was muttering about, as he stared at her wrist with almost too much concentration.

"And violets," he said quietly. "Violets are my favorite flower."

Was he... answering all her questions? Every single one, in the order that she had asked them? Maia didn't even remember what she'd asked, let alone in what order. She'd just blurted out a bunch of random questions that weren't all that important for her to have answered. If she didn't know his favorite flower, that wouldn't be the end of the world.

But now she did know his favorite flower. "The tiny purple ones?" she asked, just to clarify.

"They grow outside of caves. They're hardy and strong, and the first sign that winter is over and spring has come."

"I think that's a lovely reason to like a flower." And it was far more deep than she was expecting out of him. But then again, she was constantly surprised by this troll, who was supposed to be a beast yet seemed to be anything but.

She bit her lips and stared down at their hands. His dark claws were so close to the veins in her wrist, yet now she wasn't afraid he was going to use them. Perhaps this tumultuous start had been a good thing. She'd needed to see the worst of him, to know that his best was... well, better than just that of a murderous troll who was coming to destroy her home.

He turned her hand gently, tracing his fingers over the deep wounds in her palm. "And I think about the future constantly. I worry about what path my people will have to walk to stay alive. I fear what your people are planning to do to mine and how our numbers have already dwindled. The joining of our peoples was supposed to stem the flow of hatred that always leads us back to war. And without the binding, my powers are limited to what I now know how to do. If we are at war again, I won't be able to heal as many people as I'll need to."

Her heart broke for him. Without thinking, she turned her hand in his and laced their fingers together. "It's not up to you to save your people. One single person cannot change the hearts and minds of countless others. There would be no war if there were not so many who hated each other. The fear that causes all the strain and stress and strife was not born out of your mind. It's not up to you to fix it."

Ragnar's haunted gaze met hers. "We all have to try to fix it. If there is but one person who says they don't matter, then there are a hundred, or a hundred more than that who agree. So many people saying they cannot make a difference will lead to no one even trying," he said. "I will be the first to make the change, and others will follow suit."

There was so much more to this troll than she ever would have guessed. And it stung to know she had been so wrong about him, and perhaps his kind.

Chapter 14

He didn't sleep that night. Instead, he leaned against a tree and watched the firelight play over Maia's features. He'd decided for her to be his troll wife, and now he wouldn't go back on that. Once Ragnar gave his word, he kept that word, no matter how hard it was. But what he hadn't figured out was how to make sure that he could.

His people would be livid to find out that he hadn't killed her. They were probably all assuming he'd taken her away to make this slow. He would keep the kill for himself, then show back up with her fingers in his pockets and blood coating his skin. He would return victorious, keeping his people safe from yet another human who thought they knew how to hurt the trolls. But that was far from the case.

The seers knew something he didn't. And he was starting to understand perhaps a bit of what that was.

Maia was softer than any troll he'd ever met. His people had learned to be hard throughout years of war and hiding from the humans while they'd learned how to be people themselves. And that was the most difficult part to get over. They had hundreds of years of animalistic nature they fought against, even now. She would never understand that.

He was no better than the trolls with the least elven magic. Though those families were just starting on their journey out of the mud and the pits of darkness, they were the ones who he looked to first. They were the ones who deserved his attention more than any other. Because they still didn't entirely have their minds yet. It took time and generations to be able to think rather than react.

As the pink streaks of sunrise crested the sky, his little human woke. She scrunched in on herself at the dawning of consciousness. He'd thought perhaps she would stretch, show off more of those curves that were barely revealed through the slices in his shirt. Instead, she curled a little tighter, as if clinging to sleep for a few moments before all that tension released.

Rolling up into a seated position, she stared at him through bleary eyes with her hair tangled in a red cloud around her head.

"You're still here," she muttered.

"Where else would I go?"

"You could have just left me in the woods to fend for myself. I get that you don't want to kill me, but there are plenty of things here that would, I reckon."

It would take time for him to win her trust. And time for her to win his trust as well.

Ragnar shook his head. "I don't want to kill you, fire hair. But we do need to return."

"Are we finally going to your home?"

"Yes."

"How far is it?"

He pointed at the mountain she'd been leaning against. The monolith of power stood at her back and the massive rock had kept her safe from the winds last night. "We're already here."

All night, he'd listened to the song of the mountain. The echoing cry of the stones that recognized him. This place sang for him, and it called for him to come home. It wanted him to return to the depths, to the safety of where all the trolls lived. But it wasn't sure if it wanted him to bring a bride who might be dangerous to them all.

He wished he knew the right answer. But for now, he had to trust her. And keep an eye on her. The moment she stepped foot into his home, she would be watched by everyone around her.

Maia craned her neck and looked behind her. Her eyes widened, and he wished he knew if that was in shock or anticipation. Or if she was terrified at what she imagined lived within.

But, after the meager time he'd spent with his troll wife, he should have known she wouldn't be able to keep her mouth shut and hide her thoughts from him.

"Trollveggen," she whispered.

"Indeed. It is."

What must it look like to her human eyes? He knew what it looked like to him. The "troll wall", as the humans called it, was a wide swath of mountain that lurched out of the earth as though it was a living, breathing thing. Parts of the mountain range caught clouds within it, and that made it look like the mountain itself was breathing, exhaling smoke into the sky. The peaks were rarely visible, but he'd climbed them when he was young. He'd seen the sun pierce through the veil of clouds that shrouded the sight of the sky and he'd seen tops of those clouds as he peered over them. They looked like he could walk upon them, though he'd tripped over himself when he tried.

"They say Trollveggen is cursed," Maia whispered. "The darkness inside of the caverns will steal your eyesight if you even try to go into it."

"It is dark inside, yes."

"The rumors always claimed that it wasn't just the trolls who lived within. But giant worms that would devour an entire person in one bite. Bats the size of small horses and… other creatures that were likely just conjured up by a terrified mind." She tucked a strand of that wild hair behind her ear, as though that would do anything to make her appear more presentable. "We're taught to fear it."

Ragnar stood, kicking dirt over the fire before he reached out a hand for her to take. "There is nothing to fear here but rocks and stones."

"Those can be fearsome in their own right." She reached for his hand, her tiny fingers tucking into his as he easily lifted her.

He didn't want to bring her to his people looking like this. The tattered clothes on her back and the earrings in her ears that weren't even remotely the ones he should have given to her. But it would have to do, for now.

Daring to touch her, he brushed his fingertips over those piercings. The tiny hoops didn't move when he nudged them. Likely because they had been traveling in dirt and earth, making it hard for her body to properly heal them. Sighing, he gave her a small nudge of his magic to speed along the process before turning his back to her.

"Climb up," he said. "And I will introduce to you to Trollveggen."

She sucked in a deep breath, and then she clambered onto his back. He hooked his hands underneath her knees, and then they were off. It would be a long day. Traveling without the war band meant he had to travel faster so they could get to food and water at the end. He didn't have that with him, and his human was likely thirsty. She hadn't drunk in nearly a day, and he wanted to make sure she would survive.

So he went straight up the mountain, rather than heading toward the passes that were safer, but slower. He'd thought she would be terrified and make that little squeaking sound she often did. His fire hair rarely complained, though. She merely tightened her arms around his neck and clamped her legs tighter at his waist, and held on.

It took hours of grueling labor. Even he was breathing hard by the time the sun had reached its peak on the horizon. He paused to breathe and stared out at the beauty of his realm. The clouds were close above their heads and he could see for miles.

Her arm appeared over his shoulder. Her finger pointed to the right toward two rocky fingers reaching up toward the clouds. "We call those two peaks the watchers. It's said they see everything the humans do and mark all of our activities so that the trolls know everything about our movements."

The two peaks were well known to his people. They stood close together, thin as needles in the sky. They were nearly unclimbable, even to the mountain goats that lived in this region. The sharp peaks did not grow any trees at all, merely a few patches of pale green and yellow lichen that were difficult to see without being right on top of them.

But it was funny that the humans had thought up such a gruesome story for the twin peaks. He reached back and hitched her a little higher up his back before turning his attention to the climb again. "We call them Brura and Brudgommen."

"What does that mean?"

"It is an old human tongue. When the trolls were first made, we took on your language before creating one of our own. The old words mean the bride and groom." He felt her arms spasm around his neck, and it made him grin. "Our legends say those were the first two trolls to be made. They did not wish to fall into line as the elves wanted them, so instead, they stood on the mountain range to provide safety for all trolls. They are our guardians, in a sense. So I suppose the watchers are not all that wrong, either."

"The bride and groom," she murmured.

He glanced over his shoulder to see her looking back at the twin peaks. The breeze played with her red hair, sliding tendrils over her wind burned skin. Those green eyes never stopped looking at the mountains, though. Not even when her hair blew in front of her sight. And for some reason, he suddenly realized she could be beautiful.

A wild creature, she was. Elegant and free in this moment, unlike she'd ever been in her life, he would guess. This was what he could give her. This was what he could offer to the human who had walked into his life and commanded far more of his attention than he'd thought she would.

Ragnar continued to climb. He pushed them harder as he moved throughout the mountains. And though he would have loved to bring her to above the clouds, the sun was already on the opposite side of the horizon and he wanted to get home.

Traveling was always an adventure, but he'd grown tired of adventure at his age. He wanted a warm hearth, a mug of hot mead, and a quiet bed to rest his head for the night. A familiar place—that was all he asked for.

So when he got to the fork in the mountain, worn down by countless years of troll feet, he felt some knot inside of him release. He was so close to being able to let down his guard and finally feel safe.

"You said something earlier," Maia murmured, her voice almost impossible to hear. "Might I ask a question?"

"You don't have to ask permission to ask a question, fire hair."

She tightened her arms around his neck and then slowly released them. "Perhaps I could walk for this?"

He didn't see why not. They were so close to his home that soon she would have to, anyway. Although he did worry she would get too cold when she wasn't pressed up against his much warmer skin. "For a few moments," he relented, releasing his hold on her legs and letting her slide down to the ground.

She stomped her feet a few times, and he had to wonder if she'd lost feeling in them. "When you were talking about the spires, you said the trolls were created. That's not my understanding of your people. The humans assume trolls have always been here. I remember my father talking with some of his clients, saying that the trolls were angry at us because this mountain has always been yours and we built too close to it."

"You did build too close to it."

"That's not what I'm asking." Those big eyes stared up at him, and he hated that it softened something inside his chest. "The trolls were created? By who?"

He didn't have time for this explanation, but then again, he supposed she deserved to know the answer. It was, after all, a good question.

"It's not common knowledge that the trolls were made. Elves created us out of mud and stone and fur. They wanted slaves. We did not wish to be slaves. Because of that creation, though, the elves gifted us the smallest bit of their magic." He reached out and touched a stone that loomed over their heads. The granite created a small bridge where trolls would walk earlier in the day toward another cavern. They ducked beneath it, toward the shadows beyond. "In the early days, trolls were little more than animals. The fur and scales and wings that were used to create us were all that we knew. But that spark of elven magic gave us a hope that someday we would be more. The first troll who mated a human with a spark of elven blood, they were the ones who created more magic. That troll born, the one who'd been gifted elven blood, he would go on to become our first king."

He looked down at her, seeing her eyes grow even larger than before. She watched him with a slightly open mouth, rapt attention never moving from his lips.

"So that's why you wanted an elven bride? A woman with more elven blood than me." She blinked a few times, then looked away from him. "You're all seeking to become... elves?"

"We were born of mud and ash. We will never become elves." They approached the mouth of the cavern that led to his home. It was a crack in the very realm, it seemed. He loved it. Staring into the pitch black of something that was so eerie and terrifying reminded him that he was very, very small.

Moss hung from the top of the cavern in tendrils that reached toward their heads. A faint breeze always tunneled through it, toying with the ends of his long hair and making the shaved sides of his head even more obvious to him. It was hard to focus on words when he could smell the loam in the cave and the slight mildew scent that always reminded him of home.

The sound of chittering bats could be heard from where they stood, and beyond that, the faintest clang of metal and the rumbling of deep troll voices that echoed from so far into the earth that it was impressive they could hear them at all.

The open maw that led deep into the ground swallowed all the light.

It was easy to find if someone was brave enough to climb Trollveggen, but even then, it would be difficult to get the rest of the way down. He knew the rest of this tunnel was a labyrinth that sometimes led into only darkness and there was no getting out of it if one did not know the way.

Maia looked up at him, and he expected a question about where they were going. She was a curious little human, and he appreciated that about her.

Instead, the question that dripped from her lips was about what he had already said. "What are you trying to become, if not elves?"

He wrapped his arm around her waist, lifting her easily so they were face to face. He searched through her gaze, trying to know if she wanted to know the answer or if it would terrify her even more. Ragnar assumed the best he could do at this moment was to be honest.

"We are trying to become the darker version of them. Elves made of grit and power and mud."

"Dark elves?" she whispered.

He didn't have to reply. Instead, he drew her into the black maw of the cave, where the shadows swallowed them both whole.

Chapter 15

She clung to him, feeling a little strange with his face so close to hers. Maia had expected to cling to his back, not to be carried like a proper bride across the threshold of darkness.

Soon enough, she would find out if the rumors were true. If the curses surrounding this kingdom would affect her, then soon her eyes would be lost. Perhaps she would learn if it was just blindness, or if it were the trolls that plucked out the eyes of any human visitor who dared to step foot in their kingdom. She wouldn't be surprised. They were rather bloodthirsty individuals, in her experience, and they were very protective of each other.

Although she was coming to find it wasn't just that they sought out fighting, but that they were born into it. If they didn't fight, people took from them. Why wouldn't they stand up for themselves?

It had only been a week here, and she already didn't recognize her own thoughts.

She clung to Ragnar's shoulders, and her thoughts turned to her safe home, a little garden left behind, and all of her things that she might never see again. She feared what would happen next. Would he force her to live underground for the rest of her life?

Ragnar was sure footed as he carried her through what looked like ink. Sometimes she swore she saw things moving in the black, but that had to just be a trick of the mind. She couldn't see anything in this darkness, no matter how hard she tried. It was a little unnerving not being able to see.

All it did was give her more time to worry about what she would find in this kingdom compared to her own. She wanted to go back home more than she had so far on this entire journey. She wanted her comfortable bed and monotonous life. She wanted her freedom.

Ragnar's breath was louder that she'd remembered. She could hear her own heart thundering in her ears, and she wondered if that was because all her senses were suddenly stronger.

He said she was his troll wife, now. Maia had no idea what being a troll wife even meant. Did that mean she was meant to stay here forever? Did she service him? She'd certainly attempted to do so, and he had denied her. That rejection had stung more than she wanted to admit.

If she was to be his wife, there were no rules around the role. After all, she knew what being a wife to a human meant.

And she damn well wasn't going to let him crush her beneath his heel while she still had somewhere she could escape to.

Gasping, she struggled in his arms all of a sudden, trying to get down. He clamped down harder, grunting as she jammed her elbow into his rib, but never releasing her.

"Stop wriggling," he growled, wrapping his arms around her even tighter. "You're going to fall."

"My plants!" The argument was meager, but she could only think of a few things to shout at him that might convince him to let her go home. "My business! We have to go back."

"We're not going anywhere but deeper into the mountain."

"But the law! If a business and a home are vacant for more than two weeks, then it is forfeit to the crown. I have to go back and make sure that I get at least one client, or everything I've worked so hard for will be gone."

"You're a troll wife now, woman. What makes you think you're going back home to your flower business?"

Tears pricked at her eyes. "You don't understand. This was my life! My whole life. I spent countless hours in that garden, poured blood, sweat, and tears into the business. I never married, even after my father's death, and starved some winters just to keep it. That business is mine, Ragnar. It's no one else's."

Maia hoped he could feel the desperation in her. She had to go back. She had to get the business back on track. Her entire life—her entire being—was defined by that business. And he callously just thought she could throw it away?

His arms tightened even further until she could feel her bones creaking in protest. But then he stopped moving and just squeezed her.

Darkness surrounded them. There was just the sound of his even breathing and her heart beating out of sync. Then, all she could focus on was the tightness of his grip. How easily he held her in those strong arms and the calm, steady thud of his heart that was half as fast as hers. All those sensations broke through the panic, the anxiety, and the downright fear that she had somehow failed her father's ghost.

Her breathing slowed, until she stopped trying to get away from him and instead, just breathed.

"Are you done?" he asked.

"I guess so. I'm not happy about it, though."

"The trolls have our ways. We can get your plants from your garden, although I don't know if they will grow here. We might kill them by taking them underground, and that's something you have to consider. But your business is gone. You're a troll wife now. I'm sorry that makes you sad, fire hair. I'm sorry your king did this to you. But I cannot change what has been done any more than you can."

She leaned the side of her face against his chest. It felt a bit like giving up if she didn't at least try to argue with him. That was her life she was leaving behind. But her reality was that she'd never chosen anything for herself. She'd done what her father wanted and maybe… Maybe it was time to let that go.

"I think we can both agree that I'm giving up more than you are," she whispered. It was hard to say the words. She still didn't like arguing with anyone or even try to tell them her own opinion. "You get to go home to everything that is yours and all the familiar things that you've gathered over the years. I have nothing but unfamiliar people who don't trust me."

For a moment, she swore he hugged her a little closer. There was a gentleness to his touch that hadn't been there before, but then it was gone. He was just as cold and stoic as stone. "You will learn," he finally said. "But first, open your eyes and see the kingdom of the trolls."

She hadn't even realized she'd closed them. But then she blinked them open and a new world unfolded before her. She'd been told countless times in her life that the trolls lived in damp, dark caves. That they were little more than rats or moles living in the dirt.

But this wasn't at all what she had thought. There were trees down here. Tall trees with spiraling trunks that looked like countless trees all wrapped around each other. A dim blue glow illuminated the entire world, turning the leaves into silvery, sky blue creations that hardly looked real. They stood on the top of a rise, with a winding path that was covered in a bed of those same leaves. Far beyond that path, she could see a river running through this world that stretched as far as her eye could see. But the water... it had an almost purple glow. Above their heads, she could see the entire kingdom was bracketed in stone.

Tiny green and blue lights dotted the ceiling of stone like stars, but then she realized they must've been some kind of glowworm. She'd heard about them in a tavern once, when a caver had mentioned that sometimes there was light in the darkest parts of the realm. She'd never thought to see them herself, though.

As Ragnar moved throughout this marvelous place, stepping foot on the path and drawing them into the blue forest, she realized the leaves were larger than she was. These trees were old. And they weren't anything she would have seen outside of this place.

"Where are we?" she whispered.

"The home of the trolls," he replied. "We call it the heart of the mountain."

A wind stirred around them, and she caught a sweet scent in the air. It was a bit like honey and chocolate all mixed into one, although she thought perhaps that was her own wishful thinking. She'd wanted nothing more than a sweet this entire journey. And now, she swore she could smell them.

They didn't walk on the path for long before he turned off it. Now there were lanterns lighting their way. They were spindly in creation. She thought perhaps made of iron, but she'd never seen such a slate gray metal be used to create something so delicate. The globe on top was clearly made of glass, because there were wisps contained inside of them. But the metal that rose up over it was like a blooming spiked flower.

The pathway of leaves turned into a pathway of stone. It was this path that Ragnar brought them to, his feet sure as each clawed toe hit the stonework and drew her deeper and deeper into the forest.

"Are we going to your home?" she asked, nerves setting in again.

"No. We're going to the king."

Every hair on her body rose and every part of her suddenly turned to stone. She swore she didn't even have a heartbeat left after he said that. "Excuse me? We're going to see the troll king?"

"Of course we are. All troll wives are presented to him before they're brought back to their home."

Maia resumed her struggles. She knew what kings did when they were presented with new brides. They took, and they tore and they did everything they thought they deserved to make women suffer. No man was going to do that to her. Not after everything else she had suffered at the hands of these brutes. She would not go through that. Not in her life. She'd seen enough women go through it in her own kingdom and she knew how to get away from that future.

Run. Run fast, far, and even if that meant she had to dig herself into a rocky crevice that these trolls were too big to get to, that's exactly what she would do.

"Would you stop doing that?" he hissed, obviously trying to juggle her writhing form again.

"I will not go see your king!"

"Nothing is going to happen. I don't know why you're so—"

"I know what kings do to brides!" she shouted, her voice echoing through the trees. It was only the second time she'd shouted in his presence, but he froze at the sound of it. Perhaps she'd finally startled him into submission. "I won't let you take me there."

But then he bounced her in his arms, so high that she was afraid she would fly out of his arms, only to catch her again. "What do you think kings do to troll wives, fire hair?"

"Kings..." She gulped, swallowing down the fear of saying this to him. "They take the first taste of the wife. That's how it has always been. And I'm sorry—I'm just not... not able to..."

Her words trailed off. She didn't want the king, or any man at all right now. Not even her own husband, which was an entirely different fear. She could barely consider sleeping next to him, let alone think about how terrified she was about the differences between their bodies. She'd hardly had a chance in her life to even look at a man naked, let alone explore all of that. And now she had a troll before her, one the other troll women had hinted had a pierced cock, and it was so overwhelming. She'd tried not to even think of it, but it had been hard not to while running her hands down the impressive ridges of his abs.

Ragnar sighed, and his hands curled around her. He turned her in his arms until his hands were underneath her armpits. He let her dangle from his grip. "Listen to me, Maia. And I want to make sure you are actually listening, so you are going to repeat everything I say. Do you hear me?"

Miserable at her own fate, she sighed and nodded.

"The king does not take troll wives from their husbands."

She muttered the words, but she didn't believe them. Kings always took—that was what they did. It was their right as a king to sample brides before they were taken by their husbands. It was the way of things. If Ragnar wanted to lie to keep her pliant, then she'd let him do that. But she wouldn't believe him.

"No self respecting troll would ever let another man touch his wife."

She repeated that. But then he shook her, bringing her closer to his face so he could stare into her eyes.

"Listen closely, fire hair. If another man touches you, I will first cut off his fingers. I will make him watch as I eat them, one by one. I will savor the taste of his blood and his pain before I cut off his hand for ever having it graze your skin. If he survives that, I will hunt him down. I will run him through the forest until his breath saws from his lungs and until he knows what it feels like to be prey. Then I will skin him alive until he dies. I will wait for him to wake up if he passes out. I will continue until the end," he said. "Do you hear me? Trolls are not humans. We do not use our wives as play things, nor would we ever allow a woman to be traded around like that. You are not in your human kingdom with your foolish men."

That got through her anxiety. Maia's hands shook where she held his forearms, and she finally gave him a quick nod. "Okay."

"You hear me?"

"I hear you."

"What will I not let happen?"

"No one will touch me," she whispered.

"No one but me."

She hadn't expected that to be quite so reassuring. She shouldn't want him to touch her, either. He was a troll. A terrifying creature of the mountain who would likely drag her deeper into this realm.

But somehow, she trusted him. With the blue leaves behind his head and harsh juts of his tusks against the shadows, he looked every bit the beast she had always thought him to be. But this time, she saw him as her beast.

He would keep her safe.

Chapter 16

They continued through the forest, with Maia in his arms and a little quieter than before. He'd been carrying her all day without any signs of tiring. She would have been impressed if she wasn't so worried that he was straining himself unnecessarily. She wasn't helpless. She could walk on her own.

She'd suggested the very thing to him, but he'd scoffed.

"What I carry to make camp is heavier than you," he'd replied. "And I carry that for days on end."

And that was that. In the silence that followed, her mind started to make up stories about what would happen when they reached the castle. The troll king wouldn't be happy to see her—that much she was certain of. He'd likely take a bit of her flesh for what King James had done. And she wouldn't even blame him for wanting that revenge.

Now she understood the gravity of this bride switch. So she would take her punishment with her head held high. After all, her father had taught her that it was easy to be punished. She just had to go somewhere in her head where nothing bad ever happened, and eventually, the punishment would end.

Soon enough, the castle loomed in the distance. The base was created by roots of trees, while tall spires of stone emerged from their tangled knot. All the stones were white and gleaming in the blue light. Those spires had banners hanging from some of the windows, blowing in the breeze. As they strode toward it, she could see the roots rising out of the ground and creating what looked like stairs that led right up to the massive double doors.

It was a beautiful sight to behold. A castle not standing above all the beauty of the land around it, but part of the land. She thought of her own people's castle, the one she'd grown up in the shadow of. It always looked like it had been built on top of that field, conquering the surrounding lands. With everything flattened into farmlands and not a hint of wilderness left, it was a testament that humans could and would destroy everything in their path if it stood in their way.

As they walked through the roots, she marveled at how large they were. This tree had long ago died. She couldn't feel a single hint of its soul lingering in those thick, brown spirals that sank into the ground and held the castle in place. But she could feel the magic that still lived where it had once stood.

The true heart of the mountain was the ancient magic that fed into the people who lived here, and now she could feel it spreading. Everywhere. Every inch of this kingdom held a bit of that magic that the tree had sacrificed when its time had come.

Monolithic doors stood open to all who wished to enter, and that was a difference between her castle and theirs as well. King James loved to keep the doors closed, and people had to beg to get inside. Even if they were in dire need, the king wouldn't just let them in. He preferred for them to prove themselves to him, no matter how hard that might become.

But these dark green doors were wide open. And as they walked through them, she realized they were made entirely out of some green precious stone.

"Jade," Ragnar said as he caught her staring.

"They're beautiful."

She caught a glimpse of the carvings as well. There were elves etched into the door. Their beautiful, thin figures were easy to pick out, as they were infinitely more beautiful than any human could be. Their hands were raised and magic cascaded down out of their hands. That magic seemed to spark upon the ground, and then she caught the smallest glimpse of something that appeared to disturb the mud beneath their feet.

The king had carved his doors with the creation of his people. A reminder to all that they were not animals at their core, she supposed. Or perhaps a reminder that all the work they had done was leading them somewhere great.

Ragnar strode beyond the doors and then they were inside the castle. She'd been expecting more natural things inside. Perhaps proof that these people weren't as advanced as her own. She'd expected a lot of candles, like at home. But the trolls had made deals with the wisps who were everywhere she looked. The tiny balls of light clung in clusters at the ceiling, like chandeliers, illuminating the stunning mirror shined floors of white marble. Furniture was everywhere she looked. Seating areas were filled with trolls, and the seats were all cushioned with beautifully vibrant fabric. Hand-woven rugs, stunning in their quality, were spread out meticulously along the floor to keep the chill at bay.

Maia had to blink a few times, because the trolls here didn't look like the ones she'd already met. The war band had been clothed mostly in leathers and loincloths. But these people appeared to be wearing the finest clothes she'd ever seen. They were dyed every color she hadn't thought possible, pressed into perfect lines. All the fabric complimented their shapes, but also made them look less like trolls and more like...

Elves, she realized. They looked like elves. Just with darker skin, different colors, and stripes of tattoos. They were the wilder version of elves.

Rubbing her fists over her eyes, she watched as the trolls all turned their attention to the spectacle of a troll carrying a human through their castle. The plush rugs quieted Ragnar's movements. He must've looked out of place here, as much as she did. He was still bare chested, with all his skin on display for anyone to see.

The people here in the castle looked like nobility. They were prettier than she'd imagined, with those delicate long ears and the dangling piercings that filled their ears with gemstones.

It wasn't what she had expected from the supposedly animalistic and dangerous creatures who lived underground.

He carried her straight through the main area and all the way to the back, where there was a stunning throne. She was a little caught up in the sight of it, so much so that at first, she didn't notice the man on the throne itself. It appeared to be entirely made out of crystal. It was fractured with a hundred colors, all intertwined until the light moved through it in a strange way that made the rays warp.

Until she finally focused on the man seated on the throne and every single thought in her head burst like bubbles. The creature on the throne was not at all like the trolls she had seen. His skin was a dark slate gray. Every color all mixed together to create a grayish tone with shadows of nearly pitch black. His hair and eyebrows were completely white, as were his eyes. The long tips of his ears were even more extended than Ragnar's, but it was the shape of him that startled her most.

This wasn't a troll close to elven beauty. She was looking at an elf.

Maia had only heard of their beauty. Their faces were so perfect in every way that they were almost eerie to look at. They were tall and lean, just like the man on the throne, though he was laced with muscle. And the air crackled around them with magic that was born straight from the source.

She had no idea where the elves lived now. Some people claimed they had ascended to become gods and that they lived in some mythical city in the clouds. She thought the elves had just found a newer, better place to live and abandoned all those who once worshiped them. But now, she was looking right at what remained of those god-like people whose power had terrified her own.

Ragnar gently set her on her feet and then bowed low. He kept his hand on her back, pressing her into a bow as well, even though that wasn't the right motion for a lady. Surely he'd rather she curtsey?

But she peeked out from underneath the veil of her hair and noticed that everyone else was also bowing low. The trolls had stood as they'd passed, and every single one of them bowed to the man seated on the throne.

"Ragnar," the king said, his voice a deep bass that made the very floor shudder underneath her feet. "You have returned with your troll wife."

"I have," Ragnar replied, but then he hesitated.

She knew, in that moment, he was going to announce that she

wasn't who she was supposed to be. Right in front of all of these other trolls. If they rebelled against her, if they decided that she should die, then there was nothing her husband could do to stop them.

Her knees started to shake. She was having a hard time staying bent over as she was, and if she wasn't careful, she'd topple over onto her hands and knees before this king.

She had to trust that Ragnar would take care of her. That trust was hard to build, though.

"I have bound myself to this woman. She is my troll wife, as confirmed by the Blood Witch and the Bone Reader. My destiny stands before you." Ragnar straightened, but he kept his hand on her back. Maia took the hint to remain with her face turned toward the floor. "But she is not the princess."

Murmurs rose through the crowd of trolls behind her. Whispers echoed, bouncing from the ceiling and returning to her ears.

"Of course she's not the princess. Look at her!"

"There doesn't seem to be a single drop of elven blood inside of her."

"I could feel it the moment she walked into the room. There is no power in this woman."

Then there was silence again, other than a strange scraping sound, like claws on stone. Peeking through her hair, she realized the king had stood from his throne. She swallowed hard and tried not to shudder and quake as the sensation of his magic trailed over her. Ragnar's magic was a cool, icy water that dripped from wherever he touched. But this king's magic was so much stronger.

His magic felt like ten sets of hands, all gliding over her skin and tugging at her hair. Then she could feel his magic reaching inside of her body and pulling at her power, tugging at the very heart of her, the little gift she had barely even recognized all her life.

Then there was a clawed fingertip at her chin, drawing her head back to look at him. Her neck screamed in pain, but Ragnar's hand was still firm on her back, so she bent her neck and looked up.

Up close, the king was even more terrifying. He was taller and longer than Ragnar, all that beauty of his face so impossible to look at. But then she realized he had wings. They were crumpled, useless things, wizened and bent, so they dragged upon the ground as he walked. That was the sound. The sound she'd heard were the tips of them, where there had once been talons, scraping the floor as he approached her.

"You are an abomination in this court," the troll king said. "You should not be here. A deal was made for a powerful match. Elven blood for less spilling of human blood. Do you understand this?"

"I do," she whispered.

"And yet, you still decided to deceive me and my people?"

"They tricked me into the marriage as well. I did not know King James's plan."

The king scoffed and then released her chin. She felt a bit like she could breathe again when he turned away from her. But then his words echoed throughout the hall. "You are a liar, just like all humans. I should send you to the gallows."

Ragnar flinched beside her. "I would request that you do not."

"There are better matches out there for one with your power. She will stagnate your bloodline. It's too important that we foster your healing magic, Ragnar. Kill her and move on."

A spear of anxiety flashed through her. Maia felt her heart stammering in her chest but with it came an icy cold calm. She'd known they would want to kill her. She had felt it from the beginning.

But then another voice rang out, this one far bolder than Ragnar's. She turned to see a dark green body barreling toward them, anger on every inch of his form as he shuddered with rage. "Do not kill that woman! The Blood Witch has already declared that she is his."

Gunnar was going to get himself killed arguing with a king. She wasn't worth that.

Maia whipped back around to catch the king's apathetic expression. "The Blood Witch can bring it up the next time I see her. She rarely comes to this castle, though, and I am certain one human woman will not change that fact."

"It will weave a new future lacking the thread of a necessary color," Gunnar insisted, standing beside her and Ragnar. "You cannot deny the Blood Witch, my king. This is why we have the seers."

The king snapped his jaws, the sound echoing in the chamber. "I have made my decision. There will be no liars in the court."

"We all smelled the steel at her back. The human king held a knife to her. What was she supposed to do?"

"Not allow cowardice to force her to comply with a plan that would doom us all! This was meant to stop the fighting and the battles. Now we must retaliate because this was an act of war."

Ragnar stepped in front of her and everyone fell silent again. She couldn't see past his broad back, but she could see the expression of surprise on Gunnar's face. As everyone stopped talking, they all listened to the words that Ragnar declared.

"This is my troll wife. I have agreed to take her. I made a vow the moment I saw the Blood Witch, and she said this woman was my destiny. I have no desire to leave this place, but you will force my hand if you try to take her from me. My father's line does not end with me. Gunnar is perfectly capable of creating strong children. Therefore, I relinquish my claim to my father's birthright and I give it to my brother."

Gasps echoed in the hall, but Maia had no idea what that meant. Why was he relinquishing his birthright?

The king's voice rumbled with anger. "You would give up all that you have been given? Your father's house? Your mother's treasures? All of it would go to Gunnar and you would return to living in whatever you can afford?"

Ragnar's back tensed. "If that's what it takes."

A snap of a jaw and a scoff was the king's response. "If you are willing to risk so much for a weak magicked woman, then you can have her. What a shame it is, Ragnar. You and your bloodline have fallen so far under the guidance of emotional decisions that have always flawed your family."

Then there was the sound of the king returning to his throne, the scraping grind of his wings on the floor and the silence that surrounded them.

Gunnar turned to them, his expression a bit stunned, before he wiped it off his face and looked more like the carefree brother she had come to expect. "Ah, don't you worry about it. You can keep the house."

"I'm not keeping the house," Ragnar replied.

"Keep the house. I'm in the barracks and I enjoy being in the barracks."

"It's not my house any longer."

Gunnar slapped a hand to Ragnar's chest, and even Maia flinched from the sharp crack of flesh on flesh. "You have a troll wife, brother. I do not. Keep the house and use the treasures to your heart's content. You have my blessing to do so."

Ragnar nodded, but she could see the anger and disappointment on his face. It seemed she had caused more trouble without ever even attempting to do so.

Chapter 17

So many mixed emotions ran throughout Ragnar's head. He shouldn't have stood up for her like that. Especially not in front of King Egil. Chasing that thought was another that said he should have done more. Some part of him believed he should have postured in front of the king and threatened the man if he were to ever lay a finger on his troll wife and that wasn't... him.

Ragnar was a healer. He'd never threatened to hurt someone outside of battle, but in that moment, he'd run through every single poison he knew of. He would make the king's end terrible and swift, and that...

No. He couldn't.

This was King Egil. He had done nothing but good for their people, and he had led them into a time where there was more reason and thought than there was animalistic desire.

Maia was proof that the humans would never work with the trolls. They weren't even willing to give King James's offspring to them, even with the absolute certainty that she would be worshipped by Ragnar. By all laws of his own people, he should let them punish Maia in retribution.

And yet, as he left the castle with her tucked against his side, he was very glad that he hadn't. Because for all that she had seemed a frightened little thing who couldn't speak her mind, she never let that break her. She stood tall and strong next to him; her legs moving at a run to keep up with his pace. But he couldn't slow down, not when there were plenty of trolls behind them who wanted to say their piece.

"Gunnar..." She looked over her shoulder at the castle that was no longer looming over them. "Is he not coming?"

"No."

"But didn't you just give your house to him?"

"And he gave it back."

Her brows furrowed, creating tiny lines on her forehead as she looked up at him. "Is it really that easy to give a house away here?"

"It's just as easy for humans, fire hair. Let's not make that comparison." He ushered her away from the castle and toward his own home. "Keep your eyes down and forward. We don't want anyone giving you too long of a look right now."

"Why is that?"

"Because they all want to know if your betrayal is reason enough to kill you, Maia. The king has agreed to let you live for now, but that decree is not permanent by any means. Give the rest of them time and let me hide you so they can give up their hunt."

His heart thundered in his chest, so distracting that he barely gave himself a second to look at his kingdom through her eyes. It was all lit with the glow from above. His home was always cast in pretty blue light. Giant mushrooms grew the farther they went from the castle.

Each one was different, but all the plush caps were held up by thick, sturdy stalks. Maia brushed her fingers over the top of one before she hurried to keep up with him down the blue leaf covered path.

The farther they were from the castle, the more he could breathe. He filled his lungs with the scent of loam and earth, the headier scent of the mushrooms and the crushed leaves that crumpled beneath his feet as he moved. It was all so familiar and yet, with her standing beside him, it wasn't at all.

Finally, they reached the perimeter of the forest and came out onto the edge of a cliff that dropped ever deeper into the earth. It was then he heard that intake of breath from her again that suggested she was shocked. And why shouldn't she be? A city unfolded before them in the crevice of a mountain.

Far into the shadows, there were countless homes. Each one of them carved into the very rock face, but it wasn't just homes. There were streets and markets and twinkling lights that filled the entirety of the cavernous space. Wisps readily roamed, seeking out those who needed a light to guide them places. All of it continued as far as the eye could see until the trolls themselves were tiny dots so far out of sight that they looked like children's toys.

The sound of laughter and the pealing of music rang up throughout the cavern and filled the mountain with the sound of troll joy. It was a beautiful sound, and one he had listened to his entire life. But right now, all he could do was stare at the woman beside him, whose eyes had widened.

"This is Trollveggen?" she asked.

"It is."

"I didn't know it would look like the night sky."

Now it was his turn to frown. "The night sky?"

She gestured to all the lights laid out before them. "It's like your city is made of stars."

Then he saw it through her eyes. The twinkling starlight, the faint blue glow that highlighted everything with accents of silver like the moon itself lived in his home. The beauty of it, the way every inch of this place radiated with sound and energy—it all filled his soul with peace. Perhaps she was right. This feeling was the same one he got when he looked at the thousands of stars in the night sky.

"Perhaps it is made of starlight," he muttered. "The elves designed it, and we all know how much the elves loved the stars."

She shook her head. "I know very little about the elves, actually. My father had no interest in them, and my mother... Well, I think the meager power I have came from her, you see. So she wouldn't have been able to teach me anything."

"Why not?"

"She died." Maia's voice had turned quiet and wistful. "Giving birth to me, unfortunately. My father used to say I was bad luck for that."

Something in him twisted. She'd mentioned her father a few times, and never in a good light. The man had seemed determined to wear her down, and soon enough, Ragnar would get the entire story out of her. Even if it made him hate her kind even more.

"Would you like to walk to our new home?" he asked, his voice low. "Or would you prefer that I carry you again?"

"Is it safe enough to walk?"

Ragnar mused the possibilities before relenting, "I think you'll be all right."

"Then I'd like to walk."

Her grin lit up the entire space around them, and for a moment, he swore that her eyes glowed a little brighter green.

Stone pathways led down into the city and soon enough, they were there. Ragnar led the way so she wouldn't get too many stares walking behind him, but that didn't last very long. The moment they walked underneath the first brightly colored canopy, she was already out from behind his back and rushing ahead of him. Markets were dotted throughout the kingdom, and this was one of the smaller ones.

Without a single glance at the trolls surrounding her, his little wife was quick to race toward one of the food stalls. She lurched to a stop in front of her, her wild hair billowing around her head as she stared down at the food.

"Carrots, sweet potatoes, radish, and is that ginger?" she asked, pointing at the root vegetable and looking up at him.

He wasn't sure. Ragnar wasn't the best cook, and he'd never taken the time to learn. He preferred meat, and trolls could live on only meat for their entire lives if they wished. Raw and still bloody had always been his favorite, but there were some trolls now who preferred to add a little more fiber to their diet. He'd never understood it.

"Sure it is," he said, looking at the troll behind the stall. The woman bit her lips to stop herself from laughing. Then he placed his hand on Maia's shoulder. "Come on. We have to get to the house."

"Right," she said quietly, but he could see her mind was working so fast that her thoughts were protected on her face. "How do they grow underground, though?"

"The wisps," the shopkeeper said. Her eyes were bright with mirth, still. "The wisps help them grow with magic, although it takes a little more work than it does above."

"Fascinating," Maia murmured. Her hand stroked one of the bright green stalks. "They feel like they were happy."

"No magic in the general area of other trolls," he muttered, grabbing her hand and yanking her away.

She reacted like he'd struck her. Maia curled in on herself, as if terrified at what he would do for her for practicing even the slightest bit of magic. "Sorry. I'm... I'm so sorry."

That wasn't what he wanted her to do. He didn't want her more afraid because of what he said, but he hadn't expected her to touch things. Sighing, Ragnar rolled his eyes up to the blue glowing lights and prayed to all his gods for patience. "You're allowed to do magic here, but touching a vendor's wares who has likely used magic to grow them is a recipe for disaster. You don't know what spells have been woven to keep them fresh, and you might undo those spells. Or worse, make them stronger."

Maia swallowed, but she didn't flinch away from him like he'd expected. Instead, she seemed to take a deep breath and force herself to look at him. Those wide eyes were still full of fear, but she nodded. "All right. I won't touch anything without asking first."

"Good." He patted her shoulder before releasing her. "Let's keep going."

This time, she didn't rush away from him. She stayed at his side, staring at all the things that were laid out for others to buy. Soon they left the market area that was filled with an overabundance of food and moved into the part of the city where jewelers filled the streets. Gemstones lined some of the stalls, not placed into any piece yet but just there for others to look at and buy. The enchantments on them fairly hummed with bright energy that he could feel vibrating throughout his entire form.

It was divine to be home. He could feel the mountain welcoming them both, and it eased some of the tension in his chest. At least, until they walked by a stall that was decorated by the most stunning earrings. They all swayed in a slight breeze, the sound of their gemstones clinking together filling his ears. The sparkles caught his attention first, but then it was the song a pair of them sang.

Stones were easy for trolls to hear. He'd listened to them his entire life, and now knew that the quiet hum of their voices was something he could ignore. But these green emeralds called out to him.

Their song was a little different from the others. Sometimes gems were quite loud in their need for people to look at them, but these were quieter. He couldn't help but turn his attention to them.

They weren't the hoops she currently had in her ears. Tiny studs with small, imperfect emeralds that each had the slightest fissure through them. That was why their song was different. Because when they had been harvested, they'd still been bonded to the mountain they'd lived in and they hadn't wanted to let go of that mountain. For that, they had broken just slightly, but they were no less beautiful than the earrings surrounding them.

He couldn't help himself. Her wearing someone else's earrings had been tormenting him from the start. He paused by the vendor and gestured at the studs. "Those, please."

The shopkeeper was one he knew well. His daughter was sickly, and had been for some time now. Fluid built up in her lungs, so Ragnar knew he would see her again very soon. The shopkeeper didn't even mention payment. He just nodded at the earrings and turned to another customer, all while Maia continued walking forward without even noticing he'd stopped.

Perfect.

Ragnar wasn't sure why he didn't want her to know that he'd gotten them, only that he wanted her to be surprised. In such a short amount of time, he was coming to... like her. And he didn't enjoy that feeling in the slightest.

But then he saw the sway of her hips and how she didn't care that she was in literal rags at this point, walking through a city of trolls who were all beautifully dressed and dripping with gemstones. She didn't even notice the differences because she was so busy staring at all the new things. It was clear that she implicitly trusted he would keep her safe.

He hated how that fueled some part of him that had always looked forward to having a troll wife. She was his to protect, his to guard. That was his purpose at the end of the day. He would bring her peace, and she would give him softness. It was a partnership that went beyond reason, because it was fate that had brought them together.

And, damn it, his fate was with a human. He could see it now. He just still wasn't sure yet that he liked it.

Catching up to her before she noticed he'd stopped, Ragnar placed a hand on her shoulder and steered her in the direction of his home. They were close now, and nerves churned in his belly. What would she think of it? He was certain it wasn't the same as her home. Humans lived in squalor, it always seemed.

There were very few human and troll pairings. None that he remembered from his generation, and those who had come earlier, were usually noble. The people like him, the ones who lived in the base of the city and who had fought tooth and nail to get out of the ancient animalistic bloodlines, were not usually paired with willing human participants. His great grandmother had been human—he knew that. Her elven bloodline had fueled the many pairings that had led to his own powerful magic.

But he was still more animal than he was human. He was still too big, his ears too long, his stripes too visible.

Finally, they reached his small street. Wisps hung above them in the air, many of them clustering in the doorways to light up the homes of people who hadn't returned yet. They would leave once the owners were back.

His own door had a symbol of bear on it. His father had been the one with a bloodline of such a creature, and that was why both he and Gunnar were so massive. But alongside the bear was the faintest hint of claw marks.

His mother's tiger. The reason why he had his stripes.

Ragnar ran his own claws down the mark. It was something he'd done since he was a child, keeping his mother's legacy alive as long as he could. Then he turned to look at Maia, feeling the earrings in his pocket dig into his thigh as he did so.

"This is your home now," he said gravely, watching her features for any sign of remorse.

Chapter 18

Maia wasn't certain now what she'd expected Trollveggen to be, but it wasn't this. A hollow mountain, with clouds in the sky and stars on the ceiling. This was a different world and she couldn't stop herself from wandering around with her mouth hanging open like an absolute fool.

But she didn't care what anyone thought of her. Her mind had no room for those thoughts when she was just drinking in all the differences that she had never expected to find. This place was beyond beautiful. It was like a fairytale, or some myth that had appeared out of the pages of a book. She'd never thought she would ever see a place like this.

Which made it hard to really focus on the reasons she should have been terrified. There were trolls everywhere. But, while she was aware of them, they were so much taller than her it was easy to just wander among them without being noticed herself. Some of them had surely stared at her, of course, but she'd been more focused on observing the very world that unfolded at her feet.

Now she was staring at a massive door that was far larger than she was. The handle for it came up to her chest, and she'd have to reach high to even use it. Strange, to think that she was going to have to reach up to open a door.

"My new home," she murmured, before nodding her head. "I've only lived in one place my entire life—the house my father bought from my grandfather. It has been in my family for generations."

"That's the same as this house. Every time it changes clan hands, it receives a new carving. That's why you see the bear and the tiger claws." He reached for the handle, and Maia noticed he hesitated as well. Maybe he was just as nervous as she was.

Even though it made her feel a little odd, she put her hand on top of his. "I'm sure I'll love it," she said. "It's a home. And while it might be unfamiliar right now, maybe someday I'll think of it as mine."

A shadow passed in front of his eyes and she wondered if that had been the wrong thing to say. She wasn't very good at reading this man. Normally, she was very good at knowing what was going through someone's head. It had been a great skill to have when working with her floral customers, but unfortunately she hadn't managed to transfer that ability to her marriage yet.

Ragnar opened the door and thrust her into the house without any preamble, as if he still didn't know how to manage his strength around her. Stumbling in, Maia blinked her eyes as wisps flared to life. They were in a small parlor, she realized. Yet again, her mind had run ahead of her. She'd thought they were going into a cave. Of course, that was the reasonable thought. They were in a mountain, after all.

But this room was very clearly a parlor. Yes, the walls were made out of stone. Yet someone had carved small bricks so it looked like it wasn't stone at all. There were even carved windows. Sills with beautiful arches that led only to a shallow recess. But there were balls of wisps there to make it almost look like there was sunlight on the other side. A very thick carpet made her feet entirely silent as she stepped a bit more into the room. There was a large stone mantle to her right, carved with the images of foxes chasing each other, and thick embroidered chairs that surrounded it. It was a cozy space, filled with blue light that made everything look a little less vivid than she thought it might be in the sun.

Awkwardly, Ragnar stepped around her and gestured for her to continue down a hall. "The wisps will light themselves as you pass them."

"Oh."

She wasn't sure how to feel about the wisps. How did they know she was coming? Did they have eyes? Were they actually looking for her or did they just react to movement? Or wind?

But as she walked down the hallway, she found herself captivated by so much else. The walls here were carved, too. She paused, staring up at a bear that was so realistic she could see the individual hairs on its form. It became a story as she drifted forward. The bear left fur in the mud, and out of which a troll crawled. It was massive, with fur on its shoulders and large fangs. The terrifying creature then met another troll, who took his hand and led him into a cave.

She stopped next to a depiction of troll children, tracing her fingers over the chubby cheeks of the first one. "You and Gunnar?"

"No, my family has always had two boys." He shrugged. "It is the way of my family line. We've always sought out troll wives, rather than needing to find them husbands."

She felt some of the blood drain from her face. Two boys? It was already hard enough to think about this as a marriage, let alone knowing that she was likely to have two babies.

Babies. She'd never even considered it, at least not yet. She had so much she wanted to do before she had children, even though she knew there was limited time for her to create those children.

Ragnar nudged her. "The kitchen is over here."

He pushed open a stone wall that she now realized was a door. It had rectangular carvings around it, so she should have assumed it opened. The stone was so well oiled that it was almost soundless as it glided over the floor and revealed a room beyond. There was a large table in the center, with plenty of cabinets made out of a pale blonde wood. A strange metal contraption curved out of one of them, but she only spared that a few moments of mind before she noticed the massive stove.

It was longer than she was tall, with three doors in which to put wood and a massive pipe that went right into the wall and disappeared into the stone. He must have noticed her looking, because Ragnar cleared his throat.

"When you said the mountain looked like it was breathing sometimes? That's usually when the trolls are cooking. A small amount of smoke most people wouldn't notice, but sometimes we celebrate with food and that's when there's usually quite a lot of smoke coming out of the mountain."

Her mouth dropped open, but then she grinned. "I knew it was breathing."

"Exhaling," he corrected. She caught the small smirk on his lips before he turned to draw her down the hallway again.

"Semantics."

"Which are important when one is speaking of a magic mountain." He stopped at the end of the hallway. There was a massive bear carved here as well. It stood on its back legs, glaring down at anyone who walked toward it. But beside Ragnar was a small fox carved into the wall with butterflies dancing around its whiskers. It stared up at the bear without fear. "This is your room," he said.

He nudged the door open, and Maia felt all the breath leave her lungs.

The moment the door opened, yellow wisps burst to life. Not blue, like the others she'd seen so far, but yellow like the brightest beam of the sun. It was a sparse room, filled with very few belongings. Just a single plush bed with a yellow and green quilted blanket. A wardrobe in the corner was made out of sturdy oak, and would be more than enough room to put her things. If she had any.

But there were four windows carved here. Each of them ended in a delicate point, with carved squares down them to look like they were windows revealing a world beyond. The wisps that gathered there were so bright, it felt like she was outside.

Maia pressed her hands to her chest, wonder filling every ounce of her body. "Oh, Ragnar. It's perfect."

The floor wasn't covered with woven rugs, but thicker sheepskins, so when she stepped barefoot on the soft skins, her toes immediately warmed. He pointed to a hearth in the corner. "Would you like a fire? I assume you're rather cold."

"I'm used to the cold. Ever since my father died, I've realized that I'm rather shit at starting fires." She pressed her hands to her mouth. "I apologize. Swearing isn't lady-like."

He arched his brow. "You're married to a troll, Maia. Swear all you fucking like."

An unlady-like laugh escaped her mouth before she contained it. Well, she didn't know what to do with that. She'd been a lady her entire life, because that was what everyone expected from her. To know he didn't have the same rules?

She sank onto the edge of the bed and watched her husband crouch in front of the fireplace. She was suddenly very aware of her state of dress in this grand house. It was far easier to be fine with the wildness of her looks when they were in the middle of a forest. Maia could justify the tears in her clothing and the dried blood as simply something to expect from such a wild journey. But here, with a fine rug underneath her feet and a quilt beneath her bottom, she felt rather inadequate.

In comparison, somehow Ragnar still fit in. Though he was clothed in little more than leather pants, the blocky way his thighs bulged as he crouched or the sharp edges of his features made it appear as though this was where he belonged. The rough stone and the harsh shadows—all of it fit him.

She wasn't all that certain where it left her.

She curled her fingers in her lap and waited until the fire was roaring. He stood, and she noticed he pressed a hand against his lower back as he did so. Was his back hurting? She knew he shouldn't have carried her that long, the stubborn man.

But when he turned, she would never have known there was a single thing sore on his body. He looked strong and capable and so other that it was hard not to notice their differences.

He took a step toward her and her mind fractured with anxiety. What was he going to do next? She was on a bed. Was this their bed? Did he expect her to share it with him? He'd said this was her room, but they were married, after all.

"Your tattoos," she blurted. "What do they mean?"

"Most are not tattoos."

"Oh." She frowned, even as he walked over to the other side of the bed. He stretched his arms over his head, and she lost all rational thought as those muscles stretched before her gaze.

"Trolls were born from mud and fur, remember? My mother was striped like a tiger. Gunnar didn't get too many of that family trait, but I did." He dropped his arms, his hands sliding down planes of muscle that were so tempting.

No. Not tempting. They were simply not tempting. Maia wasn't thinking about how warm he looked and how desperately she wanted to slide her hands in the same path. She definitely didn't want to know what those abs would feel like flexing against her palms, or if he would clench like he had the last time she'd touched his stomach while moving her hand toward—

He suddenly moved again. She was frozen as he placed a knee on the bed and then prowled toward her. All the muscles in his shoulders bunched and rippled with the movement until he was kneeling right in front of her on the mattress. He stared down at her, all raw masculine energy and male pride.

She could do nothing other than stare up at him with wide eyes as he reached into the pocket hanging from his loincloth.

"Come here, wife." And those words said in that dark, rumbling tone made every part of her body stand to attention.

What was it about his voice that made her want to do anything he said? She turned on the bed, rotating until she was on her knees before him as well. It was strange to kneel on a bed like this, at least until he reached forward with those massive, clawed hands and started removing the piercings from her ears.

"Wait," she said, though holding herself as still as possible in case he ripped her ear. "Aren't those supposed to stay in?"

"These are a mark of a troll wife, so yes, they stay in. Anything else you will earn."

"Earn?" She waited until he was done removing the four new piercings before shaking her head. "Are you suggesting I'll get more of them?"

He turned his head so she could look at his ears. There were so many other things that she'd been looking at, so she hadn't gotten a good look at all the piercings he had. But there were quite a few. From his lobes to the cartilage above, there were many piercings. Even one hidden inside his ear.

Apparently, his patience ran out for her scrutiny, though, because he grabbed onto her chin and turned her head to the side. "Piercings are an honor among my people. You earn them, far more than you earn anything else. Tattoos are decorations for many, but piercings? Those you must earn through rights and trials and life lessons."

"What life lesson is being a troll wife?" she muttered.

But then his hand came down between them to reveal glittering emeralds in his palm. They were stunning. Absolutely gorgeous earrings with tiny cracks in the stone that made the bevels look like she could stare into them for hours on end and never see the end of these fractures. And if she listened really hard, Maia swore there was the faintest hum to them.

"These are the earrings you should have been given the night we met," he murmured.

Ragnar drew even closer until Maia had to press her hands against his wide chest and brace herself. He freed her chin, those thick fingers sliding along her jaw until he could reach her ear. She could feel him inserting the earring and it felt... strange. Odd to have someone taking care of her like this, but it made it so she couldn't breathe.

His heart thundered against her palm, betraying the calm in which he talked to her.

"A troll wife is a gift to her husband. A treasure that must be protected at all costs. It is his job—no, his duty and honor—to decorate her in all the elegance he can find. Gemstones do not come near to her beauty, but they can enhance it. Gold and silver are only the merest specks to make her prettier. Clothing, fabric, all of it can make her comfortable, but it's no competition to the beauty he finds in just looking at her."

"If a troll finds his wife that beautiful, it sounds like it's hard to live," she whispered. He turned her head, making quick work of the other two earrings. Maia couldn't move her gaze from his chest, terrified of what she would find in his gaze.

"It's an obsession that a male can never break free from. An honorable troll knows his wife is the most beautiful being he will ever see in his life. To adorn her with whatever he can find that might contend with that radiance is a lifelong challenge that none will ever succeed in." He leaned down, those warm lips pressed to her ear, his breath caressing down her throat. "But it's all worth it to see her in nothing but the jewelry he has given her, and the beauty that captivated him for years. When he earns that, troll wife, that is the greatest gift of all."

And then he got off the bed and walked out of the room. As though what he had just said didn't turn her legs to water and steal all the air from her lungs.

Chapter 19

Maia slept for longer than she thought she would. After Ragnar had left the room, she'd been certain that she wouldn't be able to fall asleep. After all, how was someone supposed to close their eyes after the creature she was married to said... that?

She had a million questions. Did he find her that distractingly beautiful? No one in her life had ever mentioned that she was even pretty. Did he want to buy her gemstones? Maybe that was why he'd gotten the new earrings for her, which was rather lovely of him, even though he hadn't been the kindest throughout this experience. Did that mean that he was going to be nicer from now on? Should she forgive him for how he'd acted?

Maybe that forgiveness was coming, but also she wanted answers for why he'd acted the way he had. Historically, Maia was too quick to forgive. She liked to smooth things over with people because she hated anyone being upset. Even when it was at her own detriment, she would rather someone else not be upset, even if that meant she had to be.

But not this time. This time, she wanted an apology. This time she would be stronger than she usually was, and she would make him apologize for being rude and for all the things that he'd done to terrify her.

Just... she would have to figure out how to do that. Or maybe how to be the kind of person who could do that.

With those thoughts on her mind, she had drifted into a dreamless sleep and then woke as the wisps started blinking on again. She wasn't sure why they were doing that, or if she should be concerned. What if they were giving her some kind of warning?

She sat straight up in bed, her heart thundering and a cold sweat spreading over her body. What if this was a warning? What if, after all this, she was supposed to listen to the wisps?

She didn't hear a single thing. The entire room was as quiet as a tomb, and that in itself was rather unsettling. So she stood, padded over to the door, and opened it. Peering into the dark hallway was more than terrifying. She swore there was something moving in those shadows at the end of the hall. Sure, she was working on being brave.

But she wasn't that brave yet.

Closing the door quietly, she looked around the room and tried to get her bearings. She'd given it a quick glance last night, but mostly she'd been looking at him. Ragnar. Kneeling in front of the fire and then kneeling in front of her. Those heated eyes looking her up and down, telling her that a troll wife was most beautiful wearing nothing but gemstones.

A shiver trailed over her body and all the hairs on her arms rose. She had to get a hold of herself. If she didn't, she was going to lose her mind in here quickly.

Rubbing her hands over her arms, the chill set in through the holes in the shirt. Now that the fire he'd set was out, Maia had to admit, it was very cold in this room. The stone didn't retain heat, it seemed. Which left her shivering in this shirt that wasn't much of a shirt at all.

The wisps dimmed as she stood there, looking around. She thought for a moment maybe she'd stood still for too long, but then she noticed they were dimming so she could see light under the cracks around another door. The walls of this room weren't carved, so it had been hard for her to notice the first time that there was another room attached to this one.

She pushed the door open and sucked in a deep breath. It was a bathroom. There was a lovely clawfoot tub carved out of white marble in the dead center. It was large enough to fit two people easily, likely three if they were friendly. The feet were carved into roots that sank into the floor. A lavatory in the back was the first thing she put to good use, before coming back to stare at the tub.

She would give anything to get into the bath right now. Half asleep and chilly, she wanted to wash the grime off her skin and the travel that likely lingered. Ragnar had said trolls bathed every single day. She wasn't used to that.

But she didn't feel sick after bathing nearly every day on the journey out here. So maybe he was right. Maybe she wouldn't fall ill and die if she bathed every day.

There was a metal arm that curved up and over the tub as well. What that was, she had no idea. She supposed it could be a handle to get in and out. But as she circled the tub, she didn't think it was that.

Maia mused what it could be until she heard a faint noise from the doorway. Startled, she spun around to see Ragnar leaning against the frame of the door. His arms were crossed over his chest, all those bulging muscles on display for her to see.

Her initial fear at being startled bled away as she looked at him. So far, she'd only seen him as the warrior. The troll in leather laced pants who had stolen her away from her home and carried her over his shoulder for most of the journey. Seeing him clothed was an entirely different experience.

Tight breeches clung to his legs, although he still wore no shoes, which was entirely improper. A loose white shirt tucked into the breeches, but wasn't buttoned, so she could see the powerful structures of his pectorals and the interesting hollows of his collarbone. He wore a thick necklace of silver around his throat and had bracelets tightly woven around his wrists.

He'd traded out all of his earrings as well for silver jewelry. All of this made her realize without a doubt that this was not a monster in the slightest. Every single thought of him as something other and wrong disappeared at the sight of him standing in front of her like this.

She swallowed hard, trying to figure out what she was even supposed to say to him. Her mouth wasn't working right. Words stalled in her mind as she tried to guess who… what…

"I'd like to take a bath," she said, only realizing after she'd said the words how much work she'd just asked him to do. "I mean... If you show me where to get the water for the bath, I'm happy to heat it myself. I've done so many times in my life, but you've repeatedly told me that I smell, so I assume I must be quite offensive at this point. I don't mind doing all the hard work myself."

One of his brows lifted, and yet he did not stop her rant of words that flowed from her mouth. He just listened to her mumble even more about how she really didn't mind at all and then strode into the room.

Every single word dried up on her tongue that was stuck to the roof of her mouth as he walked right up to her. She stumbled backward, her lower back striking the tub hard, and still he continued to lean. He moved ever closer—by the gods, was he going to kiss her?—before twisting something behind her back.

Suddenly, the sound of water filled the room. She was frozen where she stood, grabbing into the tub behind her for balance as she stared up into his features that gave away nothing of what he was thinking.

"How?" she asked. "Magic?"

"Your people are far behind ours. We do not use magic for everything. The trolls long ago figured out a piping system for the entirety of the city. The hot pipes are affixed to a hot spring nearby, as there are many of them and we will never deplete them in our lifetime. The cold water is run off from the top of the mountain and the snow that builds there year round."

His gaze never left hers. She had no idea what to say. The steam from the hot water was building behind her, clinging to her fingers in warm droplets.

The trolls were far more advanced than her own people could dream of. Water in pipes? She'd never thought she would hear the day that was even possible, let alone that it had already happened.

Breathing in slowly, she turned to look at the steaming water filling the tub.

All she would have to do was step into the water. Whenever she wanted a bath, she could have one. No waiting. No need to boil water and carry the heavy buckets over to the tub.

This changed everything.

The hot steam coiled into the air, and she was so focused on tracking those small plumes that she didn't notice he'd leaned closer. But then his voice rumbled in her ear and every nerve in her body fired white hot.

"Get in, fire hair."

The hairs on her arms rose. Her breath caught in her lungs because surely he didn't mean... "Now?" she squeaked.

"Is there any difference from the river?"

Yes, there was a difference. In the river, she'd always been in her clothes. Or he'd left her alone to her own devices, and she'd gotten undressed quickly and dunked herself in the water before anyone could see her. That much was easy when it came to bathing. But this...

Still, some unhinged wild woman inside of her said to do it. A part of her soul that had been trapped by society's rules and the expectations of others unfurled its wings and cried out for her to be the woman she'd always wanted to be. A wanton, needy creature who bared her body to the man she desired and, against all odds, she wanted him.

She wanted the warmth of him at her back. She wanted those big hands to touch her. She just wanted everything he offered that she'd never been able to grasp in her life.

And he was offering.

She knew he was offering.

"Would you like me to help?" he murmured, that dark, sensuous voice plucking at her senses. She didn't have to look at him at all, and somehow that made it easier.

Easier to do all the things that her father had warned her about. It was a sin to want. It was a sin to indulge herself in all of her senses, and yet...

There was an ancient hunger in her veins. An age old need that had long been denied. And sometimes, the old ways were best.

Maia nodded, answering his question.

As the steam billowed out from the tub, she felt his fingers at her shoulders. The backs of his fingers brushed against her skin, dragging down her spine as he slowly worked her out of the shirt. Her entire body shuddered at his touch as he moved down to the base of her spine, and then the shirt just slipped.

It moved down off of her shoulders, free from her form to pile at her feet. Then there was nothing left to cover her but her undergarments that had seen better days. The small strip between her legs had seemed to be the only rebellion she could have when she was still back in the human kingdom. She didn't stay true to the old undergarments that were little more than a dress. These were new and different from what other women wore. But they showed far more of her skin as well.

She thought to cover her breasts with her arms, but then that brave part of her that he'd awoken decided no. She wasn't going to do that. She was going to see what he would do next.

Ragnar groaned, the sound echoing through his chest and into her back. He leaned forward, ever so slowly, and removed the last remaining barriers between them. The fabric gave so easily to his touch, and those clawed hands came up to cup her breasts. The sight of them was enough to send heat flooding between her thighs. They were massive, clawed, and striped with colors that were so inhuman. To see those hands carefully holding onto her, to see those fingers moving to grasp her aching nipples? She wasn't sure she would survive this.

Breathing hard, she arched into his touch. It pressed her back to his chest while displaying her body for him to see. With his head leaned low, he whispered dirty things into her ear that made her see stars.

"Someday, when you are ready to earn new piercings, I will place my mark here." He pinched her nipples hard enough to make her stop breathing. "You will wear my bars, troll wife. Soon enough, I will see you dripping in gemstones."

Her heart raced as one of his hands trailed down her stomach. His palm was so big that his hand spanned the space between her hip bones, but then his fingers slid between her legs and she ceased to think.

"Troll wives are more than just pretty things to decorate," he murmured as his fingers moved. Slickly playing with her clit as he rocked his fingers back and forth, the speed too slow and yet somehow burning where he touched her. "You are an instrument to play. Your moans are a symphony to my ears, fire hair. Let me hear them."

What was he doing to her? The moment he said it, she let out a moan that made her turn bright red with embarrassment. But as a reward, he pressed his thumb down on her clit and circled it in a way that was so perfect she made the sound again.

"I will be your slave," he rasped. "I will do all that you require and more. All I ask is for one thing."

She'd give him anything at this moment with her entire body on fire and her heart thundering in her chest. "What?" she gasped.

"Tell me what you want, fire hair. I would hear you say it."

She couldn't. But the creature who lived inside of her could. She heard herself moan and then cry out, "I want you to make me come, troll."

The sound he made was part animal, part man. And suddenly he spun her. Turning away from him was easier, but now she was leaning against the tub with him on his knees before her. He gave her one long stare before he opened his mouth and stuck out his tongue. She had only a moment to blink at the piercing in the center of that pink appendage before he was on her.

He licked her long and deep, that tongue flicking over her clit. His tusks pressed against her thighs, the sensation foreign and yet somehow so right. Just as she thought she was going to explode, suddenly she felt that warm metal ball sliding against her as well.

The things he could do with that tongue. She hadn't expected him to be so talented. Obviously, she'd touched herself with her fingers before, and she'd thought she was rather good at that. No one could do it better than herself.

But this man poured every ounce of who he was into devouring her whole. He wasn't a gentleman about it. He was loud and messy, almost embarrassingly so as he groaned into her pussy and lavished her with attention. His fingers spread her wide, making her hold herself steady on the tub so she didn't tumble right into it.

He hooked one of her legs behind his shoulder, using it as an anchor to pin her in place when she ground against him. But he didn't rush her. He just enjoyed himself with pleased sounds and echoing groans that mingled with her own as the sound of this immoral act filled the room. This was wrong, but damn it, it was so right.

She wanted his fingers inside her. She wanted his tongue to plunge into her depths. Fuck, she wanted him to push his cock between her folds and make her see stars.

"Please," she whimpered, trying to rotate her hips against him. "Please, I need more."

"You'll earn more later," he gruffly replied, before palming her ass and squeezing it too hard. "This is all you get for now, troll wife. Soon you will have more than this. But for now, all we both get is the taste of you on my tongue and the bliss beyond."

With a tortured sound, he attacked her again, this time with a frenzy that made her see stars. And suddenly, impossibly, she could feel herself tighten. She wound more tense with every strong flick of his tongue, every lingering lick.

Then... There it was. Her entire body clenched as she cried out and gripped his hair. She arched in on herself, likely a horrendous sight to behold, but her entire body felt like it was seizing as the pleasure coursed through her. He didn't stop. He licked and sucked until she was shuddering and begging him to stop. Only then did he give her a break, easing back on his knees to look up at her.

Maia still had a solid grip on his hair. She loosened her fingers, almost apologizing for how she'd tugged on those strands before he silently pressed a kiss to her thigh.

Saying nothing else, he pointed to the tub and then... left. Like what they had done hadn't changed everything forever.

Chapter 20

He made himself scarce for a while after that. But even days afterward, Ragnar hadn't forgotten the taste of her on his tongue. He could still hear the little sounds she'd made and feel the way she'd twisted in his hands. He had been completely enraptured by her movements. She was the rising wave of passion that he had ridden with no hope but to be dashed upon the sands of reality.

Ragnar should have known this would happen. She was his troll wife. Already the Blood Witch's magic was connecting them. Their blood had mingled. Their magics had been drawn out of their bodies to meet the other. They were, without a doubt, bound in a way that neither of them could ever escape. Only through death, and now that he had accepted her, he would not let her die. Not without him.

Gunnar clapped a hand to his shoulder in the market they wandered through, thoroughly delighted by the conversation. "So you actually like her now?"

"I don't like her."

"You seem to be thinking about her an awful lot. And one of the vendors told me you bought her proper earrings. Sounds like you're leaving your mark on her, and that in itself says a lot about what you're thinking." The cheeky grin on his face was one that Ragnar wanted to wipe off with a jab of his fist.

"I do not like the human. She's difficult at the best of times and far too concerned about what is proper or what is right." Unless his tongue was between her legs. Then she seemed to unravel.

And now he was uncomfortable again, surrounded by trolls with the ability to smell his passion and he needed to leave the crowd before he was laughed out of it.

Gunnar wouldn't let him, though. His brother wrapped an arm around his shoulders and dragged him toward a tavern in the farthest corner of this street. "Oh, come on. You've always been such a grump. You know better than to let a woman get the better of you, troll or human. It doesn't matter."

"You have no idea the ties that already bind us." Ragnar rubbed a hand over his chest where there was an ache he could not explain. It was like a part of him wanted to go back home. Like there was a thread of his magic that was tied to her, and the longer he was away, the more it stretched and ached.

His brother chuckled. "You've been staying away from her like a snake waits in your bed. From the moment we first picked her up, you've been hiding this feeling. So I don't think going to a tavern and having a drink with your brother is going to change that."

It likely wouldn't, and Ragnar did need a drink. Maybe he could drink himself under the table and not feel like he was getting ripped in two by his mind and his soul.

They walked up to the doorway that was taller than two trolls high. It was surrounded by the antlers of deer that had been hunted on the mountain for centuries. Wisps gathered between the tines, pooling a warmer light around the space that already filled the streets with the sound of laughter. He knew beyond that door he would be greeted with the scent of warm baked bread, countless steins of ale, and friendship that would soothe the ache in his soul. Even if he would become the joke of the century, considering he was in a bar while his new troll wife waited at home.

"A few drinks," he muttered. "I don't want to give anyone the idea that I regret—"

The ground shook beneath their feet. He looked at his brother, shock on both of their features as a rumble spread throughout the mountain of Trollveggen. The mountain had never shaken before. Not like this. And then they heard it. The sound of rock and rubble falling from above.

"Run!" Gunnar shouted, shoving him out of the way as a large stone fell where they had just been standing.

More rocks tumbled out of the sky, splitting them off from each other for a moment that had his heart racing. They ran for the tavern as one, ducking into the doorway and watching as the mountain shook with rage.

Pressing his hands against the stone, Ragnar tried to understand what would bring the mountain to this reaction. But when he reached out with his magic, the magic that connected all trolls to the home they lived in, he could feel it wasn't rage. It was fear. Fear that moved throughout the entire stone of his home as the mountain did what she could to protect them from something terrible.

Another rumble shook beneath their feet. Screams echoed throughout the streets, along with shrieks of pain that filled the air.

Lights fell from behind him, crashing onto tables that sent trolls to their feet as they shouted. More shaking, more stones, until the very ceiling above their heads creaked.

He looked up, brow furrowed, as he noticed a crack spread across the stone above them. Gunnar did the same, and all the trolls in the room held their breath as it seemed like their lives might be over.

But then there was sudden silence. Dust billowed around them, a quiet reprieve from the moments of madness. Then all the sound returned as the mountain settled back into comfort.

All he could hear was the sound of his people dying. Countless of them. Their pain was something he could feel deep in his chest as his magic woke and flooded through his veins. He had to go to them. He had to get out of this tavern and help where they needed him. It wasn't a choice. His body becoming a vessel for the power inside of him when he was surrounded by the wounded and the dying, and his brother knew that.

Helplessly, Ragnar looked for Gunnar as they both staggered toward the door. He stepped over rubble that had fallen in front of him, knowing that he was going to see more of it as he walked out into the streets.

"Let me help you," Gunnar said, rushing ahead of him to get out into the streets first. This wasn't the first time they'd done this. Gunnar's magic was in control. He was better on a battlefield where minds were weaker and able to be manipulated. But he'd seen Ragnar in this state many times after a battle, and he was the one to seek out those who needed help first.

Ragnar's magic liked to find anyone who was hurt. It didn't matter if that was a small cut on their finger or their guts hanging out of their belly. He wasn't good at picking who to start with, only who would ease the sudden swelling of magic that pressed against his lips and tongue.

"This way," Gunnar said, grabbing onto his forearm and yanking him away from a small group of trolls with bloodied hands from digging people out of the rubble.

Ragnar blindly followed his brother, his vision becoming obscured by the white magic that boiled inside of him now. It hurt. It ached. His fingernails felt like they were ripping from his body, but that was the pain of his magic. It was always a little painful.

A whispered voice in his mind kept repeating the same word over and over again. He could barely hear it over the rushing sound of magic in his ears.

But he thought the word might be *Maia*.

His wife. He needed to go to her, make sure she was all right. But the screams of the dying and injured were right in front of him and he knew logically that their house was safe. She was far from here. Much farther than the quake would have reached.

If she stayed where she was, then she was safe. She had no reason to leave their house.

He took one step away from the street that would lead him to her. Then another. Even as his soul screamed to just look. All he wanted was to just check on her and make sure that he was right, and she was okay.

But so many other people needed him too. And she was fine. He would know if she was hurt, so he kept going.

Soon enough, they stopped and Gunnar pushed him down onto his knees. Clawed hands grabbed his, drawing his fingers to a wound that was warm and wet and vibrated with pain that he could feel.

The magic in him pushed out, shoving through his skin and into the body of the troll who had been injured. Though he couldn't quite see her, he could feel that she'd been caught underneath a rock. It was her leg that he had in his hands. He could feel the broken bone and how it had cracked in so many places that, without magic, it never would have healed. The blood that coated his hand was from the skin that had torn beneath the weight of the rock.

But his magic knew what to do. It knit through flesh and bone, mending and weaving the form before him like clay. Though it would never be the same as a leg unaffected by such trauma, he knew it would be walkable for her. She would still be able to stride through the city without limping.

"Good enough," Gunnar grunted, his hands on Ragnar's shoulders once again. "More."

The word echoed in his mind. *More, more, more.*

A child who had been pinned to the stone, his face scraped raw against the wall. A man who had pushed his family out of the way and the stone had landed on his torso where his guts had emptied into the cavity of his chest. An elderly woman crushed in her bed. But he hadn't been able to save her. So many trolls, so little time.

They wandered through the city, depleting his magic until his hands were shaking. There were so many trolls injured, so few people like him who were gifted in flesh weaving. He stood after hours, his knees weak and his vision back to normal. Even his magic seemed to whimper inside of him when he came across another injured child.

"Get my supplies," he said, his voice little more than a croak as he directed his brother. "The salves and herb packs—they will help. I can use them."

He'd been on battlefields like this before. His magic simply could not do more, but he could convince the body to speed things along. With the right herbs, the right poultices, he could place them on the wounds and then speed up what it would have done already. It wasn't the best option. Stitching together skin and then begging it to heal left scars that his regular magic would not leave.

Still, he had to try. There were more people who needed him.

Gunnar nodded, stretching out his back before turning down the street that would lead to their home. "Get some rest until I come back, brother. I won't know where else to find you."

Rest? He couldn't rest. Not when he could hear all of their pain and still feel it sparking throughout his body. But when he tried to walk, he ended up slumped against a wall and sliding right down it. Maybe Gunnar was right. He needed to rest his body for a few moments before he could continue this mad dash to help his people.

Then they would find out what had happened. Because the mountain had been terrified and he had felt that in the very marrow of his bones.

He must have drifted off to sleep. But even resting, his mind ran through every single injury that he'd healed. All the people he might have soothed better if he hadn't been so distracted by other screams that still echoed in his ears. He would think of this day for years to come. All the good he might have done and all the mistakes he certainly had made.

But then he blinked and his brother had returned, only he wasn't alone.

A small human trailed along behind him, her eyes wide and her face streaked with dirt. Why was she always dirty? This human seemed to constantly get herself in situations where he had to plunk her into a river or a bath and pray that she wouldn't be the small gremlin creature she always seemed to be.

But on the tail of that angry thought was relief. She was alive. She was okay. He'd been right about one of them.

Gunnar knelt in front of him. "You ready for more?"

The word continued to echo in his mind, and then his eyes met wide green ones over Gunnar's shoulder. Ragnar had no idea what he must look like at this moment. Slumped against the wall, nearly drained of all his magic, crushed by the weight of all that he must still do. The horrified expression on her face was enough for him to know he must've looked worse than he thought he did.

But he still stood. All on his own. Even though his knees shook and his back ached and his vision skewed to the side. He still did it, and there was some pride in that.

"Where did you come from?" he grumbled, as a small arm wrapped around his waist.

"I was with Rota," she replied as they started down the street. "She stopped by your home to drop off a gift from her mother. She said you helped her with her arthritis, and then the shakes happened. She barely saved me when a part of your ceiling came off and fell into the center of the parlor. Your home is... We'll figure that out later."

"That doesn't explain where you came from." Although it warmed his heart that Rota had been with her. The troll maidens were always helpful, even before they had their own families to join.

"She didn't want me to be alone," Maia murmured. "And then Gunnar came to the house hours later and when he said he was bringing you supplies, he thought I could help."

"He thought you could help? You have no magic, fire hair." He didn't mean to spit the words at her, but he knew how they sounded.

Instead of flinching, her jaw seemed to set a little firmer. He watched a muscle bounce in her jaw as Gunnar gestured for them to come to yet another person propped against the side of a building. The troll woman was holding a hand against her leg where the muscle had been cut clean through by a stone. She was already weak. He could feel it. The pool of blood puddling around her was going to be the death of her before that wound.

Maia released him and cautiously knelt beside the woman with light blue skin who was so much larger than her. He stared down at the two of them, realizing that the troll woman laid out before them was everything he had once dreamt of. Perfect tusks, long black hair that was tangled around her face, that beautiful blue skin that he might have wanted to lick only weeks ago. But now? Now he was more stunned by the presence of those strangely small hands now smeared with blood as she pressed them against the woman's wounds.

Maia looked up at him, her eyes wide. "I don't know what to do, healer. But if I can help as your brother believes, then I will."

She couldn't help him. No one could. But Gunnar tossed his bag of herbs at him and nodded at the bag. "She's a plant speaker, brother. Even if there isn't a lot of magic in her, she can still convince that bag of goodies to do more than what you've got. It'll last longer."

The theory had merit. Sighing, he took out his needle and thread and got to work. The throbbing, angry vein that had been severed by the stone was difficult to knit back together, and he had to use more magic on that than he wanted to. Then he stitched together muscle and flesh until finally he reached into his bag and took out the smallest amount of yarrow to stop the bleeding further.

He held it up for Maia to see and then asked, "Can you convince this to do more than it normally would? I can use her body to absorb it, but I need more than what I have."

She frowned, staring at the small bit of yarrow before holding out her hands. He dropped the leaves into her hand and then watched as she cupped it. Holding her closed hands to her mouth, she whispered to the plant.

He thought he could hear her asking for its help. Begging it to give them a chance to save more people, even though it was tired and had long been resting.

But when she opened her palms, the leaves in her hands were significantly larger. There was more than enough for this one troll, and perhaps even two more.

Relief spread through his chest. He set to work with the now generous amount of yarrow, placing the leaf against the woman's leg. When Maia's hand came down on his, he could feel her magic intertwining with his own. Now, it felt like he could speak to both the plant and the body. Use them both together to convince the healing properties of the plants to be stronger while convincing the body to use it faster.

When they were done, the leg was healed as though it had been weeks since the injury. And his magic hadn't been used up to the point of him shaking yet again.

"Thank you," the troll woman said, placing her hand over theirs. "Now go, healer. There are many more trolls for you to see."

He stood with his troll wife and marveled at her strength. She lifted him to his feet with what seemed like little effort and then tugged him forward. "Come on. There's a lot more of them."

"You will continue to heal them with me?" he asked, stunned.

"Of course I will."

He tugged her to a halt, needing this answer above all others. "Why?"

"Because they need help." Her brows had furrowed, but then her features softened. She reached for his hand and brought his bloody fingers to her lips. Gently, she pressed a kiss to his worn knuckles. "I'm so sorry that all you have seen of my kind is anger and hate. Not all of us rejoice in the pain of your people, Ragnar, and I know nothing I say will take those memories away. But I am here. I will help for as long as I'm able."

Together, they headed out into the city to heal who they could and to help those who needed help. And for a few moments, he allowed hope to bloom in his chest. Perhaps his troll wife wouldn't be such a burden after all.

Chapter 21

Gunnar had to drag Maia home before Ragnar was finished. She didn't want to leave him there by himself, suffering by overusing his magic. His hands were shaking with effort, his posture had curved in on himself, and his usually lovely lavender shade had turned into a strange pale color.

Maia hadn't known anyone could use magic like he did. Humans rarely ever used their power, if they even had it to begin with.

But watching him was magic in itself. She could see the trolls' bones rearranging themselves underneath his touch. All it took was a single grimace from Ragnar and the entire wound he touched would close. The power that he had inside of him… she couldn't imagine how deep it went.

"Has he always done that?" she asked as Gunnar opened the door for her to go inside.

"Done what?"

"Stretched himself too thin for others?" Maia looked up into the broad green face of Ragnar's brother, searching for something in those features that was familiar. But Gunnar was just as different to her as all the other trolls were.

He flashed her a sad smile. "That's part of who we are. We stretch ourselves thin for everyone here. Those who can, do. Those who can't appreciate the help that is given. Trolls are all a family here, no matter who came from who."

"That seems... idyllic."

"It's not all fun and games. Trolls argue. Some of them leave the mountain entirely. Bad blood spreads and festers." A troubled expression twisted his lips and furrowed his brows. He looked at the door, but then sighed. "Ragnar lost his oldest friend that way. It's not all good here, but it is mostly good. We love our home and the people around us until they don't wish to be loved any longer."

Her heart broke for them. These were good people who had been handed nothing but suffering, and they deserved more than this. She stepped further into the room. The wisps lit up, casting blue light on all the rubble that surrounded them.

There was so much to repair. The ceiling had cracked in multiple places, raining down shards of stones all throughout the parlor. She'd been seated right underneath it, laughing about something Rota had said when she'd first heard it. The crack had felt like it came from deep within her bones.

She'd lunged off the couch at the same time Rota had reached for her. With their combined effort, she'd just barely gotten out of the way. Standing here now, her heart raced with the same fear. She'd almost died.

But thoughts like that didn't help. So she pressed a hand to her chest, rubbed the ache there, and surveyed the room. There were three large pieces that she wouldn't be able to move herself. One of those had destroyed the comfortable couch near the fire.

She sighed and shook her head. "So much to fix. It feels like trying to move a mountain."

Then she heard what she said and immediately looked over at Gunnar. They stared at each other for a few moments before he burst into laughter. The dust covered troll laughed until tears tracked down his cheeks, and then he finally blew out a long breath to get ahold of himself. "It is, in fact, a mountain to move. But we've seen worse."

She couldn't imagine what worse could be. But, at the very least, Gunnar took the large stone on the couch with him as he left and locked the door behind him.

"No reason to sit in worry," she muttered, before getting to work cleaning.

First, she took the time to pick up all the stones she could and put them in a pile in the corner. Maia had no idea where she was supposed to bring them, because it wasn't like there was an easy place for them to be stored. Still, they could go in a corner until she was told what to do with them. Her husband had to have some kind of cleaning cabinet, so she spent far too long searching for that. Finally, though, she found a broom and a dustbin in the back corner of the kitchen.

Armed now against the dust, she made her way throughout the entire parlor. It took her four rounds of sweeping before she was done with it. She imagined that had taken her the better part of two hours, and he still wasn't home.

The damage in the kitchen was significantly less than the rest of the house, so she went into the bedroom. Ragnar had yet to sleep with her, and it was just this morning that she realized why. A blanket had been left on the couch. He must have been sleeping out in the parlor most nights, but now there wasn't anywhere else for him to sleep.

Unfortunately, cleaning gave her too much time to think about her new life. She mused that her husband was not who she thought he was, and that this entire situation was truly surreal. But also, would he plan to sleep in bed with her now that there was no other option? Why didn't that sound so bad?

Perhaps she had gotten too caught up in everything. Only a few weeks ago, she'd been terrified of trolls and now she'd been tossed head first into the reality of their lives. Over and over again, she was slapped with the reality that these people weren't as terrifying as she thought, and in fact, they were good people. Every bit of who they were made her want to like them.

No, it made her enjoy them. She'd been greatly enjoying her conversation with Rota while the entirety of the world had blown up in their faces.

And she found she was angry about that. These people didn't deserve to lose their homes or be injured on safe streets. How could something like this happen to good people? Weren't there supposed to be gods looking out for people who helped each other? Bad things shouldn't happen to good people.

But they did. Bad things happened every day to good people, and she knew that, but it still stung for her to see it happen in real time.

She'd gotten the bedroom clean in her frenzied anger and then there was nothing left to do. Maia got ready for bed, feeling a bit numb that she was going to try to sleep when the streets were still covered in blood. But there wasn't anything she could do. Her magic was weak, just like the trolls had said. She laid down in bed, staring up at the cracked and chipped ceiling, and something in her soul just wouldn't settle.

How could it?

Ragnar had thought she wouldn't help. That statement still rankled. He'd thought she would just let the trolls suffer, and what? Laugh in glee that they'd gotten what they deserved?

He still thought she was a villain.

Time passed slowly. Or perhaps quickly—she wasn't all that sure. All she knew was that one moment she was staring up at the ceiling, and the next, she heard movement in the room adjacent to hers. Tilting her head to the side, she watched the silhouette of her massive husband walk into the bathroom.

For a moment, she just let herself look at him. She listened to the low murmur of his voice as he asked the wisps to be dim, so they didn't wake her. His shoulders were curved in what looked like defeat. She'd always seen him with such power in his body. Even though he wasn't a warrior like some of the other trolls, Maia thought of him as strong and powerful as the others.

Now, as he limped into the bathroom and fell quietly to his knees in front of the tub, she saw him in a different light. This was a broken man. A wounded man. One who had seen too much pain from his people and who had taken it on himself. He was aching and sad, and there was so little she could do.

But she was here. So she sat up, got out of bed, and made her way to the bathroom.

His shoulders moved up and down with heavy breaths. His white shirt was smeared with dirt and blood. His clawed hands rested against his thighs, and she could see that three of his claws had cracked right down the middle.

Tears burning in her eyes, she gently placed her hand on his shoulder. "How can I help?"

"There's nothing left to do. I have nothing left to the give them and there are so many more who still need help." Even his voice was raspy, as though he'd lost his voice hours ago. "I wish to rest, wife. That's all."

Maia knew what it was like to have no more emotions to give. But she also knew this troll. She knew he didn't want to get into bed with dirt on him, even less than he wanted to get into bed with her. And that was all right. She could sleep in one of the chairs. She'd slept in worse before.

Quietly, she reached for the hem of his shirt. He said nothing as she helped pull it over his head. The moment his shoulders had to rise, he let out a long groan that made her wince. He had pushed himself too hard, even beyond using so much of his magic.

They got the shirt off, though, and she let it drop onto the floor. He used the edge of the tub to stand and then waved a hand at her. "I can do the rest."

"You don't look like you can."

"It's just a quick wash. I'm not so helpless that I cannot do that myself."

"Then you can wash all the bits that are hard to reach," she scolded.

Part of her screamed to just let him do it. Her ears were already burning bright red at the thought of undressing a man. She'd never done this before. The few and meager interactions she'd had with men had been behind her father's house. A quick, stolen moment where all their clothing had remained on. The first man to see her entirely naked had been him.

Placing her hands on the waistband of his pants, she gently tugged them down. He didn't argue further. Instead, he just let her shift them down over the round globes of his ass, down those powerful thighs that had caught her attention from the first day she'd seen him, and down to the clawed toes that gripped onto the floor even as he lifted first one leg, then the other.

Maia reached for the faucet and turned it on, just as he had for her. But instead of looking, as she desperately wanted to, she busied herself gathering up the necessary supplies of soap and towels. For a man as large as him, he certainly had tiny towels. She couldn't imagine they were even capable of wrapping around his waist.

She heard the sound of water trickling and then the long groan as he plunged himself into the warm water. It was safe enough for her to turn around now, she supposed.

And when she did, all the breath was sucked free from her lungs. He leaned against the back of the tub, his arms on the edges, his head tilted back so all she could see were the planes of his chest and the hot steam that surrounded him. She didn't care that blood streamed off of him, down his collarbone, and dripped from his claws. All that mattered were the muscles that were a feast for her gaze and the way he looked so thoroughly delicious.

Swallowing hard, she grabbed a few wash cloths and approached him. "You can't save everyone, Ragnar."

He blinked one eye open and then closed his eyes again. "I can save as many people as I can save. I learned that a long time ago, fire hair."

"Then why are you punishing yourself for not saving more of them?"

He grunted.

What a response, she thought. Dipping the cloth into the water, she lathered soap on it before tapping his hand. "Here," she said. "Take this."

He looked down at the cloth and arched a brow.

"You said you didn't want me to wash you. I'm holding you to that. If you're as well as you say you are, then you can manage it on your own, big man."

He grunted again but grabbed the cloth from her with a hand that shook only a little. She knew he'd likely expected her to wash him despite his protests, but she would not do that when he was being like this. He could earn that treatment, but she wouldn't do it just because he expected it.

Hilariously, he washed himself. He was brisk and rough, his lavender skin darkening with all of his efforts. And throughout it all, she just watched him. Cushioning her chin on the edge of the tub, she kept her gaze on his face and shoulders and not on the intriguing piercings that were surely just underneath the edge of the water if she wanted to look. But right now wasn't about that. She just wanted to look at him and note every time he winced or let out a little exhausted breath.

To his credit, he let her. She knew it must've been a little strange to have someone staring while he bathed. But he didn't ask her to stop.

Although eventually he did ask, "What are you doing?"

"Getting used to you."

"How so?"

She lifted one shoulder in a shrug. "I've never been around so many trolls. I'm getting used to it, I guess. The more I look at you, the less strange you become."

"You find me strange?"

"Well, you aren't human."

He gave her an unimpressed look. "And I'm glad for that."

Maia grinned. "I knew you would say that."

He shook his head at her, clearly unimpressed at her grin. But she swore his lips twitched a little, too.

Soon enough, he was finished, and the water was getting colder. The moment Ragnar placed his hands on the side of the tub, she jolted to her feet and held out the towels. "I'll let you dry off."

She was running away from what would be revealed when he stood. She didn't want to know what he looked like naked just yet, or to gawk at what she was certain to be terrifying. And right now didn't feel like the time for her to look her fill. Not after everything they'd just gone through.

Darting back into the room, she got back underneath the covers and yanked them up to her chin. She even rolled so her back was to the bathroom door, just so she wouldn't know when he left. He'd never slept in the same bed as her. Tonight that wouldn't change. If she saw him leaving, Maia feared she would beg him to stay.

But soon, she felt the mattress dip underneath his weight. Like he'd put a knee on the edge and then thought better of it. Because then that weight was gone for only a moment before the covers lifted.

A warm body tucked into the bed with her, and then an even warmer hand palmed her waist. She wasn't sure what was happening until he dragged her back against his muscular, broad chest. Ragnar took a deep breath, those muscles shifting along his ribs before he heaved a sigh that stirred her hair.

"What are you doing?" she whispered.

"Hush, my wife. I need to remember that something is alive tonight."

"Oh."

That hand on her waist moved up her chest, landing on her ribs. His fingers curved under her left breast. Maia held her breath, wondering if he would do more, but then she realized he was falling asleep.

His hand was over her heart. Ragnar had moved them so that he could fall asleep with her heart beating against his palm, all because he had lost so many people today that he needed to know she was alive. Just so that he could finally rest.

She pressed her hand over his, holding him a little tighter.

Chapter 22

He snuck out of their home early in the morning. She didn't need to come with him this time, because he didn't plan to heal anyone today. Maia was very unused to using her magic, and he knew that would take some time to replenish what they'd used together. As much as she'd given last night, she would realize how much that had impacted her as soon as she got out of bed later today.

Everything in Ragnar ached. His shoulders, his back, his thighs. Every part of his body felt as though he'd been training like he had when he was a young man. Unfortunately, he was not as young as he used to be. He'd spent hours upon hours every day with his brother and friends, allowing Gunnar to hit him over and over until the pain didn't matter anymore.

It made his heart hurt to think she would be suffering the same kind of pain that he felt now. But he hoped she would make use of the warm water in their bathtub, and he had too much to do today.

As expected, Gunnar was waiting outside of his home. His brother

was strapped from head to toe in warrior garb. Weapons glinted at his sides, leather strappings held them tight to his legs and torso, while an armored plate against his back would serve as a shield should anyone try to attack him from behind.

"Took you long enough to wake," Gunnar grumbled. "We've all been ready for hours now."

"That's an exaggeration."

"Probably, but everyone is waiting."

"You could have left without me," Ragnar sighed, trying to dig his fingers into a knot at the base of his neck. He'd curved his body around her the entire night, but that had left his arm and shoulder in an odd position he now regretted.

Although he wasn't sure he could ever regret sleeping beside Maia. It had been weeks since he'd slept in his own bed, wanting to give her space, yet last night he couldn't help himself. He'd forgotten how nice it was to have someone by his side and in his bed. She was so warm. In the aftermath of the quakes, the mountain felt cold. Snuggled up to her, he'd been as warm as he could ever hope to be. Under those blankets, he had felt a significant amount of comfort as well. Just holding her body, feeling her heartbeat, knowing how easily she had melted into him as though she trusted him with her life?

Ragnar wouldn't stop thinking about that moment for a long time. He'd thought, perhaps, that she would be enjoyable as a bed partner. That was why he'd caught her in the bathroom, tasted her on his tongue, so that he might at least know that she would be willing and enjoyable when it came to that. And she would be.

But last night had been something different. He hadn't wanted to just bed her, rut into her until they'd both seen stars and forgotten about all the things that they'd seen that day. She'd offered him a comfort that no one else ever had.

Gunnar leaned in close and took a deep breath. "You smell like her."

An unreasonable need to punch his brother in the chest and take that scent back filled him. Which was stupid. A scent wasn't something he could get returned just by his brother exhaling it but... Maybe it would make him feel better.

Sighing, he instead shook his head and started down the streets toward where he knew the rest of the war band waited for them. "Enough, Gunnar."

"No, you smell like her far more than you did in the past few weeks. Just living with her has, of course, left a bit of a lingering scent, but you smell like her."

"Gunnar, what did I just say?"

His brother hustled to keep up with him, a laugh bursting forth as they passed a stall being filled with hastily made meat pies. The city was already piecing itself back together enough for Gunnar to get a breakfast pie and continue ribbing him as they hurried down the streets.

"Really? What happened last night? You went back later than she, which I'd thought would mean you wouldn't even find her awake. But clearly she was. Did you finally show her the piercings you've gotten for her? I was there to hold your hand, man. I know how terrible those were for you to—"

Ragnar spun on his brother and slapped him in the throat. A quiet gurgle filled the street they were in, followed by a few surprised snorts as Gunnar struggled to get air into his lungs. But Ragnar was done listening to this teasing.

"Stop talking about my wife," he hissed.

But by the time they'd reached the other trolls in their war band, his brother was already laughing again. Shaking his head, Gunnar walked over to the other warriors who would be joining them and without a single pause in breath, his brother started talking about how good Ragnar smelled.

"You should go sniff him!" Gunnar said, his voice pitched low like he was trying to whisper but obviously projecting his voice so that Ragnar would hear him. "Seriously. I never knew humans could smell so sweet, like honey and fresh baked bread. It's a good scent on him."

Ragnar headed out ahead of the others. He couldn't stay with those warriors without trying to push Gunnar over the edge of the cliff. And it was far too early in the morning for that kind of behavior. His brother needed someone to teach him a lesson, but realistically, that person could not be Ragnar. Not yet.

The war band moved through another path in the forest that led to their home, and then out of the mountain into the sun beyond. He squinted his eyes, the bright light always difficult to adjust to when he first left Trollveggen. He looked around, trying to figure out why the mountain had been so angry. But it didn't take long for all them to see the problem.

Deep grooves slashed through the earth. He'd seen markings like this in the human villages before. They were the wheels of carts, but carrying something so heavy that it had left deep imprints that were easy to follow. Together, he and the trolls spread out to follow them.

How many times had he hunted the humans? How many times had he learned that, if they were in a group, humans would attack a troll without hesitation? Troll hide was tough. It was hard to put a knife or sword through their skin, so the humans had learned other ways to hurt. Fire, flaming acid, ballistae that threw stones at them.

Anything they could do to kill the trolls, they would. Fortunately, the trolls were harder to track down than humans were.

Silently, the war band moved across their mountain, following the tracks of the cart until Ragnar broke off from the others. He ran faster. Ragnar was able to go ahead of the rest since, as the band's healer, he didn't carry any weapons.

But then he came to the edge of a ridge and stared down at deep, black furrows that spread through an area which had once been forested. Like a fire had been lit and left to run wild, it wasn't hard to see what had made their mountain afraid. Stones had been thrown by ballistae against the side of the mountain. There were deep cracks in the rocky face where a rock slide had been triggered. So many stones that the entire tunnel into Trollveggen had collapsed. And worse, he could see the humans had coated the entrance with a thick black ooze they'd then lit on fire.

It wasn't an entrance regularly traversed by his people. Smaller than most, usually only women and children walked here to pick flowers or grow crops that simply couldn't grow underground. It did not lead back to the heart of their kingdom, but it was an entrance, nonetheless.

More signs of humans dotted the landscape. Small rings of fire where the humans had left the flames still burning. The refuse they had thrown in their retreat.

Ragnar started down into the crater left behind. Not a single shrub remained after that fire. There was no birdsong dancing through the air as he walked over stones that were easy to twist an ankle over. Even the wind didn't seem to want to disturb the ashes on the ground. And as he approached the entrance, he stopped where he was and felt his heart shatter.

Because even here, even this far away, he could see the lovely yellow hand reaching through the rocks. The hand was now limp, no life left in the troll who had desperately begged for help as the entrance had collapsed on top of them.

There was no one here he could save. No one who needed his magic even though it weakly rose in his chest as if it could try to bring this troll back from the dead. Like he could sing their soul back into their body, even though he didn't know who they were or how he would manage to do so.

Healing was an art form. He convinced the body to knit itself back together, to feel well again. He loved being able to soothe old aches or mend a cut in the skin that would have left an ugly scar. But a moment like this was when he was reminded of just how terrible it was to have been given such a gift.

To know he could have saved them if he had been here in time.

Footsteps approached. Countless trolls of the war band joined them, and together, they all sank onto their knees to honor the fallen troll.

Gunnar was at his side, and he reached to put an arm around Ragnar's shoulder. "They fought well."

The troll to his right murmured, "They fought hard."

No one wanted to say the last bit, though. No one wanted to be the one to admit that this was over and there was nothing they could have done.

So Ragnar took a deep, rattling breath that coated his tongue in smoke and tasted like defeat. "Their spirit joins the warrior's hall. Someday, we will join them, and on that day, we will feast."

Growls erupted around him. Rage made the air electric between them all. He wanted to roar at the world that would allow a troll to die like this. He knew this kind of death. It hadn't been quick. This troll had reached out a hand for help and no one had offered to help them. Not a single one of those monsters who lived at the base of their mountain had done anything when they'd set this trap. They didn't even kill the troll, so they wouldn't suffer.

Turning his head to look at the tracks, he stood. The other trolls joined him, all of their eyes on the deep furrows that would lead them right to the humans who had done this.

His brother placed a hand on his shoulder. A steadying voice to listen to as Gunnar murmured, "Ragnar. Your wife is human. Perhaps it should be us that go. You wait here, and we can make sure any injured return to you. If it was a small number of humans with a ballista, they will be easy to track."

"No. I want my revenge for this."

"She may not forgive you for it."

Ragnar knew that. He did. He knew that his troll wife was more sensitive than he was. But she had been by his side during the aftermath of what her own people had done. Surely she would understand that he had to hunt after that.

She had held his hand while he'd knit together flesh and bone. She'd heard the moans and the screams of the dying. Maia had been there while people had begged him to save them and he had known that he wouldn't be able to. If she denied him this, then she was no troll wife after all.

Baring his teeth in a snarl, he glared at his brother. "Give me a knife, Gunnar."

"Ragnar, I just don't think—"

"Your knife."

Without another word, his brother reached for the knife that he had strapped to his chest and handed it over. It was a long handled blade, wicked and curved. The glint in the sunlight reminded him of his very first hunt with his father. They had just been boys then. Young and unknowing of what they were going to get into. Ragnar had been the first to kill a deer, and when his father had handed him a knife just like this and told him to gut the beautiful creature, he'd cried.

At first, Ragnar had been ashamed of his reaction. No real hunter would have tears dripping down his cheeks while he gutted the animal that would feed his family for weeks on end.

But his father's words would remain with him for the rest of his life. "You honor the beast you killed by shedding tears for their loss. Tears show you know you have taken a life, and that is good. We do not kill without reason or meaning, my son."

And now he knew his reason. He knew his meaning.

Gunnar sighed and reached for the back of his neck. They pressed their foreheads together, two brothers who knew, without question, that they were going to risk their lives yet again. "Kill quickly," Gunnar said.

"Go for the gut," Ragnar corrected him. "I want them to die slowly."

Perhaps it was the animal in him. Perhaps he was just proving that his line wasn't so far removed from the fur and the scales. But in this moment, he did not care. He wanted his retribution, and he wanted it now.

His brother nodded. They would fight together. Ragnar would remain slightly behind the others, but no troll would argue his right to fight with them. No troll would deny his desire for blood and for the screams of a human to ring in his ears.

Together, they moved as one. He felt his blood heat with the desire of the hunt, even if it meant that his new troll wife might hate him for it later.

Chapter 23

Maia woke to someone knocking on her door. Which was silly, because she didn't have any customers today. She couldn't remember the last time someone had come to her asking for a flower arrangement. Why? In her groggy state, she wasn't entirely sure. Maybe it had something to do with her father being completely incapable of managing their accounts. Too many people had been charged twice for flowers, and eventually they were just going to find someone else to do the arrangements. She really needed to talk to her father about that.

Staggering out of bed, she blinked her eyes so slowly it was almost like she was walking down the hall with her eyes closed. She needed to go to the market today. Something in her head said that she didn't have any food in the house, and she wouldn't mind baking something today. Her father loved fresh baked bread with butter. Maybe he'd be in a better mood if he woke to that this morning.

Swallowing the cotton mouth that made her tongue feel a little thick, she made her way to the front door and threw it open.

Only to stare up into the face of a troll woman. Which couldn't be right, because there weren't any trolls in her town.

Until she finally woke up and remembered everything that had happened. This was, indeed, a troll. Because there were many trolls in this city. Because she was no longer in the human kingdom where she was surrounded by her own kind, but instead, she was surrounded by trolls.

A rush of anxiety trickled down from her head to her toes, turning her face likely bright red. What was her name again?

"Inkeri," the troll woman said. Her dark blue skin seemed almost magical in the light of the wisps. "I'm sure you remember me from your journey here, but there has been much that happened since and it's very easy to forget those you have met when you've been introduced to so many."

"I'm so sorry," Maia blurted, then opened the door even wider. "I do remember you, of course. It's just that I just woke up and I don't really know what's going on, to be honest."

"It has been a very long night for all of us."

And then it all rushed back to explain why she was so tired and sore. Every muscle in her body felt like she'd been running for hours on end, and in truth, she had. What an idiot! How did she not remember all of this?

Rushing forward, she grabbed onto Inkeri's hand and squeezed it tightly. "Are you all right? That should have been the first thing I asked. I'm so sorry. I don't know what's happening to my mind."

"That would likely be magical depletion," Inkeri said with a soft laugh. "I'm surprised Ragnar didn't warn you that using so much magic at once would lead to this. It makes memories difficult to recall, but it's also very hard to wake from. Your magical reserves will have to be rebuilt before you feel better. You had very little to give, and clearly, he expected you to give it all."

Well, that didn't settle well. "He didn't ask for all of it. I did offer."

"Of course you did. You want to fit in here. This is your new home, and you've only been here for a few days before we were all attacked and now you are living in a kingdom where nothing makes sense. You have no close friends or ties other than the husband you did not want." Inkeri's eyes cast to the rubble of the room, the stones in the corner, but at least that there wasn't as much dust as there could have been. "Did I summarize that correctly?"

She did, but... "You speak like nobility," Maia stammered. "I didn't realize that trolls were so eloquent."

"I trained with the troll princes and princesses. My mother thought I would marry one of them, but clearly, I did not." The blue-skinned troll looked her up and down. "He has not dressed you appropriately yet, I see."

Maia looked down at the shirt he had given her a few days ago. It wasn't a dress, that much was certain. But it wasn't like she was regularly running about the streets. Ragnar just continued to give her shirts, and she washed them in the tub when she needed to. "I think there's not been time."

Inkeri's eyes cast to the piercings in her ears. "Well, at least he replaced those disgraceful earrings. Hulda's thoughts were in the right place, but it was a slight against his honor. Come with me, troll wife. We will set you to rights and make sure that you fit in better than your husband has clearly intended."

Maia glanced around the room, not sure what she was supposed to do here. Did she follow the troll woman she really didn't know? Or did she stay here and wait for Ragnar, who was...

"Do you know where Ragnar is?" she asked, her brows drawing together in confusion.

"The war band has been sent out to discover the meaning of our mountain's fear. I'm sure they will return with answers for us soon enough. But that will be enough time for me to get you new clothes, and some food in that belly, as you are in desperate need of."

Food sounded good. At the thought, her stomach rumbled loudly. She didn't remember the last time she'd eaten anything other than trail rations and the few pieces of bread that had been in the kitchen. Ragnar didn't keep it well stocked, and she'd eaten what she could, but... a real meal? Warm food that wasn't out of a cabinet and questionable of how long it had been there?

Biting her lip, she nodded and followed the other woman out of the front door.

"I don't know how to lock it," Maia said as she stepped out onto the street.

"There is no need."

"Oh." Back home, she would have needed to. There were plenty of people who would wander into a house that was unlocked, and they would take whatever they could carry. But here, apparently, the trolls didn't do that.

They walked down the street only a few steps before Inkeri spoke. "I'm certain you can see that this is not like the human kingdom."

"That would be hard to miss," Maia replied with a soft chuckle.

"You would do well to forget all the rules you know and all the injustices you faced. Humans are, at their core, greedy and cruel. They take whatever they wish. They end relationships over petty arguments. They are weak-willed creatures who have no right to have as much power as they already have."

The words stung a bit. Maia tried very hard to see it through the eyes of the trolls, but she couldn't. Quietly, as they turned a corner and started up a small hill, she said, "I am human, though."

Inkeri stopped so suddenly that Maia almost ran into her back. She had to side step and nearly toppled into a bush, just trying not to run into the troll woman who stood so still, it was like she wasn't breathing.

What had she said? Was it the reminder that she was human? It wasn't like she could hide where she'd come from. Being human in this kingdom felt like uttering a dirty word. It felt as though she wasn't meant to say it in mixed company because the mere thought of humans made the trolls' skin crawl. But it was the truth.

Inkeri turned her head, eyeing her with sudden disgust. "You would do well to never say that again."

The malice in her tone made every hair on Maia's body stand on end. "I'm sorry for whatever I said, but... I am human. It's hard not to say it when that's the truth."

"You are not a human any longer. You are a troll wife," Inkeri spat. "We are the women who run this kingdom. We are the throbbing, bloody heart of Trollveggen. Every step we take, every word we say, it fuels our homeland. Our men are nothing without us. This mountain is nothing without us. We would never willingly allow a human to step foot on these hallowed grounds. You are a troll wife. You said the words and claimed them as your own. Never say that you are human again. Do you understand me?"

The words flowed over Maia. She wasn't sure what to think of them. Because yes, she was the wife of a troll, but that didn't define who she was. Without Ragnar, she was still herself, and that was important to recognize.

Inkeri started walking again, and Maia supposed she had no choice but to continue to follow the other woman. But now, she wasn't sure where they were going. She didn't want to join this rather cult-like experience of being a troll wife above everything and anything.

The leaves crunched under her feet. The breeze toyed with her hair. It was like the mountain itself was trying to calm the nerves that churned in her belly, but nothing would get rid of the wrongness that had spread from Inkeri's words. She was not owned by any man, and she never would be.

When Inkeri turned down another forest path, Maia couldn't help herself. "I don't want to be a man's property. Back home, I refused every offer of marriage so I could keep my father's business as my own. You make it sound like being a troll wife is a gift, but if that gift comes only at the hand of a man, then I do not want it."

Inkeri shook her head. "You misunderstand my words, fire hair. He does not hold all the power in your relationship. You do."

Using her arm, the troll swiped away a curtain of leaves that hung from a tree branch and revealed a glen beyond. It was filled with troll women, each one of them dotting the landscape like brightly colored flowers in a meadow. They had countless objects with them. A loom that was carved out of the tree in the far right, like the plant had grown it just so that a troll wife could use it while sitting in the grass. Other women were at a table, each of them carefully setting gemstones into complicated metal loops. There were others whispering enchantments into jewelry, armor, and weapons.

A small stream ran through the center of it. Four women stood in the calm waters, their skirts tucked up in their waistbands as they slowly moved their hands left and right. As Maia watched, a small ball of water rose between them and danced in the air with their movements.

The air crackled with energy. She could feel it toying with the ends of her hair and suddenly singing in the piercings in her ears. Like the entire world lit up with power and energy just from her walking into the glen. Or like it had been here the entire time, and all that magic had been waiting for her to arrive.

"A troll wife is not bound to her husband," Inkeri said. "You took your human ideals, and you brought them here. That is why we do not welcome your kind. You hear my words and think I mean to bind you to him. But the stages of troll lives are different. A troll maiden hears the sound of the mountain. She wishes to join us in this glen, but she has not yet proven herself worthy of the ancient foundation of our world."

Inkeri held out her hand for Maia to take, and she didn't hesitate to place her fingers in the much larger hand. She allowed the troll to draw her toward the women in the water as though in a trance.

"A troll wife knows what it is to have her magic bound to another. To feed off another's life essence, which means we can also spread that throughout the mountain. We call her Móðir, the mother of us all. She is the mountain that feeds our magic, and the one who teaches us how to use our powers and make them stronger. It does not matter if our husband has given us that power or not. He may die, and still the mountain soothes us."

Inkeri pointed to the side, where Maia recognized Hulda among a group of older women. All the trolls were weaving in that corner, some of them sewing stunning jewel toned fabrics into impressive gowns. "The troll crones have gathered all the magic they can from this place. They do not have their husbands for the most part, but we have not forgotten the crones. They are still here. They still have access to all the earth's magic, but they are an integral part in teaching all of us what they have learned. In doing so, we do not have to learn through the same hard ways that they did."

"So when you call me a troll wife…" She didn't know how to end the question. Other than knowing the accusation she had made still stood strong in her mind.

"When I call you a troll wife, I mean the wife of the mountain. We mean the mother of magic that will grow and learn and develop here. We mean a troll." Inkeri cracked the last word off her tongue, harsh and filling the word with so much emotion. "You are no longer a human if you are here with us. You are a troll wife. You are one of us, Maia."

And that was the first time she'd felt truly welcome here. As though she belonged with the trolls, rather than simply being the uncomfortable person in the room. Even though she was surrounded by people with countless skin colors and patterns and piercings. Trolls who should have made her terrified, this was the first time in her life that she had been given permission to be herself and be loved for it.

"I don't know that I fully understand," she said, looking down at the water at her feet and then up to the women practicing magic. "But I would like to."

"That's all we can ask," Inkeri said. She placed a hand on her back and drew her toward the older troll women, who were all working on many articles of clothing. "Come with me. We'll get you clothing that doesn't have holes in it and that fits you far better than this bag he's placed on you."

"What if he doesn't want me to wear your clothing?" It was something she was concerned about. Ragnar had made it very clear that he wasn't interested in her as a wife back then. And frankly, they were so new to each other that it was hard to believe he had changed his mind.

Inkeri raised a dark brow. "Then he can rot. He mingled his blood with you, which means you are ours as much as you are his. And we take care of our own."

Chapter 24

Ragnar returned home, dripping in the blood of Maia's people and riding on the high of vengeance. He had made them suffer. He had watched as countless human men begged him for mercy and he had given them none. He'd made sure to cut them in ways that they would never heal from. Ways that would take days or weeks to die before they finally had suffered enough for what they had done to his people.

And still, it didn't feel like it was enough. He wanted to wipe the stain of them from the entire face of his kingdom. The trolls deserved to live in the sun without fear, if that was what they wished. They deserved so much more than being trapped inside a mountain, knowing that the humans had figured out a way inside.

The war band stood before their king, all kneeling as they reported what they had seen. And at the end of it, their king bid them all to rise.

He was tired. Ragnar could feel the exhaustion in the old troll long before he even looked and saw the bags underneath his eyes. At some point in their report, King Egil had removed his crown. It dangled from his fingers, the truest symbol of defeat that he had ever seen.

"So, the humans know how to find our paths now." The king heaved a long, regretful sigh. "That complicates things."

Gunnar was the first to stand, pounding a fist against his chest. "I would gladly set up the first watch, my king. My warriors will ensure that no human succeeds in destroying more of our roads into this sacred home."

"It is an honorable thing you ask to do, but there are not enough trolls to watch every entrance, and certainly not enough of us to stop the humans if they try more. We will set up scouts so we know which of the entrances they are targeting and nothing more."

The words weren't enough to satisfy the war band. They were all dripping in blood. Ragnar could see the crusted, dried flakes settling on the stone floor where all of them stood. They had destroyed everyone who had dared, but there would always be more.

But then the king continued, and Ragnar realized the wisdom in this choice. "We will hide the entrances better, but first, I must know which ones the humans are aware of. Those are the ones we will allow them to destroy. Let them cave in the entrances, or even better, we will do it ourselves so that it is controlled and no one else gets hurt. I do not want even a single human knowing how to enter Trollveggen."

Gunnar nodded. "I can send out scouts to listen in on the human conversations. It shouldn't take long for us to be in the basements of the barracks yet again. Last time it took them two weeks to realize we had tunneled our way in."

"Be careful. Clearly, their king has plans. After the betrayal with his daughter, I am inclined to believe their king wanted that entire wedding to be a message." King Egil's eyes darkened, and Ragnar's skin crawled with the sensation of magic that rolled off of the king's body and onto the floor like mist. "He will learn how foolhardy that act was."

All the trolls let out a synonymous growl that echoed throughout the room, but then they were dismissed. There was nothing Ragnar could do. He wanted to destroy the damn world because of what the humans had done, and he knew the other trolls in the war band felt the same. Unfortunately, they had to wait.

He headed toward his home, pausing only when Gunnar called out to him.

"Brother!"

Ragnar turned and waited for his brother to catch up with him.

"Be gentle with her," Gunnar said, and there was worry in his eyes. Ragnar hadn't recognized it at first, but now he could see the fear. As though his brother feared he would take these emotions out on his wife.

"I'm always gentle with her," he replied with a quiet sigh. "It's hard not to be when she is so delicate."

It hadn't even crossed his mind to purge some of this anger on her. Maia had proven herself worthy of him, but it was worrisome that his brother feared what he would do to the delicate creature. Clearly, she had made an impression on Gunnar. But somewhere along the way, Ragnar had given his brother reason to worry.

Perhaps that was partly because of the wedding. Perhaps it was that the first thing he had said to his bride was that he would never be her husband. And now he was returning to her dripping in the blood of his enemies, who were *her* people.

He had a lot of explaining to do, and perhaps some healing of his own. He trudged back toward his home, knowing without a doubt that he would need to tell her what had happened. If he didn't, someone else eventually would.

Maia, up until this point, had only seen him as a healer. He feared that some part of her thought that was all he was. Dealing with someone who wasn't active in the fight was likely easier for her when she was trying to reconcile what the trolls were going to do. War was brewing. And he wasn't so much of a fool to think this wouldn't affect her.

He stopped by the public baths before he got home. At the very least, he could arrive at their doorstep not covered in blood. While he scrubbed the deaths of her people from his skin, he tried to figure out what to tell her.

Perhaps he should lead with something along the lines that he didn't want to hurt her. It might be good to state that he had no interest in making her life harder, or taking out these feelings on her, as Gunnar feared. Then she would know that he was serious. He still saw her as a human, but not like...

No, that wasn't right. He couldn't even say she wasn't like the others, because she was. He knew she was. There were both good and bad people in every species, from the elves, to the trolls, to the humans. He'd have to be a fool not to recognize that, and so would she.

He couldn't say he didn't even see her as human. She was. And it wasn't that she was different from anyone else. He knew there were countless good humans. There had to be.

So what *would* he say?

He was embarrassed at how long it took to clean the blood from his skin as he tried to figure out the correct words. But by the time he stood in front of his own house, he was still tongue tied. No path made what he had done right, but no path said he was wrong either.

Blowing out a breath, he just opened the door and walked in. The least he could do was get inside and say what was on his mind. He would tell her the truth and then see what she said about that. If she wanted to yell at him, throw things, scream and rage, then beg to go back home, he would endure it all. She deserved that.

He walked into the parlor and furrowed his brow in confusion. He'd expected there to be far more rubble in here, considering the state that it had been in yesterday. But where he had seen small rocks in the corner and broken furniture, now the parlor was nearly put back in order. The broken pieces of his couch were gone, and the stones had been removed. Even the rug had been beaten free from dust and shards that had clung to the thick weaves.

A clanking noise in the kitchen caught his attention. He hadn't expected her to cook, not when there were plenty of other trolls that enjoyed cooking and were readily happy to trade services for cooking. At least then he didn't have to do it.

He walked through the doorway and froze at the vision before him.

She wore traditional troll garb, although it was modest for his people. The dress was sewn to look like dragon scales. The pinched green fabric created triangles up and down the tightened bodice and then disappeared into the skirt that clung to her broad hips and strong glutes. Her arms were bare, a dusting of freckles covering the sun kissed skin that was just now starting to become less red and more of a tanned burnish. Her hair was swept back from her features, the long sway of the tail at the top of her head moving as she fairly flew throughout the entirety of the kitchen.

The air smelled strongly of rosemary and freshly baked bread. He could see a few loaves of it were already out, and he suspected there were plenty more of them in the oven if the entire room smelled like this.

But all of his attention was on her. On the graceful sway of her hips as she turned toward his massive oven and pulled more bread out of the heat there. On the freckles that he desperately wanted to lick, and the way her hair swayed so temptingly at the middle of her back, pointing where he could loosen that dress and rip it off of her.

He reached above his head, bracing his arm on the doorframe just so that he didn't fly at her and devour her whole.

Maia finally noticed him and nearly dropped the bread in her hands. "Oh! Ragnar. I didn't hear you return."

"I'm quiet."

"Clearly," she replied, her gaze on him like he was about to pounce on her at any moment. Maybe she could see it in his eyes.

His claws dug into the stone. "Why are you making so much bread?"

She set the bread on the counter next to the row of them that were already waiting. "Inkeri said there were a lot of families that were affected by the cave-in. So I wanted to make sure that everyone had a chance to eat. It... Well, it's the least I could do."

"You've already helped enough, Maia."

She blinked. "Why wouldn't I do more? People need help. I'm able to give it."

He wanted to say that many weren't willing to give that help. But there were no words on his tongue, only need. He barreled across the room like a man possessed, grabbing her by the waist and setting her on top of the counter next to all the bread.

"Ragnar!" she said, her hands slapping on the stone behind her as she stared at him in surprise. He stood between her spread legs, drinking in the sight of her in the garb of the trolls, and he couldn't help himself. He palmed the back of her neck and kissed her.

Ragnar had no idea how to kiss a human. With trolls, there were only certain angles that worked. Mostly because of their tusks, and no one wanted to crack those together. But with a human, kissing was all soft skin and warm, pliant lips. Maia melted into him, just like she had last night. Her arms wrapped around his neck, her back arching to press her chest against him.

Kissing her felt like the entire world ceased to be. Like he could only focus on the way her lips moved beneath his, and the way she let out a little gasp when he caught her lower lip and gently bit it.

She pulled back after that, breathing hard and staring at his tusks with curious intent. "Are you... You'll be careful with these?"

"Wasn't I careful before?" Ragnar rasped, heat flooding through his body at the memory of the last time he'd tasted her. "I don't remember you complaining the last time, wife."

"Oh, you mean to..." Her face turned bright red, and he thought that was his new favorite color. The deep blush that spread across her face, down her neck, and all the way down her chest was so lovely because he knew exactly what it meant.

He fell to his knees before her, the countertop putting her at the perfect height for him to glide the fabric of her skirt over her thighs. He took his time feeling the warm skin, drawing his claws up her inner thighs and watched the bumps raise wherever he touched.

"I have missed your taste, wife," he murmured, rubbing his tusks just beside her knee and starting a slow journey upward.

"Didn't you just..." She shuddered as he pressed a wet kiss to her skin. "You just did this."

"You think once is enough?"

"I would think once every other week would suffice."

He yanked the fabric up to her hips, using that movement to control her body and splay her out for his pleasure. And gods, she was beautiful. All smooth skin and freckles leading to a small thatch of hair that hid all the world's treasures from his gaze.

He would beg her if she wanted him to. And as he stared up her body at her red face and strangely flustered expression, he had a feeling that was exactly what she needed right now. "Weekly isn't enough. Daily is hardly enough. I will never stop wanting to taste you."

"That's…" she whispered, her cheeks going even redder.

His claws flexed against her hips. "Please, wife. Let me taste you."

Something flared in her eyes. It was like he could see another being awaken underneath her skin, suddenly discovering a desire that she hadn't realized she had. A desire that she wished to feed.

Maia licked her lips, and he watched that pretty pink tongue dart out. He wanted that tongue in his mouth, on his body, teasing his cock. He wanted to know what she could do with it, and more so, he wanted to know what would please her when she used it.

"Again," she whispered, as though the word felt foreign on her tongue.

"I am begging you," he said, dragging his tusks so close to where she needed him. Where he could see the faintest shine of her desire. "I've had a very long day, wife. I would love nothing more than to lick you here. To feed you my fingers until you beg for my cock. I want you writhing underneath me, all that pretty skin turning bright pink as it always does. I want to hear your moans again. Let me fill this room with the sound of your pleasure."

That flush spread even further. She was panting now, her chest rising and falling with need. All he desired was for her to let go. He wanted her to give him the single word that would allow him to devour her whole.

"If I say no?" she asked.

"Then I will go to the tavern with my brother. I will leave you here to bake in this room, to fill it with more of your bread." He blew out a long breath, knowing it would make her shiver. "But I'm praying you do not say no."

His muscles were so tight he felt like he was shaking. But then she met his gaze and said, "Taste me, husband."

Chapter 25

Maia had no idea what had come over her. She wasn't this wanton woman laid out on a counter with her legs spread wide and a monstrous being kneeling between them. But then, when she looked down her body and saw those strange eyes and the tusks he dragged against her skin, all she could think about was that she could be the wild and wicked thing that lived inside of her.

All she had to do was ask him. To beg, as he wanted her to do. But it was more than that.

The other troll wives had impressed upon her that troll men worshiped their wives. They were guided by a feminine hand, and in that way, she had to be the woman he needed her to be. If she wanted this to happen, then all she had to do was say so. If she didn't? She was still in control.

She'd never been in control of anything her entire life. Everyone had looked at her as this weak-willed woman who needed to be ordered around, pushed toward so much that she didn't want to do, and had to be protected by a man because she certainly couldn't do it herself.

That was not what the trolls thought. They looked at women as capable, influential, and knowledgeable creatures who had use in a society. That freedom bloomed inside of Maia's chest. It gave her the confidence to tell him to taste her. Because that was what she wanted.

The low groan that echoed out of his chest made her feel powerful. She held the reins of this troll between her thighs. All she had to do was tug at them and suddenly, he was hers. Overwhelmed. Needy. He'd been begging her for a taste and now, as his tongue slid up between her thighs, all she could think was that finally she would get what she wanted.

He flicked his tongue over her clit, the motion so light she could barely feel it until he was circling it just with the tip. She couldn't breathe with the pleasure that coursed through her body. Zings of it moved up her form, lighting in her chest as every muscle tightened at the sensation.

"I have been waiting for this moment," he snarled against her skin as he drew back. She almost complained, but then his fingers replaced his mouth.

Those broad, blunt fingertips were so much larger than she remembered. It was like a monster traced her seam, a featherlight touch moving down her folds, parting her for his gaze. She was likely red-faced and panting as she watched him, but Maia found she couldn't draw her eyes away from what he was doing to her.

Being touched like this? It was more than she could survive. She was certain of it. Because he used both of his thumbs, spreading her ever wider and nudging her legs even farther apart. The breath in her lungs grew thin, like there just wasn't enough air in the room.

And then he descended upon her. He feasted, his tongue lapping before suddenly plunging into her depths. She arched, her gaze flying up to the stone ceiling like that would provide some kind of answer for what was being done to her. Every nerve ending in her body coiled tighter, searching for something impossible and something she simply could not understand.

One massive, clawed hand trailed up her body. His hand grasped her breast, molding it into his palm before using those claws to pinch her nipple until sparks danced down her body. And then he stopped everything and made her look back down her body at him. All she could see were her own heaving breasts and the need in his eyes.

"I told you that I would wait to fill you until you begged," he murmured. "You've earned it, fire hair."

Earned... what?

She watched, breathless still, as he lifted his free hand to his mouth. With a sharp snap of those jaws, tusks flashing in the light of the kitchen, he bit off two of his claws. The middle finger and the ring finger. It took so little for him to break them, but the sound of the snapping claw filled the room.

With his gaze holding hers prisoner, he slowly sank that thick middle finger into her. She couldn't look away from that heated gaze even as she clenched around him.

Even his finger felt massive. She felt her body trying to adjust to him, strange as it was to think that it was only his finger. But when he'd gone as far as he could, he ground the heel of his palm against her clit and suddenly she felt another rush of passion flooding through her.

"Look how well you take me," he muttered, and then his gaze released her because he was staring down at where they were connected, an expression of awe on his face. "So tight. By all the gods, fire hair, you're so fucking tight."

Maybe that was a problem, but she didn't care right now. All she wanted was for him to move. She rocked her hips, a slight, keening cry moving through her throat. Maia needed him to move. She needed the friction that would give her that bright, sparkling release unlike anything else in this world. She needed.

He shushed her, a low chuckle reverberating through his chest. "Easy. I'll take care of you."

And then he pulled his finger out, only to plunge it back inside of her. Hard. So hard she rocked on the table, throwing her head back as blistering pleasure set her body alight. He moved like a man possessed, each thrust of his finger so brutal that she was nearly crying. Everything in her coiled, tensed, certain that she would fall apart.

Every muscle in her body coiled tighter, seizing up until she came. She stopped breathing, unable to even do that as she focused on the tight coil of her body and the sudden release of all that pressure. He rode her through it, every single movement sending more pleasure sparking until there was no more burning pressure or shifting across the table.

There was only the light trace of his fingers again, drifting around her clit until she was panting again. No longer crying out with every hard thrust, she was still panting with need until she looked at him again.

Maia swore there was a slight look of pity on his expression. "You're very small, fire hair."

She shook her head, nearly delirious now. "So?"

"So we will have to take our time with this. A cock like mine would break you."

She let her eyes trail down the length of him, her gaze lingering on the shape of that bar in his pants that was impressively larger than she'd even thought. She knew he was huge. Maia would have to be blind to think that trolls weren't huge everywhere, considering how tall they were. How broad. Every inch of them was bunched with muscle, but that wasn't the only reason their kind was huge. Even if he lost all the muscles that made him so bulky, he would still be a massive beast.

His fingers started moving again, and she jerked. She was so sensitive that even the smallest movement made her entire body react.

"What are you doing?" she asked, as he slid his finger back inside of her, curling it up in a way that had her gasping.

"Taking it slowly," he replied. Ragnar licked his lips, staring down at her body, and then back up to her eyes. "It is a pleasure to serve you, troll wife. Let me make you scream again."

"Scream?"

But then she couldn't talk. He'd brought his tongue back to her clit while his fingers worked inside her. This was different. The first time she'd been so caught up in the pleasure that it was hard to think, but now she was riding the high of an orgasm while he fought to bring her to another, and she wasn't sure she would survive it.

Her heart thundered. She could feel it banging against her ribs, but she couldn't focus on that right now. Not when his tongue was doing that thing against her clit that made her stomach clench so hard it almost hurt. He was circling, then flicking, circling again. All of it was too much. She was going to come too fast. It was too soon.

Maia rode the edge of pain, or at least, she thought she did. Until he drew his finger back and there was suddenly a burn.

A second finger. He was trying to put both of his fingers inside of her. She flexed her stomach, drawing herself up to look down at him in shock.

"I can't—" Maia arched when he sucked on her clit so hard that she nearly came right then and there.

Everything seemed to freeze. He drew back from her, looking up with her pleasure smeared across his face and so much desire in his gaze that she burned. He looked like a predator. Like a creature who had been caught in the midst of feeding and she was the foolish one who had disturbed him.

But then his fingers were pressing against her again, and there was the slow glide of them. It burned. She was fuller than she'd ever been in her life, but with that came the feeling of pressure. Like she was meant to do this. Like she had been born to take this much and that her body needed it.

The pain wasn't all that bad, but with that pain came the pride that she had done it. Even though she'd been afraid of it, his blunt fingers were now sliding easily inside of her.

He pressed his hand to her chest, lying her back down silently before feasting again. His lips and tongue and fingers plunged inside of her, licked her, soothed her, spun her entire body into a tight little ball. She was a writhing creature made of pleasure and pain, laid out for him to do what he wished.

Maia barely recognized her own voice as the room filled with little cries and whimpers. His hand came up to her breast again, yanking the fabric of her dress down so that he could touch the heat of her flesh. His fingers were on her nipple as well, pulling and tugging on it until she was blinded to the world. There could have been another rock slide and she wouldn't have even noticed as long as he didn't stop.

She came harder than she ever had in her life. So sensitive already, but then this one felt different. It was like her entire body tried to climb out of herself, reaching for some strange reset that made all the stress in her entire life melt out of her form.

The cry that left her lips was animalistic, and wrong, but so right at the same time. She held her breath and stayed in this moment of both pleasure and pain until the crushing wave of it left her.

Ragnar let out an answering long groan, followed by the slam of his hand against the table beside her. He stood, looming above her with his eyes closed. One massive arm shook as he braced himself over her. His other hand was pressed hard against the front of his pants, where a darkened stain had spread.

Had he...

He had, she realized. Just the mere act of bringing her pleasure had made him come in his pants like he was a young man and she was the first woman he'd spread out like a banquet before him.

For some reason, Maia had never felt more pride. She should have been embarrassed, but all she could think was that her pleasure had made him so excited that he couldn't contain himself.

Breathing hard, they both remained frozen in place until he opened his eyes and met her gaze. They stared at each other for a few moments. She wasn't sure what to say to him. Did she tell him he'd done a good job? He certainly had. There should be some kind of praise for what he'd done.

But then he wiped his hand on his pants and cupped her cheek. With the slightest huff of a chuckle, he shook his head and gave her a wry grin. "You are going to be the death of me, fire hair."

Biting her lip, Maia tried to hide her own grin. "Well, I wasn't the one who started all this."

"You absolutely did. You were standing in the middle of my kitchen, making bread for my people who needed your help. What is a man to do but offer pleasure?"

Now that was just ridiculous. People needed help, and many of the trolls had been kind to her thus far. Certainly, there were a few who were still wary of her presence, but for the most part, they had at least tried to accept that she was here.

She rolled her eyes at his antics. "Ragnar, that is ridiculous. I'm happy to help where I can. You brought me here. I want to make this place a home if I can."

"And that is worth praising." He leaned down, pressed his lips against her forehead, and gave her the slightest kiss.

It was strange to feel those smooth tusks pressed against her skin. Maybe she'd never get over the strangeness of it. But with his kiss, she felt like she'd done something right. Like she had proven herself worthy to be here.

After all, she was a troll wife now. Not human, and certainly not troll. But there had to be a happy medium somewhere in the middle of both.

Maia was a survivor. And someday, she would prove to them all that she could live here.

Ragnar pulled her bodice back up and then smoothed her skirts down her legs. "I'm off to wash. You keep baking, fire hair. Let's hope your bread doesn't taste like ash."

"Why would it—" The scent of smoke hit her nose. "Damn it! You could have warned me it was burning!"

He laughed as he disappeared down the hall, but the sound of his happiness filled her with hope. Maybe it wouldn't be so bad to be here after all.

Chapter 26

S omething has to be done!" The massive troll general slammed his fist down on the table, and the sound of it echoed throughout the room. Gorm had been a general for many years now, and he was one of the greatest of their fighters. His already reddish skin was burnished with anger as he stared at the rest of the trolls around the table. "We cannot allow them to kill our people without retribution. This was an act of war."

Gunnar pinched his nose where he was slumped beside Ragnar. The two of them were very uninterested in accusations and ridiculous attempts at fear mongering. The entire war room had been filled with blustering and anger, but no actual solutions.

They'd been stuck in here for hours on end. The king even looked exhausted. All of their colors were getting a little too vivid, and everyone with an ounce of animal blood in them was foaming at the mouth. Ragnar had seen far too many of the trolls around the table wiping their tusks free from the frothy substance, a dead giveaway that too many of them wanted to fight.

If they weren't released soon, they would all fly at each other's throats.

Ragnar leaned forward, trying to keep his voice calm and sound of reason. "We hunted down the band of humans who attacked us. They all suffered before they died. That has to be enough of a warning sent to the humans that we will retaliate if they continue to collapse our tunnels."

"Humans are stupid," Gorm spat. "They do not know their own limitations. They fight us as though they believe they can win, and as such, that means they will not stop."

Bodil, another war general who had spent her entire life fighting humans, leaned back in her chair and crossed her arms over her chest. "That is the truth. We've already heard rumblings that the humans are going to attack again. My scouts have seen many of them crawling like ants over our mountain. They seek a way in."

His brother heaved a long sigh. "And if they do manage to get in, they'll be lost in the dark. It would take them months to find a way into our city, and even if they did, there would be so few of them that we could pick them off one by one."

Silence rang after that. They all knew it to be true. Their mountain was a labyrinth to anyone who didn't know their way around it. The trolls had built it that way on purpose. Just in case the odd human found themselves wandering into their home. Ragnar had found many bodies in the dark winding tunnels, usually as dried out husks because even the trolls hadn't noticed them until it was long past the time they'd first entered the mountain.

But then Gorm shook his head. "We cannot risk it. If they send too many people, then they'll be able to find us. What would we do if a human discovered one of our children before we found them? You know the little ones play in the streams at the edge of the forest. If they're found by a human first, what do you think their kind will do? Should we teach our children to be afraid in their own home?"

They all froze as their king cleared his throat. King Egil's claws scratched the table, leaving deep grooves as he thought. The others remained silent, so they did not disturb the king's thoughts. After all, he had protected them all for many years now.

"We could easily set a rule for trolls to kill any human on sight," the king mused.

Ragnar reacted like he'd been struck by lightning. "My wife is human. You cannot ask our trolls to do that. There are many who have yet to know her."

Gunnar was quick to add, "If we wish to continue strengthening our bloodline, we have to allow more human troll wives. They should be comfortable here, as we all know, unwilling brides dilute the bloodline they carry. Magic is earned in childbirth and must be freely given."

It was a sobering reminder of their follies. Humans with elven bloodlines had always been part of dragging the trolls out of the mud and filth they had once lived in. Their people had stolen women for their bloodlines, and none of them had been willing.

For the time being, his own wife wasn't kicking, screaming, or begging him to take her to her human home. He wished to keep her like that for as long as possible, because he wasn't certain his heart could take it. She was so sweet when she was trying to be happy. He could easily see how other women could do the same. Perhaps they had just been taking the wrong human women.

But then Bodil chuckled, her dark laugh filling the room with promise. "Then keep your wife inside, Ragnar. Tell her to be a good little pet until this all blows over."

"That could be years."

"Yes, it could be. But she'll be fine in the dark for that long. And if she isn't?" Bodil lifted her hands in the air. "I heard she wasn't a good match, anyway. I thought we were going to get the healer of the ages when you were paired with the princess, but instead, all we got was the same healer and a useless worm who can make plants grow if she asks nicely."

A stunned silence followed her words. Thus far, most trolls had been accepting of his troll wife. There had been some pitying looks, of course, but none of them had been so blatant as to tell him that she wasn't good enough. But Bodil had always been a mouthy one. She'd always shared her thoughts a little too readily.

Now, as he looked at the other trolls surrounding the table, he realized many of them shared the same thoughts. They looked away from his pointed stare, ignoring the words that had been said. Perhaps some of them struggled with trying to think of something to change the subject, but it was out on the table now.

"Is that how you all feel?" he asked, suddenly outraged that his own people would be so callous.

No one at the table would look at him. Not the king, not Gorm, and certainly not his own brother, which somehow enraged him even more than the rest.

"Gunnar?" he asked, making sure that he pointed out his own kin. "You feel the same way?"

"It's not forever, Ragnar."

"It is forever, and you know that. The humans will not stop fighting us. Their king tricked us, used us to send a message that he would never let his daughter or her magic be tainted by animals. You all know this as well as I!" He caught every one of their gazes. "She is my troll wife. You all know that I am bound to do what I can to take care of her, to ensure she lives her life to the fullest. You're asking me to lock her away in a tomb."

Bodil snorted. "Our home is not a tomb. You can walk with her through the streets with a leash, if that is what you desire to do." She turned to the king. "We should lock our people in, as well. The humans are growing bold and it would only be dangerous to allow trolls free access to the outside. At least until the passes are secured and closed off."

Were they now going to continue like his problem was a nonissue? Ragnar interrupted the conversation. "I have no interest in binding my woman to me. Besides, you know as well as I, she has to go out into the sun."

The others had the nerve to look like his interruption was bothersome. Gorm was the first to reply, his deep rumbling voice stating, "Why is that a problem for us? If she dies, she dies."

"Excuse me?" he snarled.

The king sighed. "Ragnar, we all hoped for a better match for you. We've seen you struggle with the human woman as well. If she died, it would not be the end of your line. There would be another to come, and I would not allow you to remain without a wife for long."

He saw red. All of these people saw her as disposable. Or even worse, they saw her as a creature so far beneath them that her death wasn't a bother. They'd just pair him off with another, without ever asking if that was what he wanted.

At least his brother appeared disturbed as well. Gunnar shifted uncomfortably. "My king, I will happily bring her to the sun if Ragnar cannot be spared to do so. She does not need to die for this plan to work."

"That creature was a mistake," the king said, his voice low and grumbling. "She should never have been brought here. I have no interest in fostering or feeding mistakes. Get rid of her in whatever way you have to, but I thought a slow death would be more kind than asking one of ours to kill her."

Ragnar stood. His chair screeched on the floor, a battle cry of its own as every single troll surrounding the table stared at him in shock. "If you try to lay a single claw on her head, I will take her and leave. You can heal your own trolls. She is my troll wife, and the mere threat of harming her is its own act of war. You know that as well as I do, high king."

The king did not flinch. He just chuckled, knowing that Ragnar would never make good on that threat. "You will do no such thing. If I have to tie you down and force you to use your magic, I will. But we both know that your power binds you to us just as your honor binds to you her."

"So this is the kindness of trolls?" Ragnar hissed. "We have not changed so much from our ancestors, then."

The others stared at him, but Gorm was the one to laugh. "Animals? You think you are so far from the tiger, boy? Look at you, all flared up and ready to fight on her behalf."

Ragnar gave him a cold glare. "I speak of the elves, General. Heartless monsters who would stop at nothing to gain more power for themselves. Clearly, those bloodlines are still strong within us. We have fallen far to be so willing to follow in their footsteps."

Snarling, he left the war room. There was no place for him if they were going to talk about his future and his troll wife as though he had no say in it. He couldn't stand to hear them talk about her like she was beneath them, either.

Maia had proven to him that she was kind hearted. She hadn't complained once, not even when she had spoken of her home and how much she missed it. When she had begged him to bring her back, and when he'd denied her the right to do so, she had taken that with grace and moved forward.

She was as much a warrior as any of them, and she deserved to be treated as such.

"Ragnar!" His brother's voice rang out in the hall. "Stop!"

"I have no interest in talking with them or with you, brother."

"I'll talk sense into them. They're angry and suffering. You can't hold that against them."

"I can and I will," he snarled. "They have no care for me or mine. Why should I suffer to hear their opinions when you and I both know they would strangle her in her sleep if they were given the chance?"

Gunnar rushed ahead of him, slamming his hands on Ragnar's chest and throwing him back. They both stared at each other for a moment. The violence in Gunnar's touch was enough to set them both off, but Ragnar feared what would happen if he fought his brother. He wasn't certain they would ever come back from this moment.

Then they both lunged. Tusks locking, they grappled. But they were brothers, and they had fought like this many times. If there was anyone who could best him, it was Gunnar. But the same could be said for Ragnar. They knew each other's weaknesses. And as they pushed, shoved, punched at each other's ribs, they knew what to do to avoid every attack or make it hurt when one of them made a mistake.

Gunnar managed a strike that hit Ragnar's chest hard enough to knock the wind out of him. It silenced the growls coming from his throat long enough for Gunnar to shout, "You cared little for her only moments ago! What changed?"

"She's my troll wife. Mine. We're bound to protect each other until the very end."

"This isn't magic binding you to her." Gunnar grunted as Ragnar's fist hit his belly. "This is more than that. Blind loyalty isn't like you."

"She's earning my loyalty."

"Then tell them that!"

Ragnar wriggled free from his brother's grip, slithering out of his brawny arms and unlocking their tusks with a harsh click that made his very skull ache as the tips of their tusks scraped against each other. Shaking his head to clear the pain, he staggered away from his brother. "They won't listen. You know it as well as I."

They stared at each other, yet again. Both of their shoulders heaved with breath and their eyes widened in shock. Ragnar didn't know what to say to his kin. And Gunnar likely didn't understand the change that had overcome his brother, who hated humans just as much as every other troll.

Ragnar held out his shaking hands, trying to make his brother see. "She is no longer human," he said, his tones pleading. "She is a troll wife. The moment I accepted her, the moment our blood mingled, she became a troll wife."

Gunnar shook his head. "They'll never see her that way."

"Others do."

"Kinder trolls. Trolls who have never found a body buried in rubble or seen the remains of a child after the humans have found it in the forests. They've never seen the suffering her people have caused."

His mind was so twisted, so wrong now that he knew her, because his first thought flew from his lips. "But my wife has never seen the bodies we left in the forest. She's never seen how we hung them from the trees, their skin flayed from their corpses to look like wings. Should we assume she would hate us if she knew that truth?"

Gunnar's jaw dropped open before he snapped it shut. "Do you hear yourself? We gave them the justice they deserved for what they did."

And yet...

And yet.

Ragnar turned away from his brother, his mind running wild with all the wrong and the right that filled it. But he knew, deep in his gut, that what he had said was true. He just didn't know how to live with those thoughts.

Chapter 27

The market was lovely on days like this. Maia was used to the human markets, which had their own level of charm. The village near the castle was always full of vendors on any day of the week. But usually those vendors had recognizable food that she could sometimes afford.

She'd loved going into town and searching out the freshest bread she could find. There hadn't been a lot of time for her to bake, not when there'd been so much gardening to do. Some part of her missed that, as well.

Walking through the troll market was so different, namely because she was surrounded by plants. It seemed everyone had something alive they wanted to sell, whether that was flowers, green leafy beasts with long stalks, or piles of leaves the size of her head.

She missed being around plants. Nothing was more satisfying than being wrist deep in the earth, convincing the plants to grow better while she pulled weeds or rotated the soil for the next year. Of course, none of her plants had been useful for anything other than their beauty. The plants here were all food or herbs. Maia could sense the medicinal properties in some of them. The way some of them would burn if she were to put them on an open wound, but they would convince the skin to heal faster. Sometimes there was even the faintest hint of magic in their leaves, but those were usually only in roots that were bundled together by heavy twine.

The trolls were all very kind and aware of each other's presence. There was no loud shouting or screaming from vendors for her to come look at their wares. They all were merely there, waiting for someone to see what they had brought. It was a more polite way to gain customers, even if it was unfamiliar to her.

As she had for three days now, Maia wandered down the market with a basket full of her bread. She supposed she could have asked if Ragnar wanted her to start selling it, but he hadn't been all too particular about her buying ingredients and giving the bread away. After all, the city needed the help.

While there were plenty of trolls who had pieced their homes back together and were ready to sell their regular wares, many trolls still appeared to be struggling, depending on where they had been during the collapse. But Maia still walked by some homes that were little more than rubble, and it made her entire heart ache.

She walked by a troll who had a bandage around his head, still injured from when Ragnar couldn't heal him during the entire madness that had befallen this kingdom. She walked up to him first, pulling a loaf of bread from her basket with a soft smile.

"Here. I know it isn't much, and it won't help that head of yours, but everyone needs to eat."

The troll looked at her as though she had crawled out of the shadows. His eyes widened, seemingly horrified by her actions, before he staggered away.

Had she said something wrong? Perhaps it was rude to point out an injury among their people. The next person she would approach quietly, and perhaps not with so much eagerness.

So she walked to the next person, who appeared to be quite injured. The woman was leaning on a cane, wincing with every step as she made her way down the street.

Maia walked up to her, getting her attention from afar before she gestured at her basket. "I made enough bread for many people. Would you like one? I hope it will help."

The woman only looked at her with an expression of disgust before ignoring her.

What was she doing wrong?

Maia frowned, trying to find someone who would look at her in the crowd and maybe explain what was going on. But no one was even looking at her, she realized. They were all pretending that she didn't exist. Like there was a fly buzzing among them, and they were all ignoring it.

What had changed? She'd done this for the past two days, and so many people had been willing to take the bread in her hands. It was helpful, at the very least, to take food home that they didn't have to cook.

There was a younger woman down the street who had taken bread from her just yesterday. As Maia walked up to her, she could see the guilt in her eyes as the young woman looked away and started down the street away from her. Even though that meant the troll maiden had to turn and go in the opposite direction she'd originally been walking.

"What is happening?" Maia muttered under her breath, before

turning around.

It was like she'd turned invisible. No matter what she did, no one would look at her. They would not talk to her. And if this was how it was going to be, then... well, she supposed she should just go home.

With fifteen loaves of bread that would mold.

An arm wound around her shoulder, tucking her against a side that smelled like clean linen and woven tapestries. "Do not let them insult you so," Hulda said, her old voice wavering with emotion. "They do not see that you are a troll wife, and that you are to be honored as such."

Maia looked up at the old woman, seeing the kindness in her wrinkled face. "I don't understand what changed from yesterday."

"The others found out that a cave-in caused the earthquake. The humans attacked one of the entrances into our home, and there were many trolls injured because of it."

Maia's stomach churned. "And they blame me for it."

"It is misplaced blame. You did not cause the collapse, nor did you order your people to attack our home. But you are the only human here." Hulda's face wrinkled with worry. "I don't think it is entirely safe for you to be out on your own, fire hair."

Safe? The trolls had never given her reason to be afraid for her safety, but... Maia glanced back at the crowd now gathering and staring at her, and she saw distrust and fear in their movements. Both of those emotions were quick to convince people to do awful, terrible things, and she wasn't sure that she wanted to know what they would do to her if they caught her.

Swallowing hard, she nodded. "I think you're right. Perhaps it would be best if I went back home."

"I'll come with you."

"That would be very appreciated. Thank you, Hulda."

Together, they headed back to Ragnar's home. But the entire journey, all Maia could see were the hostile expressions on the trolls' faces.

Was it that hard for them to see her here? She knew that there were many who had likely lost a loved one, or who had family members injured in what happened. And she was so sorry for it. Maia had done everything in her power to help, and continued to do so. But was she the problem here?

Hulda even put her hand over Maia's head, as though she was hiding the red hair from afar so people wouldn't see her. The old woman couldn't move fast, but when she wanted to, she moved fast enough that Maia was almost jogging to keep up with her.

Until a vendor called out to them. The man was standing in front of his cart, one that was full of earrings and gemstones that weren't set in metal yet. He pointed at the two of them, calling out, "Hulda! Is that Ragnar's human?"

"She's his troll wife," Hulda corrected. "There is honor in that title, Arvid."

"It's not possible to separate their kind. She was born human, and human she will always be." There was a flash of something in the man's eyes. Something dangerous that threatened her well being and Maia felt that inner voice in her head scream.

She'd seen expressions like that before. The twist of her gut had never been wrong, not about a man. Soon enough, he would try to hurt her. Maybe he would justify it as saving his people from her kind, and she wouldn't blame him for that. Everyone was angry right now.

She was furious at her own people. Attacking the troll mountain, trying to make it seem like she was the princess and tricking them out of their deal. There were a hundred transgressions that her people were wrong for, but she did not want to take the brunt of that pain for them. She wasn't sure she even could.

Arvid growled, and the sound made every single hair on her body stand on end. "You're standing up for her, Hulda? You're a very old woman to try to keep her safe."

"But I will keep her safe. Or will you attack me first?"

"I have no interest in attacking troll kind. But I do want the human scum to get out of our market."

Hulda let out a sound that was far too close to a hiss. "Troll wife!"

"Get out of my way, crone. She could easily spy for her own people, and I won't have my family endangered because she wanted to play with the animals before returning to her cultured ways." He spat the last two words, the insult obvious behind them.

"I don't want to—" Maia stopped talking at the glare he nearly leveled her with. The hatred in that chilled her to the bone.

Arvid took a menacing step forward, the threat clear in his movements. "Get out of my home, human. You deserve to be back at the surface where you belong. I'd prefer your keeper to do it, but I'm not above angering Ragnar just to see you gone."

Another troll close by yelled, "We don't want you here!"

"Your kind isn't welcome!"

"Thief!"

"Murderer!"

Maia's heart hurt. Her chest quite literally ached as she ducked a little closer to Hulda. But she wasn't fast enough.

Someone launched a stone at her, catching her right hip hard enough to sting. Gasping, she whirled away from the pain, only to put herself right in the way of yet another stone. This one caught her shoulder, leaving a mark of grit against her skin and a red scrape where her flesh had torn. Shock had her reeling a little too close to Arvid.

The jeweler snarled with more anger. "Are those my earrings in your ears?"

Oh, no.

Had Ragnar gotten them from this man? She clapped her hands over her ears, trying to get as close to Hulda as she could. More rocks found their way to her skin, though, and she didn't want the old woman to get hit. So she tried to step around Hulda, only to find more trolls on the other side. There was nowhere for her to go.

Fear made her freeze. She wasn't proud of it. Part of her still said that if she just gave them what they wanted, they would leave her alone. She could lick her wounds in the shadows after they were done with her, whatever that looked like. She survived because she had to. There was no other choice. Surviving was what she was good at.

A rock launched through the air, and she could see it was going to hit her in the face. Squeezing her eyes shut, she prepared herself for more pain as she lifted her arms to protect her head.

But the pain didn't come.

Blinking her eyes open and dropping her arms, Maia stared at the lavender-colored hand in front of her face. It took her a moment to realize Ragnar had caught the rock before he dropped it onto the ground at her feet. His shoulders were rising and falling with rage as he stared at the crowd surrounding them. Without a word, he put his arm around her and turned toward their home.

Hulda took a deep breath, the sound little more than a wheeze before she said, "Be careful with her, Ragnar."

He growled, "I wish everyone would stop telling me that," before dragging her through the streets. He said nothing else. Not while they walked. Not when he opened the door. And certainly not when he thrust her into the waiting darkness beyond.

She worried he would scold her. Or perhaps that he was like the others who had decided to be done with her. But that thought was trailed by an edge of rage, because how dare he? He'd given her hope. He'd made her feel like this could work, even though she should have known that was a lie.

Breathing hard, she turned on him the moment he shut the door. "Did you know?"

He remained with his back to her, his attention on the closed door. "I did."

"Is that where you were? When you came back that day in the kitchen? Were you outside of Trollveggen, in the party that found out my people collapsed an entrance?"

"I was."

Her entire body hurt, like he'd been the one to throw the stones at her. "What did you do to them?"

He still didn't turn. But she could see the way his shoulders curved in on him. "I killed them, with all the other trolls in our war band. I skinned them alive and left them to die in the trees. So that when your people found them, they would be half dead and soon on their way into the realm beyond. They would be like monsters to your own people, omens of the deaths that would soon find them."

Maia's stomach churned with the brutality of the image. His people did not know how to forgive. That much she was certain of. But then she remembered all the trolls who had died here too, and the awful ways they had done so even as Ragnar had fought for hours to save them.

"What are we going to do?" she whispered, feeling more broken and defeated than she had since the day she'd married him. "Your people and mine hate each other. There is no coming back from this kind of hatred. I cannot even walk your streets, and you cannot leave this place without my kind trying to kill you. Or you killing them."

He turned at her words, staggering toward her like a man who had seen a ghost. But then, just when she thought he would reach out to shake her or yell at her for dreaming like she had, he fell to his knees before her. Ragnar's head came up to her chest when he was like this, his size was so much greater than her own. He was so infinitely gentle as he brushed his fingers against her hip.

"They struck you here?" he asked, his voice so quiet she almost didn't hear it.

She nodded, words sticking in her throat.

"And here." He touched the red mark on her shoulder where the stone had scraped her. "They never should have touched you. This is my fault."

"Ragnar." She wanted to say it wasn't his fault. He hadn't even been there until the last moment.

But he didn't let her speak. Instead, he merely tugged her into his arms and kept her silent, holding her close to his heart as his cool, healing magic filtered through her. She could feel his power convincing her body to knit together, to heal, to relax her muscles that were a little too stiff.

"I'm sorry," he whispered against her hair. "I will find some way to fix this."

But she wasn't all that certain it could be fixed.

Chapter 28

Ragnar watched her sleep with a troubled mind and a hardened heart. His people wanted Maia dead. That much was certain. Trolls were a fickle bunch, but they also desired to have some retribution for what her people had done. He could see it in the way they moved around her, in the stones they had thrown and the pain in their chests whenever they looked at what had been done to their beautiful home.

The trolls' entire culture was based around righting wrongs. They were the ones who had been injured. Their people had been killed, their homes destroyed, all the safety and comfort of Trollveggen ruined because of what the humans had done.

He supposed there was still anger left in him as well. He hadn't told her the entire truth of all that he had done. The screams of those dying men were still a song he thought of in his mind when he grew too angry at her. He had gotten his own revenge. But many of the troll people had not.

Fixing this wouldn't be easy. Ragnar had a reputation that he could fall back on. Many of the trolls might not have liked that he was married to her, but they knew what he had done for them. Healing their people had been in his bloodline for many ages, as the gift had been his mother's before it was his.

Maia had helped heal them, too. They had softened toward her when they'd realized her magic had convinced his own to keep going, and that it was her touch that had eased his torment while he'd healed them. She'd won much support in doing that, although his people had conveniently forgotten that now that hers had attacked them.

It wouldn't get better without intervention.

Maia stirred in her sleep, and he breathed out a long sigh as he tucked the strands of her hair behind her ear. None of this was her fault. She hadn't ordered her people to attack, nor did he believe that she had been sent here as a spy. Her king had used her to deceive them, proof that humans would never work with trolls.

King James likely believed that he had sent her to her death. He perhaps even intended that the trolls would quickly realize that she wasn't the princess—how they hadn't realized sooner he would never know—and kill her. There were many calling for it, so Ragnar supposed the human king hadn't been all that wrong.

Still. He wouldn't let it happen to his own troll wife. Not when there was still honor in his body and breath in his lungs.

He needed to prove to the other trolls that she was valuable and not dangerous. If he could do that, then perhaps at the next attack, they wouldn't be so quick to see her as human. Those ties had to be knotted around each and every troll. They had to see her as one of their own.

And in doing that, perhaps they would forgive her for being what she was.

He could do this. There were places he could take her, and trolls he could introduce her to who weren't so hardened that they wouldn't be able to see past her size and strange eyes. They would recognize the usefulness of her tiny hands, or perhaps see the magic that had been building in her since their blood had bonded.

It wasn't much. She would never be able to heal the masses or stop storms from coming onto their mountain. But perhaps he could still find use for her.

Ragnar stood from the bed, creeping out of the room so he wouldn't wake her. Healing always made people sleepy, and perhaps he had used a bit of his magic to convince her to rest more thoroughly, so he didn't have to talk to her about all of this. Not yet, at least. Soon, they would talk about everything. But right now, he simply did not know what to say. There were no excuses for his people's actions.

He left his home with a purpose now, though. The plan built in his mind as he strode down the streets of his home, eyeing the piles of stone and rubble that many trolls had left outside their homes. Someone would come to take those rocks out soon enough. But for now, they were a reminder of what had happened.

But then, as he rounded a corner, the entire city seemed to open up. The massive gardens as the heart of Trollveggen were filled with plants that his troll wife had likely never seen. They grew in the darkness and the meager light provided by the wisps. Massive plants that were rooted into the ground. Some of them were ancient, ones that the elves themselves had grown. Some of the brightly colored leaves were larger than he was tall and hid glowing berries that were used in medicinal spells. Flowers could easily fill his hands with their pollen, the tiny specks lifting up into the air as they passed and emitted the sweet scent of powdered sugar. So many plants turned the gardens into a veritable feast for the senses.

Neat rows lead in spirals away from the center, creating a labyrinth that many found hard to get through. He knew his way around fairly well and also knew that all the spiraling paths led to a cottage in the center. It was a small, quaint stone building that had been mortared together by years of hard labor and a troll who wanted nothing more than to be left alone by everyone and anything that bothered him.

The garden thrived under the touch of loving hands. Green magic made all the plants grow when they shouldn't, and such magic was limited. There was only so much anyone could do here. Although, clearly the plants were loving where they were. A wisp darted past him. The blue shimmering light had little striations that made it appear like a ball of lighting as it zipped along the ground. Most of the wisps ended up here. Someone had once told him it was because they liked to be in gardens where things were ever changing.

Then there was the troll at the heart of it all. The man who had taken care of this garden for decades, and who was known to be far more sullen than any other troll in this mountain.

It was a terrible plan, but it was the only one he had. If he could convince Birger to like Maia, then everyone else would quickly follow suit. If only because they were shocked the old troll could like anything.

"Who goes there?" the ancient troll called out, his voice already sullen with dislike.

"Ragnar."

"Who?"

"The healer," Ragnar replied with a chuckle. "You've seen me nearly every week for years now, Birger. You know who I am."

Finally, he could see the gardener. Birger's face appeared from behind a massive green leaf with variegated holes in it. The troll used to have tusks, but they had been lost to the humans after he'd been caught the last time he'd gone above ground. It made his face a little different from the other trolls, and that had always set him apart. His skin was a strange pale yellow color as well, which many had whispered looked a little too human for their liking. That, along with his advanced age and many wrinkles, led many other trolls to feel uncomfortable around the old man.

Ragnar had never felt the same way. There were still claws on his hands and a ferocity in his eyes that no human could ever match. Birger was far closer to being an animal than any troll ever had any right to be as well. The old man growled regularly and snapped his jaws like he wanted to bite.

As he did now—snapping at Ragnar like interrupting him was the gravest deed.

"I have work to do," Birger said. "We are not meant to see each other for a time yet."

"No, we're not. But I believe you need a helper around here, and I have someone who can help you."

Birger's eyes narrowed. "You're not going to send that human into my garden. She'll trample the garlic and feast upon the carrots long before they're ready."

Ah. So rumors had made it all the way out into the garden. Ragnar crossed his arms over his chest, glaring at the old man. "Who told you about my troll wife?"

"Everyone's talking about her." Birger batted the leaf away from his head and marched down the path away from Ragnar. "You bring too much conflict wherever you go."

"I don't bring conflict anywhere. When was the last time I caused trouble for you?"

A coughed laugh trailed behind the old man. "Always! You brought your old lovers here when you were a youngster. You made the garden quake with fear every time you let out one of those loud moans. The plants still talk about the troll who marched into battle whenever he took a lover."

Now that... that he was rather proud of.

With a wicked grin on his face, Ragnar followed the old man with the plan already falling from his lips. "She has green magic, just like you."

"She doesn't. Everyone says that girl has barely any magic at all. I won't fall for this just because you want to foist her onto someone else. Didn't the king tell you to get rid of her?"

Damn it, the old man was far too smart for his own good. He'd seen right through Ragnar's plan.

He trailed Birger to his cottage. Smoke coiled out of the small stone chimney, and ivy grew on every surface it could cling to. Ragnar remembered being able to see some stone at least, but not a single gray speck was visible beyond the plants now. Even the ancient wooden door was nearly covered as Birger pushed it open and strode into his cottage.

Well, he would not wait for an invitation. The old man needed to listen to him.

Ragnar followed him right into the home uninvited, not caring if he got an earful. But Birger didn't yell at him. Instead, the old man limped over to his chair and sank into the cushion before the fireplace.

The fire blew off a lot of heat, but it was still chilly inside the cottage. Even Ragnar felt the hairs on his arms rise as he strode toward the matching patchwork chair that was right in front of the flames.

He sank down onto it, noting that there was no longer a plush rug beneath his feet. In fact, most of this cottage appeared emptier than he remembered. Even the bed in the corner was smaller, now more like a cot.

"Are you moving?" he asked, frowning as he peered at the other details. There used to be herbs hanging in that corner, drying for the chefs that were dotted around Trollveggen, but now those were gone too.

"No. I'm not moving."

Hadn't there been a painting on that wall? It had been a picture of Birger's late wife and his girls, all of whom were now married and no longer lived with him. "Where are all your things?"

"I'm getting rid of a lot. I can feel my time is coming to an end soon, and I would like the right people to have them."

"Birger. I would tell you if your time was coming soon," Ragnar replied with a chuckle. But just in case, he reached from his chair to put his hand on the old man's.

He'd always been able to feel when a troll's body was starting to fade. If they didn't die in battle, it was rather easy to tell when they were going to leave this realm. Their magic was what kept them alive. Once it began fading in their bodies, they were likely to leave their families soon.

Birger's magic was still strong, still full of power and green magic that tasted like basil the moment Ragnar prodded at it with his own.

The old man was just fine. So at least Ragnar could lean back in his chair with a little more relief.

"I need you to take her on."

"Absolutely not."

"As a favor to me."

"I have no interest in having someone hanging around my garden and touching all my plants. She'll make a mess of the entire garden, and I'm too old to be fixing other people's mistakes."

The old man was right about one thing. He was getting older. Ragnar narrowed his eyes as he tried to figure out the best way to phrase what he needed. "She's rather good at taking care of a home. She'll clean up in here for you."

"I can do that myself. I don't need someone else's troll wife to do that for me."

"She was a gardener in the human realm." Ragnar threw that out there despite knowing it wouldn't convince the old man.

As he suspected, Birger scoffed. "I don't care what she knows. Humans cannot convince anything to grow well. She'll just insult the plants and then they'll spite me by not giving us any food for the year."

Rubbing his chin, Ragnar tried one last time. "She's kind, Birger. I think if there is anyone who can put up with your surliness, it would be her. You could yell and scream and scold her all you want, but she's not going to flinch from any of it. I've never seen a woman more capable of handling anything that I throw at her."

There it was.

The old man stilled, his breathing even stopped as the challenge burned through him. Birger had never met a person he couldn't get to leave the garden. He was famed throughout all of Trollveggen for being an absolute beast of a man, and anyone who stepped foot in the garden left with their ears blistering and their pride bruised.

If there was a single person who wouldn't let him get to them, though, Ragnar was certain it was his Maia. The woman knew how to let words roll right off her. Her father and the other humans had taught her that much.

Hopefully, she could do the same with this ancient troll.

Birger finally looked at him, the calculating expression on his face one of pure glee. "So you say?"

"I've never once been able to make her upset with me." The lie rolled off his tongue with ease. "She doesn't seem to fear our kind at all."

"Bring this human to me, then. I'll remind her that trolls are not something to fear just because of our size."

Ragnar hoped he hadn't just made all of this worse.

Chapter 29

They didn't talk about how Ragnar had killed a group of her people. Maia wasn't sure why a voice inside her head screamed for her to not confront him about what he'd done. Maybe there was some sense of self preservation in there, and the recognition that she wasn't sure she'd be able to deal with it.

She knew what trolls did to the humans they caught. She'd grown up with the stories, and unfortunately, that meant she was now faced with the reality that those stories were very much true. The trolls really did skin people alive. They really made their bodies look like strange omens hanging from the trees. Those weren't rumors—they were true.

It made something in her quiver with fear to face that reality. Her husband, the one she couldn't get away from even if she tried, had participated in those acts.

"Justify it," she muttered to herself as she walked to the garden with Gunnar at her side.

"What did you say?" he asked, though he didn't look at her.

None of them did these days. Ragnar was the only one who could look her in the eye, but he was rarely home. He wouldn't even walk her to the garden, or explain how he had convinced the owner of said garden to let her onto the property. All he'd said was that he was busy. He didn't have time to bring her, but she was going. Whether she wanted to or not.

"I didn't say anything," she replied.

At least Gunnar looked at her then. It was more of a glare, really, but at least he wasn't pretending that she wasn't standing right next to him. "Trolls have good hearing."

"I know."

"Then you know I heard what you said."

"If you heard what I said, then why are you asking what I said?" Maia wrinkled her nose up at him. "It was an internal thought, Gunnar. One that shouldn't have slipped out. Leave me to my thoughts, since you're so determined to pretend I'm not here, anyway."

"I'm just trying to make sure no one attacks us, woman. Good lord, do you always think the worst of people?"

"I don't know. Do you blame me for the attack on your city?"

His expression became grim, and she knew the answer without him saying it. Some part of him blamed her. She could see it clear as day on his face as he turned his features away. He might not have wanted to admit it to her, but there was that ugly underbelly she'd been so good at pretending wasn't here.

Blowing out a long, frustrated breath, she turned her attention back to the path. "I had nothing to do with it, you know."

"You could be a spy."

"Do you really think I'm a spy? You've traveled with me. Talked to me. You've even visited me in Ragnar's home and given me advice. Just how good of a spy do you think I am?"

His gaze narrowed on her, as though he were trying to pick apart her thoughts just by looking at her. "A very good one, if you are a spy."

Maia rolled her eyes, and then nearly stumbled on a stone that had yet to be moved. "Please. I would be a terrible spy, and you know it. Some warrior you are if you can't see that I would crack under pressure."

"I think you're far more talented than you give yourself credit for," he murmured, before pointing to the left. "We're going that way. You're going into the garden and you're going to stay there all day. No other trolls will bother you there."

"Why? Is there some kind of armed guard reminding people to go nowhere near me?" The words were said sarcastically. She wasn't some famous princess who needed an entire armed guard to keep her safe. But Gunnar seemed to take her seriously.

His expression turned grave, almost apologetic. "I'm sorry, Maia. There will be no guards to keep you safe here, and it's a shame that it has come to that for you to feel safe in our kingdom. However, there are very few who dare go into the gardens."

"Why?" Her stomach churned with nerves. Was it dangerous to be in their gardens? What plants should she expect?

"Birger is the worst," Gunnar muttered. "No one likes him, and he makes it very clear that he doesn't like anyone at all. You'll be lucky to leave this place with your pride intact."

What was that supposed to mean? She barely had time to consider Gunnar's words before he planted his hand against her back and pushed her onto a path that led deep into brightly colored plants and toward a light that was brighter than she'd seen thus far being in Trollveggen. It was so close to sunlight that Maia tilted her face back automatically, seeking out the warmth that was not there.

"Good luck," Gunnar said before backing away.

"Why does it seem like you're running?"

"Because I am. I don't want him to see me."

Another voice interrupted them, rough and raspy with age. "Gunnar! Is that you? I have a bone to pick with you, boy. Get your ass over here. The last time you came into my garden, those big feet of yours crushed a turnip!"

She swore Gunnar lost most of the green coloring in his face before he turned and rushed down the path. He was almost running, he moved so fast.

Maia had only a few seconds to whip around and find herself right in front of a very old troll who stood at least three feet taller than she did. He stared down at her, clearly unimpressed by the human who was in his garden. His mouth widened into something like a grimace, and then he snapped his jaws at her, biting the air just like the stray dog that used to live outside of her house. It was a warning, she knew. But she also knew that flinching away from a creature like that only made them believe they were the one in power.

So she stayed still. Looking at him with wide eyes, she took in the strangely yellow skin and the lack of tusks in his mouth. She'd thought perhaps he just had little ones, but on closer inspection, she realized there just weren't any tusks there after all. Maybe he'd lost them.

The troll appeared rather perplexed that she didn't flinch away from him. "You're Maia?"

"I am."

"I have no use for you. You can leave." He turned around, disappearing into the brush.

Taking a deep breath, Maia told herself to be brave. This was her one chance. She understood why Ragnar wanted her to work here. If this surly old man thought she was all right, it was likely other trolls would think the same. She had to win this man over. If she could find her place here in this garden, maybe she could find her place within the greater Trollveggen. And even better to do so while surrounded by plants.

Closing her eyes, she let her mind wander. The scent of earth filled her lungs. Most people didn't realize that dirt actually had a smell to it. They would think it was maybe a little bitter or acrid as it hit their nose, but she knew what the smells meant. The dirt under her feet was full of food for plants as they stretched their roots deep into the ground. They would feast upon all the goodness in the soil, and they would flourish with every ounce of sunlight and magic they were given.

The more she focused on the smell and the feeling of the garden, the more she swore she could sense those roots. Little sparks of bright green magic that dotted all through the ground around her. They called out to her, almost with a sound like laughter. Wiggling underneath her feet like excited little puppies, begging for a pet. They wanted her to notice them, to sprinkle some of her own magic onto their leaves and let them grow a little more.

She'd never been able to feel them like this before. Something happened here in Trollveggen that was so much more than the land above. Her garden had been kind, she knew that. Every single flower had recognized her as she'd walked the paths that she had created herself. But this was different. These plants almost felt like they wanted to know her.

Blinking her eyes open, she shrieked at the sight of a wrinkled, gnarled face far too close to her own. Stumbling backward, Maia cursed and pinwheeled her arms so she stumbled back down the path and not onto the rather impressive row of potatoes that she'd gotten a little too close to. Her foot caught on a root and sent her right down onto her bottom next to an impressive network of mole hills.

"No magic," the troll snarled. "Not with my plants."

"I wasn't using magic!"

"You were. I could feel it. The plants were humming for you and I don't like it." He glared, and then bared his teeth where she could see there were two holes where his tusks should have been. "Get out of my garden before you mess it all up."

"I'm not going to mess it up. And I really wasn't using magic!"

He continued to glare until the expression on his face changed. He went from distrustful and angry to... curious? His brows furrowed and his gaze focused on her right wrist, which had sunk into the soft earth.

Maia looked at what he was staring at and caught sight of a root that had come out of the ground and tangled around her wrist. Then she heard it again. The hum that slowly focused in her mind into something that sounded like laughter. The more she stared at the root, the more she could pull it apart from all the other sounds around her.

The plants were laughing. They were giggling as the root wrapped around her wrist, gently stroking her skin like the plant was petting her.

"How are you doing that?" the troll asked.

"I'm not doing anything," she whispered. "Can I lift my arm? Or will it hurt the plant?"

"That is a wood sorrel, and I'm sure it doesn't appreciate you not calling it by name." He crouched beside her, gently disentangling the roots that were trying to weave through her fingers like the sorrel was holding her hand. "Let go of her, now. You're only going to hurt yourself."

"Sorrel," Maia tried out the name, watching as the roots froze the moment she did so. "That's your name?"

"All plants have names if you listen to what they have to say." He tsked and sank back onto his haunches. "You've done it now. She's never going to let go."

The roots had indeed tightened around her, holding onto her fingers and gripping her with clear excitement. And now that she'd thought of the emotion, she could hear it. The sorrel was babbling about something, but she couldn't understand the words.

Furrowing her brow, Maia shook her head. "I can't understand it."

"You can hear it?"

"There's something there. I could hear laughter when the roots first came out. But now... It's like there are words, but I just can't hear them. They're so muffled."

She looked up at the troll, who wasn't looking at the plant. He was looking at her. His hand sunk into the ground beside hers, his fingers tangled with the roots just as much as her own. And there was something in his gaze that felt like she'd unlocked some part of him.

"I've never met anyone else who could hear them," he murmured.

"There are plenty of trolls with green magic, I would assume."

"There are. Lots of trolls can make plants grow, but none of them can speak to the plants. Why is it that you can?"

This didn't feel right for him to believe. It wasn't the entire truth. "I haven't ever been able to hear them. Not until I came here. Back home, all I can do is make plants grow a little better. I don't know what changed."

His hand tightened on hers. Not painfully, just like he was trying to ease the fear that suddenly made her heart stutter in her chest. "Ah. So that's how it is."

With light movements, he untangled the sorrel from her wrist and then helped her stand. The troll even brushed the dirt off her bottom before standing her up on her own and grabbing onto her shoulders. "You'll help me with the garden, lass. But if you make one mistake or crush one plant, I'm sending you home and you aren't welcome back. Do you hear me?"

"I hear you." Maia's brows furrowed as he turned and started walking away from her. "But... I have questions."

"Walk and talk."

"Right." She hurried to follow him down the path, making sure she stayed on the weaving pattern and didn't step anywhere near the troll's very precious plants. "Everyone is scared of you. Why?"

"I'm not nice."

"But..."

He glared at her over his shoulder before deviating from the path. She could see he knew exactly where to step, like the plants themselves warned him when he got a little too close.

And she supposed maybe she could do that too. All she had to do was listen a little harder.

Picking through the garden, completely avoiding stepping on any of the very important plants, she felt a bit better about herself. The greenery let her know when she was getting too close. Their sing-song voices told her where to place her feet, and where it wouldn't hurt them if she did so. Together, she wandered with the troll into an unkept portion of the garden. This place had no paths, no stones to step on, just a tangle of wilderness in the middle of the most untamed place she'd ever been.

"Do you know something about my magic that I don't?" she finally asked.

"I know nothing about your magic. Magic is hard to know if it's not yours." The troll bent and plucked a small leaf before handing it to her. "What's this?"

"Um." There wasn't anything particularly telling about the leaf. But when she rubbed it between her fingers, the soft texture gave her a small hint. Then there was the smell, like pepper. "Bee balm?"

"Monarda," he corrected, obviously disgusted, before he then added, "But bee balm is another name for it."

And off he went. Continuing through the garden, plucking some part of a plant, handing it to her, and demanding she tell him the name. She did so, over and over again, until he seemed somewhat satisfied with her performance.

"When trolls are joined, when we find our mates, our magic is mingled. You were given that gift by the Blood Witch. A true troll wife can use some of her husband's magic, just as he can use some of hers. That's why you can use this power now. He has strengthened you."

"And that... changed your opinion of me? Somehow?"

He sniffed. "You're not human. You're a troll wife—that much I am certain of. So you can stay."

The plants cheered, the sound of their happiness and mirth filling the clearing. The troll grumbled, heading away from her before he spun around again. He looked at her for a long time before finally saying, "You can call me Birger. But if you mess up my garden, I will throw you out on your ass like all the others."

"Understood."

Birger nodded, and then quietly added, "But I don't think you'll make the mistakes all the others did."

It was a start. This old troll had no idea how much his words soothed the aching hurt in Maia's soul.

Chapter 30

Ragnar couldn't see straight. He was so bleary-eyed from working on potions and elixirs and all the other things that his people needed that he wasn't sure what time of day it was. He'd been working for hours.

Days, really. Days on end where he was barely home and if he was home, he was sleeping. Eating was hard enough. But his people would need more of these healing potions and all the magic he could give them if they were going to fight the humans. The king had decided they would take the fight to Maia's people. If the humans continued to stay on their mountain, then the trolls would force them off of it.

This mountain was theirs. For years, they had allowed the humans to wander over their land. All because they'd known the humans couldn't get into their home. But now they could. Now the humans had proven they knew of at least one entrance, which meant they had been watching the trolls for too long. Now, they had to make sure that the humans couldn't continue to do so.

Sighing, he rubbed his eyes and tried his hardest to keep going. His magic was already depleted, but it had been so for days on end now. All he wanted was to crawl back to his home, get into his bed, and pray his wife turned in her sleep to rest against him.

Those were the best parts of his evening. No matter how hard the day was, at least she leaned against him. At least she sought him out in her sleep for warmth or reassurance or whatever it was. At least he could hold her while she wasn't aware of what she was doing.

Because otherwise, he didn't see his wife. And that drove him mad.

Gunnar strode into the room, carrying another armload of clean bottles that needed to be filled. "When was the last time you saw Maia?"

"I was just thinking the same thing."

His brother grinned and set the box down a little too hard. The sound of rattling glass filled the room. "She's doing well, you know."

"I would prefer to hear that from her lips."

"Too bad you don't talk to her anymore."

Ragnar was going to punch him right in the mouth and make it so that his brother stopped talking about his wife like he knew her better, like Ragnar didn't know what was going on in her life.

Because he didn't. He had been absent for the better part of two weeks now. And he desperately missed her. A human.

Groaning, he dropped his head onto the desk and rested the aching muscles in his neck. "We were getting along so well, too. We'd made progress, brother. Real progress."

"You mean you tasted her pussy, and you'd do anything to get another taste?"

Ragnar heaved a sigh. "Shut up."

"So I'm right."

"Of course you're right. But when would I get a taste when I'm always working and only return in the middle of the night?"

There came the sound of a chair screeching against the floor, and then the wood groaning under the weight of his massive brother. "Interesting. I suppose you could always wake her up."

"That feels less than willing."

"You'd know if she was willing."

Ragnar didn't want her to mistake it for just a dream, though. He wanted her ready and willing and dripping like she had been in the kitchen. Just the thought made every muscle in his body tense and his cock so hard that he thought it might burst.

"You could always go to the brothels. There are plenty of women there who would love to have you back."

But he didn't want to go to the brothel, either, because at some point his mind had shifted to wanting red hair wrapped around his wrist. He wanted to count the freckles on her shoulders and lick at them like they were tiny drops of caramel. He wanted to twist her body into every position he could think of just to see if he could get that sound to come out of her mouth again, like it had the first time he'd made her come.

And then the second.

"Fuck," he muttered. "I have no interest in a moment of release. I want all of this to be over with so I can convince my wife to fuck me."

"You could go right now."

He stared at Gunnar in silence. It wasn't fair of his brother to tempt him like that. He had too many duties, too many things to do right now that would lead his people toward victory. This was his duty to the entirety of troll kind.

And somehow, Gunnar was still staring at him like he was an

idiot.

"Well?" his brother asked.

"You know I can't go anywhere right now. I have too much to do."

"You don't have too much to do that you cannot return home, fuck your wife, and be back in…" Gunnar's lips mashed together. "An hour or two? Three hours, if you don't break her."

"There is much I could do here in three hours." But he wasn't thinking about making potions or grinding up healing herbs. He was thinking about what it would be like if he hooked her knee over his shoulder and drove into her soft, wet heat.

Three hours wasn't enough. He'd need more. There were too many things he wanted to do and so many ways he wanted her to scream. He'd need five hours, and then maybe he would be satisfied enough. At least for a little while.

She'd have to eat, after all.

"I'll cover for you," Gunnar said, grinning far too wide. "You need a break, Ragnar. You need to get all those thoughts out of your head or you're going to make a mistake."

"I don't know if she'll even want me." Or if she was even ready.

But if he spent a few hours making sure she was prepared, she could take him. And damn it, now he was drooling. Wiping at his mouth, he tried to hide the reaction from his brother, who was still grinning from ear to ear.

He had to do something about this reaction. It wasn't natural to feel this way about a woman—that much he knew. Their father certainly hadn't followed their mother around like a panting beast.

"Go on," Gunnar said. "I'll cover for you. And then we can see what to do about the rest of this business."

He didn't need to be told twice. Ragnar stood, heading out the door and up a winding stairwell. The room in the depths of the castle had always been for healing, but it was far away from the entrance. It took some time for him to walk through the crowds of people who were working, all of them finding something to keep them busy at times like these. From the people who kept the castle clean, to the blacksmiths working on weapons, to all the generals who trained their warriors, it was always bustling here.

Ragnar usually enjoyed these crowds. He would take his time walking through them all, ensuring that he said hello to everyone he had healed before. Many of them wanted to speak with him about potions or stiff shoulders. And normally, he wouldn't mind.

But right now? He wanted to get home to his woman so he could focus on them. Their relationship. The taste of her skin and the sound of her pleasure. All the things that he should have been focusing on since the beginning, and yet had been pulled away from multiple times. He just wanted and it was his greatest hope that she wanted the same thing.

He felt lighter than he had in a week. It wasn't just about the sex that he was going to please her with, because he would use one of those recovery half hours to ask her how it had been going in the garden. He'd heard she had managed to tame the impossible troll. Birger didn't hate her. He didn't like her, of course, but he didn't hate her. And that was saying something for the old man.

Every detail of her life was something he wanted to hear about. Did she like the job he'd picked for her? Did she hate it?

If he knew her as well as he believed he'd come to, she'd absolutely love it.

Ragnar inched by a group of new warriors he knew would stop him and ask about their sore muscles, trying to remain out of sight.

They were the first to complain about how they were feeling during training hours. It was always an excuse for them to return home when they were feeling lazy.

The castle doors burst open and a single scout raced in. He was covered in dirt and red mud… although on closer inspection Ragnar realized it was blood. The troll ran through the front rooms of the castle, heading toward the throne without a single word to anyone else.

Ragnar stared at the open door. He could still leave. He could head out into the city and no one would come to get him. If there was something terribly wrong, someone would get sent out to his home and they would interrupt whatever happened there. If he hurried, there might be time for a single taste.

But he could feel the fear and anger that rose in the room at the arrival of the scout. Something was seriously wrong. That man had been sent out for a good reason, and coming back like that? Clearly, the troll had a message that could only be for the king's ears.

"Wasn't that the scout sent to the base of the mountain with the war band?" a troll murmured. "I thought they were supposed to leave and come right back?"

"Damn it," Ragnar hissed, before turning on his heel and heading into the throne room with the other generals.

Too many questions burned in his mind, and none of them were going to get answered if he didn't go into that room. The guilt would hound him until he returned halfway on the journey to his home. So he joined the others standing before the throne, waiting for the scout to give his report.

The young troll was breathing heavily, trying hard to stay conscious while the king stared down at him. Scouts weren't allowed to talk until the king bid them to, and it was obvious this young man wanted to purge everything he had seen.

"Go ahead," the king said, his voice grave.

"The war band reached the edge of the mountain. They put up signs to warn humans that we will hunt them, but it seemed like the humans knew we were coming. An army attacked us almost instantly, and there was more blood than I have ever seen. They had different weapons. Arrows that rained down from the sky. Swords that were sharp enough to pierce our flesh. Many died."

Ragnar's heart twisted in his chest. He didn't enjoy hearing that trolls had died, no more than he enjoyed knowing he hadn't been there to help. The other generals shifted on their feet as well, each of them likely having similar thoughts. They should have been there. If one of them had gone, perhaps this wouldn't have happened.

"Ragnar," the king called out. "Your supplies. Have they been replenished after the cave-in?"

"Only by half, my king."

"We'll likely need all those supplies and more, if I am correct. The humans have been watching us too closely if they were able to guess our next move."

A grumble came from the troll beside him, an elderly man who had been a general for many years. "It's almost as though there is a spy in our midst."

Everyone shifted uncomfortably at the thought. But then they were looking at Ragnar. Like he knew something they didn't, or perhaps, as though he housed someone they could not trust.

He bared his teeth in anger, shaking his head so his tusks glinted in the wisp light. "Don't even say it."

"It's an explanation to a question we have no answer to."

Gunnar walked up beside Ragnar, his arms crossed over his chest.

"I've brought her to the gardens and back every single day. I've seen many humans who lie and cheat and steal. I've been around them my entire life, fighting them, losing to them, and I know a spy when I see one. That woman is no spy. But she is a troll wife, if you were willing to look."

"All humans are the same," another general proclaimed. A few other trolls nodded in agreement, grumbling under their breath about weapons the humans built and the acid they poured on innocent trolls.

He hated hearing it, but now was not the time for any of this argument. More so, it was yet another way for her to show her worth. "My king."

King Egil's eyes narrowed on him, as though he knew what Ragnar was about to ask. "Speak, healer."

"My magic is stronger with the presence of my troll wife. I would like to bring her to heal the wounded warriors. She has use to me, and thus, to the rest of the trolls as well."

Every single person in the room froze. Half of them watched their king with hatred in their hearts, willing him to say that was a boundary no one could cross. The other half perhaps knew the meaning of what Ragnar asked.

Let her prove herself again. Let her heal the trolls, the people who had taken her in. Even if they wouldn't entirely trust her after that, they would at the very least know that she wasn't the spy they thought she was.

After giving it some thought, the king nodded. "You may bring her. Gather your supplies, now, healer. Save all those you can and bring them back to Trollveggen."

Ragnar turned swiftly, rushing back to the room where he would gather his supplies. Gunnar and three other trolls went with him, knowing they would be useful in carrying all the supplies that were necessary.

Gunnar stopped him at the door. "Go get her, Ragnar."

"I need to tell you what to bring."

"We know the potions. You've used them on all of us before. Get her here safely and keep an eye on those other generals. Not everyone thinks highly of Birger's opinion, Ragnar."

He nodded, fear already spiking through him. It might not have been the best choice to bring her, but at the very least, they had to try. He wouldn't keep her in the dark forever, no matter what the others said.

Chapter 31

"Don't plant that there," Maia grumbled, trying to grab the herb out of Birger's hand. It was a very delicate breed of parsley that somehow didn't mind growing underground, and the damn thing was the only plant giving the food flavor down here. She would not allow him to plant it anywhere that would risk its life.

"This is where it goes."

"Maybe so, but it doesn't want to go there."

Birger lifted it over her head, far out of her reach, but she still jumped trying to get to it. Maybe if she stretched just a little higher, she could grab it out of his hands and take off with the poor thing. The longer she was in the garden, the more she'd learned to listen to the plants talking. Birger was a good teacher when it came to using her magic, but he was terrible when it came to listening to the plants.

"Why doesn't it want to go there?" he challenged. "This is a good place for parsley. The wisps gather here more than anywhere else. The soil is good. There's nothing wrong with this spot. You're just giving in to a picky plant. You can't do that so much when they don't know where they need to go."

"They know exactly where the best place for them is," she grunted. "This soil is too acidic!"

"It'll do just fine here. It just has preferences like you do. If you let them all tell you where they want to be planted, they'll be clustered around each other and none of them will grow." Birger gave her a glare. "You're letting the magic make choices for you."

"No, I'm listening to them, which you are not very good at. Give it here."

He grunted, then gave her his back as he planted the parsley where he had originally wanted to. "And here I was thinking that human women were meek. You're worse than the squirrels up there. Always nattering about nothing."

Her heart skipped a beat. Maia hadn't ever been told that she talked too much. She was always the quiet girl in the corner, praying no one would look at her, and when they did, she would hop to do whatever they wanted. Knowing that here she was more than that? It filled a hollow deep inside of her that had wanted to be the opinionated woman who lived in her head.

Biting her lips, she grinned as she returned to her plot of the garden, pausing only when a shadow fell across her neat row of holes that were ready for more plants to sink their roots into the soft earth.

Looking up, her lips parted in surprise. "Ragnar?"

"We're needed." He stared down at her with troubled eyes, and she could sense something had happened.

She hadn't felt another earthquake, though. Were her people attacking right now? Maia didn't know if she wanted to be in the middle of a battle between the trolls and the humans, especially not when it was so easy for someone like her to get lost in the midst.

He grabbed her arm, hauling her up to her feet and nodding at Birger. The other troll said nothing as he watched them leave, but anxiety churned more and more in her belly as Ragnar drew her away from the garden. He wasn't leading her toward home, though. He was leading her into the forest.

Were they leaving?

"Ragnar?" she asked, breathless already as she tried to keep up. "Where are we going?"

He didn't reply. Not until they were so far into the strangely colored forest that she knew she wouldn't have been able to get back if she tried. There were no footprints to follow, and certainly no path. He'd walked between the trees like he knew them by heart, and perhaps he did.

But finally he stopped, whirling on her and stalking back in her direction. She stumbled away, slamming her back into a tree as he loomed above her.

"Ragnar?" she tried again.

She couldn't read that expression on his face. He looked angry, and normally she knew why he was. But he'd taken her out of the garden, hurried her away from Birger and the job he'd given her, only to bring them right into the middle of the woods where no one would find them.

Maia watched with wide eyes as he sank to his knees before her. He was breathing hard, but she didn't think it was because he was tired. Instead, his gaze slid down her neck, her chest, to the core between her legs that instantly burned with desire. The feeling of his gaze was like a physical caress long before he actually touched her, those claws gliding up her thighs, catching on the fabric of her skirt and drawing it up.

"Wife," he said, his voice a low guttural groan. "I have need of you."

Her breath caught. "You do?"

"I don't know if we'll return alive from where I need to bring you, so I wish to taste you one more time." And then he leaned closer, pressing his nose against her lower belly, breathing in deeply. "I wish to do more than that if you'll allow it."

If she would...

Oh.

Oh.

She could make him wait, but she didn't want to. She'd been burning for him for so long, and even if it was wrong, she wanted this troll. Maia wanted to feel him between her thighs, to hold on to that broad, strong back and cry out with pleasure like he'd made her do already. She wanted to hear his moans of desire and know what it was like when he seated himself fully in her.

Even if that was terrifying. Even if she had questions whether or not they would fit. She wanted to try.

Tangling her fingers in his hair, she gave the locks a tug. "Consume me, husband."

It was like she had unleashed an attack dog. Suddenly, he was everywhere. His fingers pinched her hardened nipples through her dress, creating a friction that was equally wonderful and maddening. He surged toward her, his tusks scraping up her chest to her neck, where he growled into her ear. The hard bar of his cock pressed against her lower belly, and she was so disoriented she didn't even think about the size of it.

His mouth opened, teeth clamping down on her neck in a claiming bite that had her squirming. She couldn't move, not even if she wanted to. There was so much control in those jaws. He told her without words to stop moving as he reached between her skirts and moved them out of the way. Those long, blunt fingers found the core of her, sliding through her folds with ease.

Cool air joined his fingers, brushing between her thighs and making her see stars. She blinked her eyes open, not sure when she'd closed them, only to see the monster of him right before her. Heaving chest, massive muscles bared and ready for war, mountains of flesh that were all hers for the taking. She spread her fingers wide across his chest, trying to feel as much of him as she could.

He released his hold on her throat with a deep groan before grabbing her waist and heaving her up. The dress protected her from the tree's rough bark, but now she was even higher. She wouldn't be able to stand if he put her down, but perhaps that was the point. Ragnar hooked her legs around his shoulders, and then he was between her legs again, his head buried beneath her skirts, and then there was his tongue.

That broad, flat tongue plunged into her softness. He licked and sucked, teasing her with the flat of it. He knew what she liked already. He knew how to torment her, how to make her buck against his mouth like a wanton creature. She lost herself in the warmth of him. The heat of his tongue, the way he seemed to salivate at the taste of her. Her own wetness slid down her thighs, and she squeezed his shoulders to keep the feeling of him just a little longer.

He turned his head, biting her thigh hard enough to make her squeal before he plunged two fingers inside her.

"There's not as much time as I'd like," he said against her thigh. "I would've been gentler with you. Stretched you. Made sure you were ready for me."

"I am," she whimpered, even though she wasn't entirely sure what she was agreeing to. "I want you, Ragnar."

She'd never felt so empty in her life. Clenching around his fingers, she needed more than just those. Even as he plunged them in and out of her, even though he curled them in on that spot that made her see stars, it wasn't enough.

She wanted him rutting against her, grunting and groaning with her. She wanted to be pressed against this tree, incapable of even forming words.

"Come first, fire hair," he said, and then his tongue joined in with his fingers. Flicking and sucking and circling her clit until she didn't know which to focus on—his fingers, his tongue, or the rough sounds he made as though he were a starving man at a feast.

She splintered, shattering apart and tightening around his fingers so much that he froze inside of her. And that sound he made added to the burning pleasure, a deep groan that came from his chest at the feeling of her coming around him.

He stood, moving her body like she weighed absolutely nothing. He had her pinned to the tree so easily with just a single hand, and with the other, he freed his cock.

She'd only seen it out of the corner of her eye in the bathwater. But now, with that massive beast between her thighs, she felt the slightest bit of nerves. It really was massive. A gigantic cock that his hands somehow made look manageable, with a broad head and a darker purple than the rest of his skin. And then there was all that glinting metal that caught her attention.

He thumbed the scorching head of himself, one clawed finger smoothing over a pearlescent drop. Eight bars pierced through the underside of it. Sixteen circular beads that gave the entire beast an entirely different appearance than she was used to. Would those ridges hurt? She reached between them, trailing her fingers gently along each piercing to get used to them.

"They'll feel good," he promised, his voice a rasp. "I'll make you feel good."

She had no doubt of that, but she wondered if she'd be able to walk after.

Staring down her own body, she watched as he rubbed that massive head against her pussy. It was so hot. Blunt and swollen, appearing between her thighs as he thrust against her a little harder. Another drop of come appeared on the top, disappearing as he slid it between her folds and something about that made her moan.

She slammed her head back against the tree, shutting her eyes as the sensations danced over her. He notched himself against her, pushing just the slightest. It seemed like he was waiting for something. For her.

But words had long ago failed her. She had no idea how to tell him to keep going, that if he didn't, she feared she would die.

So she rocked her hips, lifting them, rising so it was easier for him to wedge himself inside her, and pushed down.

The burn.

The stretch.

The ache of just the head of him pushing into her body was a stark contrast to the clenching emptiness in the rest of her. Some part of her wanted him to slam inside her, to get it over with and plunge so deeply that she wouldn't know where she started and where he ended.

But then he pulled out again, and that emptiness was almost unbearable.

She whimpered, her eyes flicking back open to see him staring down at where they were just joined. Again he pushed, sliding into her just a little farther than the first time. The first bar touched her outer lips, pressing and then sliding into her.

Maia's eyes rolled back in her head. "Oh my god."

"Easy, fire hair. You're doing so well."

He pulled out again, all the way, leaving her bereft until he moved again.

This time she could feel herself stretching, aching, accommodating the massive length that slid two bars deep into her body. Out again. Three bars.

Her entire existence zeroed into counting how many of those bars had fit inside of her. To the slick glide of him entering and exiting. To her body warping, changing, demanding that she take more of him, no matter how overwhelming it felt. No matter how much more there was. She could count to eight. She could make eight work.

But then he stopped six bars deep, sunk so far inside her that she'd forgotten how to breathe. He hadn't, though. He leaned forward and pressed their foreheads together, breathing with her as he held himself in place. "That's as much as you can take, fire hair."

"More," she whimpered, grabbing onto his back and trying to convince him to go farther. The bite of pain was something she enjoyed. It felt good, beyond good, like he had reached into her soul and stolen it.

His big hand smoothed down her hair, stopping at the back of her neck where he drew her forward for a soul stealing kiss. "No more today. Someday, you'll take more. But today, that's all you get."

And then he drew back out and slammed back in.

She ceased to be. Even if that was all the cock she got, it was more than enough. He was so big, and she was so fucking full. So stuffed with every thrust in and out, pleasure and pain mingled together.

The thrusts only grew faster, stronger, so much so that she started moaning things that might have made no sense: *desire, need, please don't stop*. Words that came from deep inside of her and she didn't know where they came from.

"That's it," he growled. "Tell me what you want, Maia."

"I want to come," she groaned.

"You can do better than that."

And there it was. That wanton, wild creature she never would've believed lived inside of her. That woman grew claws and dug them into her very being. "I want to come around your fat cock, Ragnar. Please, please make me come."

The sound of his pleasure at her words was almost enough to send her tumbling over that edge. The animalistic growl that echoed against her neck made everything in her tighten, tense. And then he was reaching between them. His thumb pressed against her oversensitive clit, rubbing in a circle just like she liked.

She tightened even more, impossibly more. His thrusts stuttered, forced to no longer pound inside of her because he couldn't move, not with her clenched like that.

What was happening to her? She could feel the orgasm building and building, but why wasn't it shattering? She'd go mad if it didn't. Her fingers moved down her body as well, pausing at her belly. She could feel him moving inside her, stretching her. Looking down at her stomach, she watched the bulge of him warping her skin, sliding inside her, out, because she'd stretched to take him that much.

It all shattered. Everything inside of her burst into an orgasm that was so much more than just coming. It unmade her, ruined her for anyone else other than the troll, who froze inside of her as well.

There it was. The groan that she'd wanted to hear. As she clenched and shuddered around him, he poured himself into her as his cock swelled even larger.

Sweaty, clinging to him with every ounce of her last bit of strength, she desperately tried to pull herself together. Even as he slid out of her, every single one of those bars making her sensitive body quake even more. Even as a gush of liquid slid down her thighs that were so weak she couldn't have stood on her own.

If she'd known this was what it was like to be a troll wife, she would have agreed to do it a long time ago.

Chapter 32

Ragnar carried her to a stream where he helped clean her up. She would obviously be a little worn out after that, but he feared he had been too rough. With careful hands, he made sure to hold the cold water between her legs for as long as she would let him, before she laughed and batted his hands away.

This was new to him, though. He wasn't sure how to…be together. He wasn't sure how to do any of this now that they'd done… all that.

His mind had fractured the moment he'd felt the warmth of her surrounding him. She had been so tight, so slick, so ready for him, even though he had worried. And when he'd felt the sensation of sliding into her with those bars on his cock?

Nothing would ever be the same again. He would never survive another coupling like that, because he was certain his heart would burst. But he also wouldn't survive not doing it again. Even now, looking at her splashing through a stream of icy water, he wanted her again. More. Longer. Deeper.

She'd taken six bars, though, and he was shocked at that. She was so small compared to him, and yet she'd taken so much of him on the first try.

He'd have to research if there was a way to make it easier for her. Perhaps there was an herb to take, or a drink Ragnar could make her, something that would make it easier for her body to accept him.

Because even now, even while she was far from him, he could feel the pain in her. His magic rose to the surface of his skin, reaching for her even though she was insistent that she could wash herself. There was something off. Something...

She moved her skirts just enough for him to see a flash of pale skin and bright blood smeared between her thighs.

"You're hurt," he said, splashing through the stream to get to her side.

"I feel fine," she replied with a short laugh. But then he saw her hesitate when she noticed the blood. "Oh, well, that's... You're rather large."

"You shouldn't bleed after sex," he snarled. Ragnar scooped her out of the water and walked with her to the stones on the other side. "It's not natural to do so. If I hurt you, you're supposed to tell me."

"You didn't hurt me."

"I thought we had gotten over this. I am not owed your silence or your suffering. You argue with me, tell me what to do. If you are injured, you tell me. These are things we've already had conversations about." He set her down on the stones and then cupped her mound. "Now stop talking and let me heal you."

"I don't need healing!"

But she stopped talking, and let his magic do the trick. Her wounds were entirely superficial, he realized as soon as his magic was able to crawl through her body. None of it was life threatening, and he certainly hadn't hurt her enough that she wouldn't be able to walk. Still, blood after sex terrified him. He didn't want to cause her injury. In the heat of passion, he'd forgotten all the things that he had to keep in mind. She was small, her skin was easy to break, he could bruise her if he wasn't careful.

Maia cupped his jaw with both of her hands, pulling him forward to kiss just underneath each of his eyes. "Do you feel better now?"

"I do."

"It was nothing, wasn't it?"

"Not nothing. But you would've survived." And he shouldn't have used his magic when there were people who needed it more. Sighing, he drew her tighter into his arms and hugged her fiercely. "We have to go."

"Where are we going?"

"There was another attack at the base of the mountain. A war band was sent there to warn the humans that the mountain is now off limits to your kind, and that we'll kill any human who steps foot onto our home. The fight did not go well for either side."

He had thought she would flinch. Perhaps she would admit to being nervous and not wanting to go. But she didn't. His brave little wife straightened her shoulders and gave him a quick nod.

"Let's go, then."

"It will be a long journey."

"Just let me hold on to your back rather than tossing me over your shoulder, and I'll be fine."

They shared a small smile with each other, perhaps both of them thinking about the many times she'd vomited when they'd first met, before he turned and offered her his back. Maia clambered on, and then they were off.

He took one of the lesser known entrances to the mountain, risking that the humans hadn't found it just yet. But it was a tighter opening, and fewer people could get through it while walking beside each other. Ragnar was just able to fit through the passage with her on his back, and then they were out into the sun. He didn't pause to let his eyes adjust, he just powered forward. Lunging into the bright light and trusting his body would carry him where they needed to go.

Then there was only the sun and the wind. Blasting, cold air that scraped at his cheeks and stole the breath from his lungs. Air that reminded him they were very close to winter. That if they weren't careful, they would get stuck in a snow squall and it would be very difficult to come home.

Soon, the humans wouldn't be able to reach the mountain, anyway. Winter would protect the trolls from whatever else her people had planned.

It took them half a day to reach the others, although Ragnar was certain that was partially because they could move so quickly. He didn't have large packs to carry or equipment to bring. There were few weapons on his body, and only the lightest of humans clinging to his back.

The closer they got, the more he felt like he had to warn her about what she was going to see. "Humans are not kind to trolls when they fight," he reminded her. "The weapons your people have devised leave wounds that are hard to look upon."

"I understand, Ragnar."

"And I don't know what bodies we'll find left behind." He cleared his throat. "The bodies of your people."

"I also knew that was likely."

He just hoped there weren't bodies already flayed and in the trees.

The last thing Maia needed to see was her people like that, while he was asking her to heal the trolls who had done such terrible things. He had done them as well, but now it felt wrong. Or perhaps the act didn't hold quite as much justice as it used to.

They headed toward a group of trolls, all standing watch. They gave him small nods, but he could see their wary glances toward the woman on his back. Even now, they were afraid of what she could do, of what she might do.

He helped Maia off his back and steadied her when she landed on the ground. She was still a little weak-kneed from what they'd done in the forest, and likely from being carried such a far way. He couldn't blame her.

But as the trolls stared at her with mistrust and no small amount of fear, she walked through them without looking back. Ragnar was struck with how terrified she must have been when he'd first taken her from her home, how hard it must have been for her to be surrounded by trolls and not wonder how they were going to kill her.

And somehow, still, she had kept going. She had learned to argue with him. She'd thrown herself into working on whatever he'd given her, and even then, she'd somehow asked for more. Never once had she complained about the different clothing, food, or even the lack of light. Instead, she had wholeheartedly decided to make the best of what she had been given.

Even now, when his people thought she was little more than a monster herself, Maia stood with him. Ready to do whatever it took to save the very people who had rescinded the trust they'd given her.

His heart flipped in his chest, squeezing painfully as she looked up at him and asked, "Who do we start with?"

Swallowing hard around the sudden emotions and lump in his

throat, he replied, "We find Gunnar. He went ahead of us, and he'll have gathered those who need the most help."

"Then that's where we go." She reached for his hand, lacing their fingers together, and then they were off.

Gunnar had indeed already set up a tent where those who were the most injured were resting. And there were quite a few injuries. The majority of wounds seemed to be burns. The few trolls who were talking around them were already speaking of the fire the humans had unleashed. Great swaths of it had cut through the battlefield, making it almost impossible for the trolls to even get close to the soldiers they'd needed to attack.

Ragnar went into the tent of burn victims, and the chorus of groans that erupted at the sight of him reminded him just how much he was needed. He walked to the corner where all the healing potions had been set. He'd need to keep their use as sparse as possible, because he was quite certain these weren't the only injured warriors.

Gunnar brushed aside the tent flap and came in with them. It didn't escape Ragnar's notice that his brother wore significantly more weapons than he should have needed.

"Tell me," Ragnar grunted as he carried the jars of potions over to the burn victims. He handed one of the jars to Maia. "Put this on their burns. Lightly—we need to make it go far. You should be able to see it work quickly. Then wrap the wounds with the gauze on the table behind you. Understand?"

"Well enough. I don't think I can hurt them any worse than they already are," she replied, before turning to do the job.

Ragnar turned his attention to Gunnar, who was already shifting back and forth on his feet. His brother only moved like that when he wanted to fight, which meant there was a battle to be had.

"The humans aren't gone," Gunnar finally said. "They've regrouped at a village nearby, but they're already preparing more weapons. Our scouts have seen them making the same substance that caused all of this."

"The king said not to engage unless they were on the mountain, didn't he?"

"We can't just let them come back. We can bring the fight to them before they're able to make more of that fire. If they do and follow us up the mountain, then we can do very little to stop them." Gunnar ran his hand through the long locks of his hair, some of it getting stuck in the piercings in his ears. "I don't know the right thing to do here. Do we bring the fight to them and prevent more injuries, or do we listen to what our king has ordered us to do?"

Ragnar didn't know what to tell him. He wasn't the warlord here. He was a healer, and the magic inside of him was already blistering. It wanted to heal the people around him, and it wanted to shove aside anyone who distracted him from doing that. The thought of what might happen if the trolls attacked the humans? If he was being honest with himself, he would rather wait and see what other weapons the humans had created. His magic wanted more people to heal, and the only way to get that was to see more people injured.

But that was why he had never become a warlord. He could make choices that were a detriment to the well-being of other trolls. Such was the downside to hungry magic that just wanted to be used.

"You'll make the right choice," Ragnar finally said, clapping his hand to Gunnar's shoulder. "Let me heal these warriors first, though. If you're going to attack that village, you need all the help you can get."

Then he turned to help Maia. Together, they healed the trolls who were in so much pain.

And throughout it all, he watched her. Because he could heal a troll in his sleep, but he'd never expected someone with no healing background to do what she did. She was a natural. Where he usually grunted and healed them however he wished, she was the first person to reach for their hands. She held them through the pain of healing, whispering words of encouragement and telling them that they were doing very well.

She asked their first patient where he was from. The question startled the male out of the pain, and he stammered as he told her about his wife and children who were waiting for him back home. When he panicked, fearing that he wouldn't ever get to see them again, she smiled at him and reassured him that he would be fine.

"Tell me about your troll wife," she said.

His eyes had teared up at the question, and Ragnar was certain they were going to have a difficult patient. But they didn't.

Because Maia then said, "I need all the advice I can get. I'm sure you've heard I'm not very good at being one."

The patient had chuckled while Ragnar set in on healing him, using some of Maia's green magic threaded with his own to make the potion go even farther than it had before. Her fingers curled around his, her magic convincing the marigold to grow and spread through the man's body, healing faster than before.

And that was how it was with every patient they saw. She reassured them, quietly gave them even more strength while he made sure that they were healed. As each of those warriors fell asleep, she tucked them in. There were blankets at the foot of the cots they all lay on. Blankets he hadn't ever seen a troll use because he usually moved on to the next person who needed to be healed. But she took the time to make sure they were warm before she joined him at the next.

When they were getting close to the end of the first tent, Maia's fingers caught his just before he touched the next patient. This woman was already exhausted and asleep, but there were still burns to be healed.

"Ragnar," she said quietly. "Can we try to speak with the village first? Instead of going in and razing it to the ground without giving them a chance, can we maybe talk to them? Perhaps they will be understanding."

"They have never listened to trolls."

"What if I'm there?"

An inner voice screamed in his mind. No. No, he could not allow that. He wouldn't put her in harm's way because she wished to see her people in a better light. He knew what they would do. The humans wouldn't care that she was one of their own. They would see her as a threat.

But he could see a spark of bravery in her. That spark was one he so adored, and one he wanted to cultivate. Because she deserved to be brave. She deserved to try.

"I'll speak with Gunnar," he said quietly. "I'll do my best."

Chapter 33

"This is a stupid idea," Gunnar grumbled beside her.

On Maia's other side, Ragnar seemed to agree with his brother. Both of the trolls were on edge, and she didn't know what to say to calm them down. In truth, she wasn't feeling great about this plan herself.

But some part of her needed proof. She'd seen what humans did to the trolls, and while she hadn't seen what the trolls did in response, she knew damn well they weren't innocent. Maia needed to see how the humans of this town would react when they were faced with what they had done. Perhaps it was naïve of her to hold out hope that her people would make the right choice. But she really needed to give them the chance to not disappoint her.

One last chance. One last hope that maybe, though the kings didn't agree, that the people of this kingdom could provide some peace for themselves.

They walked toward the village. Each troll near her was armed to the teeth. Ragnar even had knives in his hair, twisted in the tall peak of the braid that fell down the center of his head. Not to mention the knives strapped to his arms and thighs, the sword at his hips, and the shorter blade on the other side. There were so many weapons on each of these trolls that it was clear they were a threat.

And yet, they were not running toward the village. They were not letting out those whooping calls that usually warned humans that trolls were attacking. The war band was calm and quiet as they walked toward the village.

A tall wooden barrier circled the town. It was crudely built—just logs that had been stood on their end and driven into the ground. The uneven heights made it seem like there were fingers surrounding the village, waiting to clamp down on the people within.

A small gap, just large enough for six men to walk through side by side, was the entrance to the town. At least there was no way for the human soldiers to be above them, because there hadn't been a second level of this wall built.

As it was, she could see there were countless soldiers on the other side of the gap. They all waited, their swords gleaming in the sunlight, ready to start yet another battle that many of them wouldn't come back from.

Gunnar shook his head. "And a fight it is."

"You don't know that yet," Maia desperately replied. "You haven't even tried to talk to them."

"They don't want to talk, fire hair."

Ragnar put his hand on her shoulder, forcing her to slow down so they were near the back of the war band. "You will stay hidden if a fight starts. I don't want you getting involved."

"I didn't plan on it. I have no idea how to fight."

"Good. Don't let them touch you."

He leaned down and pressed a kiss to her forehead before turning his attention to the head of the group. Already, a few people from the town were coming out of the safety there—two men and a woman.

The first man who led the way seemed to be the leader of the soldiers. He wore gleaming armor that was expertly molded to his body, the joints moving soundlessly as he walked. This was not a man who had grown up on the outskirts of this village. Maia had only seen armor like that closer to the city, and within the castle itself. The swagger in his step also betrayed a confidence that didn't come from a place like this.

The man and woman behind him were hesitant in their movements. Their clothing, while still nice, wasn't anywhere near the quality of the other man's armor. And they held each other's hands in a grip that was so tight she could see their white knuckles even from the distance where she stood.

"Trolls!" the man in armor called out. "This is a first. I've never seen your kind try to barter before. Have you finally learned how to speak?"

A chuckle erupted from within the village. She could only imagine those were the soldiers just waiting to pour out of the false safety behind the tree trunks.

Gunnar walked to the head of the group, pushing some of the trolls aside to be the first to speak. "We've come to warn you that the mountain is off limits. Any human who steps foot on our land will be killed. We're taking our home back."

"And just how are you going to do so? We have more soldiers than you do, and that mountain belongs to our king."

"Your king has no claim to our homeland." Gunnar placed a hand on the sword at his hip. "There doesn't need to be any more bloodshed today. We understand that you have willingly fought with our people, and that you desire to see more of us dead. But I can promise you will suffer far graver losses."

"With our new weapons, I think you'll find the battle will end in ways you could never have imagined." The soldier grinned, and an icy chill went down her spine.

Maia had met men like this before. They'd come in to speak with her father, but never about flowers. They dealt in information. Control was their drug, and any instance where they could exert control over others was where they thrived.

This soldier wanted the trolls to attack. He wanted another reason to fight them, because he had some trick up his sleeve.

The trolls surrounding her shifted. She could feel the nerves suddenly rippling through them, like the man's words were a wave that crested and swelled throughout their numbers. They knew, she realized. They knew there was something wrong, and they still came here. With the intent that they would give the humans a chance.

Perhaps she wasn't the only fool who'd hoped for too much.

Gunnar didn't let it show that he was nervous, though. Even back here, she could see the flash of his grin as he lifted his hands from his sides. "We're here to talk, and that's all. We don't want to kill any more of you."

"Is that so, troll?"

"The rest of your people are lying out there in the woods. We could hear them groaning as we healed our own. You didn't kill more than three trolls. How many of your men did you lose, soldier?"

Then, slowly, blatantly, Gunnar wrapped his fingers around the pommel of his sword.

She could see how much that affected the man. Even the one behind him flinched and shoved his wife toward the trolls on instinct. Perhaps in an offering, or perhaps to try to save himself first. The woman staggered, then fell onto her hands and knees.

And that one little movement sent the entirety of the trolls into a frenzy. Everyone around her started drooling and growling. The sounds of their anger rose into the air, filling the space around her with so much rage and tension that it made her heart race.

The soldier laughed. "You don't want to fight? You've got a pack of slavering animals at your back!"

"We don't treat women like that," Gunnar said.

"I've seen you kill women and children before."

"On accident," Gunnar spat. "We have no fight with those who cannot lift a sword against us."

They were not willingly kind to human women, Maia knew that. But she had never seen them blatantly want to harm someone, like what had happened just now. No troll would have shoved a woman to the ground, and certainly not one of their own.

Gunnar stepped toward the woman, keeping his hands raised so no one tried to attack him. And then he reached his hand down for her. What an image he made. A massive troll, skin green as the grass surrounding them and his hand the size of the woman's head, reaching out to help her.

But then the woman stood so quickly that she was almost a blur. Ragnar grabbed Maia and spun so he protected her with his body, but not before Maia saw a dart from the woman's hand catch Gunnar in the chest. He took a step back, his hand over his ribs where the weapon had sunk. And when he drew his hand away, it was coated in blood.

There were no choices after that. Not for any of them. In one rushing movement, the trolls rushed forward. Maia's hair blew in front of her face at the speed of their storming rage. She stood still in the center of all that anger, watching as the humans ran back toward their home. Soldiers stood in front of the trolls, but it didn't matter. They would go through the wall of those men like they were paper.

Ragnar cupped her cheek in his hand, a sturdy rock in the madness of all that anger. "I must avenge my brother," he said, his gaze searching hers.

And Maia knew he was waiting for her to bid him to go. He wanted her permission. If she said no, he would get her out of here and allow the other trolls to fight.

But this was his fight, too.

"Go," she whispered. "I'll be safe."

He kissed her fiercely before turning and leaping into the fray. She was left alone as an empty vessel, as the trolls took all her rage with them. They rushed into a battle she could not join, so she sent her own aching pain with them.

Maia had never wished for blood in her life. She'd never wanted to hurt someone else just because she was angry. She'd done everything she could to give them a chance. The humans weren't supposed to prove her right. They were supposed to prove that they were reasonable, and that it was just the crown who wanted the trolls dead. People on the outskirts of the kingdom could use their own common sense and know that a deal with the trolls was beneficial. But now she wondered if she'd ever been this angry in her entire life.

Finally, her feet moved. She raced across the grass toward Gunnar, who was still standing where he had been moments before. The air filled with the sound of battle. Shouts, clanging metal, screams of pain.

But none of that mattered as panic filled her veins. He was so pale. The moment she touched her hand to his shoulder, he staggered.

"Gunnar," she said, grabbing onto his arm and trying to tug him in the opposite direction. "Come with me."

"Where is Ragnar?"

She could just barely make out her husband. He was a purple blur tearing through the ranks of humans as they stood in front of him, slowly but surely carving a path into the village. "Fighting."

"Good," Gunnar wheezed. "Good, he should be fighting. Take the knife from my thigh."

"What?"

"Take the knife." His weight listed to the side, and there was nothing she could do to stop him from toppling over.

Lunging for the knife at his thigh, she grabbed it and then held it up for him to see. "What now?"

He wasn't breathing right. The air exiting his lungs rattled and wheezed in an unnatural sound. But he still rasped, "Now run, fire hair."

Run? Why would she run?

She waited just a little too long. Hands grabbed her by the hair, hoisting her up by the long strands. Kicking out her feet, she tried to cut the grip that made her scalp scream in pain. She must have caught something with the knife, because an angry curse echoed right next to her ear before she was thrown onto the ground.

Maia just barely moved the knife out of the way before she impaled herself on it. But that meant she landed hard on the ground, knocking the wind from her lungs. She couldn't stay still. She had to crawl away, if that was what it took.

Dragging herself with her forearms, she tried to get the air back into her lungs while she moved. She had just barely wheezed in a breath before a boot caught her in the ribs, flipping her over. Everything in her screamed in pain, unlike anything she'd felt before. But then she focused on the man standing over her, and adrenaline flooded through her.

A soldier. Someone who might have once been familiar. He looked like so many of the men she had known in her life. Sandy brown hair, streaked with lighter colors from years of being in the sun. Sunburnt skin across his nose and dark brown eyes that were almost handsome. A square jaw that she would have once thought was appealing, and it certainly would have made her blush if he had flirted with her.

But now? Now he was glaring at her like she was the most disgusting thing he'd ever seen in his life.

"Troll whore," he snapped, then spit onto her chest.

What did he just call her?

He pulled the sword out from his belt, and she didn't have time to think. Maia let out a startled shriek that made him freeze for the barest of moments before she sank the knife into his thigh. She didn't know if she'd gotten him good, or if she'd even hit something important. All she knew was that she wasn't going to die at the hands of this man.

"You bitch!" he screamed, grabbing for the knife and ripping it out of his leg.

But that was just enough time for her to roll and get up onto her feet. She ran. The skirts around her legs were cut on the edges, so she could run faster than she would have in her older clothing. Her breath sawed in her lungs, her heart thundering in her chest.

Troll whore.

He'd called her a whore, and she wasn't that. She was a troll wife and how dare he call her anything else?

With that fueling her, she ran faster than she ever had in her life. And still, it wasn't enough.

The man tackled her from behind. The air flooded out of her lungs for a second time, and now she saw stars. Little specks made it hard for her to focus on fighting when she wasn't even sure she could stay conscious. If she passed out now, though, she didn't know what he would do to her. Already he was wrestling her body, flipping her onto her back. Straddling her with his legs on either side of hers, she didn't have to guess what he might do.

These men all wanted the same thing. Control. She'd seen it countless times when she was under her father's roof. He'd protected her then, saying he wanted a daughter as pristine as the first snow. But the expressions on the faces of those men had been the same as the one above her now.

They all wanted to feel powerful, even for a few moments.

"Oh, don't give me that look," he hissed as he reached for his belt. "You're a troll whore. You can take me just fine."

A glint of metal appeared in the center of his throat. He looked a little shocked by that, even reaching up to touch the sharp tip of the blade that had pierced through him. A bead of ruby red blood rolled down the strong muscles of his neck, disappearing into the armor beneath.

And then more of that red blood, trickling up into his mouth as he made a choked sound. He was thrust away from her, his body forcibly lifted by the tip of the sword in his throat. She watched as the weight of his body warped the wound, stretching the wound in a wide open maw as the sword slid out and his body dropped onto the ground, before her eyes were drawn to the troll standing above her.

Ragnar stared down at her, his chest heaving with breath and slick with sweat. There was blood splattered all over his body, along with dirt and smears of things she didn't want to acknowledge.

"Troll wife," he said. "Are you well?"

No. She wasn't sure what had just happened, but she wasn't well. She didn't know if she would ever be well again.

But she cleared her throat and replied, "I'm alive."

The corner of his lip twitched above his tusk, his expression nearing a snarl. "I should have made him suffer longer than he did."

"I wouldn't have minded."

His gaze flicked to the man still drowning in his own blood, before he spat onto the man's body. The wad of spit stood out on the gleaming armor, now dripping with blood. "Or perhaps I should have let you live, soldier. I would have sent you back to your people missing all of your limbs, so that you could tell them what would happen if any of your people touch my wife again."

He lifted his sword into the air and she turned her gaze away as Ragnar hacked into the body. The sounds were enough. But soon there was no more noise, only her husband as he gathered her up to his chest and disappeared with her into the forest.

She clung to him, holding onto his form as tightly as she could. Dark shadows moved through the trees with them. Trolls who ran through the woods like they were part of this wild place, and one with Gunnar's limp body slung over his shoulder.

All of them covered in blood.

Chapter 34

He'd almost lost her. That was all he could think. He'd nearly lost her, all because he had indulged in his own battle lust. Revenge had blinded him and he'd left her alone for too long. All Ragnar wanted was to clutch her against him and hold her just a little while longer.

Her limbs were tangled around his waist, holding onto him tightly as he pressed her against his heart and ran. Still, Maia wasn't close enough. He wanted to crawl inside of her and never leave. Because if he had been just a few moments later... If he had stayed in the battle and not heard Gunnar's shout...

Thinking of what might have happened to her made him see red. He wanted to go back and kill that man again. Hacking into his flesh hadn't been enough of a punishment, not for someone who would do that. The man had had intentions, brutal intentions, and that soldier had been about to do that to *his wife*.

Blood boiling still, he pushed himself harder. Running faster through the forest in the hopes that at least if he ran, Ragnar could get some of these feelings out. He didn't have to think about them if he was running. The thoughts couldn't keep up with the speed with which he ran. But they still chased them. The memories of what had been done, and the fears of what could have happened, trailed along behind him like wolves nipping at his heels.

The humans hadn't been what Maia had wanted. His heart bled for her, but also tha the had been foolish enough to believe her. Even for a few moments. The humans would never change. He wasn't fast enough to outrun their cruelty, no matter how hard he tried.

Soon enough, they reached a clearing where the trolls could rest. Soon enough, the others of his kind gathered together with knives and swords to protect their injured

His fire hair shook like a leaf in his grasp. She trembled in his arms, her face pressed against the side of his neck as she breathed in his scent. And he knew.

He knew that she needed him to be present right now. She needed him more than his people did, even if some of them were injured.

He'd never felt more torn.

Because he could see there were trolls who needed to be healed. He could see even his own brother was wheezing and bleeding out, the breath filtering from his lungs in a way that wasn't natural or right.

And yet...

Maia sighed against his throat, her breath fanning across his skin and raising goose bumps in its wake. "They need you," she whispered against his skin. "And they can't do it without you."

Ragnar was ashamed of both the relief and the disappointment that rose in equal measure to her words. "I'll heal them quickly."

"I'll be fine."

Those were the words she kept saying. Over and over. But he could see that wasn't true. Even as he set her on the ground, his hands on her shoulders, she shook. Her arms curved around her waist, holding onto herself in a hug like she needed something to ground her.

"Ach," he muttered, yanking her into his arms again. He hugged her tightly. "We'll go. They can use up the rest of the healing potions."

"No, Ragnar."

"You're not in any state to stay here."

"Your brother is hurt, Ragnar." She peeled herself away from him to look up with those giant green eyes. "You have to heal them. That's who you are."

He hated that she was right, but he loved her for it. For seeing what he had to do and deciding to put his people before her own well-being. But that was what Maia did, wasn't it? She always put everyone in front of herself. He regretted that in this case, so did he.

Sucking in a deep breath, he nodded before rushing through the healing process. He saw to all who needed him until he got to Gunnar, who grabbed onto his arm. His brother was sitting on a log in front of a fire, his hand pressed over the wound on his chest that had already healed a bit thanks to one of Ragnar's potions. But it was still ragged and bleeding, red liquid seeping out of it in a slow, sluggish crawl.

"Take her away," Gunnar said, his voice twisted in pain.

"She's more than earned our respect," he replied. "If the trolls don't see that now, then they'll never trust her."

"No, I'm saying..." His brother winced as Ragnar started working. The healing magic was likely a little too cold against the wound, because Gunnar pressed his hand against Ragnar's, holding him tighter to the wound. "Take her away, just the two of you, for a while. I saw what that man was going to do to her. I tried to get to them, but…"

He'd seen Gunnar. His brother had attempted to stand, his back curving in a crawl as he'd forced his body to move. Just the barest amount, falling onto his face and then forcing himself back up as he'd slowly made his way toward Maia. It had been hard to watch, but that was the only reason Ragnar had known something was wrong.

Cupping the back of Gunnar's neck, he pressed his brother's forehead against his own. "You are the reason she's alive, Gunnar. I know that. You know that."

"I do."

"Thank you. Thank you for keeping my troll wife safe."

Gunnar breathed out a long exhale and then nodded as the healing magic settled into his body. "I'm fine. The rest of us will heal on our own. Take her to the illuminated glen, brother. No one will be there for a while yet. Bring her somewhere to remember that there's still beauty in this world. Heal her soul as well as her body."

Ragnar nodded. It was a good idea. Bringing her home right now would only put them right back in the same place they'd been before. He needed time away with her so the stories could start about what she'd done to heal the others, and how she'd fought bravely against that human soldier. His people would value her courage, and she would win permanent favor.

It would take time, though. And in that time, he could indulge himself in his bride.

Standing, he headed over to Maia. Some of the other trolls had bundled her up and sat her down in front of a fire. They had thought she was cold, most likely, but now he could see some were realizing it was far more than that. No matter how close she was to the fire or how many layers they put on her, her teeth continued to chatter and her body still shook.

Quite a few helpless glances were sent in his direction as he approached. Few knew what to do with a person in this state.

But there was another troll seated beside her, a warrior he admired quite a bit. Edda had a scar down her face from where a human had tried to end her life, and quite a few more on her body. Her quiet murmur held Maia's attention more than the fire did.

As he walked a little closer, he overheard what the troll woman was saying.

"It's a long journey to fight through, but you give him even more power if you let him live inside of you. You fought. You won. These are battles to be proud of."

At his approach, the warrior cut off what she was saying and stood. With a sharp nod, she left them alone.

Ragnar, in the full sight of all the trolls around him, knelt before her. On his knees before his troll wife.

As it always should be.

He gathered her hands in his, squeezing those shaking fingers. "Will you come somewhere with me, Maia? Or do you want to go home?"

She looked at him with so much hope in those eyes that it made his entire body ache. She trusted him beyond measure, this woman. Even if she shouldn't.

"I'll go anywhere with you," she whispered.

If that didn't make his heart sing, he didn't know what would.

Gathering her up in his arms, he held her against his chest and walked into the forest. The rest of the war band watched him, and he could see the relief in their posture. Ragnar was taking her somewhere to piece her back together, and they could rest easy knowing that she wouldn't be in so much pain anymore. Soon enough, he would see to it that his bride was well.

On the way, he talked to distract her. And partly to bare a part of his soul that still ached.

"When I was young, Gunnar wasn't the closest person to me. That was another troll."

Maia's head tilted against his shoulder to look up at him. "I think Gunnar mentioned something about him once. That you had suffered a loss before."

"Bjorn was a good man," he replied, picking through the forest so he could find the entrance into the mountain that was rarely used. He kept his eyes on the trees, though, and listened for any human foolish enough to chase them. "He was another warrior, like me. We trained together when we were young. The warrior who led us made us fight because we hated each other. It was hard to fight him, because he fought just like me. We had the same mind, the same plans. Beating another warrior like that is difficult, because I knew what he was going to do, but he also knew what I was going to do."

The entrance to the mountain loomed in front of them. He'd chosen a close one, knowing that it might give her more relief to slip between the stones and away from her own people.

The rocks looked like any other jumble of rocks that were all over this mountain. But these hid a tight crevice that he carefully slid them through. He had to turn to the side just to get into it, but he made sure that Maia's legs and arms were carefully tucked against him before he moved.

Once through, he continued his story. "Bjorn was the first one of us to be welcomed into a war band. He was one of the most talented fighters I've ever met in my life, so it wasn't surprising to any of us. He was quick to battle, but quick to end it, too. He wasn't the kind of warrior who would draw out a fight for his pride or the pride of another. In an instant, he would have a human pinned beneath him and dead even just with his teeth. But beyond all that fighting power, he was also kind. And a very talented jeweler, if you'd believe that."

Something in that last bit caught her attention because suddenly, she was looking up at him with a narrow-eyed gaze. "I suppose all warriors have something that makes them seem more personable."

"That we do." He walked into the darkness with her. "Are you still frightened of the dark?"

"No. I don't mind it as much as the first time I came here with you."

"Good." He took a deep breath, starting into the painful part of the story that still plagued him to this day. "In one of the raids Bjorn went on, he got injured. I was there with him. The humans had set a trap that caught his leg in it. One moment he was standing, and the next, a bear trap had nearly severed his calf. I was still learning how to use my power, but I was so certain I could heal him. Unfortunately, that caused more issues. I healed him too quickly, and he had a limp for the rest of his life."

"You couldn't have known that would happen," she said, her voice little more than a murmur. "You were trying to help him."

"But I failed. And he was no longer capable of being a warrior in the way he was before." He swallowed hard, finally reaching the end of the dark tunnel and stepping out onto a small path that would lead them deeper into the mountain. At the very least, now there were wisps to guide them. "And if I had healed him better, he would still be here today."

"Ragnar..."

"No, sweet thing. You do not have to make excuses for me. I know the truth of what I did and how I limited him. He went on another war band, against the wishes of many trolls. They didn't want to tell him what he was capable of, but he knew his own limitations. As such, he was captured by the soldiers there. They took him away, and we don't know what happened to him. But we know humans well enough. He's dead, and they killed him in a horrible way. All of that is my fault."

And that was the hardest part of this memory. All of Bjorn's bad luck led right back to Ragnar. It was why they hadn't spoken for months before he had disappeared.

Maia watched him with a careful expression on her face, like she was trying to figure out the point of this story while also having her heart break for his loss.

"Ragnar?" she asked, her voice a low melody. "Why are you telling me all this?"

"I know what it is to have a memory that has sunk its teeth into you. It's a wolf with a grip on the back of your neck, shaking you every time you think you can get away from it. This is all very new for you, fire hair. I know that. Rushing you through a experience like this will only make it sink its teeth in even deeper." He held her a little tighter to remind himself that she was alive. "And perhaps to remind myself that, unlike Bjorn, I did not lose you."

She smiled, but even that expression was a little weak for her. "I'll be fine."

"You keep saying those blasted words, but I fear that you do not believe them."

"I will be. It'll just take some time. Time that we maybe don't have." But then one of her tiny hands came up and cupped his jaw. He tilted his face into the warmth of her touch, luxuriating in the feeling of her fingers tracing the outline of his lips. "Being with you helps. I know you might not believe that, but it's true. Just being here, in your arms, chases away the bad thoughts."

"Good." He leaned down, his lips so close to hers that he could feel the heat. "I don't want to push you."

"I want to remember that I'm alive," she replied, before kissing him.

Just hearing those words made everything in him ache. Every part of his being wanted to gather her closer, to lunge into her body and worship the very ground she walked on. But first, he wanted to show her one last distraction. One last gift.

He pulled away from her kiss, breathing a little harder than before. "I want to give you a chance to forget all of this. At least for a little while. Do you think we can do that? Together?"

She shuddered against his lips. "I would love nothing more, Ragnar."

Chapter 35

Maybe it was the wrong choice. Maia shouldn't try so hard to forget all the blood and gore and terror. She'd seen so many people in battle today. She'd stabbed a man, and it was that memory that stuck in her mind more than the rest. Yes, there was the fear of what that soldier would have done to her if Ragnar hadn't gotten there. There was still a sting in knowing that her own people referred to her as a troll whore.

But the sensation of the resistance against the blade in her hand? How it had felt like his body fought against her before the sudden pop and release of flesh? The gush of blood and how, after that smallest bit of fight, it had been so easy to stab him?

Maia had never been a violent person. Even when she'd been younger and those men had made her frightened in her own house, she hadn't wanted to hurt anyone. She had just wanted them to go away.

Now? She was a little terrified of the woman she was becoming.

Because she had wanted to hurt that man. She'd been so capable of lifting that blade and defending herself. The old Maia—the version of herself she was far more comfortable with—would have laid there and let it happen. She would have gone quiet and hoped that if she just checked out of the moment, it would be over soon enough. But she wasn't that girl now.

Because the wild and wicked creature who had awoken inside her at the first touch of Ragnar's hands, the one who sometimes felt like a wild beast, had wanted to fight. That person had screamed out in anger that anyone would dare touch her who wasn't her husband. That was the same part of her who wanted to go back and spit on the man's dead body.

Maia didn't know who she was now, and that was equally terrifying. So the opportunity to avoid thinking about any of it? She'd take that in a heartbeat.

At her admission, Ragnar strode toward what looked like a wall of vines. The blueish leaves glowed in the wisp light, but he walked right through them. The ivy tangled in their shoulders for a moment, clinging to them with little cries of loneliness. The vibrant plants hadn't seen people for a very long time in this part of the mountain. They wanted Maia to linger, but she just wanted to get away for a little while longer.

And then they stepped into another world.

Light blossomed on the other side. A stream of water moved slowly, creating pools of glimmering light that were so bright, they almost outshone the massive mushrooms that grew all around them. Moss covered the ground at their bases, and they were so large, some of them grew taller than her. They created an almost forest-like effect. Some tall, some short, but all of them glowing with an internal light that bloomed throughout their thin skin.

Ragnar walked with her through this enchanting place, all the way to the edge of a pool where steam rose. It was warm here—so warm and cozy that it really accentuated how chilly the rest of the troll kingdom could be.

This man. He gave her gift after gift no matter what they endured. And for once, Maia knew she would make this choice to forget everything that had happened to them. At least for a little while.

Today was gone. Now it was just her and him.

Breathing out a long breath, she stared up at him as he sank onto the moss near the glowing water. "What would you have me do?" he asked.

She didn't want to talk anymore. Because if she talked, it was all too easy to remember the trauma they had both gone through. His friend. Her people. His people. All the memories were piling up, and she just wanted to stop thinking for a while.

So instead of responding, she wiggled out of his arms. He swung her legs down to the ground and steadied her when she weaved. But then she was right in front of him, staring up at this massive troll who had saved her life, who had been so kind now that he had given in to what they were to each other.

And by all the gods in the realm, she wanted to please him. She wanted him to please her. She wanted her mind to be overwhelmed with all the sensations that only he could give her, and whatever would make her stop thinking for a while.

Maia reached for the waistband of his hunting clothing. Banded straps of leather held his tight pants on, but she made quick work of them. She dropped his weapons, one by one, onto the moss with soft thuds until she could finally tug at the waistband of his pants. And then he helped her, guiding the leather down his legs until he was nearly naked other than the straps of weapons still held to his chest.

Ragnar got rid of those too, hungry eyes watching her as she stepped back from him. Slowly, ever so slowly, Maia peeled the clothing off her own body as well. Her gaze traced his body, her eyes following the stripes that decorated his skin and the tattoos over one shoulder. She meandered her gaze over the muscles of his body, the thick blocks of his abdomen stacked on top of each other, and the sharp-edged "v" that trailed down to his massive cock.

And it really was massive. She was shocked she'd managed to fit that thing inside of her.

The bars looked even more intimidating in this light, but she remembered how good they'd felt inside of her. How she desperately wanted to feel them again.

His massive hand fisted that cock, slowly jerking up and down as her gaze lingered on it.

"Is this what you want?" he asked.

She licked her lips and nodded.

"Then get on your knees, fire hair. Let's see how much more of it you can take."

Those words shouldn't have sent a blistering heat throughout her body, but they did. She could feel a rush of liquid between her thighs as she knelt down. Pressing her knees together tightly, she tried to create some friction even as she reached for him.

She trailed her fingers down the bars, one by one. Ragnar stepped a little closer, his breathing ragged as he watched her. Every muscle on his stomach and torso was rock solid, rigid as he held himself in place for her to play with the piercings that she'd never quite gotten time to touch.

Leaning forward, Maia trailed her tongue along the middle row of them. The metal was warm, even though she'd been quite certain that it would be cold. She had no idea what he would like, or if the metal made him even more sensitive. She wasn't sure if what she wanted to do would hurt him. Then she trailed her tongue higher, following the grooves of the metal, and stilled at the sound he made. The guttural groan was animalistic, almost painful to hear.

His eyes had rolled back in his head, she realized. He'd fisted his hands at his sides to stay still, and that was more than enough proof that he was enjoying every bit of what she was doing.

Maia moved to the head of his cock, laving her tongue over the slit that was already leaking pre-cum. She could taste it. Salty and sweet, just like he was. And then she gave her best effort to swallow him down.

Her jaw ached at being forced that wide open, but she had to try. She could fit the head of him just barely, and it stretched her jaw so much that it almost hurt. Still, she kept going when he made that wonderful groaning noise again. Saliva gathered on her tongue, dripping down the head of him and her chin. The bars were too wide to fit into her mouth anyway, so she could only take her time sucking on the head of his cock, swirling her tongue around it and gathering more of that salty sweet taste.

Another of his groans filled the clearing, and then his hands were on the back of her head. He drew her a little closer, forcing her jaw slightly wider until she whined. Only then did he ease his grip, petting his fingers through her hair as she worked him.

"Such a talented little thing," he murmured, his hands on the side of her head and drawing her away from his cock. "But right now isn't about me, as much as your lovely tongue could make me come far too quickly."

He picked her up off the ground like she weighed nothing, arranging her how he wanted her. Ragnar laid himself out like a giant mattress on the ground, sitting her right on his chest while he cushioned his head on the moss. He quirked his brow when she flattened her palms against his chest, assuming he was feeling rather rushed and wanted to get on with the main part of the show.

"What are you doing?" he asked, when she slid herself down his stomach.

She froze. "I was going to... well... you know."

"Come here," he said, grabbing both of her thighs and jerking her back up his chest. Then he grabbed her hands and lifted them forward, bracing her against the stalk of a mushroom just over her head. "Hold on to this."

"Why?"

But then his hands were on her hips again, lifting her up... up... up...

He grinned up at her between her thighs. "Sit on my face, fire hair. Fucking crush me, if that's what it takes. But I want to feel you come on my tongue before I make you scream on my cock."

And then he buried his face between her thighs.

She saw stars. Maia grabbed onto the mushroom for dear life as he licked her. He was slick and warm and groaning against her as he feasted on her flesh. His teeth nipped at her, gently scraping against her clit before circling it with his tongue. And then... fuck, he sank his tongue as deep as he could inside of her.

How was it so big? How was he able to move it like that inside of her body, licking and undulating before he pulled it out and then sank two of his fingers deep, deep inside.

She arched against him, hissing out a long breath as that talented tongue circled her clit while his fingers moved in and out, a rapid pace that already had him slamming deeper and deeper inside of her.

"I believe you've earned another piercing, troll wife," he said, drawing back only slightly to look up her body into her eyes. Those talented fingers never stopped moving, seemingly spreading her even wider as he added a third finger to stretch her even more.

"Another?" she breathlessly asked.

And then, obscenely, impossibly, he stuck out his tongue for her to look at. He really did have a tongue that was longer and thicker than a human's, and that wonderful silver ball at the tip. But then he drew it back into his mouth and wickedly said, "I'll get my tongue pierced again for you. You'll like it better when I eat you."

Oh. Fuck.

He returned to doing just that, tonguing with her a ferocity that had every muscle in her body tensing. What did he mean she'd like it better if he had more piercings? What would that even feel like?

But then she focused on the single ball sliding around her clit, and it was almost all too easy to imagine more metal on his tongue sliding against her, rubbing, smooth and hot and...

She shattered. Unexpectedly. Suddenly. All at once in a rush of pleasure that was all too consuming.

She rocked against his mouth, seeking more friction from his tongue so that this feeling wouldn't disappear. She wanted to chase it a little longer. She needed to feel him just a bit more.

And he didn't complain. If anything, he only groaned louder as she released that mushroom and instead let her hands fall behind herself to brace her weight against his abs. It gave her a different angle to grind against his mouth.

When she finally could breathe again, she looked over her shoulder to stare down at his bobbing cock. It really was intense to look at, but now she wanted nothing more than to see if she could fit the whole damn thing inside of her.

"Easy," he muttered. "We'll get it all in you this time, fire hair."

He rolled with her, looming above her for a moment and pressing his lips to hers. He tasted like her, she realized. Earthy and warm, until he broke free from the kiss and made her turn. "Hands and knees."

Hands and knees?

She supposed she could do that. But the moment she was in the position he wanted, her arms started to shake. Because the head of him pressed against her core, and she couldn't focus even on bracing herself upright. He was so big, so much, so...

She groaned as he sank inside of her. Easier this time. Though there was still the pinch of pain, it wasn't like the last time. In fact, the burn felt good as he pushed a bar deep, two bars in, more and more until she was crying out.

"Stop?" he asked, his voice a little breathless.

Frantically shaking her head, she sank her fingers into the moss. "More, more, Ragnar. Please."

"Such a pretty plea."

Then he gave her more. With each thrust, more bars fit into her. Scraping along her insides in little lightning bolts of pleasure. Five, six...

She held her breath. Ragnar let out an angry sounding groan and the last two bars slid into her. They moved so beautifully, so intensely, and all her thoughts were obliterated as his hips pressed flush with her bottom.

They both froze, breathing hard. She tried to think about anything other than how full she was, but then he moved.

It was like he'd set her body on fire. Something happened when he was inside of her like this. The pain, the pleasure, the overwhelming need that sparked with every glide in and out. Every movement. Every snap of his hips that was followed by the cracking sound of him slapping into her, turning her mind to mush.

"More," she whispered, falling onto her forearms. "More, Ragnar."

And he gave her more.

Ragnar wrapped her hair around his wrist, tugging her head back so he could arch over her and bite her shoulder like he had before. "Beg for me, fire hair."

"Please," she whimpered, the sound throaty and breathless.

He pounded into her until there was nothing but the endless search for pleasure. Nothing but him and her and the ache that built inside of her until it was too much, yet again.

Would it always be like this? Would she come so hard with him inside of her that the line between pain and pleasure blurred into something she didn't recognize?

"Fuck," he hissed. "You're so fucking tight."

The heat inside of her turned blistering even as she felt him stiffen. His cock jumped, and he sank as deep as he could just as she came around him in a clenching wave. They both hissed out long noises of pleasure as they came together so powerfully she wasn't sure she would ever put herself back together.

Breathing hard, she let him roll her into his arms. Still inside of her, he spooned against her back, holding her to his chest as he rained a thousand kisses upon her shoulders, back, and neck.

She'd needed to forget about everything. And he'd damn well delivered.

Chapter 36

They stayed in the illuminated glen for hours on end. Partially because Ragnar thought she needed the time to recuperate, and partly because he wasn't done with her yet. While he needed time to recover, she did not. And he was all too obliged to help her forget what had happened.

For hours, he learned every bit of her body. He found the spots that made her jerk away from him with a laugh—the hollow of her spine and the back of her neck. He found the spots that made her moan and shudder—the small of her back and the valley between her breasts. He discovered everything he could do to make her so wet she was dripping down his hand, and then some. There was more he wanted to do.

But eventually, she could barely even talk. The poor thing was limp and pliable as he arranged her in his arms. He'd drawn her into a hot spring, taking care with her sensitive skin even as she laid her head against his shoulder.

"Look at the mess I've made of you," he murmured, drawing her back to his chest so he could play his fingers over her breasts. "You look so perfect like this."

"Ragnar," she whispered, attempting to shake her head. "I can't. No more."

"Just one more."

"I can't."

He wasn't listening to her begging. He just needed to hear her come apart one last time, and then he would let her rest. Even though Maia whimpered when his hands slid down her front and sank between her thighs, he found her ready and willing there. She was so swollen, so sensitive, that the merest brush of his fingers against her skin had her groaning.

All it took was a few brushes of his fingers over that sensitive clit of hers and she was crying out in his ear. Hours of this apparently made her so sensitive that sending her over the edge took so little.

"Sweet wife," he murmured, brushing her wet hair back from her face. "So perfect for me. Last one. I promise."

She was a panting mess against his neck and he'd never seen anything prettier. This was what he had wanted. This was what he had needed since the moment he'd decided she was his: Hours to dedicate to her pleasure and her pleasure alone.

Hours for him to solidify that she wanted him, and against all odds, he wanted her too.

Ragnar held her a little tighter, wrapping his arms around her waist and squeezing. He wanted to breathe her in for a little while longer, but also knew that he needed to get her home.

She whimpered slightly, turning her head into his neck and going even more limp.

"You need a bed," he murmured against her neck, moving to carry her out of the water. "Do you want to sleep, fire hair?"

"Yes," she breathed.

"I'll bring you to bed, then. Tuck you in and make sure nothing touches your dreams. How's that sound?"

But she was already asleep in his arms. Sighing, he set her down on the warm moss for a few moments so he could yank his clothing on, and then helped get her dressed. She was grumpy while he did it, half asleep and making little noises of displeasure as he pulled her dress over her head and moved her arms into the right position. Adorable.

Everything about her was so soft and delicate, and he couldn't believe that he'd once thought that would be a problem. When he'd first looked at her, all he could see was a tiny person who would need his protection. But now?

"Your bravery never ceases to amaze me," he murmured as he gathered her up in his arms and started toward their home.

Not just in the battle or how she'd fought that soldier off, but in taking him all the way. He could only imagine that it had been terrifying for her. Looking at a fully grown, massive troll and expecting anything to happen between them had to be madness on her part. Yet she'd done it.

More than once now.

And fuck if he wasn't the luckiest man in the realm right now. Because his bride wanted him just as much as he wanted her, and there was nothing standing in their way now. Nothing between them. She'd fought at his side and maybe it was just the high after spending hours between her thighs, but he had more hope than he'd had in a long time.

Their future was looking brighter and brighter. With that thought, he said nothing else as his troll wife fell asleep in his arms and he carried her home. She was warm and pliable in his grip, easy to carry but also a reminder of all the precious things he had to be thankful for.

Ragnar returned her to their home safely and quietly. A few trolls gave them strange expressions. Furrowed brows and pursed lips were abound, but no one stopped them. And when he settled her on the bed, he brushed her hair back from her face and blew out a long, relieved sigh. They were home. They were safe.

Here he could keep her until the very end of time. No one would find her here, and no one would dare even touch her without knowing they would answer to him.

Ragnar went out into the parlor for another blanket and then heard a knock on his front door. A quiet one. Like the person on the other side knew they were disturbing him and his troll wife, who desperately needed her rest.

Frowning, he headed over, ready to tell off whoever was on the other side. His bride needed rest. After everything she had seen and gone through, the trolls could at least give her that.

But when he threw open the door, he sighed in defeat. The official messenger of King Egil stood on the other side, clearly not pleased to be here either.

"The king has requested you," she said, apologies in every word. "I know you would rather be here right now, Ragnar. And truth be told, I'd rather you stay here as well."

"But the king waits for no one."

"No, he doesn't."

He cast one glance behind his shoulder, but Maia wasn't going to wake any time soon. He'd made sure of that. His wife would sleep for hours on end, and deeply after what he'd done to her.

Grinding his teeth, he gave up the thought of crawling into bed with her and resting. But he wasn't going to leave her alone. Not again. So he held up a finger to the king's messenger, and returned to his bedroom.

Bracing a knee on the bed, he brushed her hair away from her face and murmured, "Someone is here."

"Come back to bed," she breathed.

"I can't, fire hair."

As much as he wanted to join her, he knew better than to ignore the king. He left her cozy in his bed, closing the door behind him and joining the king's messenger on the long walk to the castle.

Once there, he headed to the throne room, where he knew the king waited for him. What he wasn't expecting was to find the room full with all the generals and warlords who had been fighting in the town. They all watched him enter, a few of them wearing guarded expressions that he couldn't quite make out.

At least, until he stood next to Gunnar who seemed much better. Clearly the king's healers had seen to him, still, Ragnar immediately asked, "How's that wound?"

"Magic can fix a lot of things."

"And?"

Gunnar sighed. "And it still hurts like I ran straight into a boar, but I will be fine. The healers sent me home with plenty of your healing potions, and a strict order to rest."

"Good." Ragnar crossed his arms over his chest and left it at that. If the healers thought he was well, then he had to be well enough to be standing here.

His brother cleared his throat. "She is well?"

He glanced around to see every other troll in the room watching them. Waiting for his answer.

"How fickle you all are," he muttered. "Just mere days ago, you were reminding me that she could be a spy."

Gorm grumbled under his breath, "She could still be a spy."

But the general was silenced rather quickly by a few of the other trolls next to him. "She wouldn't have healed our people if she were a spy."

"Even if she would have healed them, my cousin said she held his hand through the entire thing and then tucked him in," another added. "That's not acting."

"She stabbed that human in the thigh. Right through it. I saw her from the battlefield, and that was real terror afterward." The female troll who said the words then crossed her arms firmly over her chest. "You don't pretend to be affected like that after a male attacks you."

Watching trolls stand up for Maia warmed his heart, but also infuriated him to no end. Where was this support only days ago? Why did she have to suffer for them to see her worth? Rather than encouraging their behavior, he turned his attention to the king.

Their leader wasn't sitting on his throne. Instead, he sat on the floor in front of it, his legs hanging down the stairs and his crown in his hands. Perhaps all the other trolls were focusing on Ragnar, because the sight before them was hard to look at.

Finally, King Egil sighed and looked up. He met each and every one of their gazes slowly, as though he knew this was a terrible burden for any of them to bear.

"The mountain will never be ours until we can prove to them that we can keep it," the king started. "And I know many of you would fight to your last breath to prove that this land will not be under human control. But we do not know why they fight so fiercely for it."

"It's hatred for our people," Gunnar snarled. "They don't care a mite for this mountain. All they care about is that it's not currently theirs, and that we have it."

A few trolls grumbled in agreement.

But it didn't sit right with Ragnar. There had to be more to it than just a blind hatred. King James was too cunning for that. At least, that was what he'd seen so far.

"Why send scouts to our home?" he asked. "If it's blind hatred, they would just chip away at us. One by one. Instead, they seek out entrances to our home, strategically sealing us inside of the mountain. Why?"

"That is precisely why I think we need to figure out a new way to attack the humans. We need to understand what the human king wants," Egil replied. He rotated the crown in his hands, his fingers finding each gemstone that symbolized every king before him.

Ragnar used to wonder if holding a crown like that ever made the king feel less than what he was. It was a reminder of the heaviness each king carried who had come before him, all of those who had made a name for themselves and earned those gems on the crown. They were impressive beasts of their own. Men and women who had earned the title of king and ruled the mountain for ages.

All of them were Egil's family, a bloodline that flowed through his own veins.

The king set the crown on the stone next to him and then laced his fingers together. "There are few things we know about the humans. Getting into the castle has been next to impossible. The only option we have is to trust those currently within our ranks and hope they do not betray us."

Of course, they would trust each other. Ragnar would give his life for his brother standing next to him, and he knew many other trolls shared the same opinion. There were few who weren't willing to risk their lives for the trolls who would do the same for them.

The king took a deep breath. "Ragnar. Tell me about your wife."

"She is not a spy."

"I think we all know that by now. There are some who will fight against the truth, as they have no desire to believe that humans are capable of being something else. What I want to know is how your bond has grown." The king laced his fingers together, the knuckles turning white with some unnamed emotion. "I promised you a more powerful troll wife to build your lineage and your power. For that, I am still sorry. But if this wife is yours is who you choose, then I would know this works."

"I'm sorry, my king." Ragnar shook his head in confusion. "I don't follow."

"Humans and trolls have rarely been together. The humans we have caught before, the ones who have given their blood and their bodies to create stronger troll lineages… those women were caught unwillingly. Their magic was locked in their bodies. Husbands were unable to force that magic out of them, although their children were stronger for it. I want to know if it is true that you can use her magic and she can use yours."

All eyes were on him, and Ragnar realized this had always been about more than an alliance. The king had wanted to know if the magic between mates could spread. If…

Ragnar breathed out a long sigh. "You want to know if you can make trolls more powerful now if there are more willing brides."

"That's precisely what I want to know."

Of course. All of this made sense. The king hadn't sent him just to get a bride. This had been a test to see if he could make trolls even more of a formidable enemy.

"Surely you've heard me say that my magic is stronger with her," Ragnar tried to say.

"When touching, yes. That is the same as what we expected. We can pull magic out of even unwilling brides through touch. But I want to know if you can use it right now." The king's gaze sharpened, that hawk gaze of his even more intimidating than ever before. "If it's a true bond, like a troll and his troll wife should be, then you can use her magic now. You can pull upon it without her being her. Shape it and use it in ways you wouldn't have been able to before. An unwilling bride can amplify the magic of her husband. A willing one, it is said, can share her power entirely."

"None of this was told to me before—" he tried to say.

"Then I'm telling you now. You have white healing magic, like ice on a cold winter's day. But her magic is green. I have heard from Birger that she is impressive in the gardens, and that plants grow no matter what she does. If you can do that, if you can pull on her magic, then we can know for certain none of this was a waste. We could make an army of trolls not limited by their own magic, but wielding dual weapons."

Of course, it wasn't a waste.

He'd found his wife. A true troll wife. A woman who would stand by him until the end of time and who he was so proud to be tied to. His entire soul burned for her, even when he was far from her side.

Gunnar nudged him. "You need to try, brother."

"She's sleeping. What if she can feel what I'm doing?"

"Then you'll have to wake her for this small amount of time. She probably won't even notice it." Gunnar gave him another nudge, this one harder and more insistent. "You can't deny the king's direct order."

He could. He wanted to. Ragnar knew it would end with him being forced to leave this place, though. The trolls would escort both him and Maia out of this mountain, and they would lose...

Everything. Everything he had promised her. Everything they had built together. All of that would disappear because he wasn't willing to wake her after a long day.

Sighing, he nodded. "I will try, my king. But I make no promises."

"That is all I ask."

Ragnar remembered when he'd first been taught how to use his magic. His mother had been the one to teach him, considering healing magic had been her specialty. And it was her voice he heard in his head as he reached for the well of magic that existed inside of him.

Every magic feels different. Some of them are tastes, some are smells, some are sensations. Her hand had landed on his shoulder, squeezing gently before her claws had trailed light as a feather across his skin. *Healing magic is a sensation. Ours is cold—colder than you'd imagine. Those icy tendrils are what you need to focus on, my son. Convince them to move through your body, out of your body, and reach for all those who surround you. They need to find those who desire help.*

But what would green magic be like?

He tried to sense it at first. Perhaps the smell of earth and loam would do it. But every time he conjured up the scent of a garden, nothing happened. No magic burned at his fingertips. Perhaps the sight of it? He pictured Maia standing among the tomatoes with dirt smeared on her cheek and that wild smile on her face.

Still nothing.

He could hear the grumbles of the trolls around him, all of them clearly believing that this experiment of their king's had failed. One last try—that was all he could think to do.

And there it was. The burst of basil on his tongue and the strange sensation of something foreign in his mind. Then she uncoiled, blooming like the tiniest of seeds through a link between the two of them that he hadn't realized was there. Maia's magic stretched its roots within his own, and Ragnar lifted his hand.

Someone—Gunnar, he thought—placed a tiny seed on his palm. He could sense the magic in it. The power. The life that wanted to burst free if he would let it.

So he did.

Unlike healing magic, there was no guidance in this. He just gave the seed the spark, and the plant did the rest.

By the time he'd opened his eyes, a tiny seedling had sprouted on his palm. The little roots already dangled free from the edge of his hand, and the bright green leaves were as beautiful as they were delicate.

"Magnificent," King Egil breathed. "And there's our proof. Now, I need you all to join me on this plan, because it is a risk. I do truly believe, however, that if we wish to beat this king, first we will need to find all the human women who are willing and make ourselves a stronger enemy."

The murmur of agreement from Ragnar's brethren made something in his stomach twist. And when he looked at Gunnar, he could see his brother felt the same.

The winds of change blew through the throne room, and Ragnar wasn't sure if that was good or not.

Chapter 37

Maia woke feeling deliciously sore between her legs and far more rested than she had been in ages. She wasn't sure if that was the ridiculously good sex that had filled her afternoon yesterday, or the deep, dreamless sleep that had followed. Either way, she was grateful for both.

Maybe she could convince her husband to do that again. And soon.

Cheeks burning at the mere thought, she rolled over in bed to see if he was still here. Her fingers danced over a cold pillow and blankets that were wrapped around her body and no one else's.

A pang of sadness made Maia bite her lip. She hated that it still felt like this. Ragnar was always up earlier. He headed out into the troll kingdom because he was a busy man with lots to do. Considering the trolls had used up a majority of the healing potions yesterday, she was certain he was back in the castle creating more, so he could restore what was needed.

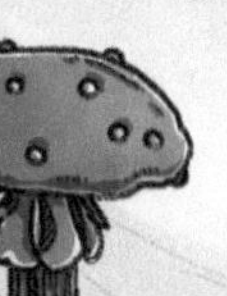

Still, she would have liked one morning to wake up in his arms. Especially after yesterday.

But that was not the life she lived. Sighing, she stretched her entire body in one big heaving movement before she rolled out of bed and padded into the bathroom. Birger likely needed her help today, and she was going to keep herself distracted. No memories of blood were going to dog her steps today. She would keep her mind and hands busy until she couldn't even see straight. And then, only then, was she going to sit down and maybe consider that what she'd seen had affected her.

As she got ready for the day, dragging on a pale blue dress that wrapped around her in little braids, a faint memory stirred. Not the one she had expected, as she'd been batting away the thought of that soldier with his hands on his belt all morning.

No, she remembered waking up and feeling a tug deep inside of her. A cool shiver had trailed between her shoulder blades, the same way she always felt when Ragnar was using his healing magic on her. But he hadn't been here then. She even remembered vaguely reaching for him and having her hands come up empty.

When had that happened?

And what had happened?

Frowning, she marched toward the kitchen, only to find that the front door was already opening. Inkeri stepped inside, her lands laden with two cloaks.

"Are you sneaking into my house?" Maia asked, bemused by the other woman's actions.

The troll woman jumped, before chuckling when she realized Maia was standing there. "Your house, is it? I believe that's the first time I've heard you call it that."

Maybe it was. She'd always considered this place to be Ragnar's home. But after last night, the fight, and... everything else that had occurred, it was so much easier to look at this place and feel like it was hers as well.

"A woman can change her mind," Maia finally replied.

"Especially when she fights like a warrior in battle. The entire city is talking about you, you know." Inkeri held out the cloak for her to take.

"I didn't fight that hard—trust me."

"You fought hard enough that those who came back from the war band were quick to correct anyone speaking ill of the human among us. Did you know that quite a few trolls were claiming you were a spy for the humans? Anyone who says that now is quick to have their mouth closed."

Which meant the entire city also knew that she had been attacked. Those memories clawed at the back of Maia's mind, a wolf just like Ragnar had said. This one wanted to hold her in its jaws and shake her hard enough that she saw stars.

"What's this for?" she asked, gesturing to the offered cloak, but even she could hear the desperation in those words. She needed a distraction, anything, from those memories. Her hand shook when she reached out for it. Even worse, she was pretty sure her voice warbled as well.

"We're going back to the safety of the troll wives. You deserve to be there, not here alone."

"I think here is fine. I like being here." In the dark. By herself. The anxiety and worries could consume her here, and no one would know.

Already she could feel the wolf at the back of her throat. It was like the beast lived inside of her, aware of her terror that it would soon enough rear its ugly head. The more she tried to shove it aside, the more those memories wanted to fight back.

She hardly noticed Inkeri move. But then the woman was right in front of her, draping the cloak over her shoulders. "You cannot stay here. You will come with me, and the others will see to it that you are taken care of."

"I thought Ragnar might be back soon…?" Even she could hear the hope in those words.

"Ragnar is busy. But we will take care of you, fire hair. Now, keep the hood up, otherwise people are going to recognize you and I don't think you're in the mood to talk to anyone right now, are you?"

No, she wasn't. She didn't want to talk to anyone who wanted to speak of what had happened just yesterday. She didn't want to think about it just yet.

Looking at the room that should have been her shelter, she followed Inkeri out onto the street and down the stone paths that would lead to the safest place in this mountain. Along the way, she tried to convince herself this was a good thing. The troll wives would understand what she was going through. At least, she hoped so. They were women as well. Surely they knew what it was like to have experienced… that.

As she walked into the hidden area with Inkeri, all Maia could focus on was that these women might want her to talk about it too. They might push her, thinking it was the right choice, that maybe she needed to talk about it and they were doing the right thing by forcing her.

But she didn't want to talk about it. Not yet. Maybe never. Maybe she just wanted to keep it all in her head and let it roll around in there until it was as soft and smooth as a river stone.

There weren't as many troll wives as there had been before. Some of the elderly troll crones were weaving in the corner, some of them sewing from where they sat on logs that were strategically placed around a warmer fire. A few troll wives were practicing magic in the stream, just as she had seen them doing before. Others were laid out on the grasses on blankets. There were even a few troll wives in the trees, although those women appeared to be picking fruit that were hanging there. Fruit she hadn't noticed since the first time she'd been here.

One of the troll wives waved at her, calling out, "Maia! We were wondering when you were going to come back."

She hadn't... well, she didn't really think they would notice that she hadn't returned. There were so many of them, and she wasn't necessarily wanted. A human in here felt wrong, on some level. But she was appreciative they even remembered her name.

"Come on," Inkeri said, reaching out to grab her hand. "I know just the thing you need."

"Inkeri, I really just want to go back to the house and pretend I don't exist for a while."

"That won't help you. But I know what will."

She didn't think the other woman did. She wasn't up to this. Being around people somehow made how she was feeling even worse. The churning nerves in her stomach at being around so many trolls were suddenly impossible to control when she knew that they were looking at her. They knew what had happened, too. A few of them cast pitying glances her way, and she wondered if it showed on her face.

Was it so obvious to see what she had gone through?

The popping of flesh suddenly burst in her mind, and she sucked in a sharp breath. Inkeri glanced over her shoulder at her, tugging her along the edge of the stream and deeper into the woods. "Stop that."

"Stop what?" Maia asked, a little breathless even though they weren't moving all that fast.

"If you're going to use your magic, then you can't be using it in a state where you're worrying or anxious or afraid. Magic doesn't work right when you're like that. So clear your mind."

"It's a little hard to do that, considering everything that's happened," she muttered.

Inkeri walked her all the way to a soft, mossy area of the glen and then sat her down. The shove would have taken her off her feet regardless of where she was, so Maia was distinctly glad that there even was a soft area for her to fall into.

Letting out a little grunt of displeasure, she crossed her arms over her chest and glared up at Inkeri.

The troll wife returned her look with a glare that was more terrifying than Maia's. "Listen to me and listen well. What you went through, what you saw, was something no woman should ever have to deal with. It's terrifying to know what might have happened, and your mind is going to go down that path whether you want it to or not."

Inkeri lifted her hand and stopped Maia from speaking.

"You shouldn't have been there, Maia. That soldier should have known better than to touch you, as well. I know there's guilt in you. For hurting him. For being there in the first place. For the way that Ragnar likely tore that man apart and then ran with you through the woods. But none of it is your fault."

Somehow, that hurt to hear. It made every part of her being ache to hear those words, when others were bubbling up inside her mind. Words that her father would have said.

This is your fault.

If you weren't there, that man might still be alive.

If you hadn't insisted and gotten yourself caught up in the trolls' drama, then there would be more humans alive. This was your fault, Maia. No one else's.

Swallowing hard, she tried not to let his voice get any louder. Because if Ragnar had named him a wolf, then she didn't want to give her father any more power than he already had in her mind.

Inkeri watched all these emotions play across her features. The troll wife stared at her with far too much intent before she tsked. "I can see the ghost of someone is still clinging to you. That's why I brought you here, Maia. You are not alone."

"I'm very much alone. Half of the trolls still think I'm a spy, the other half are worried I'm going to shatter into a million pieces." She sighed and looked down at her hands, stretching her fingers as though she didn't recognize the palms. "I'm not certain that I'm either of those people, but I don't think they're wrong, either. They have a reason to fear me. Maybe they should. I saw what my people did to the trolls, and what they would do to so many others if they were given the chance."

Inkeri crouched in front of her, tipping her chin up with a single finger so Maia had to look at her. "You are not one of them anymore. I've wondered about how I could prove that to you, and all I could think was to do this."

"This?"

Maia watched as the troll grabbed her hands. Inkeri's fingers were so different from Ragnar's. Where her husband's hands were blunt and broad, Inkeri's were thin and graceful. Her fingers were long and delicate, tipped with sharp claws that were so much smaller and less hooked than the male version of her kind.

But then Inkeri sank both of their hands into the moss, holding onto her fingers gently. "You have green magic. There is much of it here. For centuries, we troll wives have come to the same place and left bits and pieces of our own magic. We let it linger long after we are dead. And there were so many of us, Maia. So many you couldn't even dream of the number."

"Why are you telling me this?" she whispered, feeling the wet moss between her fingers and the way it almost thickened at her touch already.

"Because there is nothing any of us can say to make this better. Nothing any of us can do. You don't want to talk? We respect that. You don't want to be held or cry with those of us who have suffered similar fate? That is fine as well. You will heal as you wish to heal. But if I can give you anything to help, it is to let you be held in the arms of the ancestors. Even if they cannot touch you physically."

That sounded... nice. Less terrifying than having to face what had happened to her. At least ancestors weren't actual people. They weren't standing in front of her looking at her with pity she wasn't sure she deserved.

Eyes wide, she gave Inkeri a curt nod. "I think I might like that."

"Good. All you have to do is let your magic join with theirs."

"I don't know how to do that."

Inkeri's fingers squeezed around hers. "Of course you do. Every troll wife does."

And just like that, the knowledge seemed to bloom in her head. Because she did know what to do. She knew all the ancestors required was that she use her magic on the moss. Let it seep into the ground around her in bright green sparkles that only she could see, but that fell from her fingers like snow. All that green magic sank into the moss and suddenly, she could feel them.

Her eyes widened even more as her sight disappeared. Inkeri

was no longer crouched in front of her. Instead, all she saw was the blooming of flowers and the unfurling of leaves. She could finally, effortlessly breathe. It was like someone had reached into her heart and taken all the stress away from her.

She hadn't realized how heavy it was.

Maia let out a long, slow sigh. Her shoulders curved forward and she could faintly feel Inkeri propping her up.

"There," the troll woman's voice sounded so far away. "Let them guide you, Maia."

But it didn't feel like guidance. It felt like someone had taken all her burdens for a little while. Not forever. She knew that soon enough they would hand them back to her. When they did, she would be more ready.

She'd needed a few moments to breathe. Just a few moments where she wasn't the woman this had all happened to, and instead, she was just herself again.

"I'll be here with you," Inkeri said. "Don't worry about anything. I'll be here with you the entire time."

And something in her soul relaxed at that. She wasn't alone. She didn't have to fear.

Maia could just *be*.

Chapter 38

Ragnar hadn't stopped working for nearly a week since the king had decided on their new plan. The generals were all very forceful about what their thoughts were for next steps, and that meant he had little time to even go home. But Inkeri had sworn she was taking good care of Maia, and he had to trust that there were some trolls with her best interest at heart.

Even if it hurt to think that she was on her own. His little human wasn't all that good at being alone, and certainly didn't like being too far from him. Though he'd seen her strength come back in waves, he wasn't sure that it was the same as it had been before the battle.

She'd seen too much. And part of that was his fault.

But now, he finally had time to go back home to her. Even though it was the middle of the night.

He was careful not to be too loud before he reached the bed, namely because he wanted to surprise her by sliding under the covers. Lifting the blankets carefully, he tried to make sure not too much cold air got underneath. If he could just get a little closer to her, then he could pull her against his chest. She would make that sweet little sound she did in her sleep when he showed up, and then sigh in that way that made every part of him clench in happiness.

Gods, he loved her. So much. And he wasn't sure how to tell her that, or if there was a way for him to tell her that without her thinking he was joking or lying. It shouldn't have been possible for either of them to fall in love with each other. Not considering their start, who they were as people, or all the other things that had led them here.

But he did. He loved the little noises she made in her sleep, the soft look in her eyes when she looked at his people, and the absolute wild abandon with which she threw herself into every single thing she did. When she got something in her mind, she did it. That was who his little human was.

Ragnar slid his arms underneath her limp form and gently tugged her into him. He just wanted to feel her for a little while. Then he would wake her up and tell her everything that was going to happen. But first, he wanted to enjoy her.

Until she willingly rolled against him and draped herself across his chest in a very not tired way. "You're too big to be that quiet, you know."

"You should be sleeping."

"I couldn't sleep." She nuzzled her head on his chest, pillowed by all the thick muscles there. "You've been very busy."

"The king keeps me busy." Even though he wanted to be anywhere but in the castle. And maybe... Maybe she wanted to hear that. "I'd rather be here with you. That's what gets me through the day, you know. I imagine taking you back to the illuminated glen. Or perhaps we'd go on a journey across your lands, camping underneath the stars.

I'd catch you rabbits, just like the first time."

She made a face he could feel pressed against his skin. "No rabbits—thank you."

"You liked the rabbit I gave you then."

"Because I was starving. I'd much rather find something more palatable than an adorable little creature." But he could feel her laughter even as she tried to hide it. "Unless you're insistent on killing small fluffy things."

Ragnar ruffled her hair and curved an arm around her a little tighter. "I have absolutely no need to kill fluffy things if you're not interested in eating them."

"Good. I thought maybe we could use a pet around here, anyway. Maybe a cat?" She sat up on his chest, using her hand against his collarbone to push up. "Do you even know what a cat is?"

"I do not."

"Oh, I don't think you'll like them. But they're fun pets and I wouldn't be quite so alone all the time."

He heard the words she didn't say. She wouldn't be so *lonely* if she had a pet. And that broke his heart. He knew he hadn't been around much, but... Ragnar caught a curl that had fallen in front of her face and tucked it behind her ear. "If that would make you happy, Maia, you can get all the terrifying creatures you want and fill this home with them."

"I think they need sunlight."

"We'll bring them above to keep them happy."

"Every day?"

Solemnly, he nodded. "If that is the burden I must bear, then I will carry you and all of your strange foundlings into the sun every afternoon."

It was as much of a declaration of love as he knew how to give. For her, he would do anything if it would make her smile.

Just like she was smiling now. That ridiculous, beaming grin that said she thought he was being silly. And he was. He knew the words he said were foolish and perhaps a little lovesick, but he couldn't stop them from coming all the same.

He had fallen so hard for this woman, it was almost embarrassing.

She watched him with those bright green eyes, shadows playing across her face like a loving hand trailing along her features. Ragnar traced those shadows, watching his massive hand dance across her features as though he'd never seen either of them before.

"What are you thinking?" she asked.

"Thoughts I will tell you eventually, fire hair. But not tonight."

Her smile softened. "Troll things?"

"Troll things." And that was why he was here, wasn't it? He was supposed to talk with her about this plan of the king's, one that required her to be a large player in this game.

But he didn't want to talk to her about that. He wanted to exist in this bubble where it was just the two of them and no one else. He wanted her to be "fine", as she kept insisting that she was, and to smile at him like that for a little while longer.

Maybe she knew him better than he realized. Because that smile he so adored fell from her face. "What's wrong?"

"Nothing is wrong."

"I know that expression, Ragnar. Something is very much wrong, and you don't want to tell me."

She read him too easily. Scowling at her, he tried to play it off like it was nothing. "You're too shrewd of a woman. Were you not afraid of me only a little while ago? You should measure that fear before you demand more of my attention."

"Ragnar."

"Fine," he muttered. But he couldn't look at her while he talked about it. So he let his head fall back on the pillow and stared up at the ceiling. "The king has a plan and you're part of it."

"A plan for what?"

"To strengthen us against the humans. Likely to figure out what your king is up to as well. Although I have my doubts we'll be able to successfully do that. Humans are very good at hiding what they're doing when they want to keep such information secret."

He let the silence between them fall, knowing that she was going to start asking questions soon. He wasn't disappointed.

"What is his plan?" she quietly prodded.

"Because we have successfully bonded as troll and troll wife, he believes that proves such a bonding is... worthy of pursuit."

That was a stupid way to say it.

Maia laid her head back down onto his chest, her cheek pillowed by her hands. "A bonding like ours? What does that mean?"

"Haven't you noticed your magic is stronger with me? It's not the place, it's us." He laid his hand on her back, drawing slow, measured circles there. "Apparently, with significant more practice, we can use each other's magic without touching."

"Really?" She popped back up again, her hair falling in front of her face with the movement. "Are you saying I could heal people?"

"You could try."

"I could do what you do?"

"With practice," he replied with a chuckle. Ragnar palmed the back of her neck and brought her back down to his chest. "Because of this, he wants to encourage more bonds like that. Previous human and troll pairings were rarely, if ever... willing."

She stilled against him, and he knew this was a sensitive subject to bring up. Considering what she had just endured, there were likely better ways for him to have said it. He just hadn't thought the words through until they were out of his mouth.

His brave little wife was quick to reply, "So other pairings couldn't do that because one of them really didn't want the other to use their magic?"

"Or neither of them did. My people have done horrible things to crawl out of the mud from which the elves made us." He resumed rubbing her back, hoping she didn't mind that he was doing so. "None of us are proud of that. But I cannot say that I regret what I was born from. I wouldn't be here today, capable of such a conversation if not for all the work my people did in the past."

Her fingers curved against his chest. "I don't know what to think about all of that. I feel sorry for the poor women who were trapped here."

"So do I. I know my lineage is full of human women who were terrified of their husbands, likely even hated them." He flexed his stomach, drawing up to press a kiss against her hair. "But I honor their fear by treating you in the way they should have been treated all those years ago."

She nodded against his chest. "I don't have an ounce of that fear. At least, not anymore."

"Good. Now the king sent a message to yours, stating that he would like an audience to prove that the... gift he gave us is still alive and well." At her silence, he added, "That's you."

"Oh, yes, I realize that's me. Your king wants to send me home?"

He tried to hear if there was hope in that tone. A part of him feared she would want to return home, that she would take any opportunity she could get to run.

But he didn't think that was what he heard in her voice. This would be easier if there was light in the room so he could read her expression. But the darkness encouraged a strange and brutal honesty between the two of them as well. He wanted to tell her the truth. He wanted to tell her everything that she wanted to know, all because it was easier with the darkness blanketing them.

"You will not stay there," he rumbled. "Your place is here with me, Maia."

"I don't want to stay there. But I'm not sure that the humans will let me return." Again, those tiny claws of her dug into his chest. "They gave me to you as a joke. They thought you would kill me, and likely assume that had already happened, considering the timeline. Bringing me to them, proving that I am well, don't you think that will just make them more angry?"

"That's not the point of you going." And here was the mad part of this plan. "King Egil wants you to make a declaration before the court. That you are alive and well, and that we have treated you as you have always wished to be treated. You can embellish. I'm sure saying we treated you like a princess would raise people's hopes a little too much. But he wants you to make it clear that there may be another path for them to choose, and a good one." Ragnar swallowed hard. "He wants you to convince the women of your kingdom that there is a life here, and that we will take them willingly."

Again, that silence. He had no idea what she was thinking, or if this plan was even possible. Maybe she didn't believe that human women would come here at all.

"Those with elven bloodlines are rare among humans," she

whispered. "Getting them to come here when there are many options among the humans for their pairings... It's no easy task, Ragnar."

"The king wants you to make it clear that we are not only looking for those with strong, elven bloodlines. Ones with even a drop, like you, those are the people we wish to marry. And even those without. We will take them here in the mountain and provide them with work and a home."

A soft gasp followed his words. "The king would take... all of them?"

"All of them."

Maia sat up yet again, staring down at him in confusion. "Why would he do that? The mountain has always been off limit to humans. Few of the trolls here trust my kind, especially now that the humans are actively hunting them down, even on the mountain. That's asking my people to come into a kingdom where they will most certainly be killed."

"He is prepared to cast a decree that humans are allowed here. But they must marry us for access to this place, and they must do so willingly. That's where you come in, fire hair." He sank his hands into the curls on her head, allowing himself to feel the silken strands as they curved and tangled around his fingers. "You are the one who needs to convince them that we're not monsters, and that we take care of what is ours."

Ragnar drew her closer, his gaze on those plush pink lips. Lips he desperately wanted to kiss so that they could forget this conversation for a while. If only she would allow him to do so.

Her breath hitched, and he knew from the way her pink tongue darted out that she was thinking the same thing. "I don't know if I can do that, Ragnar. You're bringing me into a court full of people who are so incredibly pampered that the mere thought of leaving their comfort will seem foolish."

"We don't care if the nobility hear you. It's the servants, the handmaids, the people who walk with those pampered fools that rule your kingdom. Those are the people we want to hear you say that there is another life with trolls who will worship the ground they walk upon."

That lovely, beautiful mouth curved into a smile. "Is that what you do? Worship the ground I walk on?"

"Was that not obvious?"

"Well, you might have done a better job of it. If you wanted me to think you worshipped me, after all."

He was done talking. They would continue this conversation after he'd made her scream in pleasure.

Ragnar rolled them until he was above her, braced on his forearms and pressing her down with his hips. "Would you like me to worship you now, wife?"

"If it pleases you."

A hungry growl rumbled through him. "It would please me greatly."

Chapter 39

Four days had seemed like more than enough to prepare herself. Maia had thought it would be easy to think of all the things she would say to the countless people who would hear her speak at this banquet. Four days would be plenty to get her outfit picked out, and to gather all the bravery she could muster around herself so that she didn't feel like her heart was going to stop.

She'd been wrong.

Four days flew by faster than she could even think the words. Every moment of every day leading up to leaving was filled with trolls. The generals lectured her on safety. Inkeri made sure she met with the other troll wives who sewed her a dress so beautiful, all in white, just like the day she'd been taken. They cut her hair, made sure there wasn't a speck of dirt underneath her nails, buffed her skin until she glowed.

All of it was exhausting, and every day she laid her head on the pillows and told herself she'd think about what she was going to say while she was falling asleep. Which she did, but then promptly forgot in the morning when she woke.

Then, the day before they were supposed to leave, she had to pack. Everyone became a whirlwind, all the hopes of the trolls landing on her shoulders even though Ragnar repeatedly told her that they all knew this was a longshot. None of the trolls had ever seen a human willingly choose them.

But she saw the young men who had joined their company to keep everyone else safe. She saw the way they had shaved the sides of their heads, and how their armor was well waxed or brand new. Maia knew they were trying to impress the women there, in the hopes that maybe, just maybe, a human woman would see them and think they were handsome enough to leave their homes for.

Gunnar had decided to go with them, against the wishes of all the healers who were seeing him. He swore he was fine, the whalers thought the should rest a bit more. But he was far too much like his brother. There was no waiting, in Gunnar's opinion. He should be in the fight.

She stood with Ragnar now at the base of the mountain, wondering where all that time had gone. She swore she'd had a few moments where she should have been able to think of what she was going to say and yet... now all that time had run out. Now they were here, ready to head to the castle that she could already see looming on the horizon.

Maia was surprised at how much she feared returning home. Part of her had thought she'd want to go back to her father's house. Maybe even beg to go back to her home, where she was sure someone else now lived. An empty building like that wasn't left empty for all that long. And yet...

She didn't want to. She didn't care if someone was living in that building, or if her garden had been destroyed. Because now she had another home, one without the ghost of her father looming over her head. She had a garden as well, although that was shared with a grumpy troll who didn't like listening to her or the plants. But that didn't matter, because it was a garden full of wild grown plants rather than cultivated flowers.

Ragnar reached for her hand, squeezing it tightly before they started off. The troll king had made it very clear that Ragnar and Maia were to be at the front of the pack. He wanted their entire entourage to walk through the city streets before they made their way to the castle. A spectacle, apparently. That was what King Egil wanted them to be. Every single person in her old home would stare at them, and somehow that made her want to turn right back around and leave.

"You're still doing okay?" he asked as they approached the city gates.

"I just don't want people to look at me."

"You're a troll wife. You can be proud of that."

"I just worry that they're..." She paused and then glared at him when he stiffened. "I'm not ashamed of walking in with a lot of trolls— you can get that out of your head."

"Well, that's what it seems like."

"I just don't like them looking at me! I didn't when I lived here, and I definitely don't now. I know the mean and aggressive things they're going to say, not just about your people, but about me." Maia rubbed her arm with her free hand. "That soldier called me a troll whore. It's quite the difference from wife."

They headed into the city and there was already a crowd of people gathered there. So many vaguely recognizable faces. The baker's wife, and the baker himself. A painter who had once done a portrait of her father for above the mantle. A kindly old woman who had once begged Maia's father for a few flowers to put on her husband's grave. Countless people who'd once been part of her life, and they were all standing at the edge of the street, staring with open mouths as Ragnar stopped the entire train of trolls to turn to her.

He framed her face with one hand, carefully, gently. And then he turned her to look at only him.

Leaning close, just like he had on their wedding day, he moved like he was going to kiss her so that only Maia could hear him. And for a moment, she thought he was going to say again that she would never be his wife.

Until he rumbled low and almost impossible to hear, "If there is any troll whore, it's me. Even now, I want you, my wife. Don't tempt me to show them just how much."

Her jaw nearly dropped open at the same time her entire body flared with heat. He couldn't just say that in public, could he? The man was dastardly. Wicked. Awful.

But he'd made her forget that there was a crowd of people staring at them like there was something wrong with what they were doing.

Grabbing his shirt, she tugged him down for a real kiss. As though it was only the two of them standing in this crowded space, and no one else mattered. Because at the end of the day, no one else did.

They were here. They were alive. And she was going to kiss her husband when he said something like that.

The crowd gasped, and a few people even made little shrieking noises of shock as she kissed the troll who had given her the world. Maia didn't let it be a quick kiss, either. She held him there with his shirt in her fist, making sure that she got a good taste of him before she drew back. And then, with a grin on her face that she was certain made it clear that she was pleased with herself, she started up the hill toward the castle.

Let everyone stare. Let them think whatever they wanted of her, because she had a husband who wasn't ashamed to kiss her in front of a crowd of people and lay his claim. Just as it should be.

With her head held high, she walked with Ragnar and the other trolls to the castle. In her white gown, she must have looked quite the sight. A forgotten bride returning to the scene of a crime where both she and her husband had been the victims. And then they strode into the same throne room where the wedding had taken place.

Countless people waited for them. Maia had been so nervous during that wedding, she hadn't looked around to see if there'd been any people she recognized. And there still weren't.

But Ragnar grumbled beside her, and she heard a few distinct growls from the trolls surrounding her. But they weren't growls of recognition. She wondered if the trolls didn't see any familiar faces, either. The thought made the hairs on her arms stand on end.

Rather than an open space like the wedding had been, packed full of people who had no idea they weren't about to see their princess get married, now the room was full of tables. Just banquet tables that were laden with food, so much so that it was piled on top of each other. At least three whole pigs, their mouths stuffed with apples. More vegetables than she could count—eggplants, peppers, asparagus, potatoes…all laid out among sausage links and platters of fish.

She'd never seen so much food all at once before, and she knew that wasn't a coincidence. King James was making a point, and that was a point very, very well made. Even the trolls seemed a little taken aback by the amount of food that was on those tables.

Her gaze made its way between the tables, all the way up to the king who sat on his throne. He didn't look bothered by the massive amount of trolls who were entering. Nor did he seem all that surprised that she was still alive, but she had to believe that was all a mask.

King James had given her away because he didn't believe that she would make it. He'd thought, and perhaps even hoped, that the trolls were every bit the animals he believed they were.

Her breath caught in her lungs when she locked eyes with him. Because this was a very powerful man, and he knew they wouldn't ask for an audience for no reason. He had to know the trolls had a plan. What would he do when he realized she was here to convince people to leave his kingdom? Would he try to kill her?

"Bravery and strength," Ragnar said before placing his hand on the small of her back. "Come with me, troll wife. Let's show them why it's better to be a troll."

She could do this. With him at her side, she could do anything.

Breathing in slowly, she walked between the banquet tables and made her way to stand in front of the man who used to be her king. She dropped into a small curtsey while Ragnar remained standing beside her. He did not show the king any kind of respect whatsoever. And that alone should have told her that this wasn't going to be as easy as she'd thought.

"Welcome home," King James said, his voice low and soothing. "We were so worried about you, Maia."

Ragnar's snarl echoed in the chamber. "You do not get to use her name, King. Not without permission."

"What am I meant to call her, then?"

She glanced over at Ragnar to see him cross his arms over his massive chest. "You can address me."

Something dark marred the king's expression, but he nodded like that wasn't an issue. "How lovely. I forgot that your people are more barbaric than ours. I wish to speak with the woman who came from my kingdom, and to ensure that she is healthy and well. How else am

I supposed to ease the fears of our people?"

Maia understood that Ragnar was trying to keep her safe, but if she wasn't allowed to speak, then her people would never believe that she wanted them to join her under the mountain.

So she took a step forward, farther from Ragnar's side and right in front of the king. All of his attention turned to her, and the weight of it was nearly overwhelming.

Brave and strong, she reminded herself. That was what she was going to be today, because that was what a troll wife would be.

"My king. I came here with the trolls in a bid for peace. I know there have been struggles at the border of Trollveggen, but I thought perhaps it would ease people's minds to see that I am alive and well." She tried a smile, although she was sure it was a little shaky. "More than well, honestly."

"More than well?" His brow raised. "I fail to see how that is possible with such... creatures at your back."

The insult did exactly what the king thought it would. The trolls growled behind her. She knew they couldn't help the unbidden sounds that came from the other side of their nature, but those growls sounded terrifying to the humans here.

This was going to work, she told herself. All she had to do was tell the truth.

Maia turned toward the people in the crowd, looking over them and measuring the differences between the trolls and the humans. "They do look very different from us, don't they?"

A few tittering laughs rose from the humans in the crowd. Her words stopped the growls as well. The trolls were now looking at her with confusion, likely unsure why she was joining in on poking fun at them.

But then her smile curved into something soft. "Since going to Trollveggen, I have found nothing but beauty and kindness. There is so much we don't know about them. It's hilarious to think, really. Did you know the trolls were impressive jewelers? Their piercings are not just marks of beauty, but all the deeds they have done in their lives."

She turned her head so the light could catch on the emerald gems in her own ears. A few women in the crowd leaned closer as though they were trying to see the markedly beautiful adornments.

"The trolls are more than we ever thought them to be." She turned back to the king, that soft smile still on her face in a way she desperately hoped was believable. "And their king sent me here with an offer that you should take."

He was flustered. Bright red splotches appeared on his cheeks, and she knew that he wasn't going to let this go easily. "Why would I do that? What offer could the trolls have that would tempt people like us?"

"A promise of peace. If there are some brave women in this kingdom, just like me, then the trolls will take them." She turned again to the crowd. "The trolls are not what we have been told. They are kind and true-hearted. They worship their women and the ground we walk on, and they amplify the natural magic that we carry with us. The troll king has offered to take in any woman who is interested in coming to the troll mountain. I am here to speak with any of you who might show interest."

Silence. That was all that answered her.

Maia cleared her throat. "Of course, maybe there are no brave women in this room. Which is fine."

A feminine voice rose from the crowd. "Why should we marry animals?"

Maia had never been able to answer a question more honestly than right now. "Because they aren't animals. They are descendants of elves, and we're lucky that they would ever consider marrying us at all. You cannot tell me you'd rather be chained to the bed of an overweight man fifteen years your senior who only sees you as breeding stock. The trolls are young, virile, and I can promise you that you will never lie there and stare at the ceiling, waiting for it to be over."

That did it. The outrage roared in the crowd as countless human men who were exactly what she had described started shouting at her. The trolls stepped in, enraged any man would ever speak to a woman like that, but there were a few women who were inching closer to her. They were interested—she could see it. If she could just get a few minutes with them, then she could make this work.

"Enough!" the king shouted behind her.

Everyone froze and looked at the man who had lost his temper on the throne.

But maybe he hadn't. Because he drew himself together and pinched the bridge of his nose. It took a while, but eventually, the king started to laugh.

"I thought we could have a banquet with you animals," he said. "I thought we could all be civilized and be together for at least a few hours without tearing at each other's throats. I see now that I was wrong."

"Your highness—"

He lifted his head, and she saw a flash of cunning in those eyes as the plan that she had been so worried he might have bloomed.

"Thank you, Maia. For giving me the chance to do everything I've always wanted."

And then the world exploded around her.

Chapter 40

Debris flew in his face just moments before he heard the cracking sound. The blast of air sent Ragnar staggering before a second blast knocked him onto his back. He saw the dust that rose in the air and all the clutter from stones that were suddenly shattered into a million pieces. And then he heard it. The harsh ear clap of an explosion and the screams that quickly followed it.

Then sudden silence. He could hear nothing at all as the entire room was tossed backward into the rubble that rained down around their heads.

His ears were ringing. At first, he thought it was the screams of the humans around him, but no. The blast had damaged his hearing.

Maia.

Where was his wife? He'd been standing right next to her and then... His hands slapped at the ground, trying to find anyone and anything that was next to him.

His fingers found a warm, breathing body. But that broad shoulder belonged to a troll. Blinking the dust out of his watering eyes, he tried to see through the clouds of dust and dirt. But he couldn't. The air was a wall of white and gray, filling his lungs with stones and rocks that were sharp bites every time he inhaled.

"Maia," he croaked, his throat finally working well enough that he could call her name. "Where are you?"

But no one replied. The only thing he could hear through the ringing in his ears were the groans of all the trolls laid out across the floor. Although some were humans, too. So many of them all crumpled together like their king had broken their wings and thrown them in a corner.

"Maia?" he said again, crawling over one of his own as he tried to figure out where she would have been thrown. She was smaller, but she'd been standing right next to him. She must've been in the same area he had ended up in.

Hands grabbed onto his shoulders. Fire burned where they did, and it was like his body woke up at the touch. Suddenly, he could feel all the stone shrapnel that filled his back and shoulder. Bruises spread down his muscles where he had hit the floor, and there was definitely a rib somewhere it shouldn't be. All of that and more pain, waves of it, crested over his head and sent him back down onto his forearms. His thighs quaked, shaking with the effort to keep himself at least somewhat crouched.

But then those hands grabbed onto him and hauled him to his feet. There were four of them. Four humans, all of them grunting as they lifted him off the ground and threw him onto something with wheels.

His head reeled. He'd hit it against the ground, he realized. Because the moment they made him move faster than a slow crawl, the entire world spun. Ragnar blinked rapidly, trying to get everything to come back into focus, but his vision remained so foggy. No matter what he did, the world continued to spin and he could only lie there and wheeze in pain.

He was still moving. Somehow. They were hauling him across bodies, because he could feel the bumps when they hit someone and heard the groans of those trampled beneath whatever carried him. Then another body hit the wood next to him.

Tilting his head, he looked over to see his brother there. And then another general who had come with them landed beside Gunnar, half on his brother and half on him.

Ragnar couldn't handle the pain anymore. His eyes drifted shut, and the world went dark.

When he came to, he had no idea where he was. It was darker than he remembered, but that helped with the splitting headache that threatened to take his head off his shoulders. When he groaned and rolled onto his side, he could see he was surrounded by stone. The floor was wet, dripping from the ceiling in singular plops that were so loud they made his skull splinter.

Ragnar took quick stock of his body. He was injured, but not enough to stop him from fighting if he had to. Already the wounds on his back were healing, likely his own power trying to take care of him in his sleep. It wasn't enough to waste an ounce of his magic on. The head, though, that he had to fix.

With the greatest amount of effort he'd ever used, he healed himself. Even his magic felt sluggish, because it was almost impossible to concentrate long enough for him to figure out what had happened. His head had hit the ground—he knew that. But there was a small amount of bleeding in his brain, it seemed, and thankfully he had woken up before it could do even more damage than it already had.

A wave of exhaustion hit him the moment he finished. Groaning, he slumped back onto the ground, using his forearm to pillow his head.

He had to rest. At least for a few moments, but then he would get up and figure out where he was, how to get out of it, and how to find his bride.

"They put us in a prison," his brother's voice quietly interrupted his rest. "Under the castle, it seems."

"Under the castle? Why?"

"Don't know. The whole thing was a trap."

"I realize that," Ragnar groaned, but then forced himself upright. If his brother was awake, then he needed to be as well. But when he finally sat up, he realized even more trolls surrounded him. Each of them were lined up against the wall in varying states of injury, and not nearly the same amount of trolls he'd come here with.

"Our king should have guessed this would happen," Gunnar growled.

"I'm sure he did." He had to believe that. Their king was no fool, and if he wanted this to happen or expected it to happen, then he would have made plans for it. What his plan was, however, Ragnar did not know.

"Maia?" he asked, the name sticking in his throat as fear rioted through him.

Gunnar shook his head. "None of us saw her when we were taken. It's a small reassurance, but I think someone would have noticed if she was still there. Her hair is hard to miss."

That was a small reassurance, and he had to take what he was given. Maia had to be alive. He would feel it if she wasn't.

He used a bit more of his magic. Just the barest hint of it, and reached out his hand toward a small weed that was growing on the floor. If Maia was alive, that plant would grow. It would spread its leaves, brighten with life that only she could give it. Because there was no sunlight here, no wisps, nothing to help the plant grow other than her.

"Come on," he whispered, knowing that the others were watching him just as intently. "Come on, Maia."

Just as he was about to give up hope that the plant would ever grow, it did. The stalk twitched just a little, moving like there was a breeze, and then it grew an inch in size.

"Not dead, then," Gunnar said with a grunt. "I don't know if that's better or worse than what I was hoping."

He wasn't certain, either. Maia deserved so much more than this, and he had led her right into a trap. He had to get out. Perhaps the others had already looked, but he would as well. In case they'd missed anything. So he stood and first walked the perimeter of the room. He checked all the stones along the edge, knowing that he was essentially in a tomb with all the trolls who were in this room.

There were two doors, one leading out into a hallway with the smallest window that he could peer out into. The hallway led into darkness, but he was certain that meant there were more cells. There was still a chance that the other trolls were still alive.

The second door was behind him, and it had no window. But there was a faint metallic scent coming from underneath it that sent an ominous ache throughout his stomach. He knew, without a doubt, that whatever was on the other side of that door was evil.

Gunnar stood as well, wincing as he approached Ragnar. "We've looked everywhere. No way out other than through one of those doors."

"Can we break one?"

"Tried that too, while you were out." His brother leaned his shoulder against the wall. "They've got us trapped here."

"Of course they do." Ragnar spat on the ground. "But we'll be ready when they try to take us out."

"Who needs weapons?" Gunnar flashed his teeth in a grimace, but Ragnar knew better than to believe that expression. His brother preferred fighting hand to hand. He'd seen what Gunnar could do to a human without a single knife or blade on him.

Footsteps echoed down the hall. Slight clicks that were not the boots of a soldier. Ragnar turned to peer through the small window and saw a stunning woman walking through the dark with a light in her hands.

She was beyond beautiful, as close to an elf as he imagined anyone could get. Golden hair spilled down her shoulders and chest. She wore little more than a white nightgown, and for a moment, he thought perhaps she wasn't supposed to be here. The lantern in her hands revealed the image of her form through that white nightgown. Lithe and stunning, a creature made to tempt a man.

He knew better than to trust her. Elves weren't trustworthy, and certainly humans were infinitely worse than them.

A low growl built in his chest as she approached their cell and then paused in front of him, just out of reach.

"Are you Ragnar?" she asked, her voice a lilting melody.

"I am."

"I'm so sorry they did this to you. I have found your bride, and I thought you would want to know what happened to her." She set the light down on the ground, and then almost seemed to pose where she stood, waiting for his response.

He didn't trust her. Not a bit.

Ragnar looked her over, letting his eyes linger on every part of her body. She posed even more when he did that, cocking her hip to the side and setting her hand on the swell there, as though she could make him look even longer. Then he got to her face and those pointed ears.

"Princess," he said. "We finally meet."

All of that prettiness disappeared the moment he realized who she was. One moment she was smiling at him, demure and kind. The next, her face twisted into the reality of disgust and contempt that she really felt. "Oh, you didn't let me have any fun."

"I have no interest in games. Where is my troll wife?"

"Wouldn't you like to know? Unfortunately, you're stuck here. And my father is going to make use of you just like all the other fighters that he has trapped here." She grinned. "You see, my father was the first one to realize there was more we could do with you trolls. Of course, we could fight you and battle you back into the shadows, but... why would we do that when we could do so much more?"

He hated that he had to entertain her at all. "My troll wife. Where is she?"

The slender blonde in front of him lifted a single shoulder gracefully. "What will you give me if I tell you?"

"When I get out of here, I will not kill you. That's the only thing you'll get from me."

"I just want to know why she was so interested in staying with you. That's all." She pouted and took a single step closer to the cell door. "Can I just look at it? I've always heard trolls are... impressive. I want to know the truth."

Could she look at...

He reeled back in disgust. "No."

"Really? Not even if I tell you where they're keeping your—what did you call her?—your troll wife?" She laughed. "What a silly name. And to think my father almost made me one of those. But he wouldn't ever part with me, not really. Why would he do that when he could just give you the gardener from down the street and you'd be too stupid to notice?"

"I look forward to killing you," he snarled. "Slowly, as I peel your skin from your flesh. I will hang you up from the highest part of this castle so that all who see your dangling body will know that you are hated by the trolls."

"Oh, I don't think you'll do any of that. But I will enjoy watching you die." She bent down to pick up the light she'd left on the floor. The candlelight spun inside of it, showing that there was a longer hallway, with many, many more doors. "Since we were supposed to marry, I'll give you a little hint at where you are. My father likes to watch people fight. He used to bring in warriors from across the realm who were renowned, but none of them were as good as trolls."

What? Gunnar shifted beside him, leaning closer to listen.

"What do you mean, princess?" Ragnar asked.

"Oh, I like it when you call me that," she said with a smirk. "I mean, my father enjoys watching people fight who are better at it than anyone else. Eventually, humans became boring to watch. Now, he enjoys watching your kind fight until there is nothing left inside of you but beast. It's a shame that he has to gather you all up with so much drama. I'm sure the nobility will be angry for a time. You were just supposed to eat the poisoned food, and then we'd bring you all down here nice and quiet. But this works too. What a show."

She turned to leave, and every part of his body screamed for her to return. He needed more information. He needed to learn where Maia was without violating his own bodily rights.

"Wait!" he shouted.

She paused and looked over her shoulder at him. "Did you change your mind? I'm not telling you anything about your little gardener unless you make good on what I want."

"No, I'm not doing that," he snarled. "Why tell us any of this?"

"Because we were supposed to be married, and because I want to see a good fight tonight. You've been injured—we can all see that. At least if you know what's coming, then maybe you'll be more prepared and give us a better show."

She turned again and disappeared into the darkness down the hall. His stomach twisted with the reality of what he was facing.

"A fight?" he muttered.

But Gunnar had gone white. "All those trolls we thought the humans had killed. The ones who disappeared. Are they here?"

They stared at each other and Ragnar had to wonder if the trolls were even alive. Had they abandoned so many of their own, unknowing that they were fighting for their lives? And all for human entertainment.

Chapter 41

She rolled onto her side, not entirely sure what had happened. One moment she'd been standing, and the next... She swore there had been a blast. She knew she had been standing right in front of the king, staring into his stupid, smug expression, and then...

Where was her memory of the rest?

And was she lying down?

Maia stretched her fingers out, not opening her eyes just yet. She was lying on what felt similar to a bed. But scratchy sheets met her fingertips first, and then there was the sensation of a hard mattress beneath her. Her hand dipped off the edge of the mattress and into thin air, so she was at least raised off the ground.

Had something happened? She tried to blink, but there was a grit that made it hard for her to open her eyes. Every blink felt like she was grinding glass beneath her lids. Still, she forced herself to look at the world around her. Though tears made everything appear hazy, she could see she was in a jail cell.

Shit.

Something had happened, and she had been out of it the entire time. Breathing slowly, she noticed there were a few other forms on the side of the room. More cots, maybe?

Hissing, she forced herself to sit up. At least if she was upright, then she could convince her body to give up the wrong feeling that made her heart stutter in her chest and her breathing difficult. There was something... not quite right about this.

The world tilted to the side, but she wasn't injured. She didn't feel any wounds. Maybe her shoulders and back were a little stiff, but only because she'd been sleeping on an uncomfortable cot. But the way everything was warping and listing to the side, all she could think was that they had given her something.

Some kind of magic or medicine had made her sleep.

Maia tried to reach inside of her magic. Just like Ragnar had told her she could do. He had claimed she could use his magic, and if she could, then that white light inside of her could maybe tell her if there was something wrong.

She wasn't sure she'd ever be able to heal like he could. There just wasn't enough magic inside of her to do so, but she felt like she could at least diagnose what was wrong. So she tried to focus on the feeling of his magic. That icy cold water that dripped down from her head to her shoulders, and then slid down her spine as it worked its way through her.

And then she swore she could see it. The poison that worked its way through her entire body. It was in her stomach, in her veins, all of it slithering through her exhausted body as it tried to make her go back to sleep.

So they had given her something. She didn't know what. But it felt like there was residue in her throat, which she could only assume meant they'd poured it into her mouth while she had been unconscious.

Memories filtered back. An explosion, the sound of people screaming and crying, the trolls groaning too far behind her. And then the sensation of someone grabbing the front of her dress and slamming her head into the stone stairs that had led up to the throne where the king had sat.

Was this all the king? Surely it had to be.

Still, she allowed the magic to flow white hot through her entire body. It burned through the rest of the drug that had taken up residence where it was not wanted, and suddenly the world steadied. She was far more capable of seeing what was right in front of her.

Cots with blankets that were tossed to the side, like two people had sat up rather quickly and then... left. She looked to her right, seeing a door with small bars for a window. The entrance to the cell, most likely, considering the guards would want to be able to look in and see if their prisoners were still alive. To her left, there was another door. This one had no bars, though.

Interesting.

Maia had no idea where she was. She'd never heard of a prison anywhere near the castle, which meant the king didn't want the rest of his people to know that this was here. He had to be hiding something terrible here.

Her gut said that she was still in the castle. Maybe that was wishful thinking, but she could feel it. They hadn't moved her far.

She sat there on her cot, waiting for something to happen until the mystery door opened. A woman fell through it on her hands and knees. Her hair was matted and tangled, full of dirt and red smudges that Maia didn't want to focus too hard on. Her clothing appeared worn and torn, aged beyond reason as she slowly crawled toward one of the cots.

Maia couldn't stop looking at the woman's hands. Her nails were chipped and dirt streaked. There appeared to be blood underneath them as well, although she couldn't guess why there was blood there. But the cracked tips looked like she'd been clawing at stone.

"Hello," Maia said, trying to say the word quietly.

The woman's head came up, her bright blue eyes wild with fear. This newcomer looked every inch a wild animal as she stared at Maia before suddenly flying backward. Her back hit the wall with a sharp crack that made Maia wince as the woman seemed to press herself against the stone as though she could sink into it and get away from whoever Maia was.

She had no idea what had caused this woman's panic, but she could only assume it was terrible. Slowly, Maia drew her legs up onto the cot and wrapped her arms around them. She made herself even smaller, trying to not be intimidating.

Silence filled the room. Maia would not fill this void between them with more words, not when the woman was panting with terror and staring at her like Maia had screamed. Fear like that couldn't be reasoned with, it could only be sat with until it eased.

Finally the woman blinked, her eyes barely visible through the tangled locks of her hair, and Maia could see the terror ease.

"Who are you?" the stranger finally rasped.

"Maia."

"Why are you here?"

"I don't know. I was hoping you might be able to answer that."

"Oh." The woman's eyes filled with tears. They dripped down her cheeks in massive drops, sliding through dirt and grime to leave tracks there. "Oh, no."

"Why Oh no?" Maia wasn't sure she wanted the answer to that question.

"You shouldn't be here. You don't want to be here." In a sudden burst of motion, the woman darted to one of the cots and threw the blanket over herself. She disappeared under the fabric, although even that shuddered with the weight of her emotions.

"No, I don't want to be here." Maia waited a few more moments before she moved from her own cot. She made sure that her steps made noise, so the woman knew she was coming over.

And then she crouched at the head of the cot, looking at the spot where the woman's head should be. She'd completely hidden herself underneath the fabric. Biting her lips, Maia reached forward and picked up the smallest edge of the blanket. Just enough so she could peer underneath it at the woman with haunted eyes.

"What's your name?" she whispered.

"Rose."

"It's nice to meet you, Rose. Would it be easier if I came under there with you?"

She shook her head, and then hesitated. "Maybe. I don't know if there's room, though."

A plan formed. When Maia was little, she used to hide under the blankets, too. It was hard to face the world sometimes. Hiding under the blankets made it feel like the world didn't exist for a little while. She twisted and grabbed the blanket behind her, throwing it over her head and the woman, so she made an extension of the safety Rose had created for herself.

"There," Maia said. "Now we're both under the blanket."

Rose breathed out a long sigh. "You're too nice for this place."

"I don't even know what this place is."

"It's where the king sends people to punish them," she whispered, her eyes going wide again. "You must have done something to make him very, very angry."

"I did. I came back when I was supposed to remain dead."

"Oh. That would make him furious." Rose tunneled further into the blankets. "You really don't know where you are?"

"Has anyone else heard of this place?"

The other woman seemed to consider her words. Her brows furrowed while she thought, and then she shook her head. "Probably not."

Maia needed an explanation for where they were, though. This woman had been through a lot, and talking about it would not be easy, but Maia needed to know what she had gotten into. "Rose? What is this place?"

A shadow darkened Rose's features, the remnants of what she had been through bleeding through her form until the hollows underneath her eyes appeared bruised. "The king sends us here to run the labyrinth."

"The labyrinth?"

"He keeps fighters here. They all battle each other in the center, and nobility watch from the stands around it. The men here fight to the death. But the winners..." She swallowed, her throat working hard. "They get their prize."

Fuck.

Oh, fuck, that was awful. She hadn't thought...

Maia closed her eyes, squeezing them shut as she reminded herself that she was a troll wife. She would get through this, just like she had gotten through so much in her life. "I'm sorry, Rose. That is an awful and terrible thing."

"It is."

"You were…"

"I am a prize," Rose whispered. "Myself and another. She had just arrived here, like you. But she was so terrified that she wouldn't stop screaming, so he gave her to… to…"

Silence. Just a sudden silence that was full of so much meaning. She had no idea who this mythical warrior was who killed women, but she intended to find out. Maia knew that was likely her own fate.

The king hated her. He'd made that very clear when he'd attacked his own people with that explosion just to punish Maia and all the other trolls. He would stop at nothing to get his revenge. For what reasoning, she had no idea. All she knew was that she was stuck in this place and she had to find a way out.

She had to find a way back to Ragnar. No matter the cost.

"Okay," she said. "Okay, so there has to be somewhere to go. There has to be a way out of here."

"There isn't."

"There's always a way out. Maybe if we talk to the guards, we could find one who could cast some pity on us. Someone here doesn't agree with what the king is doing. If we can just get them to help us, then we can get out of here. We can tell other people what the king is doing, and maybe then we'll be able to get everyone else out. If we can get out of here, then we can send help."

Rose was shaking her head vigorously. "The guards don't care."

"One of them has to care! You just said you're being given to people as a gift, Rose. And then whatever the…" She stopped speaking the moment she saw the expression on Rose's face.

She'd said something wrong. Rose sank in on herself even more. She curled tighter into a little ball, the grimy texture of her hair leaving streaks on the cot beneath her. "No, Maia. You don't understand. If any of us try to rebel or make anyone angry in this place, they'll just give us to him."

The words were said in complete and utter panic. Rose shifted away from her, like she didn't want to be anywhere near Maia, just in case someone had overheard them. Like no matter what happened, Rose was not going to be involved.

"Okay," Maia murmured, trying to get the other woman to calm down. "It's okay."

"It's not okay! They'll give you to him!"

"Who is he?" she finally asked.

Rose said straight up, ripping the blankets off both of their heads. Her hair stuck up in every direction and her voice deepened with intensity. "The troll. They'll give you to the troll."

The entire world seemed to pause.

The troll? There was a troll in this place?

Suddenly, it all made sense. Of course there was a troll here. The king hated their kind, and he'd been attacking them for ages. But in the end, a troll was always going to be a better fighter than a human. They were bigger, more aggressive, more attuned to all the abilities that humans had never had. Maia had seen the trolls fight. She knew how powerful they were and how easy it was for them to fight through an entire group of human men. Any one of them could cut through a crowd of ten without weapons. She had no qualms about that.

But clearly, this was worse than she believed. If the king had captured trolls and was making them fight, giving them women as a gift as though that was a worthy endeavor, all she could think was that they wanted to be freed.

Humans weren't going to help her. But a troll might not have lost hope. Not yet. Not while there was still a fight possible. And even if they had given up, maybe she could convince them to fight one last time.

Standing, she straightened her shoulders and went right to the door with the small window. Banging on it, she screamed at the top of her lungs. The sound would carry, she knew that. And if no one would come to see her just yet, then she would keep screaming until the guards were so annoyed they had to come and get her.

It didn't take long. Soon enough, there was the thundering sound of boots as Rose whimpered in her corner. She'd fled from the cot the moment Maia started screaming.

The guard on the other side of the door swore at her. "Shut the fuck up, bitch!"

"What you're doing here is wrong." She spat through the window, pleased when her aim held true and it struck his cheek.

The man winced and then glared at her. "You're on thin ice."

"Good. Fuck you. Fuck this place. And fuck the king."

His eyes widened. "If you're not careful, we'll give you to the worst creature you've ever seen. I was going to give you to one of the newer fighters first. He might even be a little gentle with you."

"No, thank you," she snarled. "Do your worst."

And she could see it in his eyes. He was going to.

Good.

When he walked away, Rose stayed shaking her corner. "You don't know what you've done!"

"I know exactly what I've done," Maia replied, before sitting primly on her own cot. "I've given myself to the troll."

Chapter 42

Ragnar bided his time. Every single troll tried to figure out if there was a way out of this prison, but there wasn't. Even those who had stone magic, the ones who could sing to the very mountain, were unable to move the stones in this place. They were uniquely trapped. Perhaps there were even spells to prevent them from getting out.

He and his brother could wait for hours until it was the right time. Soon enough, he would find his bride again. Soon enough, he would destroy all who stood between him and Maia.

Time had no meaning in this place. Therefore, Ragnar had no idea how long it took for the door with no window to open. All he knew was that they had not been given any food or water. Perhaps they weren't expected to live long enough to need such things.

The door opened and revealed bars on the other side— a barrier between them and three guards, who stood there looking rather bored. There was no way for the trolls to get them, but it was very easy for them to corral his people wherever they wanted them to go. Unless the

trolls refused to move, that was.

One of the guards snickered. "If you want to eat, you'll come out of that room. There's food at the end of the hall. If you don't want to eat, that's fine. We don't care if you starve."

So there wasn't a choice after all. He looked around at the trolls with him, then at his brother. Gunnar was already looking rather pale. They had to eat. They had to stay healthy if they were going to get through this.

Ragnar was the first to stand. He cracked his back, taking his time so the humans didn't think they could just order him around. Because they couldn't. He made this choice for himself and for his people. No other reason.

He was the first to exit the room and start walking down the long stone hallway. Unfortunately, that also meant he was the first to see the mess that awaited them.

The floor was stained with old blood that made the air metallic. He could almost taste it on his tongue. No one had cleaned in ages, so he wasn't sure if the floor was dirt or if it was just months on end of people bleeding as they walked this same path. But then he stepped through a door into what appeared to be a well lit room.

Bars still stood between him and a crowd of people who were all drinking wine out of goblets, eating from plates that filled the air with delicious notes of meat and cheese. Humans, all of them in clothing that was far too fine for them to be anyone other than nobility. Each of them wore masks, but they stared at him with hungry gazes.

"Look at that one!" a woman said, stepping dangerously close to the bars. The mask on her face was of a raven, with feathers sweeping out over her cheeks and hiding her features. "I'd like to place a bet on him. He's so big."

"You think he'll defeat the Bull?" The man beside her snorted, before taking a bite from the overflowing plate he held. He had a mask that looked like a pig. Hilariously, it seemed to fit, considering his figure.

"I think he could fight the Bull."

"I don't think anyone can win against the Bull. That's what I'm saying, darling."

She reached for his plate and grabbed the massive turkey leg balanced on top. She dangled the food close enough to the bars that he could grab it if he reached quickly enough. "You'll win for me. Won't you, beast? I have a lot of money on you."

He bet she did. Growling low in his chest, he was about to lunge for her when he felt Gunnar step up behind him.

"Leave it," Gunnar said in the black tongue. "They're not worth it, brother."

The woman flinched away from them, pressing her hand against her chest. "By the gods. Did you hear that one? He speaks like a wizard!"

"Warlock, darling."

"Either! Do you think he was trying to cast a spell on us?"

Gunnar snorted. "Ridiculous humans."

"We'll speak in the black tongue from now on," Ragnar said. "And we'll get out of here as soon as we can."

He continued walking down the halls, heading toward the end without knowing what he would get to see. The Bull? He wasn't sure who that could be, but he was certain it was one of the missing trolls.

Gunnar muttered behind him a quickly laid plan. "We aren't likely to get out of here soon. They won't let us fight together. That wouldn't be much of a show for them to watch. Win your battle, brother. And quickly. Once we figure out what to do, we'll stop killing our own. But you have to know that is the direction we're heading. They aren't giving us a choice."

"It's been a long time since I've killed another troll."

It was a rarity. Sometimes there were trolls who left the mountain. Ones that went rogue and decided to take whatever they wanted. Their king would send them out to hunt down the deviant troll who needed to be ended. Ragnar had only gone on one of those war bands. It was infinitely harder to kill his own kind than it was to kill humans.

"I feel the same," Gunnar muttered. "But we have no choice."

Finally, they reached the end of the room, and it opened up into a massive arena. There were countless doors, all of them leading into more hallways, it seemed. Movement at the top of all those walls caught his attention.

There were seats up there. Stands that were now filling up with humans. The same people he had seen in that room, all of them still carrying food and wine as they meandered to their seats, still talking and gesturing as though a bloodbath wasn't about to unfold before them.

The king himself walked out into the stands and every single troll around him started to growl. The sound of their anger filled the room, and the human king seemed to only revel in the power that he had over their emotions.

"Trolls!" the king shouted. "Welcome to my labyrinth. There are no rules here, only that you are to try to live. Fight until the end, and I will reward you."

A band of women walked out onto the stands beside him. All of them were dirty, trembling, terrified creatures. But from somewhere deeper in that labyrinth, he heard the thrilled shouts of human men.

Men who likely knew that these women were to be their prize if they managed to beat a troll.

"Now, I know the humans in this labyrinth have been fighting hard," the king continued. "Today, you may hunt in packs! I have many new trolls in this arena, and I want to see who fights the best. If you wish to share your prize among five men... well, that is up to you."

More shouts.

More pleased cries that were so dastardly, so wrong, it made Ragnar's head spin.

Gunnar hissed beside him, "They use women as prizes here? What for?"

"You know what for," he murmured.

Ragnar kept his gaze on the women, moving down the line of them even though they were so far away it was hard to see them. He wasn't sure why he was bothering. But some part of his soul screamed that he was so close.

And there, at the end of the line, a woman stood with her chin raised. She looked proud standing there, unbroken. Her fire red hair blew in the wind and he knew, he just knew, that was his bride.

"Maia," he said, his voice cracking around the word. "She's alive."

Gunnar's head whipped up, looking for his troll wife and finding her just as quickly. "Would you look at that?"

"I knew he wouldn't kill her."

"No, but he's going to give her away as a prize." Gunnar hissed out another angry sound. "Now you really have to win."

He did. And that meant hunting humans through the entire labyrinth and killing as many as he could.

A feral grin split across his mouth. "Happy hunting, brother. Tear through flesh and bone if you have to, but destroy them all."

"Hunt well." Gunnar cracked his neck. "Let's see how many we can kill together. Just like the old times."

Well, not entirely like the old times. They had hunted through a forest, free and wild, as the mountain sang beneath their feet. Here, they killed for the enjoyment of the humans in the stands above them, their cries for blood thirst rankling and harsh.

Still. He would do it. If that was what it took for him to get a few moments with Maia? He would do anything. Anything at all.

"Let the battle begin!" the king's shout echoed above the labyrinth.

Ragnar bolted down one of the tunnels. He didn't care where he started. He'd studied labyrinths like this before. As long as he continued turning in the same direction, he would make it to the center. Whether that was the goal or not, he didn't care. He'd kill anyone who stood in his way.

He came upon the first group of three human men in mere moments. They had weapons; he did not. But he'd never needed weapons to kill a human.

Ragnar tore through the three of them with all the pent up rage that burned in his chest. He wanted them to die. He wanted to hear their screams as he plunged his hand into their hearts and ripped them out of their chests. Bloody and still beating, they heated his hands with fresh blood as he turned to the next. They never stood a chance.

The three of them had no idea what they were getting into when they were fighting a troll. Though they had swords, those were inefficient unless someone knew where the weakest part of his flesh was hidden. They didn't know anything about trolls.

The next two men were more cunning. They were slower in their approach, far more deliberate. At least one of them knew Ragnar was more sensitive underneath his arms, and that the skin was thinner there. The man kept trying to shove his blade in that direction, but had no luck as Ragnar continued to turn. They died screaming, and he left them on the ground, barely breathing. One of them was missing an arm, the other with a broken neck that would leave him to die slowly.

Perhaps tragically. Ragnar didn't care.

He fought through more and more people, all of them blurring together until he had a moment of reprieve. There was a lull in humans who wished to take a chance on fighting him. A fact he was grateful for. Ragnar was covered in sweat and blood—some of it his, he was certain. Breathing hard, he leaned against the wall of the labyrinth and tried to gain his bearings. He was closer to the center now. He was certain of it.

Closer to her.

With every battle, every time someone charged him, he kept his eyes on Maia. She stood strong where he had last seen her, her fiery hair blowing in front of her face as she watched him. He fought for her. She must've known that.

The human audience members were chanting, as they had been for much of his battles. Some of them shouting for him, others for more of the trolls he'd seen around. But now he could pick out a particular word they were chanting.

"Bull! Bull! Bull!"

Wasn't that what the woman had said? She'd wanted to see him fight the Bull?

Hairs raised on the back of his neck, and he knew there was someone standing on the other side of the hallway looking at him. Part of him hoped that the Bull was a massive human. Perhaps someone who could actually give him a fight, considering the others really hadn't yet. He was so angry, so frustrated, that throwing fists seemed the only way to get through. But another part of him already knew that when he lifted his head, he would be looking at someone who was not human.

Ragnar let his gaze go to the end of the hall, picking out the silhouette of a massive troll who stood at the end. He wore little more than threadbare trousers that barely clung to his massive thighs. A scarred chest was shaped like a barrel, flexing with every breath. His shoulders lifted up and down in rage, likely already blinded by the need to destroy everyone and everything that he could. Especially if this troll had been here for a long time. He would fight until his last breath for whatever it took to stay alive.

But there was something familiar about this silhouette. Yes, the troll had the same massive shoulders and broad form as the rest of them. But this one had horns. Curled ram horns that stuck out from the crown of his head. There were few trolls who still had horns. Most of such animalistic qualities had already been bred out of their lines.

Ragnar only had a second to prepare before the massive beast lunged at him. The horned troll sprinted down the hallway exactly like what the people called him. A bull. If he struck Ragnar, then he had no wonder if the beast would harm him. But there was something familiar about his shape, and even more familiar about the lumbering, awkward gait that propelled him forward.

Ragnar darted to the side, twisting so the new troll couldn't grab onto him, and then hooked a hand around the troll's horn. Holding onto it, he forced the troll to spin around and look at him.

"Bjorn?" he asked, his voice low with terror at what he had found.

Because it was Bjorn. It was his oldest friend, the young man he had fought and trained with. The same person he had looked up to, the one who had helped him learn how to use his magic by breaking his own arm, was here.

But this wasn't the Bjorn he knew. This troll in front of him had lost his mind. Drool dripped from his tusks. His eyes were wide with rage and blinded by all that stood in front of him. He didn't even react to his own name.

"Bjorn!" Ragnar shouted, then threw him by the horns into the wall. "Don't you see who's in front of you? It's Ragnar, damn it!"

The troll lunged at him again, grappling with him the moment their arms locked. And damn, he was strong. Much stronger than anyone Ragnar had ever fought, but he supposed that made sense.

Bjorn had been fighting a lot longer than he had.

Ragnar wrestled with him, fighting to get the other man in a headlock so he would at least look at him. With a quick twist of his body, he used his old move, hooking his knee behind Bjorn's and bringing his friend to the ground. In the old days, Bjorn would have laughed and heaved him off of him, but this version of his friend did not.

With another twist of his body, Ragnar planted himself on top of Bjorn, pinning his friend to the ground. But he just remained there, frozen, staring down into Bjorn's face, which almost seemed... accepting. Like Bjorn wanted to die.

"It's me," Ragnar tried again. "It's me, brother."

And for the barest moment, his friend was back. Bjorn seemed to recognize him. The fog of rage cleared, and it was like looking at his old friend once more.

"Ragnar?" he asked.

"Listen to me. My troll wife is here. She's one of the prizes for the fight today. I need to get out of here with her, and I need your help to do it."

"You can't get out."

"I can, Bjorn. I can and I will." Ragnar wasn't sure how yet, but he would. "Will you help me?"

Bjorn shook his head, once, twice, and then seemed to relent. "If she's given to me, I'll keep her alive. That's the best I can do."

"It's all I can ask."

Ragnar got off of him, helping his friend to his feet. They stared at each other for a long moment before taking off in opposite directions. They both knew they had the same enemy to fight. Unfortunately, there was no way to win that battle together.

445

A Darkness So Sweet

Chapter 43

Maia watched the blood bath before her with hatred burning in her chest. There was a time in her life when she would have been just like Rose standing next to her—shaking like a leaf, willing to do whatever it took to be given to the kindest person here.

But she wasn't that woman any longer. She was going to fight until there was no more breath in her lungs. She would battle with any person who tried to touch her, troll or not. Just as Ragnar fought for her down there. She watched him as he killed countless people with a fury unmatched.

So Maia stood, and she watched. She marked every single injury that happened to her people, and she kept faces in her memory. Every person in those stands would die by her hand or her order. Every single noble who thought it was fine to put anyone in a situation like this where they had to fight to stay alive. Human or troll. Both were so incredibly wrong.

She committed to memory the faces of the women standing beside her. Each one of them was weary. They had likely been here a long time. Each one of them deserved more than to live like this, wondering when they would finally die.

At first, she thought the king would look at her. Perhaps he would goad her, saying that this was what she got for returning. But he didn't. She was so beneath him that he never even looked at her. He just drank his wine, spilling it all over the floor as he gestured at the deaths that were taking place in the labyrinth he had built.

Maia wanted him dead. She wanted him writhing underneath her foot as she ground her heel against his throat. And then she wanted Ragnar at her side, to watch her mate kill him in the most gruesome way a talented troll like him could think of.

She wasn't sure how long the whole process took. Only that she stood there until her legs were aching and turning purple. But she endured. Watching every single death so that she would never forget this moment.

Until the guards moved up behind them. Then she looked over at the king, who stood and raised his hands. He shouted, although she wasn't sure how anyone could hear him over the crowd's cries for death.

"And that concludes the fight of the labyrinth! Those who are alive, I will gift you a prize for the evening!"

He gestured to the line of women, and Maia could only hope that she would be given to Ragnar. She'd seen him down there. She was going to get to him. No one could stop her.

The guard she'd spat at grabbed her arm and gave her a little angry shake. "You're the one who wanted the troll, weren't you? Come on, bitch. Let's see if you're as angry once you spend an evening with one of those monsters."

"They aren't monsters."

"This one is," he muttered, dragging her away from the others.

Rose tried to catch her hand, though her fingers slipped through Maia's. "Be careful, Maia!" she called out. "He's killed everyone else!"

Killed everyone else? What would lead a troll to do that? All the trolls she'd met valued the lives of women far more than just to… kill them. She staggered after the guard, disappearing into the shadows that blinded her after standing in the bright lights for so long.

Before she even knew where they were, the guard was already shoving her in a direction with an angry grunt. "Good luck, troll whore."

And then there was only silence. She stood very still, waiting for her vision to come back. If this had been Ragnar's cell, she was certain he would already have gathered her up in his arms. Which meant this wasn't Ragnar's. Which meant…. It could be anyone.

Taking a deep breath, she started with honesty. "If you're one of the trolls I came with, then know I am Ragnar's troll wife."

A rustling noise came from the corner. Slowly, ever so slowly, she turned her head to look at the troll who crouched in the corner. He had his back to her, and there were horns stretched over his head. Not features she'd ever seen in their kind before, and that was enough to give her pause. She had an idea who he was, and how dangerous he was.

But she'd heard the other women whispering about him. The Bull, they called him. And he'd certainly torn through every single person who'd tried to fight him. Even Ragnar, although they had both stopped at the last second. Much to the disappointment of the surrounding crowd.

He shifted a bit more, and the light caught in his eyes, an eerie glowing green staring at her over his shoulder. "Don't scream."

"I wasn't planning on it."

"I don't like it when they scream." He seemed almost to be talking to himself as he straightened.

By the gods, he was big. Bigger than any troll she'd ever been around. He was so much taller than she was, broader, and with more rippling muscles that were painfully on display. But she could also see his ribs. Too many of them. Too easy to count because he'd been starved for so long.

He took one lumbering step forward, awkwardly moving. She feared other women might have thought he was lunging at them, but she could see he was limping. His right leg was so stiff, he could hardly walk, let alone approach her without looking terrifying.

She stayed where she was, not screaming or allowing herself to even feel fear. She let him come to her, as slowly as he needed to.

And when he stopped so close that his chest almost brushed hers, she looked up at him. "My name is Maia," she said. "I'm Ragnar's troll wife."

He leaned down, all deadly intent and flashing eyes. Closer and closer until she could feel his puffing breath against her face. "They gave you to me."

"A troll wife cannot be given to anyone other than her husband."

It seemed to shake him out of whatever state he was in. One moment he was glaring, and the next, he let out a long breath that sounded like a sigh. He curved in on himself, all that anger draining out of him until he took two of those staggering steps away from her. Gesturing to the cot, he finally said, "Sit, troll wife."

She still wasn't certain if he would harm her. Rose's warning ran through her head a little too loudly for her to trust this troll. After all, he had killed other women.

But, as she perched on the edge of the cot, she remembered he had asked her not to scream. That he didn't like it when they screamed.

Perhaps that was part of the issue. The women they tossed in here reeked of fear. They screamed when they saw him, antagonizing every animalistic part of him just by existing. Maybe, just maybe, he didn't have as much control as the other trolls.

A low, keening sound echoed in this throat. "You smell of fear now. Why?"

She shook her head. "I don't know you. This is a unique experience for me."

"I would not..." He blew out a long breath. "I do not want to harm a troll wife."

She noticed the word switch and the way he emphasized the words "do not", as though he needed to convince himself that they were true. He didn't want to harm her, or at least, some part of him didn't.

So she forced herself to relax, tried her best to drain all thoughts of fear from her mind, and watched as he limped to the corner. He had to bend awkwardly to reach something on the floor, though she couldn't see what it was in the shadows. Then he was limping back to her with a small brass cup in his hands. It was dented on all sides, making it almost impossible to tell what it once might have been.

But it was full of clear water. He awkwardly knelt in front of her again, holding the cup out with clawed hands.

"A troll wife should always be offered refreshments," he seemed to murmur to himself. As though he had to remember the rules for all this. "They drink before we do."

Swallowing hard, she reached for the cup in his hands. But instead of grabbing it, she touched the gnarled claws that tipped his fingers. They were curled in toward his palms. Sharp-tipped and cracked on almost every single one, they looked painful.

His hand trembled under her touch, but he remained where he was. Painfully crouched there, his bad thigh already shaking, but allowing her to touch his sharpened nails like this was normal like he should expect her to do this.

"My heart bleeds for you," she whispered. "You should never have been here this long, warrior."

"I was taken many years ago. This is my life now."

"It's not your life. You don't have to stay here any longer than we let you. The trolls have come to take you away."

He looked up at her, his dark hair falling in front of his features as though he wished to obscure what he looked like. "I wouldn't know how to live outside of this place, troll wife. It has been too long, and I have been too damaged."

Yet again, her heart squeezed. The things that had been done to this man, to all the people here... they were wrong. So incredibly wrong.

Maia hesitated. She reached for his face and cupped his jaw in both of her hands. This man had seen too much pain and torment and deserved a soft touch. She tilted his face up to look at her, smoothing his hair away from his features so he could see her well.

"What is your name?" she asked.

"Bjorn," he replied. "Although I did not remember it until Ragnar reminded me of a life before this."

She knew that name. Ragnar had told her stories about him in the dead of night, but he'd thought that this friend was dead, not that he was just missing.

"I'm sorry they let you stay here this long," she said quietly. "But if they had known you were alive, they would have fought until their very last breath to get you back. I hope you know that, Bjorn."

She could see the pain in him. The ache that he wanted to believe her words but also was terrified to believe them.

"I have kept myself alive for many years on the anger at my own people for dooming me to this fate," he growled. "You're asking me to let go of the very thing that kept me alive."

"I am. Because it is not the truth that's keeping you fighting. If you wish to fight, if you wish to help us, then you can. But if you have given up all hope for your people, then I understand that as well. You are a good man, Bjorn. Or you once were. Whatever you have done to stay alive does not make you any less of a good man."

His dark eyes stared up into hers and she saw something break. Some bitter part of him that had remained just so that he would continue fighting shattered at her words.

"I have been here for many years. There are few ways out of this place without being caught. I have found... one way." He straightened, but then placed the cup in her hands. "It will not be easy, but it is a way out."

"You know how to escape?"

"I know how to get some people out while one person remains behind. It was my idea to leave myself, but..." He took a deep breath. "If what you say is true, then that means the trolls will come back for me. They will know that I am here and help will eventually come."

Oh no.

No, she couldn't ask him to do this.

She stood, the cup shaking in her hands. "This was your escape, you mean?"

"I have been planning it for many years. Just waiting for the right moment."

She took another step closer. "I can't ask you to give up your freedom for everyone else here. You know that. You've been here for far too long, and asking you to do that…"

"You can ask it. Because you are a troll wife and if anyone can ask me to do so, it is you." He nodded toward the cup in her hands. "Drink. You will need your strength."

"Where did you even get water?"

He nodded toward the wall. "We are near water, but not enough that it flows freely. I gather it for days and then have a single cup to drink."

She stared down at the water he had given her. His single cup of water. She had no idea what it was like to not drink for days, but she knew she wouldn't survive it. She took one mouthful of blissfully cold water before holding it out to him.

Bjorn shook his head. "Drink it all."

"I can't do that. When was the last time you drank?"

A low chuckle filled the room. "It has been a long time since I have had water, but trolls are hardier than your people. We can go many days without water or food. I will not die, but you might."

Her eyes filled with tears. "It's not a choice anyone should have to make."

"No, it isn't. But it is the one I make in honor of your husband who saved my life."

Again, her heart hurt. Because that wasn't at all how Ragnar remembered it, and she desperately wanted these two to have a moment where they could clear the air. And perhaps, a lot of the guilt they carried between the two of them would finally disappear.

She drained the cup and then sat back down on the cot. "All right. What's the plan?"

"There's a portion of wall in the labyrinth that is flimsy. A group of trolls crashed through it in the early days, and I know for a fact they didn't rebuild it strong enough. The only problem is that a group of trolls and yourself will need someone standing in the way for you to get all the way out. Once you're out of the castle, the trolls should be able to fight their way out."

"How were you going to do that on your own?"

He flashed her a grin that revealed a missing canine. "I was going to run very fast."

"You were going to get killed."

"Maybe. But at least then I would be free."

She swallowed hard. "All right. Tell me everything you know about this section of the wall, where it is, and how long it's going to take us to get through."

"You really aren't afraid of me," he murmured.

"I'm a troll wife." Maia laughed a bit before trying to get herself together. "And this is rather an unusual circumstance, isn't it? It feels like a story people would tell in Trollveggen to scare their children at night."

He hummed low under his breath and then used a curled claw to start drawing on the floor. "Let me show you the labyrinth, Maia, wife of Ragnar. And together, we will make a plan."

Chapter 44

He's gone, Ragnar," Gunnar said, grabbing onto his arm and tugging him away from the body of what had once been a troll he trusted. A troll who had fought beside him countless times.

Now, there wasn't much left of him to save. Ragnar's magic was depleted from days and days on end of trying to save those who'd been injured in this labyrinth. There wasn't much else he could do, not with his magic hanging by the thinnest thread. He could heal bruises, but not a nearly severed head.

He allowed Gunnar to drag him away, staring at the blood splattered walls of the labyrinth that surrounded them. The king had quickly realized that with this many trolls, he couldn't release them all together. It had taken him what felt like a week to find new human warriors for them to battle, and then he pulsed the trolls in. There was enough time for the trolls to get overwhelmed before another troll was released into the arena. Each new troll ran to the one who had come before them, trying desperately to reach them before the worst happened.

Ragnar had just done it for Gunnar, and Gunnar had done it for the trolls before them. But in the few weeks that they had been here, the multiple times they had suffered through this exact situation, they had lost too many. Six trolls out of the twelve who had been in the cell with them. Ragnar knew there were more in other areas of the prison. Trolls who had been captured with him, and likely others as well.

He just hoped they all reached the realm of the dead with their heads held high. They had fought well. They had died in glory and valor.

And someday, he would fight until his last breath to kill this king.

Breathing in deeply, he nodded and turned to his brother. "Let's go. Where are the others?"

"In the center. It's easier to defend."

He took only the briefest moment to look up at the stands. He did it often these days. Anytime he paused to catch his breath, he stared up at her. His pillar of fire. A beacon to tell him he could keep going.

They ran. The humans were given better weapons, and they didn't want to get caught by a larger group of the men. He and his brother were tired, hungry, thirsty. He didn't know how much longer the trolls could all keep going like this. Soon enough, they would all make a mistake that would be their last.

When they made it to the center of the labyrinth, there was another familiar face waiting for them. Bjorn stood there, his horns tarnished with age and smeared with blood. His chest rose and fell with each breath, barely leashed rage gripping him as he stood there looking at the other trolls.

They'd all had run-ins with him. Bjorn did not give anyone even a hint of mercy. He'd killed multiple trolls already, or at least, that was what they were told. Ragnar had a feeling they were mercy kills, considering the details he'd heard. Bjorn only killed those who were already weak, or so injured they wouldn't make it back to the others.

Easy pickings, a few of the trolls had told him. But Ragnar knew it wasn't that. Bjorn gave the trolls a quick death, where the humans wouldn't have.

"What are you doing here?" Ragnar asked, nodding for Gunnar to return to the others and make sure that their old friend hadn't done any damage while they'd been gone. Gunnar was quick and light on his steps, skirting by the angry beast.

Bjorn couldn't be reasoned with when he was like this. This was a troll who had been broken in so many ways. No one could get through to him, no matter how many times Ragnar had tried.

"Getting you out," Bjorn snarled.

"Getting us out?"

"I need you all to head to the back right corner of the labyrinth. The wall is a different color. Wait there for me. I'll return when it's time." Bjorn started to leave, only pausing when Gunnar made a sound of disbelief.

His brother had never known when to keep his mouth shut. "Why should we trust you? After all the troll blood you've spilt, I'd rather take my chances here than with you."

Bjorn merely looked over his shoulder at him, the glare turning his eyes to chips of obsidian. "I'm not doing it for you. Maia needs to get out of here. They aren't going to give her to me again. We haven't been giving the Watchers enough of a show."

"The Watchers?" Ragnar repeated, his body lurching forward at the sound of her name.

"There are humans who pay to see what we do to the women gifted to us. They are the worst of the lot." Bjorn gestured to the crowd above them, many of the humans already pointing at the gathering of trolls and shouting with excited tones. "These are the ones who are here for blood. Some of them are here to see the prowess of trolls in other ways."

No wonder Ragnar and Gunnar had been getting worse and worse places in the labyrinth. Just two days ago, Ragnar had been the first one in the arena and they'd made him wait nearly double the time for another troll to get in to help him. He'd nearly been pinned by a group of seven humans with weapons that could pierce through his skin before help had arrived.

He'd nearly died. And all because he wasn't touching the human women that the king had gifted him.

But that meant…Blinding rage seared through him. Bjorn had been given Maia. Multiple times.

"Did you–" He couldn't even say the words. Couldn't get them out.

His old friend eyed him with pity. "No, Ragnar. She is a troll wife. I have lost many of the old ways, but not that one."

Blowing out a long breath, he squared his shoulders and told himself they were all struggling here. The humans had put them through the worst that they could, and at least Bjorn hadn't touched her. "Fine. Where in the labyrinth?"

Bjorn nodded to his feet, and Ragnar could see that he'd already drawn a map on the floor. It was drawn close enough to the stone that it was mostly obscured by the walls, so the humans in the stands couldn't see it.

Ragnar nodded, and then turned his attention to the other trolls as Bjorn headed back into the labyrinth. "We don't have a choice."

"I don't trust him," Gunnar replied as he helped one of the other trolls stand. The woman was pale and had her hand pressed against her side where a stab wound sluggishly bled.

"Can you make it?" Ragnar asked her.

"I can."

He studied the map as much as he could, then nodded. He knew where this was. It had been a recently reinforced area of the labyrinth. The new mortar and stones still smelled, although he hadn't understood why. They'd all guessed that the king had the labyrinth changed regularly, just to make it harder for the warriors who were battling for their lives to memorize the layout.

Maybe they'd been wrong.

Together, they all slipped out into the looping halls. He hoped they would be able to get away without any of the humans finding them, but he'd been very wrong. The first turn led them head to head with a group of nearly ten humans, all armed to the teeth.

They all paused, staring at each other for a few moments before Gunnar stepped up beside him. Lifting a sharp claw, he pointed at one of the men who held a curved sword. "I'm going to take that. Such a blade is too good for the likes of you."

The man was bigger than many of the warriors they had met so far in this place. His shoulders were broad, packed with muscle, and his entire body slick with sweat. A splattering of blood covered his ribs, which Ragnar didn't know if that was from a troll or from another human who he had taken the sword from.

Still, the human's face curved into a smile and he gestured with the sword. "You can try, beast."

It was a good enough reason for them all to lunge into an attack.

Gunnar flew at him first, his body a blur of motion as he barreled toward the humans. Ragnar followed him closely, making sure to take the other side so there was nowhere the humans could escape. He picked up the first one that came at him, throwing the man over his head toward the hungry pack of trolls who waited for him. They tore him apart, limb by limb, until he was little more than a mist of blood in the air.

And so they fought. Continually. Over and over until his breathing was ragged and his mind was fuzzy with rage. He wanted them all dead. Every single one of them.

Until they were. Until Ragnar stood on a pile of meat and bones.

The pain registered first. A large gash across his ribs, one nearly through his thigh. One of the humans had gotten him across the face with a wicked blade that shouldn't have been able to slice through his leathery hide. Breathing hard, he stared at the others, who were looking worse for wear as well.

But alive. They were all alive. And that meant they could continue forward.

They kept going, all of them injured and limping. Finally, they made it to the area Bjorn had told them to wait in. Ragnar pressed a hand against his side to staunch the bleeding and turned his back to the wall. "And now we wait."

"We wait?" one of the trolls said, his voice shaking. "For what?"

Ragnar didn't know. But he had a feeling it was important to trust Bjorn. There was a long way for them all to go, but trusting their own kind was the best start they had.

A rumble of sound shook the labyrinth, but it seemed to come from above them. Ragnar looked up and to the right, his eyes widening in shock as he saw a woman launch herself from the stands above them. Her tangled hair and dirty clothing marked her as one of the "gifts". And then he heard Gunnar suck in an angry breath.

The women couldn't survive that fall. The stands that contained those women were significantly higher and besides, once the women were in here, he had no idea what the human men would do.

"Is this part of the king's plan?" he asked, staring up to see many guards were already rushing toward the line of women who always stood up there.

Where was Maia? She was usually with them, but today she wasn't. He didn't see her shock of red hair, nor did he get the comfort of knowing she was near.

His stomach churned in fear that perhaps the king had done something to her. At the end of the day, that was the only thing that would tear him apart. He wouldn't be able to come back from that, and the king knew it. The only way to hurt him was through her.

The rumbling sound happened again, although now he swore it came from within the labyrinth itself. Anxiety churned in his gut, making it hard to focus when all he could think about was her. The image of her red hair had kept him going, kept him fighting. And now?

Now he would tear this entire building down if it meant he could get to her. He would fight, tusk and claw, to get to her. If he had search the entire castle he would. He would revel in their death, paint the walls red and make the cavernous halls ring with their shrieks of pain.

The noise got closer, so he squared his shoulders, then shook out his hands. "This is it," he muttered. "It ends here, or I end here."

"Ragnar—"

"Enough, Gunnar. This is my choice." And he would end this battle in bloody glory.

Until bright red hair rounded the closest entrance in the labyrinth and his entire world stopped. A mirage, surely. Her red hair was more tangled than he remembered, but parts of it were woven in braids. Her white dress, that had once been so stunning, was smeared with dirt and blood. But her expression was filled with rage and determination.

She didn't stop running, not even when she saw him. She darted right for him, rushing into his arms with the force of an earthquake. He staggered back a few steps, his arms still held out for her. Part of him couldn't believe she was really here in his arms.

But then he smelled her. That sugary sweet scent that was only slightly marred by the death and decay that surrounded them. Her heart beat frantically against his belly, and her hair tangled against his chest. She was here. Just as she was supposed to be.

With a horrible groan that wrenched from his very soul, Ragnar gathered her up in his arms and held her tightly against him. He squeezed too hard. He could tell, but he wanted to feel that she was alive. He needed to know that the warmth in his arms was really her.

Tears burned in his eyes, trailing down his cheeks before dropping into her hair.

"Maia," he whispered, his voice ragged and raw.

She pressed a kiss over his heart, her lips a welcome change to the anger and rage that filled this place. "Ragnar, we have to go."

"How did you get here?"

"I jumped." She shuddered. "I was lucky enough to not break my leg, but I was the first one to jump. Did you not see me?"

He must not have been looking. He was ashamed to admit that his eyes weren't on her at all times. "Listen to me, there is something I have to say to you."

"Ragnar, there is no time–" She tried to say, but he pressed his hands over her mouth.

"I love you," he said. "I love you so much. I should have said it a thousand times before this moment, and I am ashamed that I have not.

I love you more than the mountains beneath our feet, my fire hair."

Those big, green eyes stared up at him and he swore there was laughter in those depths. "I know."

He blinked. "You what?"

"I know you love me." There was a giggle in those words. "I've known it for a while, I think. But I love you too, you know."

A knot in his chest eased. He had no idea it was even there, but it felt like it had been there for a long time.

She kissed him, sweet and slow and everything he had missed. She was alive in his hands and a missing piece of his soul slotted back into place.

Foreheads pressed together, he breathed her in before saying, "There's no way out."

"The wall behind you is breakable, according to Bjorn."

Gunnar burst into motion at the words. The other trolls were quick to follow suit, slamming their shoulders against the brand new brick and mortar that moved with every heave. Damn it, Bjorn had been right.

And then the troll himself was right there, his massive bulk taking up nearly the entire space between the two walls, and in his arms was the other woman who had jumped. One of her legs was at a terrible angle, but she was still alive.

The wall crumbled. That easily. They'd missed it, although there were countless walls that looked identical to this one all throughout the labyrinth.

Bjorn handed the woman over to Gunnar and then stood there with his hands flexing. "Give me a weapon."

"Come with us," Ragnar said.

"Someone has to give you enough time to run. The passages are small and your people are injured. Give me a weapon."

It didn't feel right to just leave Bjorn with a weapon and expect him to do all of this for them. He was meant to come with them. He was one of the trolls they had lost and now they were supposed to just... abandon him?

"No," Ragnar said. "You're coming with us."

Bjorn strode right up to him, that awkward gait reminding Ragnar of all of his faults until the massive horned troll stopped right in front of him and pressed their foreheads together. Maia was pressed between them, safer than she'd ever been before. "You will go with your troll wife and you will keep her safe. I am broken and bloody, brother. I have been for a very long time. But your troll wife reminded me that I still have some honor left. Let me do this for you. Let me go."

Ragnar heaved out an angry breath. Because he knew there was nothing he could do.

At the sound of more humans approaching, this time with clanking armor and the sound of swords being drawn, he backed away with Maia in his arms.

"Thank you," he said.

"Be safe," Maia added. "We're coming back for you."

He could see Bjorn didn't believe that. His old friend, or perhaps the man he no longer knew, turned toward the sound of chaos that approached them and let out a roar of rage.

Ragnar gathered Maia in his arms, turned, and plunged into the darkness with the sound of battle ringing in his ears.

467

Chapter 45

aia clung to her husband, pressing her face against his neck as they ran at a speed that turned the world into a blur. It was eerie to run like this. Because the moment they escaped the castle and came out on the fields beyond, she had a sense of déjà vu.

It was the same direction he'd carried her after their wedding, so different and yet so similar. She'd been terrified then, too. Staring over his shoulder at the castle as it faded into the distance. Back then, she had been scared of what waited for her after they hit the trees. Now, she was terrified of what might follow them there.

A wall of soldiers ran after them. The sunlight caught on their armor, blinding her as it reflected into her eyes. She still stared at them, though. She wanted to watch and make sure they didn't get too close.

Once the trees hid them from the sight of all the humans, the trolls shouted directions. She couldn't make out what they were saying. It was hard to pick out any words in the black tongue, even though she'd heard it many times now. With all that had happened in these past weeks, there hadn't been time for anyone to teach her their language.

Ragnar held her a little closer when he felt her shiver. Or maybe he just needed to feel that she was alive, just like she needed to feel him. Her hands continued to wander over him, like she couldn't believe he was the one holding her. Not yet. Not when she knew there was still a chance they might not make it out of this.

But soon enough, they were plunging into the mountain. The cold air blasted her back, only for it to be covered by his warm hands as he protected her from the icy chill. He never once let her go. Not on the entire run, and not as they fled the humans. Not even when they were finally in the light of the wisps with the forests surrounding them. He just kept her plastered against his heart.

Eventually, they slowed. Gunnar walked up next to them with Rose in his arms, murmuring a quiet word to her when the other woman seemed to flinch at the sights.

"It's different," he was saying. "I know it's different. But you've survived worse than this."

"So that's the troll she was talking about," Maia murmured against Ragnar's neck as she watched his brother disappear with Rose in his arms.

"Hm?"

"She had mentioned that they'd given her to a troll, but that he wasn't cruel like the others. She wasn't sure how to act around him, because she was waiting for him to attack her like all the others. He never did."

"Gunnar knows better." Ragnar started off in another direction, but she knew already that he was taking her home.

Soon enough, they would need to go to the king. But the trolls all deserved a few moments of peace before they had to relive what had happened to them.

They strode through the forest, the brilliant blue leaves filling her gaze with otherworldly beauty. A reminder that they were, without a doubt, here. Home. Not in that place that had made them fight for their lives.

She wished she could heal the mental pain all the trolls carried. Or perhaps, she wished that she could bring them to the troll wives glen and allow them all to no longer carry those memories. At least for a little while.

For now, though, she allowed herself to be selfish. She tucked her head against Ragnar's shoulder and breathed him in.

When he took a turn away from their house, she hesitated before asking, "Where are we going, Ragnar?"

"We're getting clean. Washing away all that was done to us."

Maia hadn't the faintest idea what that meant, but she had learned to trust the way of the trolls. If this was what he deemed necessary, then she would go along with it. Even if her eyes were drooping and exhaustion rode her shoulders in a mantle of weight that pressed her down into his body. Perhaps she dozed, because the next moment when she was truly aware, they were in a different cave.

Rather than the wide open expanse she was used to in the main area of Trollveggen, this one was an actual cave. There were stones above their head only a few feet higher than Ragnar's head. He had to duck beneath a few stalactites as they went farther into the cave. She could smell the strange, musty scent of the wet stones, but there was also a slightly sulfuric scent mixed in with that.

The sound of voices soon filled the air. Hushed sounds and quiet reassurances that were murmured in the deepest of voices.

Maia turned in his arms, trying to find the source of those sounds. Hot springs dotted the cave. Each pool had a different shape, depth, and a different amount of coiling steam, which made her think they were all a different heat as well. There were already multiple trolls in each one. Some of them were the trolls who had been in the labyrinth with her. Others were trolls that she recognized from the surrounding town.

Already she felt herself cringe. But she had suffered alongside many of the other trolls here. So maybe, just maybe, she deserved to find peace in the hot springs just as much as they did.

Ragnar didn't hesitate. He walked over to one of the pools far in the back. No one was in this one yet, and perhaps the others knew to give both Maia and Ragnar a little space.

He got onto his knees before her, his hands braced against her hips. For a few moments, he just looked at her, those dark eyes seeing so much. All the way through her soul and into the fear that still lingered there.

She remained frozen as he lifted a clawed hand and gently brushed the back of one over the peak of her cheekbone. She could still smell the metallic scent of blood underneath them. He was still splattered in blood from so many humans he had killed. "We are not there any longer," he murmured. "We are home."

Maia didn't know if he was saying that for himself or for her. Perhaps it was for both of them.

Tears pricked her eyes. She desperately needed that to be true. She needed to know that they were safe, and they were home, and that nothing was going to change that. No matter what, she was safe here. With him.

Squeezing her eyes shut, tears dripped down her cheeks, and she nodded. "We're home."

"We're safe."

Why did repeating those words feel so hard? They stuck in her throat like they didn't want to come out. But she forced them to come out. Just to hear herself say them. "We're safe."

"Good. Now trust me just a little more, fire hair. Let me take care of you."

She kept her eyes shut as he reached for the braided shoulders of her dress. Carefully, in front of all the other trolls, he drew the dress off her body. Shame burned in her chest. She didn't want to show them all the bruises that were there. She didn't want them to see the hours of torment that she'd put her body through as she'd tried to break down the door with her shoulder that was still slightly numb. Abrasions on her knees and palms still stung from where she'd launched herself over the edge of the stands and landed hard on the bloodied dirt in the labyrinth.

There was no sound, though. No murmurs of pity or disgusted noises as the trolls stared at her. So she blinked her eyes open, telling herself that she was still that brave woman who had braved an unknown troll to get them all out.

When she opened her eyes to look around, resolving herself to fiercely staring back, she found that not a single troll was looking at her. They were all in little family units, some of them just friends who were gathered around those that had returned with her and Ragnar. Each troll who had survived that place was surrounded by loved ones.

Ragnar stripped as well, and she had to force herself to look at his chest and not everything else he revealed.

Somehow, her husband knew what she was doing. He chuckled, a bright grin flashing at her as though he knew her struggles.

"Come, wife," he said, holding out his head. "The waters are enchanted."

"What do you mean by that?"

But she took his hand without hesitation. Because he had never harmed her. Not even when he hadn't liked her.

Ragnar led her into the water. She stepped first one foot, then the other, into the heat that sent relaxation into the arches of her feet. Then her calves were finally not so tense, her thighs finally didn't hurt any more. She sank into the depths, all the way up to her neck, and let out a long, relieved sigh.

Finally, all the tension in her body eased. She hadn't realized she was still carrying so much of it.

Ragnar leaned against the stones beside her, resting his head against the edge. The strength of his throat caught her attention. Powerful muscles worked in a swallow, almost graceful if his build wasn't quite so blocky.

Enchanted waters, she mused as she tilted her head back as well. This was what it felt like to have magic surrounding her. As she let her eyes drift shut, she could feel it. All the sparking energy of magic, but none of the strangeness that she'd thought to feel. Instead, she luxuriated in the sensation of unknown power slowly healing her body. It was more than that, though. This was strangely similar to how she'd felt in the troll wife glen, when she'd mingled her magic with all the troll wives who had come before her.

The burden of what they had been through didn't disappear entirely. It was still there in her head, not gone, just dormant. The magic flowed through her body. Healing all the pieces that were broken, but not just in the flesh. It helped her to let go of her anxiety.

"Why don't you bring patients here?" she asked.

"I do."

"Mortal wounds?" She peeled one of her eyes open to look at him.

"They won't heal in these waters. Aches, scratches, bruises—all of that can be helped here." He tilted his head to the side to look at her. "It helps us relax. It eases the pain of emotional turmoil as well. I'm sure you've noticed that."

"I have."

Dark green feet padded around them. Maia closed her eyes as Gunnar dropped his pants on the stones, and then she waited until she heard the sound of splashing water before opening her eyes again.

He looked exhausted. There were deep rings around his eyes and a pain that was bone deep. "She wouldn't come," Gunnar said before she could even ask. "I tucked her into bed in the barracks and left her there. I think she'll do better alone."

"And her leg?"

He grunted. "Very much broken. I offered to bring a healer to her, and even to get Ragnar, but she wouldn't stop shrieking, so I just left her alone for now."

Maia wasn't sure what the connection was between Rose and Gunnar, but she had a feeling it was one that was more long lasting than either of them was willing to admit. Such a bond was hard to break, after all. They'd both been through a nightmarish experience, and now they had each other.

She startled when fingers sank into her hair. Ragnar's hand landed on her thigh, holding her in place when she might have splashed into the center of the pool. But Maia still covered her chest with her arms and found herself breathing a little too quickly.

"Sorry," a light, feminine voice said. "I thought you knew I was here. I forget humans aren't as aware of their surroundings as we are."

Maia relaxed when she recognized Rota's voice. "We just don't have the same hearing as you."

"I wasn't that quiet."

Tilting her head back, she looked up into the soft smile that made Rota's face even prettier than before. She knelt on the lip of the hot spring, her knees pressing against Maia's shoulders.

"What are you doing here?" Maia asked.

"This is what we do after a harsh battle, or after something tragic happens. Ragnar didn't explain it?"

When Maia shook her head, Rota sent a glare over to her husband. "You can't keep throwing her into situations and not explaining them, Ragnar."

Her husband shrugged. "She's doing fine now, isn't she?"

"She's naked in a pool with your brother. You know how sensitive humans are!" Rota huffed, but then tunneled her fingers back into Maia's hair. "Let me take care of you, sister."

"Sister?"

Rota slowly pushed Maia's head, sinking her under the pool's surface so her hair could get wet before coming back up. Blinking the water out of her eyes, Maia looked up at the troll maiden, who smiled down at her. "Yes, sister. I thought you knew that."

Looking over at her husband, she looked back at Rota. "You're related?"

"No. I adopted you. That's what happened when Hilda, Inkeri, and I welcomed you into Trollveggen." Rota's finger traced over Maia's ear piercing. "We marked you. You're family to us. One of ours, even if we aren't blood related."

Blinking back tears, she shook her head. "I had no idea."

"Well, now you do. And when you return from battle, family will care for you. So let me wash your hair, Maia. It is the least I can do. Washing away the memories of that place will take time, but I can help."

Maia melted into her hands. An older woman arrived to take care of Gunnar, washing his hair in the same way that Rota was doing to Maia. Even Ragnar soon had a younger male troll behind him, and at her questioning glance, he introduced her to him.

"Leif is one of my newer trainees. I have taught him how to fight in many ways, and soon enough, he will join the war band."

Now was not the time to tell her that. Maia's heart twisted at the thought of the handsome blue troll going out into battle with her people and possibly not coming home. What would happen to his family? Would they worry they had lost him and then have all of their nightmares proven correct when they did?

Ragnar sent a wave of water toward her, and when it crested over her chin, she felt all those worries melting away. Even Rota scooped some up and let it pour over Maia's head, a crown of relief from the anxiety that had threatened to grab her by the throat.

And they were right. Because right now wasn't the time to sink into those fears. Right now, they were together. They weren't in that awful labyrinth where they had all seen too many horrible things.

"We're home," she said, meeting Ragnar's gaze and reaching for his hand. Their fingers intertwined, and she really felt the words for the first time since they'd made it back.

He nodded. "We're safe."

Chapter 46

Ragnar knelt before his king with the other trolls who had been taken by the humans, each of them waiting for their leader to release them. They wanted to return to the labyrinth. King James had done too much with this transgression, and they wished to fight.

In his opinion, it wasn't that much to ask. They wished to avenge all those who had been killed, tortured, and maimed. But the king seemed very much against going into battle yet again.

The trolls had lost a great amount of their people. Not to mention there was the significant fear that they would get captured again. It was hard enough to understand that there were trolls in a labyrinth being forced to fight. Let alone the sheer numbers of trolls who had died within those winding walls. This horror was all a reminder of their failures, and that would affect their king more than anyone else.

But Ragnar would not kneel here and wait for permission. Not when he had promised Bjorn that he would return. Tilting his head up, he looked his king in the eyes and held his gaze.

The others kept their heads down. They were terrified of what the outcome would be. Some of them didn't want to go back into battle. Many of them hadn't yet dealt with the memory of what they had endured. Even more of them were still feeling the effects of what they had seen. He knew that would all take time.

Returning to the labyrinth seemed like madness, but his king had to know that Ragnar would not rest. He wouldn't let Bjorn remain there when the other male had potentially given his life to get them out. The human king would not allow that heroic act to go without punishment, and they all knew that.

"Everyone out," the king said. "Ragnar, stay with me, if you don't mind."

Gunnar gave him a look on the way out. He knew his brother was trying to tell him to behave himself. The king was just as raw as the rest of them. They'd all failed in this.

King Egil took a deep, steadying breath. "You think we should go back."

"I do."

"Give me a good reason."

"We cannot leave the trolls there. They're our people. We've fought too hard for all our people to be safe, and now the battle is only going to get worse. To leave them there would be to go against everything we fight for." Ragnar pressed a hand to his chest. "I know it's personal for me. Bjorn is an old friend, but he also saved our lives. Without him, none of us would have gotten out of that place."

The king rubbed a hand over his mouth. "I cannot risk more of our people. With the humans attacking regularly now, we're already spread thin, having our scouts watching over each entrance into this mountain. We're closing off passages, but that will take time."

"I can't leave him there."

Suddenly appearing tired and every year of his age, the king slumped forward on his throne. "There is an option. My son has been... absent for a long time. I sent him away to another troll clan far from this kingdom in case there was ever an attack on us. I have known for a very long time that the tensions between us and the humans were only going to get worse, Ragnar. But I do know that something must be done."

"You would have the prince return?" he asked, stunned by this revelation. "We all know how important he is to the royal bloodline. He should remain where he is."

"He's not a child. He's a grown man these days, and from what I've heard, the exact thing we have all been hoping for. The closest we've ever been to a new future."

Every part of him froze. A new future? Surely the king did not mean they had finally, after all of these years, become what they had so desired?

"What is he?" Ragnar found himself asking, his voice shaking a bit with fear.

"I do not know what to call him yet. Only that there is so much hope for the child he and his future wife would bear. But I need to find him a bride who is half elf. Their child would then be more elf than troll, and that..." The king blew out a long breath. "That is the struggle. But this has been years of royal bloodlines bringing us here. Years upon years of searching for the right brides and ensuring that our line remained true. I cannot risk all of that to attack a kingdom who keeps our people hidden away from our eyes. Surely you understand?"

Of course he did. He knew that there were bigger things in this realm than his friend, who had given up hope. He'd seen the loss in Bjorn's eyes. He'd known that there was a chance his friend wouldn't even be alive when Ragnar returned for him, but he had to still try.

Ragnar looked at his king, feeling the hopelessness of the situation grow between them. "I can't leave him there."

"I know you can't. But there is only so much I can do. We need you here, Ragnar. We need you to provide assistance when they attack us, because you know they are going to attack very soon."

"I might be able to help." A voice interrupted them, followed by a very familiar cursing voice.

Frowning, Ragnar turned to see the doors had cracked open as a young woman darted through the small part. She was prettier than he remembered, but he'd set her leg rather quickly after she'd been mostly hidden underneath Gunnar's blankets. She hadn't wanted him to look at her, let alone touch her. And yet, she'd managed with the healing well enough.

Now, Gunnar's Rose was pretty. Her hair was a surprisingly light shade of blonde, her face smooth and cheeks bright pink. She was painfully emaciated, but she moved with a grace that he hadn't expected from a young woman who had gone through so much.

His brother charged after her, apologies already dripping from his lips. "I'm sorry, my king. I didn't realize she was at the door, or I never would have let her listen in."

King Egil lifted his hand for silence. "If she thinks she can help us, then let her speak. Who are you?"

Rose marched up beside Ragnar, pretending bravery because he could see her shaking. The scent of her fear was a cloying acid burning in his nose. But she stood there still, shoulders squared as she looked up at their king.

"My name is Rose, your highness. I was in the labyrinth as a prize for those who remained alive. I was there for over six months."

The king's brows rose. "Six months?"

"Yes."

"And how often were you... given as a prize?"

"At least once a week. Sometimes more than that, depending on when the king got bored."

Ragnar winced. He had no idea what this woman had gone through, but he could guess that it would scar her for the rest of her life. Being here would help heal her, but not for a long time yet.

The king spat on the ground at the words. "Barbarians. Your people did you great harm. You are welcome here for as long as you wish it, to heal and to take the time you need. Now, you said you may be able to help us?"

Rose swallowed hard. "My sister, your highness. I come from a very long line of women who serve the king directly. There are many of us. Priestesses, is what he calls us, but we are anything but holy. Our order is used as a way to control all the nobility in the kingdom. Once we prove ourselves worthy, we're given to one of the noblemen to aid them in all manners of the court."

"A courtesan?" the troll king asked.

"No, your highness. A spy." Rose shuffled her feet on the ground, seemingly uncomfortable with what she was about to say. "The priestesses are trained to do whatever it takes to get information to the king, and they are very good at it. Some of them are courtesans, but most are trusted advisors who were gifted to help the nobility manage... all the things nobles do in this kingdom that they shouldn't be doing."

"And your sister can help us?"

"I think she can. We were very close, you see. When I was taken, she promised to do whatever she could to get me out." Again, Rose seemed uncomfortable with what she said. "Perhaps you can use that to your advantage."

Gunnar stepped up beside her, leaning around Rose's body to look down at her. "What are you suggesting?"

Ragnar knew exactly what she was suggesting. "You want us to negotiate with your sister? We could let her know we have you, and that we won't give you back unless she helps us get Bjorn and the others out."

Rose nodded. "It's a good option. Better than going in and trying to fight your way out. The opening that the troll created for us, that'll be gone by the time we get back. The king won't make that mistake twice. You're going into a hornet's nest, but it's full of traps for you. My sister can get in, though. Her noble is one of the men who runs the entire place."

Standing, the king walked down the stairs and stood right in front of the young woman. She was so small compared to their king. Barely coming up to his chest, and she shook like a leaf. He leaned too close to her, obviously trying to intimidate her.

"Why should we trust you?" the king murmured.

Even though she was clearly terrified, Rose didn't back down. Instead, she opened her mouth and quietly said, "Because you got me out of there. I owe you my life. If I can help those who were in there with me, then maybe some of the nightmares will stop."

Nightmares. That was something Ragnar knew about. Maia had been having them as well. He knew she hadn't been subjected to the same thing this woman had, namely because she'd been given to Bjorn over and over. But he couldn't imagine that had been easy, either. Bjorn was a barely leashed monster of rage. He'd caught wind from other prisoners that Bjorn was known to kill the women he was given.

It wouldn't be easy for Rose's sister to get to him.

But when Ragnar looked at the king, he already knew the answer. This was the only way they could even try to get the other trolls out without risking their own home. There were too few warriors here already. They needed to gather in Trollveggen, lick their wounds, and start again.

The king nodded. "I will send for my son, and you will get us all the information we need about your sister. The scouts should be able to find her easily enough, and we'll leave her all the information she needs. I will not stand for any more innocent bloodshed of our people. If you are leading us into a trap, I will personally take your head myself."

Rose nodded, but it didn't escape his notice that Gunnar seemed a little flustered by what the king had said. Even as their ruler turned to head back to his throne, Gunnar's hand curled perhaps a little possessively around Rose's arm before he tugged her back to the door.

The three of them headed out of the castle, and Ragnar waited a while before he said, "Would you like to come back to our house? We'll have dinner together."

Gunnar obviously didn't want to do that. His brother was still angry at what the king had said, and that was surprising. Gunnar didn't respond like this to any woman, at least, not that Ragnar had ever seen. But Rose looked up at Ragnar with hopeful eyes, and he knew his brother would give in.

"Would it be too much of an imposition? I would like to see Maia."

He grinned. "I'm sure you would enjoy spending time with another human. How long has it been? A week?"

"I wouldn't know," Rose replied. "There isn't a sun here. I can't tell how long it has been since I've been here."

Gunnar shouldered him aside and started walking to their house with Rose in front of him. The space he made between Ragnar and her was ridiculous. Still, he hadn't seen his brother this upset over a woman before and it had Ragnar grinning as he followed them.

"It's been a week," his brother grumbled. "You know how long it's been. I wake you up and tell you every morning."

"Oh. I just don't remember—that's all."

"I try to make sure you know exactly how long it's been and where you are," Gunnar said as they reached Ragnar's home. "I take care of you."

"You do!"

What an adorable conversation he was listening to. Ragnar didn't even try to get ahead of them. He just let his brother lead the little woman up to their front door and push it open like he owned the place. Which, in the eyes of the king, Gunnar technically did, most likely. But that was a bridge they would cross later.

All three of them strode into the house that was filled with the scent of fresh baked bread and some sweet thing that had gone into the oven recently. While he'd been gone, Rota, Inkeri, and Hilda had taken time to put the entire house back together. His couch and chairs were plush again. The rugs were perfectly clean, and no stones remained. Although his ceiling now had a massive chunk taken out of it, the women had convinced the wisps to gather up there like a dripping chandelier.

"Stay here," he said as he headed toward the kitchen. "We'll bring the food out to you."

He wanted to give them a few moments to themselves, but also, he wanted to see his wonderful troll wife.

Maia was in the kitchen puttering away, making the bread that she was so good at and leaving the rest for him to cook. Ragnar had learned recently that while his wife was an incredible baker, absolutely anything else she made was so overly cooked that it was burnt to a crisp. After a few meals like that, he'd taken over cooking the meat and she could manage the desserts.

He caged her in his arms, reveling in the tiny squeak she made before spinning around to press her back against the countertop. "Ragnar!" she scolded. "I'm just finishing up."

"I know you are." He lifted her fingers and licked the sugar off them. "But I wanted a few moments with my wife."

"You can get those moments when I'm done."

"How long until the pie is finished?"

She blinked up at him. "I'm not sure. Likely ten minutes or so. Why?"

He tilted his head to the side, measuring the time before grinning down at her. He grabbed her waist and lifted her up onto the counter, just like he had all those weeks ago. "It's a challenge I'm willing to take."

Tossing her skirts up, he bit the inside of her thigh. But when she moaned, he tsked, "We have company, wife. Keep yourself quiet if you can."

"We have company?"

"The door's closed. Now stay quiet, fire hair. I want to have dessert before dinner."

Before agreeing to marry her, he hadn't known how easy life would be with her in it. Not because she cooked or cleaned, but because he could indulge every sense in her for hours on end if he wanted. And because moments like this, where the both of them were giggling and laughing, trying to remain quiet while they sought out pleasure as well, were sparks of light in his life.

Even if the pie ended up burnt.

Epilogue

The shadows clung to him. He wasn't sure when they had woven themselves into his very soul, but at this point, they were part of him. A darkness writhed in his chest, wriggling deep into his bones. The shadows were who he became in a place like this.

"What are you doing, beast?" a soldier snarled.

The human held a nasty whip in his hands. The cat-o'-nine-tails had made itself very familiar with Bjorn's back, but he didn't mind it as much this time. Because now he remembered his name. Now he knew who he was.

Bjorn, son of Dag the Destroyer. He came from a long line of trolls who had killed hundreds of humans in their days. He was not a weak troll, and he would survive this.

He knelt in the luxurious room with far too many humans surrounding him. His arms were chained to the ceiling, his legs bound so that he was on his knees before them. Countless people wearing half masks that revealed their mouths, all of them sipping wine and watching his torture. Already his blood pooled on the floor in front of him, and their long dresses dragged across it, leaving smears across the pretty marble floor.

As the troll wife had reminded him, hope was a dangerous thing. Bjorn was terrified that someday he would lose himself again. He had for many years in this place. He fought, he survived, he killed. That was all he lived for. He was the creature they loved to send out to perform, and he had performed for them far too much. If the humans had their way, he would continue to do so.

But he was not the same creature he had been a few weeks ago. He was himself again. A troll with many layers, and much to do in this lifetime.

Bjorn had been meant to be a good man. He was meant to be somebody who would make a difference. Where his father had only left a trail of blood behind him, his mother had bid him to be kind.

As the whip came down upon his back again, only the tenth lash out of the fifty he would suffer in front of a private audience, he remembered his mother.

The burning pain was lessened only a bit while he thought of her. His human mother had been stolen from her village, terrified of the trolls who had taken her. But while she had always been afraid of the "monsters" as she'd called them, she had loved Bjorn with every ounce of her being.

She used to tell him stories about how she'd cried the day he'd been born. His father had liked to remind him that his mother had cried at the sight of his ugly face, but that hadn't been why she'd cried. His mother had said she'd felt an overwhelming sense of love. Even for the little monster that had come out of her body.

He'd looked up at her, even after tearing her open with his horns, and she had known she would love him for the rest of his life.

These were the memories he needed to hold on to. He needed them to ground him as he moved forward through this torture. At one point in time, he had done this before.

He remembered talking to her at night. Perhaps her spirit had guided him in those early days until he'd finally lost all memory of who or what he was. Bjorn was not the animal they had taught him to be, though.

And now, he just had to wait.

Gritting his teeth, he endured the lashes and stared at the pool of his own blood that continued to stretch forward, seeking freedom.

Soon enough, he would find his own freedom. He would heal. He would gather forces.

And then he would return here and tear the whole fucking castle to the ground.

492

Follow me on socials or Amazon to keep your eye out for the next book!

Acknowledgements

No book is the same without all the people who help work on it. From my beta team, to my editors, to my dear friends who worked with me through every nonsense question - I adore you.

About the Author

Emma Hamm is a small town girl on a blueberry field in Maine. She writes stories that remind her of home, of fairytales, and of myths and legends that make her mind wander.

She can be found by the fireplace with a cup of tea and her two Maine Coon cats dipping their paws into the water without her knowing.

For more updates, join my newsletter!

www.emmahamm.com